The Secret of the Kingdom

Also by

MIKA WALTARI

THE EGYPTIAN

THE ADVENTURER

THE WANDERER

A STRANGER CAME TO THE FARM

THE DARK ANGEL

MOONSCAPE
and other stories

A NAIL MERCHANT AT NIGHTFALL

THE ETRUSCAN

THE SECRET OF THE KINGDOM

Mika Waltari

TRANSLATED BY NAOMI WALFORD

G. P. Putnam's Sons New York

Published simultaneously in the Dominion of Canada by Longmans, Green & Company, Ltd., Toronto.

Library of Congress Catalog

Card Number: 61-5714

MANUFACTURED IN THE UNITED STATES OF AMERICA

H. WOLFF • NEW YORK

The Secret of the Kingdom

First Letter

MARCUS MEZENTIUS TO TULLIA: *Greeting.*

In my earlier letter, Tullia, I wrote of my journeys along the river of Egypt. I stayed in Alexandria for the winter, after waiting for you in vain until the autumn gales set in. I was childish in my lovesickness, for not the richest merchant nor the most inquisitive citizen could have visited the harbor more diligently than I to meet the ships from Ostia and Brundisium. I hovered about the harbor all day until the end of the sailing season, so that at last I became a nuisance to guards, customs officers and port officials with my inquiries.

It is true that my knowledge was hereby increased, and I learned many and varied things from distant countries; but when one has gazed out to sea in vain one's eyes begin to water, and after the last of the ships arrived I was forced to acknowledge to myself that you had failed me. It is now a year since we met, Tullia, and you persuaded me, with what I now see to have been false vows and promises, to leave Rome.

I was filled with bitterness when I wrote you that letter, in which I bade farewell to you forever and swore to sail for India, never to return. Greek kings still rule there, in strange cities:

descendants of Alexander's officers. Yet already I am willing to admit that I can hardly have meant what I wrote; it was just that I could not endure the thought of never seeing you again, Tullia.

A man who has passed the age of thirty ought no longer to be the slave of his love. I have grown calmer, indeed I have, and the highest flames of my passion have died down. In Alexandria that passion led me into dubious company and caused me to wear myself out. This I do not regret, for no one can alter the course of action he has followed, or the deeds he has done. Yet all the more deeply do I know that I love you, since nothing could satisfy me. Therefore I would remind you, Tullia my beloved, that one day your flowering youth too will fade, your smooth face wither, your eyes' gaze grow dim, your hair turn gray and the teeth fall from your mouth. It may be that you will then regret having sacrificed your love for the sake of ambition and political influence. For that you did love me, I am persuaded; of those oaths I can feel no doubt. Were it not so, nothing in this world would mean anything to me any more. You loved me, but whether you love me still I do not know.

In my better hours I think that it really was for my own good only, to save me from danger—from losing my property and perhaps my life—that you induced me with deceiving promises to leave Rome. I would never have gone if you had not vowed to meet me in Alexandria, where we were to spend the winter together. Many other distinguished ladies before you have made the voyage to Egypt for the winter, without their husbands, and will continue to do so if I know anything of Roman women. You could have returned home now that the sailing season has come round again. We might have had many months together, Tullia.

Instead I wore out both body and soul during those months. For a time I traveled, until I wearied of carving your name and the sign of my love on ancient monuments and temple columns. In my listlessness I even allowed myself to be initiated into the mysteries of Isis; but I must have been older and more hardened then than on that unforgettable night in Baiae, when together you and I dedicated ourselves to Dionysus. I found no such ecstasy. I cannot bring myself to believe in these priests with their shaven heads. Afterwards it simply seemed to me that I had paid too much for a very insignificant piece of knowledge.

Don't imagine that I have kept company only with priests of Isis and their temple women. I have acquaintance among players and singers too, and even among bullfighters of the circus. I have also seen some ancient Greek plays, which might well be translated into Latin, and adapted, should one desire that sort of fame. I mention all this to show that time did not drag in Alexandria. It is a capital city; more sophisticated, more faded, more devouring than Rome.

Nevertheless, I spend most of my time in the Museion, the library near the harbor. It is really a number of libraries: a group of buildings which make up a whole quarter of the town. The old men there complained to me of the wretched state of the collections, for they live in the past. They declare that the library can never regain its former glory, since Julius Caesar was besieged here and set fire to the Egyptian fleet in the harbor; for some of the library buildings were also burnt, and with them a hundred thousand irreplaceable scrolls of the works of the ancients.

Yet it took me many weeks to learn to use their catalogues and hunt down the things I wanted to read. There are tens of thousands of scrolls of annotations on the *Iliad* alone, to say nothing of commentaries on Plato and Aristotle, each housed in its own building. Over and above this there are countless scrolls which have never been entered in any catalogue and which probably not a soul has ever read since they were added to the collections.

For political reasons, understandably enough, the authorities were not particularly eager to search out the predictions of the ancients or even help me to find them for myself. I was obliged to feel my way by indirect questioning and win their confidence with gifts and dinners. Their grants are meager and they themselves are poor, as the wisest among the learned usually are, and as those always are who love books more than their life, more than the light of their eyes.

In this way I succeeded at last in rummaging out a whole series of predictions, both famous and forgotten, from hidden corners of the library. It is clear that in all ages, among every people, the same sort of prophecies about the future have always been made. They are all as obscure and irritatingly ambiguous as the utterances of an oracle. Truth to tell, I often set aside the whole jumble of them and lost myself in some Greek tale, with its carefree lies about travel and adventure. And then I would be seized by a desire to leave these conflicting prophecies to their fate and to write a book after the pattern of those others, but out of my own head. Yet despite my origins I am too much of a Roman to start writing anything of my own.

In the library too there are writings on the art of love which would have made our old Ovid feel like a child. Some of them are Greek and others translations into Greek from old Egyptian books, and I know not indeed which should be given pride of place. Yet having read a few one soon tires of them. Ever since the days of Augustus the god these writings have been gathered together in special secret rooms, and one is not allowed to make copies of them. Only research workers may read them.

But to return to the prophecies. There are both old ones and new. The old ones have been arranged to fit even Alexander, to say nothing of Augustus the god who gave peace to the world. After reading the interpretations of these prophecies, I begin to perceive ever more clearly that the greatest temptation that besets a scholar is the temptation to interpret such writings in the light of his own times and his own desires.

Nevertheless I am convinced of one thing, and all that has happened in our own day only strengthens me in this conviction; even the stars bear witness to the same. The world is entering a new era, of which the signs are different from any that have gone before. This is so clear and evident a truth that astrologers in Alexandria and Chaldea, Rhodes and Rome are agreed upon it. It is therefore natural and understandable that one should connect the birth of a world ruler with the sign of the Fish.

Perhaps he was Caesar Augustus, who in the provinces was worshiped as a god even during his lifetime. But as I told you in Rome, my foster father Marcus Manilius in his *Astronomica* mentioned a conjunction of Saturn and Jupiter in Pisces. It is true that for political reasons he omitted that passage from the book he published; but here too the astrologers bear the conjunction in mind. Yet if the coming world ruler was born at that time he would now be thirty-seven years old, and surely something would have been heard of him by this time.

You'll be wondering why thus openly, in a letter, I remind you of something I whispered in your ear as the deepest of secrets one morning when the roses were blooming in Baiae, and when I believed that no one in the world understood me better than you, Tullia. But I am more experienced now, and can take prophecies like a grown-up man. A half-blind old fellow in the library remarked to me sarcastically that predictions belong to youth. After reading a thousand books, a man begins to sense the crushing truth; ten thousand make him melancholy.

I write openly for another reason too, and that is that in our time no one can succeed in keeping anything to himself. Even the most private conversation can be overheard and passed on, and there is no letter which cannot be read and if necessary copied. We live in an age of mistrust, and I have come to the conclusion that the best way to survive is to speak and write openly, exactly as one thinks.

Because of the Will you know of, I am rich enough to satisfy all my needs, but not so rich as to be worth killing. Because of my origins I cannot aspire to any State post, and would not even wish to. I am lacking in that sort of ambition.

The stars pointed eastward. To be rid of me, false Tullia, you made me leave Rome because I had become troublesome to you. Did I not even then swear to seek out the future ruler of the world? For it is really high time he appeared. I was to be one of his first companions; I was to enter his service and take his pay, so that one day I might be worthy to become your fourth or fifth husband. How you must have laughed at me in your thoughts!

You need not be anxious. Not even this purpose of mine gives anyone reason to seek my life. No sign of a world ruler has been seen or heard of. Such a thing would be well known in Alexandria, the navel of the world, the center for all the world's gossip, philosophy and intrigue. Moreover, Tiberius himself is aware of that conjunction of Jupiter and Saturn thirty-seven years ago. And he whose name it is needless to mention in a letter knows of all this. But he believes firmly and fully that the ruler of the world will not come from the east.

Tullia, my beloved, I know very well that this study of prophecies has been but a substitute for something I have lacked—a means of escaping from thoughts of you. When I awake in the mornings you are my first thought, when I fall asleep at night my last. I have dreamt of you and lain awake on your account. No man can be content with a scroll instead of the woman he loves.

From prophecies I drifted into the holy books of the Jews. There is a Jewish philosopher working in Alexandria, named Philo, who interprets these writings as parables, as Greeks and Romans interpret Homer. In this way he thinks to render the Jewish religion intelligible, with the help of Greek philosophy.

You know the Jews and their faith. In Rome too they keep themselves apart from others and do not sacrifice to Roman gods. For this reason many fear them. A number of families has already adopted the custom of setting aside every seventh day as a day of rest, in the Jewish manner. But most people despise the Jews because they have only one god, of whom so far as is known there is not a single image.

At any rate, one prophecy from the very earliest times has

persistently survived in their sacred books. It relates to a future ruler of the world. Their prophets have all repeated it, so that it is the best preserved of any. This ruler they call Messiah. When he comes to power the Jews will rule the world. Such arrogance no doubt originates in the dreams of the whole race, so wretched and shameful has been its destiny, with a period of slavery in Egypt and another in Babylon, until the Persians allowed the Jews to return to their own country. Their temple too has been destroyed several times, most recently by Pompey, unintentional though this may have been. They differ from other people also in that they have only one temple. It stands in their holy city Jerusalem. The synagogues they have in every town in the world are not temples but meeting houses, where they sing their holy scriptures together and explain them to each other.

Because of this prophecy that a king of the whole world will be born among them, so that through him they will rule all nations, there are many who hate them. Therefore they no longer talk openly of it, but keep the knowledge to themselves, and hold themselves apart from others.

Yet they make no secret of the prophecy. When their scholars find that one's attitude is friendly, they willingly help the stranger to understand their holy scriptures. At least this is so in Alexandria. Certain learned men, including Philo, interpret the Messiah prophecy as a parable; but others have assured me that it should be taken literally. To be honest, one ought I think to have been reared in their religion from a child to have any real faith in these obscure writings. Yet when I compared all the world's confused soothsayings with each other I had to acknowledge that this Jewish prophecy was the plainest.

The Jews of Alexandria are free in thought, and there are indeed true philosophers among them who are even willing to break bread with the stranger. I became good friends with one of them and drank unwatered wine with him. Such things happen in Alexandria. When the wine loosened his tongue he spoke with great emphasis of the Messiah and of the Jewish world-sovereignty that was to come.

To prove how literally all Jews, even to the rulers, believe in the Messiah prediction, he told me that their great King Herod, a few years before his death, caused all the male children of a town to be slaughtered. Certain learned Chaldeans had followed a star and journeyed to this town, which was in Judea, and declared in their innocence that the future ruler had been born there. Herod wanted to reserve his throne for his own family. This story seems to show that he was as suspicious as a certain ruler in times gone by, who retired in solitude to an island when he grew old.

You will understand, Tullia, that this brutal tale captivated my imagination. From the year of King Herod's death it was easy to calculate that the massacre must have taken place just at the time when Saturn and Jupiter met. The story proves that the relative positions of the stars caused as much uneasiness among the Jews and the scholars of the Orient as in Rhodes and Rome.

I asked, "Do you think, then, that the future Messiah was slain in his cradle?"

The young Jewish scholar, his beard wet with wine, laughed and said, "Who could slay the Messiah? Herod was sick, and his reason befogged."

All the same, he was a little frightened, and glancing about him he added, "You mustn't imagine he was born then. No time was ever mentioned in the prophecy. We should certainly have heard of him by now. Besides, in every generation some false Messiah is born, and stirs up unrest among the simple folk of Jerusalem."

Yet the idea lingered to plague him, and when we had drunk more wine he said meaningly, "In Herod's day many fled to Egypt from Jerusalem and elsewhere. A number stayed on here, but most returned to their homes again after Herod's death."

"Do you mean that the Messiah was born and carried away to Egypt, out of Herod's reach?" I asked.

He answered, "I am a Sadducee." This he said to emphasize that he was a man of the world and not unduly bound by Jewish traditional customs.

"Therefore I doubt," he went on. "I do not believe in the immortality of the soul, as the Pharisees do. When a person dies he lays himself down and no longer exists. So it is written. Since we live no more than once it is only sensible to try and derive some enjoyment from it. Our great kings denied themselves nothing, although a superabundance of pleasures saddened the heart of the wise Solomon at last. Yet even in the most learned mind a corner of childish piety lies hidden. When drinking unwatered wine, especially—and that too is a sin—one believes things which one does not believe when sober. So I will tell you a story which I heard when I completed my twelfth year and became a man."

He began:

"On our day of rest no one may work with his hands. In the time of King Herod there was an old craftsman in Bethlehem of Judea who fled with his young wife and a newborn boy. They halted in Egypt among the balsam gardens, and settled down. The man kept himself and his family by the work of his hands, and no one had any ill to say of them. But one Sabbath the three-year-old boy was caught by the other Jews in the village as he was baking clay images of swallows. They fetched his mother, because he was breaking the Sabbath and the law. But the boy blew upon the clay models, and they flew up and away as live birds. Soon after that the family disappeared from that place."

"Do you expect me to believe that sort of nursery tale?" I demanded in amazement; for I had regarded him as a dispassionate man.

He shook his head and stared in front of him with his bulbous Jewish eyes. He was a fine-looking man, as many Jews of ancient lineage are. "I don't mean that at all," he said. "I simply mean that a nursery tale like that indicates that in Herod's day a particularly pious, or—for all its unpretentiousness—a particularly noteworthy family took flight here, into Egypt. A rational explanation of the origin of such a legend might be, for instance, that the mother of that little Sabbath-breaker defended him with such winged words from the scriptures that the accusers were silenced. But the true explanation may be so complex as to have been lost in oblivion. With the help of our scriptures one can prove anything. And later, when the family had vanished as unobtrusively as it had left Judea, people embroidered the story so that children too might understand it."

He brought our conversation to an end by saying, "Ah, had I but the mind of a child still, to believe the words of scripture as a child believes them! To live thus would be easier than to totter on the boundaries of two worlds. A Greek I can never be, and in my heart I am no longer a son of Abraham."

Next day my head ached and I felt ill, but not for the first time in Alexandria. I spent the day at the thermae. After bath, massage, gymnastics and a good meal I was seized by a dreamlike sensation; the world of reality seemed to have withdrawn from me, and my own body had become like a shadow. This is a feeling I know well; it comes of my birth. I am not named Mezentius for nothing. It is in such a state that a man is most susceptible to omens, though even then the hardest thing is to distinguish true signs from false.

When I stepped out of the cool colonnade of the thermae the heat from the street struck up at me and the evening sun hit me in the eyes like lightning. My mood continued. I walked along the swarming streets without thinking of where I was going. As I was wandering thus absent-mindedly in the glare, I was mistaken for a stranger by a guide, who seized my cloak and began very glibly to propose a visit to the houses of pleasure in Canopus, or the lighthouse of Pharos, or the Apis bull in his temple. The guide was importunate, and I did not get rid of him until he was interrupted by a shout. Then he pointed a dirty finger at the shouter and laughed, saying, "Look at the Jew!"

At the corner of the vegetable market stood a man clad in skins. His beard and hair were matted, his face was gaunt from fasting, and his feet were sore. Over and over again he shouted the same monotonous message in Aramaic, and his eyes rolled in his head. The guide said, "I don't suppose you understand what he's saying."

But since my youth in Antioch I have spoken and understood Aramaic, as you know. In those days I was seriously thinking of a career as a scribe to some proconsul in the east, before I went to school in Rhodes and gained a better understanding of what I want from life.

Thus I understood very well what this Jewish sectary from the desert was proclaiming. He was shouting again and again in a voice already hoarse with effort, "He who hath ears to hear, let him hear! The kingdom is at hand! Make the path even."

The guide explained. "He is announcing the coming of a Jewish king. So many of these addlepates swarm in from the desert that the police do not even trouble to flog them all. Besides, it is good policy to get the Jews to quarrel among themselves. The longer they belabor one another the longer we gymnasium people are left in peace. There are no more murderous people than the Jews. Luckily for us, their different factions hate each other even more than they hate us, whom they call heathen."

All this time the hoarse, cracked voice was shouting the same words, so that at last they were stamped on my memory. The voice proclaimed that a kingdom was drawing near, and in the state I was in I could not help taking the cry as an omen for myself. It was as if, in a single moment, the prophecies I had studied all the winter long had cast off their disguise of obscure verbiage and gathered themselves into one clear phrase: "The kingdom is near."

The guide prattled on, still clutching a corner of my cloak.

"The Jewish paschal feast is approaching," he told me. "The last caravans and ships are on the point of leaving with pilgrims for Jerusalem. We shall see what sort of rumpus there'll be again this year."

"It would be interesting to see the Jews' holy city sometime," I remarked idly.

This so stimulated the guide that he began to yell: "A wise wish, lord, for Herod's temple is a wonder of the world. He who has never beheld it on his travels has seen nothing. As for riots and disturbances, you need have no fear; I was but joking. In Judea the roads are safe, and in Jerusalem, Roman law and order prevail. A whole legion is stationed in that country to keep the peace. Come with me a few paces only, and I with my good connections can surely get you a passage on a ship bound for Joppa and Caesarea. Of course you will be told at first that all places are sold out for the passover; but I will speak for you. It would indeed be a scandal if a distinguished Roman like yourself could not find room in a passenger vessel."

He dragged me by the mantle so eagerly that I went passively with him to a Syrian shipowner's office, which indeed lay not more than a few paces from the vegetable market. I soon found that I was not the only foreigner who wanted to go to Jerusalem for the passover. Besides Jews from every corner of the world, there were many ordinary travelers who just wanted to see something new.

When the guide had haggled on my behalf as furiously as only a Greek can haggle with a Syrian, I became aware that I had bought myself a berth on board a pilgrim ship bound for the Judean coast. I was assured that she was the last vessel sailing from Alexandria this Easter. She had been delayed because she was brand-new and was still awaiting a few last items of equipment, but early next morning she would start her maiden voyage; therefore I need have no fear of the ingrained filth and the vermin that usually render voyages along this coast so distasteful.

The guide mulcted me of five drachmas for his services, but he was welcome to them since I had had an omen and made my decision. He stayed behind, well content, to extort a commission also from the shipowner's clerk. By that evening I had called on my banker for a draft for presentation at Jerusalem, being a sufficiently experienced traveler not to carry needlessly large sums in cash when visiting a strange country. I paid my bill at the inn, and various other debts, and in the course of the evening said goodbye to certain acquaintances whom I could not well leave without a word of farewell. To avoid sneers I told no one where I was going, but simply said I was leaving on a journey and would return at latest in the autumn.

I lay long awake, and felt more keenly than ever before how this febrile winter in Alexandria had corroded soul and body. Alexandria, with all its sights, may be a marvel of the world; nevertheless, it seemed to me that I was leaving it at the eleventh hour. Had I stayed longer I should have succumbed to the fever that prevails in this town which is so greedy for pleasure, so wearied by the wisdom of Greece. A man who had begun to grow soft, as I had, might easily have lingered on in Alexandria for the rest of his life.

Therefore I thought that a sea voyage and a couple of days' effortless wayfaring along the Roman roads of Judea would do me good both in body and soul. But, as usually happens, when I was roused early next morning to catch the boat, after all too short a sleep, I could only curse myself for a madman to be leaving all the amenities of a civilized life for the sake of visiting the alien, hostile country of the Jews, in search of a mirage born in my own mind of a few obscure, oracular phrases.

I was far from pacified when, on arriving at the harbor, I found that I had been cheated more outrageously than I could have imagined. I discovered the ship only after long searching and many inquiries, for at first I could not believe that this wretched, rotten old tub was the brand-new vessel described by the Syrian as being in process of fitting out for her maiden voyage. That her equipment was incomplete was true enough, for she would never have stayed afloat at all without calking and pitching up to the last moment. The smell of her reminded one of the houses of joy in Canopus, for the owner had caused cheap incense to be burned everywhere to smother the other odors on board. Pieces of colored cloth were hung over the rotten sides, and a load of withering flowers had been brought from the market to celebrate the departure.

In a word, this scantily pitched, ill-found tub looked like an old harbor drab who dares not venture into the light of day until she has swathed herself from head to foot in gaudy veils, painted over her wrinkles and seen to it that the smell of her cheap scent is wafted far and wide. I seemed to see the same crafty, cold look in the eyes of the purser when he vowed and protested that I had come to the right ship and showed me my bunk, amid yelling and bawling, tears, quarrels and shouts of farewell in many different tongues.

I couldn't even be angry; I could only laugh. After all, no man is obliged to seek out perils; he can let his good sense lead him round them. On the other hand, by shunning every danger he makes his life unbearable. I have heard the teaching of so many philosophers as to be confirmed in the opinion that not even by the greatest caution can a man prolong his allotted span by so much as a handsbreadth.

It is true that even in our day there are still a number of superstitious rich people who break Roman law and sacrifice a young slave to the three-headed goddess, to prolong their own life by the life he loses. In any of the great cities of the east one can find a magician or a renegade priest who knows the magic words and is willing to perform this kind of sacrifice in return for a substantial fee. But in my view this is but self-deception and cruel error. Mankind certainly has an infinite capacity for self-deception and for putting faith in its own desires; yet I believe that not even if I live to grow old shall I fear death so much as to become the victim of such credulity.

In my ludicrous situation it was a comfort to know that the vessel would be hugging the coast and that I am a good swimmer. I was filled with mirth and bore no grudge for the fraud that had been practiced on me. I resolved to make the best of everything and enjoy the voyage, so that later I might have an amusing story to tell—with appropriate exaggerations—of the hardships and troubles I had endured.

Anchor was weighed, the rowers pulled and knocked their oars together all out of time, the stern swung away from the quay, and the captain emptied a goblet overboard in libation to the goddess of fortune. He could have sacrificed to no more suitable divinity, for he must have known that we should need good luck to arrive at our destination at all. Jewish passengers raised their hands and in their sacred language cried upon their god for succor. On the foredeck a garlanded girl begun plucking at a lyre while a young man with her played upon a pipe, and it was not long before the current song favorite in Alexandria was in full swing. The Jewish pilgrims discovered with dismay that we had a troupe of wandering play-actors on board, but it was now useless to complain. Moreover we, who in their estimation were unclean, formed the majority of the passengers, and the belated pilgrims were not rich. They were compelled to put up with the shadows that we cast and resign themselves to the incessant purifying of their food vessels.

In our day solitude is the rarest of luxuries. For this reason I have never been able to endure slaves about me, watching every step I take, and my every glance, and I pity those who because of their rank are obliged to live surrounded by slaves for twenty-four hours a day. Aboard ship I had to whittle down this luxury of solitude and share sleeping space with the most diverse and shady characters. Fortunately the Jewish passengers had their own sleeping quarters, as well as fireplaces in sand-boxes where they cooked their own food. But for this they would have stepped ashore on the Judean coast in so terribly defiled a condition that they would hardly have dared to travel on to their holy city, so strict are their laws and their rules for purification.

Had we not been helped by a gentle and favorable wind, I believe we should never have reached our destination, for the oarsmen—ramshackle as the vessel herself—were wheezy, breathless, lame and maimed old men. Not all of them were even slaves, but dregs of a yet lower order who, for lack of other employment, had let themselves be hired for this hard physical labor. Yes, this mob of rowers might have formed the chorus of a satirical play. Even the overseer, beating time on his raised platform, laughed himself sick when he saw them bumping each other and themselves with their oars, or lying down and slumbering in the midst of their toil. I believe he used the whip merely for form's sake, for it was just not possible to get any more out of them than had been taken already.

Of the voyage itself I have no more to say than that it was hardly calculated to promote piety or prepare my soul for the holy city of the prophecies. The devotion and reverence of a Jew for the temple was needed for a man to raise his arms in prayer morning, noon and night, and incessantly to chant melancholy or joyful psalms to the glory of his god. At other times of day, Greek popular songs rang out from the foredeck, where the players were rehearsing. And when the rowers were ordered to their oars for a time, the noise of their hoarse lamentations arose from the lower deck.

The Greek girl, who had begun the voyage with a wreath about her head and a lyre in her arms, was called Myrina. She was a thin, short-nosed girl with cold and searching green eyes. For all her youth, she could not only sing and play, but was also an accomplished acrobatic dancer. It was a delight to watch her daily practice on the foredeck, though the pious Jews hid their faces and wailed aloud at the abomination.

Myrina is an Amazon name. She told me quite candidly that it had been given her because she was so thin and flat-chested. She had appeared before, in Judea and beyond Jordan in the Greek cities of Peraea. She told us that there was a theatre in

Jerusalem which Herod had had built, but that they had little hope of appearing there as few performances were ever given, because of the lack of spectators. Jews hate the theatre, as they hate all Greek civilization, even to water conduits, and the eminent persons in the city were far too few to fill a theatre. For this reason the players were now bound for the other side of the Jordan, where the Romans had established a furlough-town for the twelfth legion, and where there was always an enthusiastic if rough audience. They hoped to perform also in Tiberias, the seat of the Governor on the Sea of Galilee, and on their return journey they could try their luck in Roman Caesarea on the Judean coast.

After I had chatted in this friendly way with Myrina, she came stealing to my bunk that night, whispering that I could make her happy with a couple of silver coins, since she and her companions were very poor and found it hard to procure all the clothes and shoes they needed for the stage. But for this she would not have so turned to me, as she was a respectable girl.

As I rummaged in my purse in the darkness I came first upon a heavy 10-drachma piece, and this I gave her. She was overjoyed, she hugged and kissed me, and said that because of my kindness she could not resist me and that I might do with her as I would. When she saw that I wanted nothing of her—for truth to tell, I had wearied of women during my winter in Alexandria—she was greatly surprised and inquired innocently whether instead she should fetch her brother, who was still young and beardless. I have never felt drawn to this Greek vice, though naturally I had had my own Platonic admirers during my school years in Rhodes. When I assured her that I was quite content with just her friendship, she assumed that for some reason I had taken a vow of chastity for the time and importuned me no further.

Instead she told me of the moral customs of the Jews, and assured me that she had met some who did not regard fornication with foreign women as a sin, so long as they kept away from

Jewish women. In proof of her words she whispered a few stories into my ear, in the darkness of the sleeping cabin, but I didn't really believe her. After all, I had learned to respect Jews during my intercourse with their scholars in Alexandria.

When the Judean hills were already looming like a mirage above the jeweled sea, Myrina confided to me her life's dream, as a young girl will sometimes confide in an older friend. She knew very well that for a dancer the season of blossom is a short one; therefore she hoped to save money and in due time establish a modest scent shop in some free and easy coastal town, and adjoining it a quiet house of pleasure. She regarded me with innocent eyes as she explained that the time of waiting would be shortened if she had the good fortune to fall in with a rich lover. I wished her this good fortune with all my heart. And whether because of the captain's sacrifices, or because of a lucky chance, or because of the persistent devotions of the Jewish pilgrims, we made port at Joppa—vermin-bitten, hungry, thirsty and dirty, but otherwise unharmed—three days before the Jewish feast of the passover. The Jews were in so great a hurry that they barely had time to purify themselves and eat a meal with their kinsfolk before setting out for Jerusalem, although night was already falling. But the air was mild, numberless stars burned above the sea, and by moonlight wayfaring was easy. The harbor was crammed with vessels, among them great ships from Italy, Spain and Africa. From this I might have gathered, if I had not already done so, that the Jews' love for their temple is a profitable business for all the shipowners in the world.

You know that I am no snob, yet I felt unwilling to continue my journey in company with the Greek players next morning, although they begged me earnestly to do so in the hope of securing my protection, for not one of them was a Roman citizen. So I decided to finish this letter in peace and quiet at Joppa—I had begun it on board ship—to pass the time and to explain to you the impulse that sent me out upon this journey.

I have rented a private room where I am resting after the

miserable voyage, and writing these words. I have had a bath and used plenty of vermin powder. The clothes I wore on board I have given away to the poor, having seen that people were offended by my intention to burn them. I am now beginning to feel myself again; my hair has been dressed and oiled and I have bought new clothes. My habits being simple, I have little baggage, though plenty of new papyrus, writing materials and a few souvenirs from Alexandria as gifts to bestow upon suitable occasions.

Both high and low can hire means of transport to Jerusalem at the market here in Joppa. I might have hired a litter and escort, or traveled in a wagon behind a team of oxen; I might even have clambered onto a camel led by a guide. But, as I said, solitude is my greatest luxury, and so I mean to hire a donkey early tomorrow morning, load it with my few belongings, a wineskin and a food bag, and set off for Jerusalem on foot, as befits a peaceful pilgrim. I gladly welcome this bodily exercise after the relaxing period in Alexandria, and I need have no fear of robbers, for the roads are crammed with people bound for the passover feast and are guarded by patrols from the twelfth legion.

Tullia, my beloved; it was not to vex you or make you jealous that I have told you of Myrina and the women of Alexandria. If you could have been hurt by it—if it wounded your heart in the very slightest—but I fear that you feel only satisfaction at having so cunningly rid yourself of me. Yet I do not know your thoughts, and it may well be that something prevented you from sailing. Therefore I swear to await you again in Alexandria next autumn, until the end of the sailing season. I have left all my possessions there; not so much as a book have I brought with me. You may obtain my address from the Roman travel bureau or from my banker, if I should not be at the harbor when you come; but in my heart I know that I shall be going down to meet every ship from Italy, just as I did last autumn.

I don't even know whether you have been able to take the

trouble to read this letter to the end, though I have tried to make it as varied as possible. In fact I am in a more serious mood than might appear from this. Throughout my life I have vacillated between the doctrines of Epicurus and the Stoics, between enjoyment and asceticism. The exaggerated pleasures of Alexandria, the vain gluttony of body and spirit, scorched my soul. You know and I know that voluptuousness and love are two different things. In lust one can train, as for running or swimming, but lust by itself engenders melancholy. It is strange, incredible, however, to meet the person for whom one was born. I was born for you, Tullia, and my foolish heart tells me still that you were born for me. Do not forget the nights in Baiae, in the time of roses.

At any rate, do not take too seriously what I have written of prophecies. Your mocking mouth is welcome to smile and whisper "Marcus is still the incorrigible dreamer!" Yet if I were not so, you might not love me; if indeed you still do. I don't know.

Joppa is a very ancient port, entirely Syrian. But while I have been writing this to you I have felt at home here. Tullia, my beloved, do not forget me. I take this letter with me and will send it from Jerusalem, for no ships return to Brundisium until after the Jewish passover.

Second Letter

MARCUS TO TULLIA:

I write this on the Jews' feast day of the passover in their holy city, Jerusalem, in the Antonia fortress. Something which I could never have dreamt of has befallen me, and I still do not know what it really is. Tullia, I am utterly bewildered, and so I am writing to sort out for myself and for you what it is that has happened.

I no longer despise omens, and indeed in my heart have never done so, scornfully though I may have spoken and written of them. With alarming certainty I believe that my steps have been led upon this journey and that I could not have avoided it even had I so wished. But what powers have guided me, I know not. I will begin at the beginning.

I hired a donkey in the market, to be my traveling companion, resisting all enticements to make a more comfortable journey, and set off to go up to Jerusalem with the last of the pilgrims. My donkey was a well-schooled and amiable beast, so that never once was I at odds with it the whole way.

As far as I could make out, it had plodded back and forth between Joppa and Jerusalem so often that it knew every well, and every halt, village and inn along the road. I could have wished for no better guide, and I think it came to feel friendly toward me, because I never rode it, even on downhill stretches, but walked on my own feet to refresh myself by exercise.

From Joppa to Jerusalem is barely a two days' march for a legionary, although the hills are more tiring than level ground for the traveler on foot. But the road is all the more varied for that, and Judea is a beautiful and fertile land. The almond trees have already finished flowering in the valleys, but along the road the slopes are covered with blossom, and their bittersweet fragrance accompanied me all the way. I had rested, I felt rejuvenated, and it was a pleasure to tire my limbs, just as it used to be on the sportsground in my youth.

Both my upbringing and the caution which, as you know, my destiny has forced upon me, have taught me to shun displays. Neither by my behavior nor by my dress do I wish to single myself out from the crowd. That sort of vanity makes me laugh. I have no need of servants and runners to proclaim my arrival. In the course of my journey I drew my donkey meekly aside when great folk came hurrying by, busily urging on their slaves and animals. I derived more pleasure from the intelligent way my donkey pricked its ears as it turned to look at me than I would have felt if the rich and exalted persons had halted and greeted me, and invited me to join their company.

The Jews wear tassels at the corners of their mantles, and by this they recognize each other anywhere in the world, even though in other respects they may dress as we do. Yet this road, which Rome has improved and turned into an excellent army route, is so old and so well accustomed to many races that no one paid me any attention despite my lack of tassels. At the wayside inn to which the donkey led me, I was given water, like all the rest, to water my beast with and to wash my hands and feet. In the throng the inn servants could not stay to discriminate between foreigner and Jew. It was as if every race besides that of the country had been on the move to celebrate with joy and mirth the liberation of the Jews from slavery in Egypt.

I might easily have reached Jerusalem by the evening of the second day if I had made any haste. But I was a stranger, untouched by the fervor of the Jews. I enjoyed breathing the fresh air of the hills, and the splendor of the flowers on the slopes delighted my eye. After the feverish life of Alexandria my spirit felt lightened and I enjoyed every moment, so that a plain loaf of bread tasted better than all the delicacies of Egypt. Yes, I did not even desire to mingle wine with my water on this journey, lest I should blunt my senses; water alone tasted good enough to me.

So I purposely lingered on the road, and the sound of the shepherds' reed pipes upon a hillside as they gathered their flocks together for the night surprised me when I was still some way from Jerusalem. I might have rested for a while, and then gone on to Jerusalem by moonlight; but I had heard of the marvelous spectacle that meets the wayfarer who approaches the city by day and beholds it rise beyond the valley, with its dazzling white and golden temple lit by the sun.

It was thus that I wished to see the Jews' holy city for the first time; and so, to the astonishment of my donkey, I turned aside from the road and went to speak to a shepherd who was on his way to a cave in the hillside with his close-packed flock. He spoke the country dialect but could understand my Aramaic, and he assured me that there were no wolves in this populated region. He had not even a dog to protect his flock against beasts of prey, but said that for safety's sake he slept at the mouth of the cave in case of jackals. His provisions consisted of sooty barley bread and goat cheese kneaded into a ball, so he was delighted when I broke wheaten bread for him and offered him a honeycomb and some dried figs.

Seeing that I was not a Jew, he would not share my meat, but he did not shun me for that. We ate together, sitting at the mouth of the cave, while my donkey cropped avidly among the thorny bushes of the hillside. Then the world suddenly turned as purple as a slope of anemones, darkness fell and the stars were kindled in the sky. At the same time the air turned cool, and I felt the concentrated warmth of the sheep wafting out of the cave. The smell of wool and tallow was strong, but I did not dislike it; it gave me a safe feeling, like a breath of childhood and of home. I was astonished to feel tears forcing themselves from my eyes. But they were not for you, Tullia. These were tears of weariness, I thought, because my wayfaring had tired my weakened body. Yet I suppose I was really weeping on my own account, for all that lay behind me and was irrevocably gone, but also for what still lies ahead. In that hour I would fearlessly have bent down and drunk from the spring of oblivion.

I slept on the ground outside the cave, with the starry sky for my roof, like the poorest pilgrim. So soundly did I sleep that the shepherd had taken his sheep to pasture when I woke. I could not remember one ill-boding dream, and yet everything seemed different from what it had been when I lay down to rest. The hillside faced west and still lay in shadow, although the sun lay upon the slopes opposite. I felt bruised, limp and listless; and the donkey stood near with drooping head. I could not make out how this change of mood had come about, for surely I was not so pampered that a couple of days' walking and a night's hard couch should so exhaust me. I supposed it must betoken a change in the weather, for I have always been as susceptible to that as to dreams and omens.

So listless was I that I did not want to eat. I felt unable to swallow a single morsel. I took a few mouthfuls of wine from the wineskin but it did not revive me, and I began to fear that I had drunk polluted water and was falling sick.

Away on the road I saw travelers climbing the next hill; but a long time passed before I could overcome my revulsion, load up the ass and return to that road myself. It was an effort to toil up the hill, but when at last I reached the top I realized what had happened. A scorching wind was blowing in my face, the persistent desert wind which, once it has risen, continues day after day, bringing sickness with it, and causing heads to ache and women to vomit; the wind that howls through the chinks of the houses and rattles the shutters all night through.

This wind parched my face in an instant and made my eyes smart. The sun, already high, was darkened to a glowing red disk. It was then that I saw the holy city of the Jews rising beyond the valley, girdled by its walls. With smarting eyes and a salt taste in my mouth I beheld the towers of Herod's palace, the clusters of great houses on the slopes, the theatre and circus buildings and, loftier than all, the white and gold temple, with its walls, outer buildings and colonnades.

But beneath this darkened sun the temple did not shine, as I had been told it would. The marble was dull and the gilding devoid of luster. It is unquestionably a vast and mighty structure, an incomparable creation of modern architecture. But I did not feel what the Jews feel on beholding it. Instead, I looked at it from a sense of duty, because it was the thing to do after the long journey I had made. I was no longer young, as I was when I first saw the temple at Ephesus. I did not feel the same veneration for the miracle of beauty now, with a hot wind driving salt dust into my eyes.

My donkey turned its head and looked at me in surprise when I urged it forward once more. It had halted of its own accord on the crest of the hill, at the best view-point, surely expecting me to devote some time to cries of wonder and joy, to songs of praise, and to prayer. I accused myself of arrogance and of being a slave to comfort, because I failed to be enraptured by a vision which for countless people was the most sacred of any, just because my body was weary and the wind malevolent. The donkey twitched its ears in annoyance and set off down the winding road to the valley. I walked beside it holding the bridle, so weak in the knees did I feel.

The farther down we went, the less were we vexed by the

wind, and at the bottom we hardly noticed it. At about noon we reached the point where the Joppa road joins the road from Caesarea and becomes a Roman highway. A whole throng was walking toward the city. Near the gate I saw that people were halting in groups and staring at a nearby mound, though many others covered their heads and hurried on. My donkey began to shy. On raising my eyes I saw three crosses standing on the thornbush-clad hill, and could discern the twitching bodies of the crucified men. Quite a large number of people had gathered on the slope opposite the city, to look on.

The road too was crowded, and I could not have made my way to the gate even had I wanted to. I had seen crucified criminals before, of course, and had paused to watch their torments, to harden myself against the sight of suffering. In the circus arena I have beheld yet crueler forms of death, but there was something exciting about those. A crucifixion offers nothing of that sort: it is merely a degrading, protracted method of depriving a man of his life. If I feel any satisfaction in my Roman citizenship, it is that at least I am sure of being executed by a swift swordstroke, should I ever be condemned to death.

In any other frame of mind I believe I would simply have averted my eyes, tried to forget the evil omen and pressed forward as best I might. But the sight of the three crucified men somehow intensified the feeling of distaste which the weather had engendered in me, although their fate was no concern of mine. I don't know why I felt compelled to do as I did, but I led the donkey off the road for about a furlong and shouldered my way uphill through the silent crowd.

Some Syrian soldiers of the twelfth legion were lounging on the ground by the crosses, throwing dice and drinking sour wine.

It did not seem as if the victims were ordinary slaves or criminals, for at a little distance from the soldiers a centurion was also on guard.

At first I glanced only casually at the convulsively jerking figures, but then I noticed that at the top of the middle cross, above the head of the condemned man, an inscription had been fixed. On it, in Greek, Latin, and the people's own language, was written: JESUS OF NAZARETH, KING OF THE JEWS. At first I didn't take in the sense of what I read, so greatly was I disturbed. Then I saw that a wreath of thorns was pressed hard down about the drooping head of this man, to represent a king's crown. His face was streaked with dried blood which had trickled from the wounds made by the thorns.

Almost at the same moment, both the inscription and the face of the crucified man grew dim before my eyes, the sun disappeared, and the day turned so dark, though it was about noon, that I could barely make out the people nearest to me. The birds fell quite silent, as during an eclipse, and so did the voices of the people, until all one heard was the clink of the soldiers' dice on their shields and the gasping breath of the condemned men.

I had set forth in search of the king of the Jews, Tullia, as I half jokingly told you in my last letter. I found him outside the gate of Jerusalem, still alive but nailed to a cross on a hill. When I understood the inscription and saw the crown of thorns on his head, I never for a moment doubted that I had found the man I sought: the man whose birth had been foretold by a conjunction of stars; the king of the Jews who, according to their scriptures, was to rise up as ruler of the world. How I came to understand this at once, and so clearly, I cannot possibly explain, although certainly the depression I had felt ever since early morning had prepared me for this somber sight.

I was glad of the darkened sky, which spared me from witnessing his shame and torture too closely and indiscreetly. I had already noticed that he had been struck hard in the face and flogged in the Roman manner. He was therefore in a considerably worse state than the two others, who were powerful, tough men of the people.

For a little while, as the sun was darkened, all the voices of men and nature fell silent. Then exclamations of wonder and fear broke out here and there. Even the centurion raised his eyes and scanned every quarter of the sky. My eyes grew accustomed to the darkness, and I began to make out something of the ground and the people about me. Now a few Jews of high rank began to press through the crowd, whose terror they had observed. From their headdresses I saw that they were leading men and scholars, and they wore splendid tassels at the corners of their mantles. They shouted loudly and cheeringly to the throng and began to deride the crucified man, bidding him show himself a king and step down from the cross. They shouted other spiteful remarks as well, plainly alluding to things which at some time he had said to the people.

In this way they tried to carry the crowd with them, and here and there one could hear a few shouts of abuse. But the greater part of the crowd remained stubbornly silent, as if wishing to hide their feelings. To judge by their clothes and faces they were mostly poor folk, among them many countrymen who had come up for the feast of the passover. I had the notion that in their hearts they were favorably disposed toward their crucified king, although they dared not show this in front of the legionaries and their own leaders. There were a number of women in the crowd, and many of them had hidden their heads and were weeping.

When the crucified man heard the shouts, he lifted his trembling head and braced himself upward on his nailed feet. He had been fixed to the cross with his knees bent, so that he should not die too soon, of suffocation. Now he gasped for breath, and his bleeding body was shaken by convulsive jerks. He opened his eyes and looked dazedly around as if in search of something. But to the words of derision he returned no answer; he had enough to do to endure his more immediate suffering.

The two other men had a fair degree of strength remaining. The one on the left took the opportunity of pulling faces at the crowd. To show his own stamina he turned his head to the king, perhaps seeking some miserable gratification of his pride by joining in the mockery. "Weren't you the anointed?" he shouted. "Then surely you can help yourself, and us too."

But he on the right cursed him from his own cross, and taking the part of the king he said, "We suffer for our deeds, but this man has done no wrong." Then he turned humbly and sorrowfully to the king and begged, "Jesus, remember me when you're in your kingdom."

At that moment, faced with an agonizing death, he could still speak of a kingdom. My old self would probably have burst out laughing at so obstinate a faith, but now I was in no mood for mirth: there was something far too piteous and moving in those words. But still more did I marvel when the king of the Jews turned his head toward him and in a half-strangled voice comforted him, saying, "You shall be with me in the garden of the king."

I did not know what he meant. Just then a learned man came by, looking searchingly and suspiciously at the crowd. I stopped him and asked, "What does your king mean by his garden? Why has he been crucified if he has done no wrong?"

The scribe burst into mocking laughter and said, "Are you a stranger in Jerusalem? Do you put more faith in the testimony of a thief than in the Supreme Council, or in the Roman Governor who condemned him? It is he alone who calls himself a king, and he has blasphemed against God. Even now, on the cross, he blasphemes in speaking of the king's garden."

He wrapped his mantle more closely about him, so that not even a tassel should brush against me. Offended, I said, "I mean to look into this matter."

He gave me a menacing look and replied in a tone of warning, "Have a care to yourself, rather. Surely you are no follower of his? He bemused many, but will do so no more. Do not pity him. He is a demagogue, an agitator; he is worse than either of the criminals beside him."

Then my distress found vent in wrath; I thrust him aside,

forgetful of my donkey and my rank, walked over to the centurion and, speaking in Latin to be on the safe side, pointed to the Jewish scribe and said, "I am a Roman citizen, but that Jew there is threatening me."

The centurion regarded me curiously in the half-darkness, sighed, and with clanking equipment walked a few paces along the edge of the crowd, forcing it to move back and leave more room in front of the crosses. Then he returned my greeting in Latin, to show his education, but changed immediately to Greek and said, "Peace, brother. If you are in truth a Roman citizen it does not become your rank to quarrel with the Jews, now, before the Sabbath."

Then turning to the people, without particularly addressing the leaders or scribes, he shouted, "Be off with you now, and go home. You've wagged your tongues long enough. There'll be no more miracles. Trot along to your roast mutton, and I hope it chokes you."

From this I realized that besides hostile bystanders, there were those among the crowd who really were awaiting a miracle, and were hoping that their king would step down from the cross of his own accord. But they were compelled to keep silence, for they feared the authorities. Many seemed to obey the centurion, and set off for the city. The throng upon the road had dispersed too.

The centurion nudged me in a friendly fashion and said, "Come along and have a mouthful of wine. This affair does not concern us at all; I am just here on duty. The Jews have a habit of slaying their prophets, and if they're bent on having their king crucified with Roman help, no Roman has any reason to interfere."

He led me to a place behind the crosses, where the condemned men's clothes lay upon the ground. The soldiers had shared them out among themselves and made separate bundles of them. Picking up the men's wineskin he offered it to me; for politeness' sake I took a gulp of the sour legionary wine, and he drank too. Then he puffed and said, "The best thing is to get drunk. Luckily the job ends this evening. It's the eve of the Sabbath, and the Jews don't let corpses hang out overnight."

He went on, "Jerusalem is one huge, hissing snakes' nest. The more I know of the Jews, the more I believe that the only good Jew is a dead one. So it's just as well to have a scarecrow or two hanging by the roadside before the feast, as a warning to trouble-makers not to stab the life out of any of our men who happen to be careless. But this man is an innocent man, and a prophet."

The darkness continued, though from time to time it was lit by a fleeting, reddish glow. The air was scorching hot, and heavy to breathe. Looking up at the sky, he said, "The desert wind seems to have driven up a sand cloud, but I've never seen so dense a one before. If I were a Jew I should believe that the sun was hiding its face and the heavens mourning the death of a son of God. That's what this Jesus says he is, you see, and that's why he's being tortured to death."

He addressed me without particular respect, and did his best in the twilight to scrutinize my clothes and face and discover what manner of person I was. Then he tried to laugh, but the laughter stuck in his throat and he looked once more at the sky.

"The animals are restless, too," he said. "Dogs and foxes run up into the hills, and the camels have been restive ever since this morning and refuse to pass through the gates. Today is an evil day for the whole city."

"An evil day for the whole world," I said, seized by a sense of foreboding.

The centurion was dismayed. Raising his hands in deprecation he protested, "This matter concerns the Jews alone, not the Romans. The Procurator had no wish to condemn him, and would have let him go. But his enemies shouted with one voice: 'Crucify him, crucify him!' Their Council threatened to refer the matter to Caesar, and to lay a complaint that an agitator was being aided and abetted. So then the Governor washed his hands in a basin of consecrated water, to cleanse himself from innocent blood. The mob howled, and swore that they would gladly take the prophet's blood upon their own heads."

"Who is Roman Proconsul in Judea now?" I asked. "I ought to know, but I am a stranger in this country. I've come from Alexandria, where I've been studying all the winter."

"Pontius Pilate," he answered, with a superior glance. No doubt he took me for a wandering sophist.

I was astonished. "But I know him," I exclaimed. "Or at least, I met his wife in Rome. Is she not Claudia, and her family name Procula?"

Once, long ago, I was a guest at the Proculus house, where I had to listen to a boring reading from a work designed to show what great service the family had rendered Rome in Asia. But the wine and the rest of the entertainment were excellent, and I had had a lively conversation with Claudia Procula, although she was considerably older than myself. She had impressed me as a sensitive woman, and we had both warmly expressed our hope of another meeting some day. This was not merely out of politeness. Yet somehow we never did meet again. I dimly remembered that she had fallen sick and left Rome. You, Tullia, are probably too young to remember her. She was often at the imperial court before Tiberius moved to Capri.

I was so greatly astounded by this piece of information that for a moment I forgot time and place, and was lost in recollections of my youth and of my earliest disappointments. The centurion brought me back to reality by saying, "If you are truly a friend of the Proconsul's, a Roman citizen and a stranger to the city, I would seriously advise you to confine yourself to Roman society during the passover. The Jews are always extremely excitable during the religious festivals; that is why the Proconsul himself has come up from Caesarea to Jerusalem so that he may quell any disturbance immediately. It may be that the people will calm down now that they have had a holy man crucified; one never knows with them. At any rate his followers have gone into hiding, and they're not likely to start anything: and *he* won't be coming down from that cross now."

He walked around the crosses, stood before them looking attentively at the thorn-crowned king and the two criminals, and said with the air of an expert, "He'll die soon. He was well knocked about last night when he was arrested and brought before their Council. Then the Proconsul had him scourged in the Roman manner, so that the people might pity him, or at least that death might come to him more quickly. As you know, a sound flogging before crucifixion is an act of mercy. But we shall have to break the bones of those other two, so that they hang without foot support and suffocate before evening."

At that moment I heard a most frightful braying, such as I had never heard before. The darkness lifted, giving place to a ghastly red shimmering, and the crowd stirred in fear. I saw that my donkey had bolted, load and all, along the highroad away from Jerusalem. Some passers-by caught it and held it fast, but it stretched out its neck and brayed once more, with a horrifying noise, as if voicing the agony of all creation. I ran down to the road. The animal was quiet now, but trembling all over and drenched with sweat. I tried to pat it and calm it, but this peaceable beast of mine tossed its head angrily and tried to bite me; and one of those who had caught it remarked that all animals seemed bewitched today. It happens sometimes when the desert wind blows.

From his place by the gate the leader of the donkey drivers came hurrying up, examined the beast's harness and earmarks and said heatedly, "This is one of *our* donkeys. What have you been doing to it? If it falls sick and has to be destroyed, you must pay compensation."

I myself was shocked by its behavior, for never had I seen any animal in so strange and shaky a condition. I began to unload it, and said defensively, "All of you here in Jerusalem are mad. I've done nothing to the donkey. It's afraid of the smell of blood and death, because you have crucified your king."

But our dispute was broken off and the saddlebags fell from my hands, for at that moment the whole world was filled with a curious sound, like a vast sigh, and the earth shuddered beneath my feet. I had encountered this phenomenon before, and I thought I understood now why the sun had been darkened, why the animals had neighed and brayed and I myself gasped with fear. I realized that to enter the city and go under a roof was not the wisest plan, although what I most longed to do was to throw myself on a bed, wrap my head in a blanket and try to forget the world about me.

I gave the donkey driver a silver denarius and said, "Let us not quarrel at such a moment as this, when the earth quivers in pain. See to my belongings; I will fetch them from you at the gate."

With blows and kicks he tried to get the donkey to move but it would not budge, and he had to be content with hobbling its forelegs. Taking the load upon his own shoulders, he went back to his pitch by the city gate.

I know not whether it was fear of the earthquake that kept me from entering the city or a compelling need to return to the hill and the crucified men, repugnant though it was to me to behold that suffering. In my heart I prayed to the gods, both known and unknown, and to the veiled gods of my kin, and said, "Of my own will I have studied the prophecies, but it was your omens that sent me from Alexandria and led me to this place at this time. I came hither to find the king of the future, to enter his service and to be rewarded. Let me at least have fortitude enough to do him honor until his death, even should I receive no reward at all."

So I walked lingeringly up the slope to join the crowd. It had thinned, and beyond it I saw a group of women who stood and wept. I did not see their faces, for they had veiled them. To comfort and protect them there was but one young man, whose handsome face was distorted with fear and anguish. I asked who they were, and a scribe's servant told me readily that these women had come with Jesus all the way from Galilee, where he had stirred up the people and offended against the law.

"The man is one of his disciples, but no one can molest him, for he and his family are known to the high priest, and he's but a misguided youth," the servant explained; then, pointing contemptuously at a woman whom the young man was supporting, he said, "I believe that is the mother of the crucified man."

Hearing this I felt too diffident to approach and speak to them, though I was very curious and would gladly have heard something of this Jesus from his own followers. But I was horror-stricken by the thought that his own mother should behold her son's shameful death. Even the king's enemies seemed to feel too much respect for her agony to disturb the group of mourning women.

Therefore I loitered where I was among the others, and the time went by. The sky darkened once more, more deeply than before, and the dry heat of the air made it difficult to breathe. Persistent flies and crawling insects had gathered about the eyes and wounds of the men, whose bodies quivered with cramp. Then King Jesus raised himself up once more on his cross and cried aloud, "My strength, my strength, why did you forsake me?"

His voice was so broken that it was hard to distinguish the words. Some declared that he had said that God had forsaken him, but others that he called upon Elias. Elias was a Jewish prophet who went up to heaven in a chariot of fire. Therefore the most ill-disposed among the onlookers reviled him once more and shouted to him to mount up to heaven likewise, if I rightly understood them. But the curious ones, and those who expected miracles, whispered together and hoped in earnest that the prophet Elias would descend from heaven and come to his aid. Many were so much afraid at this thought that they withdrew a little from the cross, and prepared to cover their faces.

The king said something else, and those who stood nearest

cried that he was complaining of thirst. Some merciful person came running, soaked a sponge in sour wine from the soldiers' wineskin, impaled it on a stake and held it up to his mouth. Neither soldiers nor centurion tried to stop this. I don't know whether he was still able to drink, for it was now too dark to distinguish his face. At least his lips were moistened, for his voice was clearer now, and even in that ghastly death struggle it sounded as if released when, in a little while, he braced himself up on his feet again and cried out, "It is fulfilled."

Again people began arguing about what he had said. One affirmed this, another that. But in the darkness I heard a cracking sound as his body slackened and hung from the stretched arms, and his head fell upon his breast. It was a most dreadful sound in that darkness; I knew he was dying and would not be able to raise his head again. I was glad on his account, for surely he had suffered enough, however grievously he may have offended against his people's laws.

That he really was dead I knew with certainty, because the earth sighed again and trembled under my feet. A muffled, subterranean roar, fainter but more menacing than a peal of thunder, sounded from beneath us and died away toward the city. Then I heard a rock split and the crash of a landslide, and I threw myself on the ground like everyone else; for although this earthquake was brief and quickly over, it was very frightening.

Then utter silence rested upon the earth, until from the road came the sound of hoofbeats from draught animals that had broken loose. The sky slowly cleared, the day grew comparatively light again, and people scrambled to their feet and shook their clothes. The crosses stood upright, but Jesus of Nazareth, the king of the Jews, hung by the arms, tortured and haggard, and breathed no longer. Even the soldiers stood up and gathered together to look at him in wonder and fear, whispering among themselves.

Presumably the centurion voiced their feelings when he said

boldly, "He was a good man." As he stared at the frightened Jews he became angry with them and disgusted at his own task, and he shouted, "Truly he was the son of God."

But I called to mind the prophecies which I had studied during the winter, marveled greatly, and whispered to myself, "Peace be with you, ruler of the world, king of the Jews. Nothing came, then, of your kingdom."

At the same time I resolved to find out as well as I could how and why all this had happened, and what acts of his had caused him to be nailed to the cross and executed in so shameful a manner, without a hand being raised in his defense. It seemed to me that his political plans must have been very simple, and that he could have had no adviser well versed in statecraft. This in itself was understandable, for surely no one in his senses would ally himself with a Jew to conquer the world.

The sun reappeared but its light was still strange and unfamiliar, and in it people's faces looked pale and queer. And one thing I must confess to you, Tullia. It must be something in myself, but I cannot describe to you what the king of the Jews looked like. I saw him with my own eyes, and frightful though his torment was I ought to be able to recall his face. But with the best will in the world I can say no more than that it was swollen and blue from blows, and bloodied from the wounds made by the crown of thorns, yet there must have been something divine about that face, since, having read the inscription on the cross, I never for a moment doubted that he was really the king of the Jews.

Now, after the event, I should like to say that he had a sort of gentle dignity, but I am much afraid that those are words I have thought of since. I can better remember the meek resignation which showed that he had become reconciled to his fate. Yet how can a king who knows that he is born to rule the world be meek and resigned when he has failed, and dies a disgraceful death? What was it that he felt had been accomplished? Or was it just that he knew that he was breathing his last?

I didn't scan his face as a keen observer therefore, for I was disturbed in my own mind. It was as if a sense of reverence forbade me to scrutinize him too closely as long as his sufferings endured. You must remember also that it was fairly dark all the time—now and then so dark that one could barely discern the men on the crosses at all. When the sun came back he was dead, and reverence forbade me to stare rudely at his lifeless face.

When the king was dead, many people went away, so that there was then plenty of room around the crosses. The Jewish scribes and leaders likewise hastened off, to make ready for the Sabbath, leaving only a few servants to watch the course of events. One of the crucified criminals began wailing piteously in his intolerable agony. Two compassionate women went up to the centurion carrying a jar, and begged leave to give him more of the drugged wine. They used the same sponge and stick as before, soaked the sponge in the jar and gave both criminals a drink.

The sun showed that the ninth hour of the day was already past. The centurion began fidgeting, for his main task was at an end and he wanted to be rid of the thieves as well, as soon as might be. And presently from Antonia there came two men, a soldier and an executioner who carried a board. He looked expertly at Jesus, saw that he was dead, and then cold-bloodedly began to snap the shinbones of the two others with the board. The cracking noise was cruel to hear and both the victims shrieked and moaned, but the executioner consoled them, saying that this was a work of pure mercy. The soldier who accompanied him was named Longinus. He was not satisfied with the executioner's verdict, and thrusting his spear up into the king's side he drove it in practiced fashion well through the heart. When he withdrew the spear, blood and water ran out of the wound.

The guards began gathering their belongings and the clothes of the condemned men together, joking in relief among themselves because their tedious spell of duty was nearing its end. But as the thieves' cries were stifled and died away, some agitators who had slunk in among the crowd took the opportunity of shouting anti-Roman slogans. The soldiers moved easily into the throng and began buffeting people aside with their shields and the butts of their spears. In the course of this clash, one of the agitators had his jawbone broken. This cowed the rest and they drifted away, threatening to slaughter all Romans and their lackeys in the temple next time they had a weapon handy. These were not followers of King Jesus, the centurion explained to me, but fellow criminals of the other two crucified men.

He decided to be polite, and coming up to me he apologized for the little disturbance, and hoped that I had noticed how easily he had put a stop to it. The Proconsul has forbidden the troops to kill Jews except in the gravest emergency. It is not thought worth while even to arrest ordinary demonstrators, for a yelling mob always collects and follows them to the fort, and there stays by the gate, bawling and clamoring. Any disturbance is to be avoided, especially at the Jewish festivals. At least such is now Pontius Pilate's policy, though at first he tried sterner measures and reaped nothing but trouble, and even reprimand from Caesar.

At last the centurion said, "My name is Adenabar. When I've finished this spell of duty I will gladly take you to the fort, and present you to the Proconsul when I make my report. It would be unwise for you to walk through the city alone: those oafs have seen us talking together and know that you're not a Jew. It would only make for unpleasantness if they molested you, or killed a Roman citizen. It would mean inquiries and punishment, and in this accursed city there are a hundred thousand hiding places."

He laughed, and hastened to soften his words: "So in that way we shall avoid unnecessary trouble; but apart from that I like the look of you, and I respect all learned men. I can read and write myself, though my Latin is shaky. The fort is fairly crowded, but I think we can find you quarters befitting one of your standing."

The Proconsul lives very simply, he explained, and when visiting Jerusalem is usually content to stay with the garrison in Antonia. The mighty palace that Herod has had built would be a far more splendid residence, but the garrison is so small a force that, after some unpleasant experiences, the Proconsul is unwilling to divide it into two. Antonia is an impregnable fortress, commanding the temple area, and it is in the forecourt of the temple that disturbances usually start.

Adenabar jerked his thumb at the body on the cross behind him, laughed loudly and said, "I never saw anything funnier in my life than when that Jesus looped up a rope into a scourge, drove out the dove sellers from the temple forecourt and upset the money-changers' tables. The authorities dared not oppose him that time, for he had brought a good many followers with him. When he rode into Jerusalem on a donkey, people were so beside themselves with joy that they spread their garments on the road before him, waved palm branches and hailed him as the son of David. It was the only way they dared show him that they regarded him as their king. And indeed he was descended from David both on the father's and the mother's side."

He nodded almost imperceptibly toward a group of women who had remained on the hillside, and remarked, "There's his mother."

When the press of people had dispersed, the women had sunk down upon the ground as if exhausted by an overwhelming anguish. But they no longer hid their faces; they were looking up at the cross, and I did not need to guess which of them was his mother. She was not old, and at that moment her face seemed to me the most beautiful of any I had ever seen. Stony with sorrow though it was, it was in some way both transfigured and unapproachable, as if never again in her life would she utter an unnecessary word. She had no need to prove her royal descent; her face was evidence enough, though her dress was as simple as that of the other countrywomen.

I could have wished that her companions would lead her away from that place; I would have liked to go and comfort her, and tell her that her son was dead and would suffer no more. But her face was so exalted, so beautiful and so contained in its grief that it was impossible for me to approach her. On the ground at her feet lay another woman, whose feverish face quivered and whose eyes stared at the cross as if she had not yet fully grasped what had happened. The third woman seemed the eldest, and her stern Jewish features expressed more of wrath and disappointment than of sorrow. It was as if up to the last she had been awaiting a miracle and could not be reconciled to the fact that nothing had happened. The rest of the women stood behind these three.

My eyes returned to Jesus' mother, and I gazed at her as if bewitched, without hearing what Adenabar was saying. Not until he touched my arm did I escape from the spell. "Now that my task is finished, I'll not stay in this gloomy place any longer," he told me. "The Jews must see to the bodies themselves if they don't want to have them hanging there over the Sabbath. It's no longer any concern of ours."

Yet he left a few men on guard by the crosses. Presumably he went for the sake of the executioner, who dared not return to the fortress with only two companions as the robbers' friends might have been lying in wait for him. The road was emptier now, and there was no throng by the city gate. From the houses the smell of roast meat wafted all the way to the hill, but I was very far from hungry.

Glancing at the sun, Adenabar remarked, "There's some time to go before evening. The Jewish Sabbath does not begin until just before the sun sets in the west. This evening they eat their paschal lamb, though there is a sect among them that did so last night. Their temple is one great slaughterhouse. Yesterday and today they have been letting blood from thousands upon thousands of lambs, as is their custom. From every beast slain their priests receive a shoulder and their god the tallow."

My belongings were in safekeeping by the gate, and curtly he ordered the reluctant donkey driver to shoulder my bundles and carry them to the fortress. The man dared not protest. So we made our way up to Antonia, the iron-shod boots of the legionaries clashing in a steady rhythm on the paving. The men were in good training, for none of them seemed to get breathless on the way. I did, however, by the time we reached the arched gateway of the stronghold, for in places the road had been very steep. The Jew set down my things in the archway, and refused to pass through it. I gave him a coin or two in reward, although Adenabar told me that this was quite unnecessary, and in spite of my liberality the fellow stopped at a safe distance from the gate, shook his fist and loudly cursed all Romans. When the sentry raised his spear threateningly he made off, and the legionaries roared with laughter as they watched him run.

When we reached the solid paving of the forecourt, Adenabar halted uncertainly and looked me up and down. I was aware that my appearance made a poor impression and that I could hardly present myself before the Proconsul in my present state, whatever the centurion and I might have agreed upon at the place of execution. Here in the courtyard, Roman discipline and order prevailed, and I smelled the barrack smell. This odor of metal, leather, polishing materials and smoke is not unpleasant, but it makes a man glance at his dusty feet and adjust the folds of his mantle. Here too was the altar of the legion, and I saluted it with respect; but nowhere did I see the image of Caesar.

Adenabar regretted that the fortress had only meager facilities for washing, as water had to be used very sparingly, but he took me into the officers' mess and ordered the slaves to look after me. Meanwhile he would go and report to the Proconsul, he said: and he promised to mention my arrival.

I undressed, washed, oiled and combed my hair; slipped into a clean tunic and had my mantle brushed. I also thought it well to put on my thumb ring, though it is not my custom as I dislike attracting needless attention. I hurried through all this and returned to the courtyard, arriving there just as the Procurator Pontius Pilate came down the steps from the tower, attended by his suite. He looked impatient. Some rich Jew wanted to speak with him but would come no farther than the forecourt, lest he defile himself on the eve of the Sabbath.

He must have been an influential man and on good terms with the Romans, since the Governor was willing to receive him like this at dusk. I drew nearer and joined the staring soldiers. The visit seemed to be connected with the events of the day, for quietly and with dignity the rich old man asked leave to remove the Nazarene's body from the cross before the Sabbath began, and bury it in his garden, which lay near the place of execution.

Pontius Pilate asked the bystanders whether the king of the Jews had indeed died upon the cross, and then said, "We have had trouble enough over him already. My wife is quite ill with all this unnecessary fuss. Take him and carry him away, and let me be rid of the whole wretched business."

The Jew gave his present to Pilate's scribe and went his way with as much dignity as when he had come. Pilate in surprise asked his suite, "Is not Joseph of Arimathea a member of the Council that condemned Jesus? If Jesus had sympathizers of such standing they might have used their influence in time, and spared us an affair which does us no honor."

Now Adenabar signed to me. I stepped forward with a respectful greeting, addressed him as Proconsul and gave my name. He acknowledged my greeting carelessly, saying, to show how good a memory he had, "Yes, of course, of course; I know you. Your father was the astronomer Manilius, but you are related also to the renowned Maecenas family. This has been a dismal day for your arrival in Jerusalem. Fortunately the earthquake has caused no damage worth mentioning. Well, and so you too saw Jesus of Nazareth die. But enough of him. In another year he will be quite forgotten."

Without waiting for my reply, he continued, "My wife will be delighted to meet you. She is a little indisposed, but is sure to get up and dine with us. I myself am not at my best; I have an attack of my old rheumatism, and as you may see for yourself my duties in Jerusalem consist chiefly in running up and down steep stairs."

He moved no less briskly and freely for that, and there was such a restlessness in him that he could scarcely stand still. He is slight of build and is beginning to go bald, though he tries to hide this by combing his hair forward over the top of his head. His eyes are cold and searching. I knew that his career had not been a particularly brilliant one, but thanks to his marriage he had managed to secure the post of Procurator; and this, in spite of everything, is fairly lucrative. Of course he is no true proconsul, but a subordinate proconsul for Syria. Yet he is not an unlikable man. He can smile dryly and jest at his own expense. I believe he has a very strong sense of his duty as a Roman to dispense justice among refractory foreigners, and so the case of this Jesus of Nazareth was troubling him.

He said bitterly, "If I so much as try to go up to my rooms I can wager that the Jews will soon be here again with more festival business, and oblige me to come running down into the courtyard. It's easy for Rome to urge me to respect their ways and customs, but it makes me their servant rather than their master."

He began pacing impatiently about the courtyard, and with a gesture gave me leave to walk beside him. "Have you seen their temple yet?" he asked me. "We heathen have free access to the forecourt, but no uncircumcised may set foot in the innermost court on pain of death. One would never think we were living within the Roman empire. We may not even display Caesar's likeness. And the death penalty is no empty threat, as we have found to our cost. Now and then some mad traveler takes it into his head to dress up as a Jew out of sheer curiosity, just to look at the inside of the temple, though there's nothing particular to see there. In the thick of the festival crowds he may be lucky, but if he's found out they stone him without mercy. They are entitled to do this, and it's not a pleasant death. I hope you have no such project."

Then he asked cautiously for news from Rome, and was noticeably relieved when I told him that I had spent the winter in Alexandria, studying philosophy. He realized then that I was politically harmless, and as a mark of favor he took me into the inner court, forgetful of his rheumatism, and accompanied me up into the great tower, which commands a view of the whole temple area. The temple was magnificent in the evening light, with all its many courtyards and colonnades. He pointed out the brokers' and foreigners' courts, the women's court and the Jews' court, as well as the central building in the sacred precincts where the holy of holies is situated. To that place even the high priest may go only once a year.

I asked whether there was any foundation for the story that in the holy of holies the Jews worshiped a wild ass's head made of gold. One comes upon this tale firmly rooted among every race. The Proconsul declared that there was no truth in it. "There is nothing there at all. The place is quite empty. When the old temple was burnt down, Pompey went in behind the veil with some officers and found nothing whatever. This is a fact."

Now more people came to see him and we went down into the outer courtyard. There, attended by Jewish temple guards, a representative of the high priest was waiting to demand in a stubbornly whining voice that the bodies of the crucified might be taken away before sunset. Pontius Pilate bade him carry away whatever remained to be carried away, and for form's sake they argued together as to whether this was a matter for Jews or Romans, although the envoy had evidently made ready to perform the unpleasant task himself, and for this reason had brought the temple guards with him. Their purpose was to take the bodies to the Jewish refuse place and destroy them in the fire that burned there day and night, and in which all rubbish was incinerated.

The Proconsul pointed out with some sharpness that the body of Jesus of Nazareth was not to be touched if it had not yet been buried, as he had already promised it to another. This was no agreeable news to the emissary, but he could not begin a dispute about it, having plainly been given no more than a general order to remove the corpses before the Sabbath began. Nevertheless he tried to discover who had wanted to take charge of the body, and how and why; but the Proconsul wearied of the man and said curtly, "What I have said I have said," and turned his back to show that the interview was at an end; and with that the Jew and his guards had to depart.

I said, "The king of the Jews seems to be troublesome even when dead."

Pontius Pilate, deep in thought, replied, "You're right. I'm an experienced man, and don't usually bother my head about trifles, but this perverted judgment is more painful to me than I could have expected. Early this morning this Jesus himself owned to me that he was the king of the Jews, but he added that his kingdom was not of this world. This showed me that he was politically harmless, and I had no wish to condemn him, but the populace compelled me."

He struck his fist into the palm of his hand, and said in anger, "Yes, truly, I have been the victim of Jewish agitation and intrigue. They arrested him in the middle of the night and just managed to scrape together a quorum of the Council, to condemn him. They might easily have stoned him themselves for blasphemy, though they have no right to carry out a death sentence. But this sort of thing has happened before, and then they made the hypocritical excuse that they couldn't restrain the righteous indignation of the people. But this time I suppose they dared not, because of those same people, and wanted to involve Rome in the affair. Yes, I sent him to the Tetrarch of Galilee, who is a Jew himself, to be sentenced; but that sly old fox, Herod Antipas, merely reviled him and sent him back to me, so that I might bear the blame of it."

"But what did he mean," I ventured to ask, "by saying that his kingdom was not of this world? I'm not superstitious, but it is a fact that the earth trembled when he died. The sky darkened, too, in mercy, so that his sufferings should not be seen too plainly."

The Proconsul gave me an angry look, and rebuked me oversharply. "I trust that you, a stranger, are not going to start nagging as my wife has been nagging ever since this morning. I'll have the centurion, Adenabar, locked up too if he goes on romancing about a son of God. That Syrian superstition is intolerable. Remember that you are a Roman."

I thanked my good fortune that during our confidential moment in the tower I had said nothing of the prophecies that brought me to Jerusalem. But his irritability confirmed me in my resolve to go into the whole story as thoroughly as possible. It is not like a Roman procurator to let himself be depressed by the crucifixion of a Jewish agitator. The king of the Jews must have been an unusual man.

Pontius Pilate started to go upstairs to his apartments, bidding me welcome to his table when darkness had fallen. I returned to the officers' mess, where the after-duty wine drinking was in full swing. Judea is a fine country for wine, the officers told me, and I could well believe it after tasting theirs. Mixed with water it is fresh and light and not too sweet. I chatted with officers, technicians and experts of the legion, and realized that it was indeed with reluctance and only because of Jewish pressure that Pontius Pilate has sentenced the king of the Jews to the cross. It is true that he had been scourged and mocked by the soldiers in the courtyard, but only for their amusement and because it was the custom. Afterwards they had been ready to let him go. They all seemed troubled by a feeling of guilt, for each of them was anxious to defend himself and blame the Jews. The earthquake had made a deep impression upon them, and when some of them became tipsy they repeated stories they had heard from the Jews about the wonders the king had wrought. He had healed sick people and driven out demons; and only a few days before, so it was said, he had revived a dead man who had lain for some days in his tomb, not far from Jerusalem.

I regarded this story as a classic example of how quickly rumors can grow after any sensational event. I could hardly hide my smile when I saw how readily these fairly enlightened men listened to and believed such absurdities. One even thought he knew the name of the resurrected man. They affirmed in all seriousness that this resurrection—of which the story spread throughout Jerusalem—had been the crowning stroke for the Jewish authorities, and that after it they decided to take the miracle worker's life.

As a further example of Jewish intolerance, the officer commanding a camel troop which had been summoned to Jerusalem from the edge of the desert, for the passover, told how only a year or so earlier the Tetrarch Herod of Galilee had ordered the execution of a prophet from the desert. This man had persuaded crowds of people to be baptized in the river Jordan and so be made subjects of a future kingdom. The officer had seen the man with his own eyes: he wore a mantle of camel's hair and ate no meat.

I also heard that a Jewish community of several hundred men had been founded in an inaccessible part of the desert by the Dead Sea, to search the scriptures and await the new kingdom. These austere men follow a time reckoning different from that of orthodox Jews, and have many different degrees of initiation.

Darkness fell, the lamps were lit, and it was time for me to go up to the Governor's apartments. I came in for a good deal of banter over this, but was also told in confidence that the officers had managed to smuggle some musicians and a couple of Syrian dancing girls into the mess. When the Proconsul had retired I would be welcome to come back and join in the general gaiety. They felt they deserved some enjoyment during the Jewish feast, which had caused the legion so much extra trouble.

An attempt had been made to disguise the gloom of the Governor's tower rooms with costly mats and hangings, and the feather beds of the couches were covered with fine fabrics. The dinner service was Syrian and the wine was served in glass goblets. There was another guest there besides myself, the garrison commander, a taciturn man who may well have been an eminent strategist but who felt so ill at ease in the presence of Claudia Procula and her lady in waiting that he couldn't open his mouth. Adenabar and the Proconsul's secretary were there too. The lamps were filled with sweet-smelling oil, and both women vied with them in fragrance.

I was glad to meet Claudia Procula again, although truth to tell I would hardly have recognized her had I caught sight of her in the street. She was haggard and pale, and to hide her graying hair she had dyed it henna-red. Her eyes alone were familiar, and when I looked into them I was aware of the same restless sensibility that had once enchanted me for a whole afternoon of my youth, at the Proculus house in Rome.

She gave me both her thin, well-tended hands and looked long into my eyes. Then, to my utter amazement, she flung her arms about my neck, pressed close to me, kissed me on both cheeks and burst into tears, sobbing, "Marcus, Marcus! How glad I am that you have come to comfort me on this terrible evening!"

The garrison commander turned away, embarrassed on his host's account and on mine. Pontius Pilate was painfully disturbed and rebuked her, saying, "Now, now, Claudia. Try to control yourself. We all know you're unwell."

Claudia Procula loosened her arms from about my neck, her beauty a little disarranged by the running of blue eye-shadow and tears down her painted cheeks. But she stamped on the floor and retorted, "It is no fault of mine if I am beset by evil dreams. Did I not warn you against touching that holy man?"

When I saw how troubled Pontius Pilate was, it struck me that he must now be paying a high price for the position his lady's connections had procured for him. Another man would no doubt have bidden his wife withdraw and compose herself a little, but the Proconsul merely patted her awkwardly on the shoulder. The lady in waiting, a strikingly beautiful woman, began hastily repairing her mistress's make-up.

Taking a ladle handed to him by a slave, the Proconsul poured wine from the mixing bowl into the glass goblets, of which he seemed justifiably proud. The first cup he handed to me, past the garrison commander. This was a sign that he had caused my luggage to be searched. I had purposely left visible the brief letter of introduction which I had been given, simultaneously with a hint that I would do well to shake the dust of Rome from my feet. At the head of the letter is a name which I will not mention here, but which I now find to be a name of power in eastern lands as well. So I thank you yet again, Tullia, for having at least obtained that name for my protection when you dismissed me from Rome.

When we drank the toasts, Pontius Pilate attempted a pale smile and said half aloud that he had begun to understand at least one custom of the Jews, namely the one forbidding women to eat in company with men. But Claudia Procula had by now calmed herself, and bade me recline next to her at table so that she could reach to stroke my hair. "And there's no harm in that," she said. "I am old enough to be your mother. And you, poor orphan, have never had a mother."

"For the gods nothing is impossible," I said, "so we may take it that you might have borne a son at the age of five." It was gross flattery, of course, but that is what women like. Claudia Procula eyed me coquettishly beneath her brows, called me a humbug and warned her lady in waiting against believing a word I said, because I was the craftiest seducer in all Rome, and by the age of fourteen had known my Ovid by heart. Luckily she gave no hint of the Will that made me rich.

The Proconsul took no offense at the jest. On the contrary, I had the feeling that he welcomed anything that might put his wife in a good humor. He urged me to hold myself in check and to remember that the wife of a proconsul was beyond reproach. He did really call himself Proconsul. Besides, he assured me, Claudia Procula had grown more staid from her sojourn among the Jews, and had cast off the frivolity of Roman society.

Prattling thus we began to eat. I have had better suppers, but there was no fault to find with this one, though the Proconsul is moderate in his habits. At least everything that was served was fresh and made from good ingredients, which is surely the basis of all culinary art. But the most amusing part of it was the climax of the meal, when a great pot with a lid was brought in and set on the table, after which the Governor sent the slaves out of the room. With his own hand he removed the cover, and from the vessel arose a delicious aroma of roast pork and rosemary. Both Adenabar and the garrison commander uttered a shout of delight.

Pontius Pilate explained to me laughing, "Now you can see how completely we are under the Jewish thumb. The Roman Proconsul is compelled to smuggle his pork into Antonia illegally, from beyond Jordan."

I learned that east of the Sea of Galilee whole herds of swine are bred for the use of the garrisons, but that it is strictly forbidden to bring any pork into Jerusalem, for that would offend the Jews. The customs officers are obliged to enforce the prohibition, however friendly-disposed they may be toward Rome. Therefore pork for the Governor's table is smuggled into Antonia as courier-mail, under the seal of the Roman State.

"That reminds me," remarked Adenabar, to get his word into the conversation, "that the only real harm that king of the Jews did was at Gadara, east of Jordan. He wasn't at all bigoted; he broke the Jewish laws and even the Sabbath, with all his might. Still, he must have shared the Jewish prejudice against pork, for one day, a couple of years ago, when he was journeying through the Gadara region, he and his disciples drove a whole herd of them—about a thousand—over a cliff into the water. The pigs were all drowned and their owner lost quite a bit by it. But the culprits fled back over the border into Galilee. It would have been difficult to bring them to trial and one couldn't have got compensation out of them anyhow, for they were all poor men. They lived on what their followers gave them, and did a little work from time to time. So the owner of the pigs just had to suffer his loss. I don't suppose one could have got hold of any witnesses even, for his reputation had spread across the border and people feared him because of his miracles."

Adenabar told his story animatedly, sitting up on the edge of his couch, and at the end of it burst into noisy laughter. Only then did he perceive that we had not been in the least entertained by his narration, for here we were back at this Jesus, whom we had succeeded in forgetting for a while by talking a lot of nonsense, as society manners require. Although it may be that we had not forgotten him entirely.

Adenabar looked abashed, and his laughter died abruptly. Pontius Pilate spat: "We've talked quite enough about that man already."

But Claudia Procula began to tremble, and losing her self-command, she cried, "He was holy—he was a healer and miracle worker such as has never been seen in the world before. If you had been a man and a true Roman, you would never have sentenced him. What if you did wash your hands afterwards? That doesn't absolve you. You said yourself you found no fault in him. Who rules in Jerusalem, the Jews or you?"

The Proconsul whitened with rage, and he would have flung his winecup on the floor had he not bethought himself that nothing would be achieved by smashing a valuable glass. He reflected, looked about him, and noting that the company was small and select and that no servants were present, he answered with forced calm.

"I believe only what my own eyes see and witness. He performed no miracles before me or Herod, although Herod expressly asked him to give proof of his powers. The whole affair was political in an underhand sort of way, and I saw nothing for it but to sentence him. Indeed, legally speaking, it was not I who sentenced him at all. All I did was to let the Jews have their own way. Politics are politics, and there it is expediency rather than any formal tribunal that determines the issue. In minor questions it is expedient to let the Jews have their way; it satisfies their national pride. In all important matters it is I who exercise control."

"What about the water supply for Jerusalem?" Claudia Procula put in, with feminine malice. "Wasn't that your idea—your pride—a monument to your period of office? Well, where is it? You had all the plans drawn up and the fall calculated."

"I couldn't rob the temple treasury," the Proconsul retorted defensively. "If the Jews don't know what's good for them, the blame is theirs, not mine."

"My ruler!" said Claudia Procula sarcastically. "All these years you've had to yield to the Jews time after time in any serious matter, whether great or small. Just this once you might have shown yourself a man, and you would have had right on your side. Why wouldn't you believe me when I sent word to you not to condemn an innocent man?"

Adenabar tried to save the situation by remarking jocularly, "The aqueduct came to nothing through the obstinacy of the women of Jerusalem. Fetching water gives them their one chance to meet and gossip at the wells. The longer and more toilsome their way, the more leisure they have to chatter."

"The women of Jerusalem are not quite as simple-minded as you think," Claudia Procula replied. "Had it all not happened so quickly, in such a hugger-mugger fashion, and had one of his own disciples not betrayed him for money, he would never have been convicted. If you'd been man enough at least to postpone the decision until after the passover, things would look very different now. He had the working people on his side, as well as all those throughout the country who call themselves the quiet ones and await the kingdom. There are more of them than you think. Even a member of the Supreme Council came and asked you for his body, that he might lay it in his own tomb. I know a great deal that you don't know; I even know things that not even his simple disciples are aware of. But now it's all too late. You have taken his life."

Pontius Pilate raised his hands, called upon the gods of Rome and the genius of Caesar to aid him, and cried, "If I hadn't sent him to the cross the Jews would have complained to Rome and said I was no friend to Caesar. Claudia, have I not forbidden you to meet those women who go into trances? Their dreams only make you worse. Men, Romans, I appeal to you. What would you have done in my place? Would you have hazarded your position and career for the sake of a Jew who made trouble over his religion?"

The garrison commander opened his mouth at last and said, "Jews are Jews, snipers, snakes in the grass. In dealing with them, scourge, spear and cross are the only policy."

Adenabar said, "The earth shook as he died. I believe he was a son of God. But you could have done nothing else. He is dead now, and won't come back."

I said, "I would like to know more about his kingdom."

Claudia Procula looked at us with widened eyes and asked, "What if he does come back? What will you do then?"

She said it so gravely that a shudder ran through me: the hairs on my body stood on end and I had to remind myself that with my own eyes I had seen the king of the Jews yield up his spirit on his cross.

Pontius Pilate looked pityingly at his wife, shook his head and said, as if to a simple-minded person, "He's welcome to come back. Sufficient unto the day . . ."

A servant entered cautiously with a message for the secretary. The Procurator sighed with relief and said, "Soon we shall have news. Let us leave this tedious topic."

We finished the meal in an atmosphere of constraint, the table was cleared and we drank more wine. To amuse the ladies I hummed the latest songs from Alexandria, and Adenabar contributed, in a quite well-trained voice, a shameless ditty originating in the twelfth legion. Then the scribe came back, and Pontius Pilate, showing that we had his confidence, bade him tell what he knew in our presence. Evidently the spies that the Proconsul kept among the Jews stole back to the fortress after dark to make their report. The secretary told us this:

"The earthquake has caused great alarm in the temple, for when it happened the outer veil was torn from top to bottom. The man who betrayed the Nazarene returned to the temple today and flung the thirty denarii he had been given back at the priests. At the high priest's house, great indignation has been aroused by the fact that it was two members of the Council, Joseph and Nicodemus, who removed the body from the cross and together buried it in a prepared sepulcher near the place of execution. Nicodemus paid for the winding sheet, and also for a hundred pounds' weight of myrrh and aloes for the burial. Apart from that the city is quiet, and the eve of the passover is being celebrated in the usual way. Jesus' followers have vanished. The Council has issued a slogan: *It is better that one man should die for the people than that all the people should perish.* This has had a calming effect on the city. At any rate, no one talks aloud about Jesus any more. The superstitious awe in which he was held seems to have evaporated, since he performed no miracle but died a dishonored death."

The secretary glanced at us, cleared his throat, gave a forced little laugh and continued. "Then there is one more thing which I wouldn't even have troubled to mention if I hadn't heard it from two separate sources. This man Jesus is said to have threatened to rise up from the dead on the third day. Where the story comes from I haven't found out, but it is known to the high priest too. In his house they are now wondering what they can do to prevent it."

"What did I tell you!" exclaimed Claudia Procula in triumph.

The secretary hastily corrected himself. "I don't mean they believe he will rise again, of course. But his adherents might try to steal the body, so as to deceive simple folk. That is why the priests and the Council are annoyed that the body was not burned on the refuse-tip with those of the other two criminals."

Pilate said bitterly, "I might have known that even my night's sleep would be spoiled by that man."

So much disturbed was he by this foolish tale that he took Adenabar and me on one side to assure himself yet again that King Jesus was really dead. We had seen it with our own eyes; we had also seen the soldier thrust his spear into the heart of the lifeless body, and we both swore, "That man died hanging on the cross and will never take another step."

I had a restless night because of the wine and all that I had experienced so that, weary though I was, I slept badly and had evil dreams. The drunken bawling from the officers' mess disturbed me too, all night long. At dawn I was finally aroused by shrill trumpet blasts from the temple precincts which resounded over the whole city, and all that I had seen and heard the previous day returned immediately to my mind.

To sort out my thoughts and to recall everything just as I had seen it, I sat down to write and went on writing until Adenabar came, puffy-eyed and still fuddled, to bid me come down to the forecourt to see some fun. And there indeed stood a deputation to the Proconsul from the Council and the high priesthood, although it was the Sabbath and a very great Sabbath, at that. Pontius Pilate kept these people waiting and then reviled them for all the trouble they had caused.

But they were really desperate, and vowed that the latest uproar would be worse than the first if the followers of Jesus succeeded in stealing his body from the tomb and then proclaimed that he had kept his promise and risen up from the dead on the third day. They begged and implored the Governor to set a guard of legionaries on the sepulcher for a few days because they did not entirely trust their own men, and for safety's sake to seal the tomb with his own procurator's seal, which no Jew would dare to break.

Pilate called them old women and half-wits and mocked them, saying, "You seem more afraid of a dead man than a live one."

But they promised to send him rich gifts directly after the Sabbath, since during the Sabbath they were not allowed to bring anything with them. At last Pontius Pilate yielded, and sent two men and the legion secretary to the tomb. The secretary was given the task of sealing the tomb, not with the procurator's seal but with the official signet of the twelfth legion, which Pilate thought quite good enough. He gave orders that at night the guard should be increased to four or eight if the officer of the watch thought it necessary, for he well knew that two Roman legionaries on their own could never feel safe outside the city wall at night.

I felt that a walk would do me good, and so I went with the secretary to the tomb. At the place of execution the bloodstained uprights still stood, though the crossbeams had been removed when the bodies were taken down. Only a little way off was a beautiful garden, and in it a tomb hewed in a wall of rock. A great millstone had been placed on edge in a groove before the opening. To roll it aside would have needed the strength of two men, and it was a hot day. The secretary saw no need to open the tomb, for the Jewish guards assured him that no one had touched it since the traitors of the Council, Joseph and Nicodemus and their servants, had rolled the stone into place.

While the secretary was sealing the entrance, I seemed to smell a strong fragrance of myrrh coming from it. But it may only have been the garden flowers that gave out so powerful a scent. Both the legionaries made coarse jests about their task, but they were evidently glad to stand the daytime watch and be relieved at nightfall.

On the way back I went to see the Jews' temple, leaving the

secretary, for he told me I might safely go as far as the forecourt. I crossed to the holy hill by a bridge over the valley, and was admitted, with a great crowd of others, through a mighty arch way into the court of the heathen. People had been flocking in from the city all the morning, but in the forecourt there was still room for more, and I admired its colonnades. At last the endless chanting and loud prayers, the smell of sacrifice and the excitement and ecstasy of the Jews began to sicken me. I thought of the body of the crucified man lying in the cold rock tomb and my sympathy was all with their king, little though I knew of him.

I returned to Antonia, and I have now been writing far into the night to free myself from dismal thoughts. Yet I feel none the better for it, Tullia, for while I have been writing I have not felt your presence in the same way as before.

So far as I am concerned, the story of the king of the Jews is not yet at an end, for I long to know more of his kingdom, and already I have certain plans for getting in touch with his followers and hearing what he taught while he was alive.

Third Letter

MARCUS MEZENTIUS MANILIANUS TO TULLIA:

I have written my name above, and yours, Tullia; yet seeing my own on the papyrus I cannot but wonder whether it is I who write, or some stranger within me. I am no longer myself, and now and then during these longest days of my life I have suspected that Jewish sorcery has cast a spell upon me. If indeed all has happened as I myself have seen it, then either I have witnessed things which have never happened before, or I shall be forced to believe literally in many tales of which philosophers and cynics long ago revealed the symbolic meaning.

I don't know whether I dare send you this letter. My previous scrolls still lie here undispatched; and perhaps it is as well, for if ever you read this you will scarcely escape the conviction that poor Marcus has lost the last vestiges of his reason. Yet I don't regard myself as a dreamer, even though—albeit with unsleeping skepticism—I have sought for something in this world beyond the pleasures both of virtue and of the senses. I confess that because of my origins I went to extremes when young, and never succeeded in finding the truly wise man's balance between renunciation and self-indulgence. There was immoderation in my vigils, fasts and bodily exercises during my school days in Rhodes. Immoderate too was my love for you, Tullia; there I was insatiable.

In spite of all this I can assure you that at the core of my being is something cool and watchful which prevents me from destroying myself. Had it not been for this sober sentinel I would hardly have left Rome: I would have forfeited my possessions and perhaps even my life rather than give you up. Now, as I write, this sentinel is at his most alert, for I try continually to distinguish between what I myself have seen, what I have merely heard, and what I may regard as conclusively proved.

I feel it necessary to record all my experiences in detail, even though I may never send you this letter. I shall include much that is immaterial, being not yet able to discriminate between the irrelevant and the essential. I believe I have witnessed the coming into the world of a new god. This of course will seem madness to anyone who has not himself experienced the event. But if it be so, then the veriest trifles may later prove to be significant. Let this be my excuse for so much verbiage. For if this thing is true, the world will be changed—is changed already—and a new age has dawned.

My sentinel is awake, and warns me against believing what may be no more than my own hopes. But could I ever have hoped and wished for anything so inconceivable? No. It would have been impossible for me to invent or dream of such a thing. If I thought of anything, it was of a new realm on this earth, but there is no question of anything like that. This is something quite different which I don't yet comprehend.

I warn myself against reading more into what has come about than is really there, from sheer vanity. For who am I, Marcus, that such a thing should happen to me? I have no illusions as to my own importance. On the other hand, I cannot deny my experiences. Therefore I relate them.

When I finished my last letter it was late; I had cramp in my fingers and at first I could not sleep. Later I slept well, but only for a short time, for before dawn I was awakened by another earthquake, longer and more frightening than the first. The tinkle of smashed jars and the crash of shields falling from the wall racks brought everyone in Antonia from their beds. The stone floor rocked beneath my feet so violently that I fell headlong. Guards sounded the alarm in the courtyard. I can only admire the discipline of the legion, for however drugged with sleep the men may have been in the dead of night, not one dashed out without his weapons, although their first thought must have been to escape from under falling roofs.

It was still so dark that torches had to be lit in the courtyard. When the first flurry and confusion had subsided, it was found that the wall had split in one or two places, but that no one in the fortress had been killed. Only minor sprains, bruises and wounds were reported; and even these had resulted rather from the stampede in the darkness than from the earth-tremor itself. The garrison commander at once sent patrols into the city to discover what damage had been done, and alerted the legion's fire brigade; for the fires resulting from earthquakes usually cause more havoc than the tremors themselves.

The Proconsul came straight from his bed, a mantle thrown round him, and stood barefoot on the stairs, neither descending to the courtyard nor adding his voice to any of the commands. As there was no repetition of the earthquake and one could hear the cocks in the city beginning to crow, he did not feel it necessary to send the women to safety beyond the walls. Nevertheless, it was understandable that after this alarm no one felt inclined to return to bed. The sky grew lighter, and as the stars faded there came again the powerful blasts of horns from the Jews' temple, showing that their religious ceremonies were continuing as if nothing had happened.

The soldiers were sent back to their regular duties, but only dry rations were issued to them, the cooks being forbidden to light fires for the time being, for safety's sake. One patrol after another returned with the report that alarm and confusion reigned in the city and many people had fled to open country outside it, but that except for a few house walls that had collapsed, no real damage had been caused. The earthquake seemed to have been confined chiefly to the area around the fortress and the temple.

The guards were relieved, and with only slight delay the first cohort marched through the city to their exercises at the circus. No contests of gladiators or wild beasts have been held in this costly building for years; the arena is used solely for the drill and training of the legion.

I walked back to my room over crunching fragments of crockery, washed, and dressed myself properly. While I was still doing this a messenger came to summon me to the Proconsul. Pontius Pilate had had a chair moved out onto the steps for the day's audience. I think he was glad to stay out of doors, though he gave no sign of being afraid that the earthquake might recur.

Before him stood the garrison commander and the legion secretary, as well as Adenabar and two legionaries who, in the Syrian manner, were gesticulating vigorously as they spoke, while still trying to stand at attention out of respect for their commander in chief.

Pontius Pilate said to me irritably, "The changing of the guard was delayed this morning because of the earthquake. It was these two Syrian oafs who were sent to relieve the men at that accursed tomb. There had been six fellows there all night, and they were supposed to keep watch two at a time while the others slept. Now they've come back from the place to report that the legion seal has been broken and the stone rolled away from the tomb, and that the men of the night guard have vanished."

He turned to the legionaries and snapped, "Was the body still in the tomb?"

Both men answered with one voice, "We never went into the tomb. We had no orders to go into the tomb."

Pilate asked, "Why didn't one of you, at least, remain on

guard while the other ran back with his report? Now anyone may have entered it."

Without attempting an excuse they confessed, "Neither of us dared stay there alone."

The garrison commander felt he must speak in defense of his men, for the ultimate responsibility was his. He said curtly, "They have strict orders to move always in pairs outside the fortress."

But from the faces of these legionaries it was plain to see that it was not danger to their lives that they had feared; it was the tomb that had terrified them, while the disappearance of their comrades had filled them with superstitious dread.

The Proconsul seemed aware of this, for he said vehemently, "There is nothing supernatural about what has happened. Naturally the earthquake shifted the stone before the sepulcher. Those superstitious Syrian cowards have taken to their heels and dare not return. They must be hunted down as deserters. They deserve the most rigorous punishment."

Turning to me, he explained, "The legion's honor is here involved, so I will trust no interested party. And I am not to be fobbed off with windy talk. What we need is an impartial witness. You, Marcus, are a clear-headed man with sufficient knowledge of the law. Take with you Adenabar and these two men. You may have a whole cohort to attend you if you like, so that you may cordon off the place and guard it to be sure that these two don't make off as well. Find out what has happened, then come back and tell me."

The garrison commander at once shouted for his trumpeter. This made the Proconsul angrier than before, and pounding his palm with his fist he yelled, "Have you all taken leave of your wits? You don't need a cohort—just a few reliable men. It would be madness to attract attention and make a to-do over this thing, which brings shame upon us all. Now perhaps you will be good enough to start."

Adenabar summoned ten men or so, and having paraded them

in the courtyard he ordered them to move off at the double. The Proconsul had to shout Halt, and remind us that the best way to collect a mob of inquisitive Jews was to cross the city at a run. I was glad enough not to do this, for, out of training as I am, I could hardly have kept up with the legionaries even without equipment, though we had not far to go.

People who had fled beyond the walls were now returning to the city. However, they had enough to think about already and we attracted no attention. The Jews even forgot to spit after the legionaries and shout their usual curses.

The garden partly concealed the tomb, yet while we were still a long way off we could see two Jews coming out of the opening in the rock. They were undoubtedly followers of the Nazarene, for I am fairly sure that one of them was the handsome young man I had seen protecting the sorrowing women at the place of execution. The other was a big, bearded, round-headed man. When they saw us coming they fled and disappeared, although we called after them.

"Now the fat's in the fire," exclaimed Adenabar. But he sent no one in pursuit, thinking it wiser not to disperse our force and knowing that the Jews could easily lead the legionaries astray among gardens, thickets, hillocks and clefts.

But we had seen enough of them to be sure that they had carried nothing away with them from the tomb.

On reaching the sepulcher we saw that the stone had broken the edge of the groove with its weight. It had rolled outwards from the opening and begun to run down the slope until it was brought up short against the edge of a rock, where it had split in two. We could see no marks of any tools. Anyone wishing to open the tomb from outside would have rolled the stone sideways along the groove, as was intended. A piece of cord still hung from the broken legion seal. It was thus evident that the earthquake had shifted the stone from its place. A strong scent of myrrh and aloes wafted out of the dark tomb into the damp morning air.

"You go first and I'll follow," said Adenabar. He was gray with fear, and trembling all over. The legionaries halted at a respectful distance from the sepulcher and huddled together like a flock of sheep.

We stepped into the outer chamber and thence through a narrower opening into the grave chamber itself. We could barely make out the white graveclothes on the stone bench until our eyes grew accustomed to the darkness. At first we both thought that the body was there; then, when we could see more clearly, we found that it had left its winding sheets and disappeared. The linen had stiffened with the myrrh and aloes and still showed the contours of the body that had lain in it, while the sweat cloth that had covered the face lay somewhat apart.

At first I did not believe my eyes, and put my hand in the space between shroud and sweat cloth. There was nothing there. But the linen had not been unwound; it had merely sunk a little, and still held the shape of the body. It would have been impossible to remove the corpse without unfolding the linen. Yet it was gone. Our own eyes bore witness.

"Do you see what I see?" Adenabar whispered.

My tongue would not obey me. I simply nodded. He whispered again, "Did I not say he was a son of God?"

Then he recovered himself, ceased trembling, wiped his face and said, "I haven't seen this kind of sorcery before. It might be as well for you and me to be the only witnesses, for the present."

I doubt if even threats would have induced those legionaries to enter the tomb, so great was the terror that had seized them at the disappearance of their comrades; for there was no sign of any struggle outside.

Adenabar and I did not point out to each other that no one could have wriggled out of stiffened graveclothes without disturbing them. And if those pieces of linen, which were gummed so firmly together with myrrh and aloes, had been unfolded, we should certainly have found signs of it. The most skillful hand could not have replaced them so as to preserve the shape of the body.

As soon as I had fully grasped this I was filled with a sense of profound peace, and was no longer in the least afraid. Adenabar plainly had a similar feeling. Yet I cannot explain how it was we felt no fear, considering that we had just become aware that a miracle had taken place and that we ought, by all human reasoning, to have been more terrified than ever. Calmly we left the tomb and told the legionaries that the body was not there.

The men showed not the smallest wish to enter the tomb and verify this for themselves, nor would we have allowed them to do so. Some of them, calling to mind the honor of the legion, looked about them and pointed out that stones had also rolled away from two other old tombs hewn out of the same rock. It was evidently here that the earthquake had been most violent, and this did not surprise me. They suggested that we might take a corpse from one of the old tombs and lay it where the king of the Jews had lain. I forbade them sternly even to think of such a ruse.

While we were still in doubt as to what we should do, a couple of legionaries appeared among the bushes and came hesitantly toward us. Adenabar saw at once that they were two of those who had run away, and shouted at them to lay down their arms. But they protested vehemently, vowing that they had performed their duty and watched the tomb closely from a safe place within sight of it. And indeed no one had stated how near to the tomb they were to stand.

They said, "We two and two others were asleep, and two were on guard, when toward morning the earthquake began. The stone up here loosened and came bounding down over us, and it was by mere chance that none of us were crushed. We moved farther away—still within sight—for we were afraid that there might be more tremors. Four men hurried off to tell the Jews what had happened, for it was on their account and not the legion's that we were guarding the tomb."

They excused themselves with such energy as to suggest that they were keeping something back. They said also, "We saw those two Jews coming to relieve us but we didn't show ourselves, although they called us, for we were waiting here for our comrades and guarding the sepulcher; and we legionaries stand by each other. If there is anything to be explained we'll do it together, and agree amongst ourselves what to say and what not to say."

Both Adenabar and I questioned them and learned that at dawn they had seen two Jewish women approach the grave, carrying something. They hesitated outside and but one of them entered, only to come out again soon. Just then the sun rose and dazzled the eyes of the guards, yet they could take their oath that nothing had been carried either in or out of the tomb. The women had set down their burden outside; on leaving they picked it up and ran away, although the soldiers had not chased them.

Just before our own arrival two Jews, also running, came to the place, a young man first and an older man, breathless, a little behind. The young one had not dared to enter the tomb alone, but just peered in through the opening. The older man, however, went in, and the younger took courage and followed. The women had clearly given them the alarm, but the men too lingered only for a moment in the sepulcher and brought nothing out of it. The soldiers assured us that they had observed them closely from their hiding place, so as to arrest them if they attempted to remove the body.

"For we were put here to guard the body, and this we have done to the best of our ability and according to regulations, and not even the earthquake made us run away; we only moved to a safe distance from the tomb," said they with one voice.

But I was watching them keenly, and from their looks and

their restless eyes I saw that they were hiding something. "At any rate, the body has gone," I said sternly.

Then they began waving their hands in the Syrian manner and crying, "That is not our fault. Not for a moment have we been out of sight of the sepulcher."

There was no more to be got out of them, and the interrogation was cut short, for now from the city came the four other guards and with them three Jewish elders, whom one could recognize from afar by their headdresses. When the four soldiers saw their two comrades in our midst they began shouting to them while they were still a long way off, warning them and saying, "Hold your tongues now, and don't drivel! The matter has all been straightened out with the Jews. We've confessed everything and thanks to their kindness and understanding, our mistake has been pardoned."

All three Jews were evidently members of the Council, for when they came up they greeted us with dignity and said, "We have been long in coming, but we desired first to call the Council together hastily, to debate this matter among ourselves. The legionaries guard the tomb upon our account and at our request, and we do not wish them to be punished for their stupidity. How could they guess that the disciples of this accursed Nazarene would be so crafty? We have settled the affair between us, and we allow the guard to go in peace. And do you yourselves also go in peace, for neither we nor the Romans have any further business here. The damage is done and we will leave it at that, to avoid trouble and needless gossip."

"No, no," I said. "Roman military law is here involved and we must have a formal inquiry, for the body of your king has disappeared and these sentries are responsible."

They asked, "Who are you and why do you argue with us? You are clean-shaven and still a young man. You should respect our rank and age. If the matter must be discussed with anyone, we shall discuss it with the Governor, not with you."

But having looked into the tomb I felt only repugnance for

these astute old men who had condemned their king and forced the Proconsul to crucify him. Therefore I replied stubbornly, "Your king has vanished from the tomb, and for that reason the case must be thoroughly investigated."

They contradicted me in vexation. "He was no king of ours. He alone called himself so. We have investigated the matter already. Foolishly the guards lay down to sleep, and while they slept his disciples crept up and stole his body. The guards are willing to confirm this and so atone for their fault. We pardon them, therefore, and do not demand their punishment."

Their words were so much at variance with common sense and the evidence of my own eyes that I knew they must have hit on some stratagem and won the soldiers over to their side; so I appealed to Adenabar, saying, "According to Roman military law a soldier who sleeps at his post or deserts it without leave must be flogged and executed with the sword."

Our two legionaries started in fear and goggled at each other, but the four who had returned in company with the Jews nudged both their comrades, winked at them and signed to them with much gesticulation that they had nothing to fear. The Jews repeated their assurances: "It was for us they stood watch, not for Rome. It is for us to demand their punishment or acquittal."

But I was overmastered by the desire to know what had really happened, and so I made a mistake. To frighten the Jews I suggested, "Go into the tomb and see for yourselves. Then question the guards again if you will—and dare."

Adenabar was cleverer, and said hastily, "Why should such righteous men as you defile yourselves to no purpose by entering that place?"

Yet from both my words and his the Jews realized there was something in the sepulcher that was worth seeing. After consulting one another in their sacred language, which I did not understand, one after the other stooped to enter, and naturally we could not prevent them. They remained within for a long time, although it must have been cramped in there for the three of them, until at last I went over and peered in. I saw their bowed backs, and heard their animated conversation.

At length they emerged again, red in the face and shifty-eyed, and they said, "Now we have defiled ourselves so that we may be able to testify that all has come about as the guards described it. And as nothing can make us uncleaner than we already are, let us go straight to the Governor and have the matter out with him, to prevent the spreading of lies and false information."

Seized with misgivings I quickly entered the tomb. As soon as I could make anything out in there I found that they had torn up all the grave clothes in their frenzied search for the body.

I flew into a rage, for my own stupidity had led them to destroy the only piece of evidence which showed that the king had left the tomb in a supernatural manner. But at the same moment I felt a giddiness resulting from exhaustion and lack of sleep, and from the drugging scent of myrrh in the narrow grave chamber. I was aware of a shadowy feeling of unreality, and a powerful sense of the presence of a superior force. It was as if invisible hands were holding me by the shoulders, and preventing me from dashing out and accusing the Jews. I recovered my self-control, and with it my peace of mind, so that I came out again with my head bent, saying nothing to the Jews and not even looking at them.

Briefly I explained to Adenabar what they had done. He looked at me appealingly, as if wanting to consult me as to our next step; then threw up his hands in resignation. Once more he bade the guards lay down their arms, but they talked excitedly in their own defense and asked, "Is that an order? If we lay down our arms it will seem like an admission of a breach of duty. In the name of the ox-god, this is a Jewish tomb we have been guarding, at the Jews' request, so it can be no crime to sleep at our post; it shows rather that we are brave men and not afraid of the dark. If you allow us to keep our weapons and leave the Jews to explain the thing to the Proconsul, you shall not regret it. This we guarantee, and so will the Jews."

Again Adenabar gave me a dubious look, as if to suggest that I too ought to try to gain some advantage from a situation which was now past altering; but he dared not open his mouth. So we returned in an orderly manner to the city and the fortress, the Jews following behind. They stood rigidly by their decision that since the body had been stolen there was no longer any need to guard the tomb. The six guards walked in a tight group by themselves, whispering eagerly to each other all the way.

When we reached the fortress, Pontius Pilate was still seated in his red-covered chair of justice at the top of the steps. He had had a table brought out and set beside him, and wine too, and his mood was entirely changed.

"Come before me, all of you," he bade us in the gentlest of voices. "You, Marcus, who are a man of learning and an impartial witness, stand here beside me and try to remember that the Jews are liberal people. In serious matters they are very pleasant to deal with. Bring seats for these honored Councilors, who do not despise the Romans. My own secretary shall take down the minutes, and you there, the scapegoats of the legion, draw nearer. Have no fear of me, but tell me without disguise what happened to you."

The soldiers glanced from him to the Jews and back again, and a broad grin overspread their rugged Syrian faces. They shoved forward a spokesman, who began his story with the assurance:

"By Caesar's genius and the bull-god, these are the words of truth. With your approval, the Jews hired us to guard the tomb in which the crucified Nazarene had been laid. All six of us went there last night. Having seen that the seal was unbroken, we let the day watch go and camped on the ground before the tomb. Thanks to the generosity of the Jews we had plenty of wine with us to keep out the night cold. We had intended to keep watch two at a time while the other four slept, but that evening none of us wanted to sleep. We threw dice, sang and made merry, and only girls were lacking to our enjoyment. But, lord, you know yourself that the wines of Judea are treacherous. During the night we lost count of the shifts and fell to quarreling over them, not knowing for certain who were to watch and who to sleep. In fact we were so tipsy that we all six seem to have slept, although each believed that two of the others were at their posts."

He appealed to his companions, who nodded brazenly and said, "That is what happened. That is the truth."

The spokesman continued his tale. "We didn't wake until the earthquake, and then we saw that the disciples of the crucified man had broken into the tomb and were just carrying the body out. There were many of them: cruel, bloodthirsty-looking fellows. When they saw that we were awakening, they rolled the stone from the mouth of the tomb down upon us, and so made their escape."

Pilate inquired with apparent curiosity, "How many of them were there?"

"Twelve," declared the man firmly. "They clashed their weapons, and shouted, to scare us off."

One of the Jewish Councilors joined in the conversation, saying, "There can scarcely have been more than eleven, for the twelfth—the man who deserted them—has been murdered in revenge. At least his body was found near the city wall early this morning by herdsmen. He had been strangled with his own girdle and thrown into a gully, so that his belly had split and his entrails burst out."

Pilate asked, "Did they carry the body away as it was, or had they removed the graveclothes inside the tomb?"

Disconcerted, the spokesman glanced sideways at his companions, and then said, "Oh, the body must still have been in its shroud. They were in a hurry because of the earthquake."

The Jews rose from their chairs and cried vehemently, "No, no, that is a mistake. They removed the linen from the body while it was still in the grave chamber, to make people believe he had risen from the dead. We saw it lying there higgledy-piggledy."

"Maybe, maybe not," the soldier said. "How could we have seen that in the darkness, confused as we were by the wine and the earthquake?"

"Yet apart from that you saw and observed plainly all that happened, despite the darkness," said Pilate approvingly. "You are excellent men, and a credit to the twelfth legion."

His tone was so ominous that the soldiers glanced at each other, stared at the ground and wriggled. Then they nudged their spokesman, who looked guiltily at the Jews and said, "Well, in fact . . ." Then repeated, "In fact . . ." But the words stuck in his throat.

"Sir," I began, but Pilate signed to me to be silent, and pronounced his verdict.

"I have listened to the account given by these trustworthy men, and I have weighty reasons for believing that they have spoken the truth without deceit. They have satisfied our Jewish friends also, and no punishment has been demanded. Why then should I interfere in questions of internal discipline within the legion? Have I spoken rightly?"

The Jewish elders answered warmly with one voice: "Rightly indeed!" The soldiers too stamped their feet: "Rightly have you spoken. May the gods of Rome and our own gods bless you with all good things!"

"I have now dealt with this matter," the Proconsul said, "and it is closed. If anyone has anything to add, let him speak now and not afterwards."

"Allow me to say one thing," I begged; for this farce of a trial seemed to me more like a scene from an Oscan comedy than an episode in real life.

Pilate, in feigned astonishment, turned to me and said, "Oh, you were there too, then, and saw it all?"

"Of course not," I returned, "and I don't pretend I was.

But you yourself sent me there afterwards, as a witness, to find out what did happen."

"So you didn't see it," the Proconsul remarked. "The soldiers did, however, so you had best not speak on matters of which you have no knowledge. When I sent you, I thought the soldiers had run away and brought dishonor on the legion. But here they stand, as gentle as lambs, and have made full confession."

He rose from his place with ironical reverence, to show the Jews that he had had enough of them, and they thanked him and withdrew through the archway. The soldiers too were about to leave when the Proconsul signed to them casually and said, "Wait a little." He then turned to the garrison commander, remarking, "From your gloomy looks I conclude that the high priest's treasurer did not deem it necessary to secure your friendship. It is not for me, as I said, to interfere in matters of discipline within the legion. I have indeed shown clemency to these fellows, but that need not prevent you from taking appropriate action against them by way of a lesson. In my opinion you might well put them under arrest for the time being and let them meditate upon what really occurred."

He added in a low voice, "Nor need anything prevent you from discovering how much money the Jews gave them in token of their love of truth."

The commandant's somber face was split by a cheerful grin; he gave a few orders, and the guards were disarmed before they quite grasped what was going on. They were taken down to the detention cellar, and the commandant followed to assure himself that the money was correctly counted.

When they had gone, the Proconsul smiled to himself and said, "Adenabar, you are a Syrian. Go and find out what those rogues really saw."

Stiffly he started up the steps and beckoned to me most benevolently to follow. I went with him to his office where he ordered the others to withdraw, sat down puffing, rubbed his knees, permitted me also to be seated, and said encouragingly, "Speak. I can see you are bursting to do so."

Absently he took up a leather bag, broke the sealed cord and let the pure gold coins, stamped with the head of Tiberius, run through his fingers.

"Sir," I said after a moment's reflection, "I don't know why you did as you did just now, but I take it that you have your reasons. I am not in a position to judge your actions as a Roman official."

He jingled the coins and answered, "As I have already explained to you, I have sound reasons—the weightiest reasons in the world, so long as the world remains what it is. You know yourself that the censors keep a sharp eye on procurators. One can no longer grow rich in the provinces as one could in the days of the republic. But if the Jews insist on forcing presents on me, out of sheer friendship, I should be mad to refuse them. I'm not a rich man, and Claudia keeps a firm hand on her own property. So far as I know, you are well enough off not to envy the gifts that I receive."

Of course I did not envy him anything, but my mind was so full of what I had seen that I exclaimed, "So long as the world remains what it is, you say. I believe the world will no longer be quite the same, for the king of the Jews whom you crucified has risen from the dead. The earthquake rolled the stone away from the doorway and he left the sepulcher, passing through winding sheet and sweat cloth despite whatever lies the legionaries and Jews may tell."

Pilate looked at me searchingly, and concealed his thoughts. I told him what Adenabar and I had discovered by examining the ground outside the tomb, and what we had beheld within it. "The folds of the linen were still stuck together and had not been loosened," I cried. "To conceal this, the Jews tore up the graveclothes in a rage, or you might have satisfied yourself that he kept his promise and rose up from the dead on the third day, and walked out of his tomb. Adenabar too can testify to this."

Pontius Pilate smiled with open sarcasm, saying, "Do you imagine that I would have stooped to go there myself and look at the Jews' conjuring tricks?" He said this so pityingly that for a moment I doubted the evidence of my own eyes, and recalled all the illusionist arts of Egypt with which simple folk are cheated.

The Proconsul poured the money back, drew the cord tight and tossed the bag down with a jingle. Then he said gravely, "On the other hand I know perfectly well that the guards are lying and that they have concocted this story in return for Jewish bribes. No legionary sleeps at his post when he has the seal of his own legion to guard. Besides, Syrians are so superstitious by nature, so afraid of the dark, that they would hardly have dared to sleep. It must have been the earthquake that opened the tomb, as you say; what I would like to know is what happened afterwards."

Resting his elbows on his knees and his thin chin on his hands, he stared before him. "He impressed me too, of course, that Jewish miracle worker," he admitted. "More deeply than you know—than Claudia knows. But there have been miracle workers, prophets and Messiahs in Judea before now. One and all stirred up the people and made trouble before they were rendered harmless. But this man was no agitator. He was so humble that I found it hard to look him in the eye when I was interrogating him. Remember that I had the opportunity of questioning him privately, with no Jews listening. According to their accusation he called himself a king, thereby setting himself up against Caesar. But it was obvious he regarded his kingship as something purely symbolic, and so far as I know he never even refused to pay tax to the Roman State. His kingdom was not of this world, he told me; and he said also that he had been born into this world to bear witness to the truth. Naturally this moved me deeply, thick-skinned though I may be. But the

Sophists proved long ago that there is no absolute truth in the world; that all truths are relative and must be measured against each other. In fact, I asked him what truth was. But to that he either would not or could not make any reply.

"No, I found no evil in that man," Pilate went on thoughtfully. "In the wretched state he was in after the Jews' ill-treatment he seemed to me on the contrary the most innocent and, in a noble way, the humblest man I have ever met. He was not at all afraid of me—he never even defended himself. There was strength in him. I may say that in a sense I felt inferior to him, for all my position. But it was no humiliating feeling. Rather I felt cheered as I spoke with him and he answered in his temperate fashion. He never defended himself or tried to argue."

Pilate looked up at me, smiled again and added conciliatingly, "I think it best to tell you all this so that you may not misjudge me. I desired his own good, but the political situation was hopelessly against him. It was not possible to save him, since he would not lift a finger to help himself. On the contrary, it was as if he had been merely awaiting his fate, and had known beforehand what it would be."

His face hardened; he looked darkly upon me again, and said at last, "An exceptional man, perhaps a holy man; let us call him that. But, Marcus, he was no god; cherish no illusions of that sort. He was a man, a living human being like other human beings. You yourself saw him die as men die. Not the furies themselves could persuade me that a corpse can rise again, or vanish into the air through a shroud. Everything in this world has a natural and usually a very simple explanation."

Thus he spoke to me, for the matter continued to trouble him, and as a Roman official he wanted to confine himself to tangible facts. He had to do so. I perceived this and did not contradict him, but maintained a stubborn silence. Afterwards I regretted it, for if I had asked him he would surely have been willing to tell me, in this moment of self-examination, all that had happened during the interrogation, and what the Nazarene had answered.

Presently Adenabar entered. The Proconsul nodded to him and said, "Speak."

Adenabar rubbed his hands in embarrassment and asked, "Sir, what am I to tell you?"

Pilate said sternly, "This is no cross-examination at the bar, but a confidential conversation within four walls. I don't say to you 'tell the truth,' for truth is something that neither you nor I knows much about. Just tell me what those fellows really think they saw."

"Each of them was given thirty silver pieces," said Adenabar. "For that price the Jews put into their mouths what they were to say. In fact they were afraid and hardly dared sleep for fear of ghosts at the tomb. Quite certainly two of them were awake, as they were supposed to be, when the earthquake came. The shock knocked them over; they all awoke just as the stone in front of the tomb broke loose, and they heard it rolling toward them in the darkness. And then—"

Adenabar broke off in embarrassment and said apologetically, "I am but repeating what I heard. They didn't even have to be flogged, so eager were they to talk, for they were most indignant when we took their money away. Having escaped the stone they were all trembling with fright and they saw a light like a lightning flash, though they heard no thunder. The lightning struck them to the ground again, and they lay there like dead men, dazzled for a long time. But they heard no one moving, no noise and no footsteps, when they ventured to approach the tomb again. They saw no thieves, and they believe that no one would have had time to go in and out of the tomb without their seeing him. After consulting together they left two men on guard, and the other four went to tell the Jews what had happened, not daring to enter the tomb themselves to find out whether the body was still there."

Pilate pondered what he had heard, then turning to me he asked, "Marcus, which story do you find the more credible: the one the Jews believe to be consistent with the truth or the one you have just heard?"

I answered frankly, "I know the logic of the Sophists and the truth of the cynics. I have also been initiated into mysteries, although these—for all the beauty of their symbolism—never convinced me. Philosophy has made a doubter of me, but earthly truth has always been like the stab of a knife in my heart. Now I understand it completely. With my own eyes I saw him die. Today with my own eyes I saw that no earthly power had broken open the tomb where he lay. The truth is simple, as you said just now. His kingdom came to this world this morning. The earth shook and opened his tomb. His light dazzled the guards when he rose and came out from it. How simple it is. Why should I rather believe doctored stories which bear no relation to the facts?"

"Marcus, don't make a fool of yourself," said the Proconsul. "Remember you're a Roman citizen. Now you, Adenabar, which story do you choose?"

"Sir, in this matter I have no views," returned Adenabar diplomatically.

"Marcus," the Proconsul repeated pleadingly. "Do you seriously mean me to make myself a laughingstock by alerting the legion and all the garrisons in Judea, and bidding them capture a man who has run away from his tomb? Such would be my duty, if I believed you. Distinguishing marks: a wound in the side, penetrating the heart, and nail holes in his hands and feet. Calls himself king of the Jews."

He went on more mildly, "But we can make the choice easier for you. I did not ask you what you think is the truth, but which of the stories is the more credible in the world in which we find ourselves? Or, even better, which story is politically the more expedient, from both the Jewish and the

Roman point of view? You surely understand that whatever my own opinion may be, I must act in a way that is politically expedient."

"Yes, and I can see why you asked him what truth is," I returned bitterly. "Be it as you say. You're evidently satisfied. The Jews have decided for you and have given you both a credible story and a present to help you swallow it. Of course their version is the more expedient. I don't intend to run my head into the snare and let you charge me with political conspiracy. I'm not such a fool. But perhaps you'll allow me to reserve my own opinion. I won't noise it abroad."

"Then we're all three agreed," said the Proconsul serenely. "The sooner we forget the affair the better. Adenabar, you and the commandant may each keep a third of the Jews' money—that's no more than fair—but give the men ten silver coins each, to stop their mouths. Tomorrow they may be released, and in due course transferred to the border, preferably to different places. But if they start spreading absurd rumors we must take immediate steps."

I took this as a hint that I too would be wise to remain silent so long as I remain in Judea. But on thinking it over I realize that nowhere in the whole of the civilized world could I speak openly of my experiences. I should be regarded as a crank, or a liar wanting to attract attention. If the worst came to the worst, Pilate could denounce me as a political troublemaker who was meddling in Jewish affairs in order to harm Rome. Citizens have been executed for less than that in our days.

These thoughts depressed me, yet I was consoled by the reflection that I wanted to know the truth for my own sake rather than to tell it to others. So when Adenabar had gone I said meekly, "But you will let me investigate this matter of the king of the Jews? Not his resurrection; I will keep silent about that. But I want to know something of what he did and taught. There may be something to be learned from it. You yourself said that he was an exceptional man."

Pilate scratched his chin, looked at me kindly and answered, "I think it would be best to forget all about him; I wouldn't like you to addle your brains with the Jewish religion. You're still young, you're well off and free, you have influential friends and life smiles upon you. But to each his destiny. I shall not stand in your way, so long as you satisfy your curiosity discreetly, without attracting attention. Jerusalem is full of talk about him just now, but you can have no idea how short a memory the people have. His disciples will soon disperse in all directions and return to their homes. Believe me, in a few years he will be quite forgotten."

I realized that our conversation was at an end and went down to the officers' mess to eat, since he did not invite me to his own table. I was tormented by such uneasiness that I hardly heard what was said to me, and after the meal I couldn't rest as the others did. Irresolutely I walked through the gateway and strolled about the city. The streets were full of people on their way home after the festival. I saw folk of every race, and tried to look at wares from every country in the shops of the Jewish merchants. But I had seen the same before in other great cities, and found nothing to amuse me.

Some time later I noticed that I was looking at nothing but the beggars squatting along the house walls; at their maimed limbs, blind eyes and ulcerous sores. This surprised me, for a traveler becomes so well accustomed to beggars that he notices them no more than he notices the flies that beset him. They sat in rows on each side of the street in front of the temple, and each of them seemed to have his own special place. They held forth their hands and cried out their woes, and cuffed and jostled one another.

It was as if there had been something wrong with my eyes, for instead of observing the gorgeous merchandise, the Pharisees with their huge mantle tassels, the oriental traders, the graceful walk of the women water carriers, I saw only the maimed and wretched beggars. So, wearying of the city streets, I went out through the gate and once more saw the hill of execution before me. I walked past it quickly and into the garden where the tomb was. I noticed that with its fruit trees and herb garden it was more lovely than I had thought. Now, in the time of the midday rest, it was empty of people. My steps took me to the rock tomb; I entered it once more and looked about. The linen cloths had been removed and I was aware only of the fragrance of ointments.

When I came out again I was overwhelmed by a feeling of weariness such as I never remember having felt before. I had had no proper sleep for two nights, and it seemed to me that the past two days and this third one had been the longest of my life. Reeling with exhaustion I went over to the shade of a myrtle bush, lay down on the grass, rolled myself in my mantle and at once fell asleep.

When I awoke, the sun had declined and it was already the fourth hour by Roman reckoning. The sound of twittering birds surrounded me, and the scent of mignonette, and fresher air. I sat up, feeling marvelously rested. My unease had vanished and I felt no need to torment myself with foolish thoughts. I inhaled the cool air, the world looked younger to me, and I suddenly realized that the dry, oppressive desert wind had ceased and that all was different. The wind may have changed that morning, though I had not noticed it. But now my head ached no longer, my eyes no longer smarted from lack of sleep and I was neither hungry nor thirsty. All I felt was the wonder of breathing, living, existing as a man in the world of men.

I saw a gardener moving about the garden, lifting the boughs of the fruit trees and feeling the setting fruit. He was dressed like a man of the people in a simple mantle with small tassels, and he had covered his head to protect it from the sun. I thought I might have annoyed him by lying down without leave to sleep in his garden, for Jewish customs are very complex and I know little of them. I therefore rose hastily, went up to him, greeted him and said, "Your garden is glorious, and I hope you didn't think it wrong of me to rest here without asking leave." At that moment I would not have offended anyone in the world.

He turned and smiled more kindly than any Jew had ever smiled at me, a clean-shaven Roman. But his reply surprised me even more, for he answered gently, almost shyly, "In my garden there is room for you too, for I know you."

I thought his sight must be bad and that he mistook me for another.

"But I'm not a Jew," I said astonished. "How should you know me?"

He beckoned as if inviting me to go with him. Thinking that he wished to show me something or offer me something in token of friendship, I accompanied him willingly. He walked ahead and I saw that he was limping badly, though he was not at all an old man. Where the path turned, he again lifted a hanging fruit bough and I saw that he had hurt his hand. He had an ugly wound at his wrist that was not yet healed. Seeing this I stood as if petrified, and for a moment my limbs refused to obey me. Again he looked at me as at someone he knew and then continued along the path around a steep slope.

When my feet obeyed me once more I gave a cry and ran after him, but when I rounded the slope he had vanished. I saw that the path continued, but he was no longer to be seen, nor could I spy any place where he might have hidden in so short a time.

My knees gave way and I sat down in the middle of the path, not knowing what to think. I have written it down exactly as it happened. Now that I have written it I confess that for a while I firmly believed that I had beheld the Jews' resurrected king, in the shape of this gardener. The ugly wound at his wrist was just at the place where the executioner drives in the nail at a crucifixion, so that the bones may support the weight of the limp body.

He said that he knew me. How could he have known me unless he had seen me at the cross? But the moment of rapture passed, the earth faded to gray again before my eyes, and my reason returned. I was sitting on a dusty path and a kindly Jew had smiled at me. Why had I been so bemused by that? There might well be numbers of Jews who were friendly to strangers. I had seen plenty of lame men in the city, and a gardener often hurts his hands at his work. I must have misunderstood his gesture; he may not have meant me to follow him at all, and had slipped away into some hiding place.

Above all, if he had been the king of the Jews, why should he have shown himself to me, of all people? Who am I that he should do such a thing? And on the other hand, if he had had some special reason for it, surely he would have explained what he wanted of me; otherwise there was no sense in it.

Next I thought that I had just been dreaming. But when I scrambled to my feet and walked along the path I saw the place by the myrtle bush where I had slept. No, it was no dream. I lay down again and my reason, sharpened by intellectual training, rebelled against the pointlessness of my vision. Naturally I should have been more than glad to see the crucified king resurrected and alive, but I had no right to take my wish for reality, and fancy that I had seen him.

In this way were my thoughts divided, and I was seized by a frightening feeling of being split into two different creatures, one desiring to believe and the other deriding such credulity. The mocker told me that I had lost some of my youth and stamina. The wear and tear of that winter in Alexandria, spent by turns in wine drinking and frivolous company and in the study of dim prophecies, had addled my brains. The journey on foot from Joppa, the shattering events that I had witnessed, added to wakeful nights and excessive writing, had proved the last drop in a brimming cup, or the feather of the sophists that breaks the camel's back. I could no longer trust my own senses, far less my powers of judgment.

Pontius Pilate is older than I, and an experienced, judicious man. If I were sensible I would take his advice; rest, view the sights in the holy city of the Jews, and forget.

I thought of the demons which according to Jewish tales enter into weak people and take possession of their bodies. I had slept near tombs and exposed myself to peril. My difficulty was to determine which part of me was the demon: the part that wanted me to believe that the king of the Jews had risen from his grave and that I had seen him in the shape of the gardener; or the part that so fiercely condemned this idea.

I had hardly had time to think thusly before the reviler within me flared up. "You're so far gone that you believe in the Jews' demons. You've seen the physicians of Alexandria dissecting human bodies, and you've heard how they have cut open condemned criminals to find their soul. But they found nothing. You imagine that one man among men has risen from the dead, although you saw him expire on the cross and watched a seasoned legionary pierce his heart with a spear. Such things are not possible, and what is not possible cannot be true."

But my credulous self rebelled against this: "Marcus, if you give up now and turn away, you will never in your life know any peace, you will always be tormenting yourself with the thought that something happened before your eyes which had never happened before. So don't be too clever. Cleverness is limited and misleading, as the sophists have proved. There is nothing to prevent you from investigating the matter, in a humble, practical way. Examine first, then think. The fact that nothing like this has happened before doesn't prove that it can't happen. This is something more than the signs and omens of which you have always believed at least half. Rely more on your sensibility than on your reason. You are not one of the seven wise masters, and no one has ever won success in anything by means of reason alone. Sulla relied on his luck, Caesar did not believe that the Ides of March would bring him destruction. Even the dumb brutes are wiser than man, as when the birds fell silent and the donkey bolted before the earthquake, and as when rats desert a ship that is fated to be wrecked on her next voyage."

It is hard to describe this duality, for I believe no one can apprehend it without having experienced it himself. The sensation is terrifying, and I might have gone out of my mind were it not that in the innermost part of me there dwells a coldness that has protected me through even the worst emotional storms. But I knew from experience that it was best to be silent and to shun futile brooding.

When I had collected my thoughts, evening was already near and the valleys were filled with the shadows of the hills, though on the lofty height of the city the temple of the Jews shone with a ruddy light in the sun. I went now and sought out the house of the Jewish banker, to present my draft, for I guessed that I should need money to continue my researches. The building stood near the theatre and the high priest's house, in a recently rebuilt quarter of the city.

The banker himself received me when I had stated my business to his servant. He came as a real surprise to me after the Jewish contumacy that I had so far encountered. He at once invited me to address him by his Greek name, Aristainos, and said, "I have heard of you already. I had a letter from Alexandria and wondered whether you had fallen among robbers on the way, as you didn't call upon me at once. Foreign travelers usually come to me first of all to change money and ask advice about how best to squander it; for gloomy though Jerusalem may seem, it is gay and full of variety during the feast. Then they come back to borrow money for their return journey, and truth to tell I make more by that than by cashing bankers' orders. If you should meet with any difficulties during your stay here, don't hesitate to call upon me. I'm never surprised at anything merry-minded young travelers may do. Sometimes in the morning, when the horns of the temple sound and my gate is opened, some client of mine may be found asleep outside with his head on the bare stones, having lost both mantle and sandals."

He talked easily, like a man of the world, and for all his position he was not much older than myself. For form's sake he wore a little beard, and the tassels of his mantle were almost too small to be seen. He had curled his hair in the Greek manner and smelled of fine ointments, and he was in every way a handsome and agreeable man.

I explained that I had been staying in Antonia fortress as the guest of the Proconsul, because the Romans were afraid of disturbances and had warned me against lodging in the city during the feast of the passover. He spread out his hands in surprise, and with an exclamation said, "That is a lie; that is false, malicious talk. Our Council has a fully adequate police force to keep order. I believe our own priests deal more competently with agitators and fanatics than the Romans do. Naturally the people of Jerusalem dislike the Syrian legionaries, but that is chiefly because of their arrogant behavior. A traveling foreigner who brings money to the city, respects our customs and complies with city regulations is given the best possible reception. He is waited upon and cared for; guides vie with one another in showing him the sights, while many scholars are ready to expound to him the truths of our faith; he can choose any inn at any price from the dearest to the most moderate, and within the walls of certain houses all imaginable pleasures are permitted and available to him, whether of the Egyptian, Greek or Babylonian kind. You may even find Indian dancing girls here, should you wish to experience something very special. But of course the traveler would be wise to lodge in the new quarter near the forum."

I said that the east wind had given me an unpleasant headache, and that it was disagreeable to be roused at dawn by an earthquake and the clatter of falling shields.

He spoke yet more warmly in defense of his city and said, "Those two little shocks were of no consequence. They caused no damage. If you had been living here in the better part of the city I believe you would hardly have noticed this morning's tremor. I never even troubled to get out of bed, but it must have been more violent in the Antonia district."

I knew I was being discourteous, but I wanted to lead the conversation around to Jesus of Nazareth, and I said, as if making a further complaint, "And then you went and crucified your king just when I arrived, and that was no pleasant sight."

Aristainos' face darkened. He clapped his hands, ordered honey wine and pastries and replied, "You're an odd sort of traveler, to notice nothing but unpleasant things in this the only really holy city in the world. Be good enough to sit down and let me explain a few points, since it is evident that you don't know what you're saying. We Jews are weary of holy scriptures and prophecies, and that is natural enough, for our doctrine is the most remarkable one in the world and our history is incredible. Of all the nations, ours is the only one that worships the one God, who permits us to have no other gods; and of all the countries in the world we are alone in having one single temple here in Jerusalem, where we worship our God according to the laws which he himself has revealed to us through the great leaders of our people."

Smiling, he bade me take a goblet and taste the cakes, but he did not offer me the cup with his own hand, and I noticed that his cakes and mine were on different plates.

He followed my glance and said, laughing, "You see I'm a bigoted Jew. But it's only on the servants' account that I don't drink from the same cup as you or touch the same dish. Don't imagine that I think myself any better than you. I'm an enlightened man and break the law in many ways, though outwardly I try to keep it. We have our Pharisees who make their own and other people's lives unbearable by insisting that tradition must be followed to the letter. This is our conflict. Our law holds our people together. In all the cities of the world the same law holds all Jews together and prevents them from mingling with others and being swallowed up by them. Were it not so, this race, which has known slavery in both Egypt and Babylon, would long ago have been wiped out. I myself am an educated man, Greek at heart, and I cannot agree that the spirit should be bound by the letter, although if it came to the point I would let myself be hacked to pieces in defense of our God and our temple. Our history proves that we Jews are God's chosen people, but a sensible man must appreciate that in comparison with the infinite glory of our God, it matters little how one eats or drinks or washes hands or vessels. But these complicated customs and traditions, circumcision, observance of the Sabbath, and all the other things that are too troublesome to explain to a stranger—these things hold our people together here in this little land between east and west, so that we do not merge with other races, but will be ready when Messiah comes on earth and brings in the millennium."

He glanced at me sideways and added hastily, "That is what our prophets have foretold, but on no account take it literally, or even as some political dream, that one day the Jews, led by Messiah, will rule the world. It is only the simple people—the plebeians, as you would call them—who cherish dreams. Speaking generally, we Jews are enthusiasts, and so one Messiah after another appears among us to try his luck, and there is no miracle worker too inferior to gather a few simple souls about him as long as he has confidence in himself. You may be sure that we shall be able to distinguish the true Messiah from the false ones when and if he comes. We have had some experience. Our own Maccabean king had three thousand fanatical humbugs crucified. Do you then mourn just one who tried to fool people into believing that he was a king and Messiah?"

I had been drinking honey wine and eating cakes as he talked. The wine went merrily to my head, and I laughed too, saying, "How much and how heatedly you talk about so trivial a matter!"

He declared, "Believe me, Messiahs come and go, but our God

stands eternal, and the temple gathers all Jews together throughout the ages. We have reason to be grateful to the Romans, who have recognized our especial status among nations because of our doctrine, and allow us to govern ourselves. Both the emperors Augustus and Tiberius have been gracious to us and heard our complaints, so that our position is now consolidated. In fact, we prosper better beneath the wing of Rome than we would if we were an independent state and had to waste money on a standing army and continual wars with envious neighbors. As it is, we have supporters and spokesmen in every city of importance throughout the world, as far away as Gaul and Britain and the Scythian coasts; for barbarians too respect our commercial ability. I myself, by way of pastime, busy myself with the export of fruit and nuts to Rome. The only thing that vexes me is that we have no shipping of our own, because for some reason we Jews mistrust the sea. But every devout Jew who is able will always journey to the temple to offer sacrifice there, and with him comes ever-increasing wealth in the form of gifts for our temple. So you may perhaps understand that we cannot afford to allow the people to be stirred up by dreams of kings."

He was intensely concerned to convince me of the justice of the Council's policy, and leaning forward he went on, "And yet we live on the brink of an abyss. Any greedy procurator is prepared to rule us by dividing us, yes, and to lend some measure of support to ambitious men of the people, so that later he may accuse us of sedition and revolt, curtail the powers of our administration, and take his own share of the temple funds. But it is to our advantage, and really to Rome's too, that the present situation should be preserved and strengthened so that the politically unprejudiced Council may receive all possible support. You may best understand just what the Council is if I say that it corresponds to the Roman senate, and appoints its own members. These consist of the high priesthood, the most learned of the scholars, and, as lay members, those we call elders, though they are by no means all old, but qualify for membership by birth or fortune. The people are politically unschooled and we can allow them no decisive voice. Therefore we must stifle at birth any attempt of theirs to extend political rights and reintroduce the monarchy, however innocent such an attempt may seem—as for instance when it is made under cover of our religion or, let us say, from love of mankind."

My scornful silence stung him to defend himself with even greater heat, as if he did nevertheless feel guilty in some way. He explained, "As a Roman, accustomed to worshiping mere images, you cannot conceive of the vast influence that religion has here. Our religion is our strength but at the same time our greatest danger, for a political enthusiast is forced to hold fast by our scriptures, and with their help demonstrate that his aims are right and proper, whatever his secret purposes may be. Now of course, you will say that Jesus of Nazareth, whom we had barely time to crucify before the passover feast, was an innocent and righteous man, a great healer and a great teacher. But it is just such blameless idealists, who by their personality induce the people to embrace their program of reform, that are the most dangerous. Being politically inexperienced, such a man believes the best of everyone and becomes the tool of ambitious men—men who care not a farthing if our whole society collapses and the people perish under the wrath of Rome, so long as they themselves may for a time satisfy their greed for power. Believe me, a man who makes himself Messiah is a political criminal and deserves death, however honest and sincere he may be as an individual."

He hesitated, and then added hurriedly, "Of course at the same time he incurs the guilt of blasphemy, which by our law is punishable by death. But among enlightened people like ourselves that is a secondary issue. If he had shown himself in the temple once more, during the passover, rioting would have broken out, fanatics would have seized leadership with him as their figurehead, and blood would have flowed. Then the Romans would have interfered and we should have forfeited our self-government. Better that one man should die than that the whole people should perish."

"I've heard that slogan before," I remarked.

"Forget him," urged Aristainos. "We're not proud of his execution; indeed, I myself am grieved that he had to die, for he was really a good fellow, that Galilean Jesus. He should have stayed in Galilee, and then he would hardly have come to any harm. There, even the tax collectors liked him, and the commandant of Capernaum is said to have been one of his friends."

I saw that there would be no use in hinting that Jesus had risen again; he would only have lost all regard for me and thought me a credulous fool. I reflected for a little, and then said, "You have convinced me, and I understand perfectly well that from the Jewish point of view it was politically desirable that he should die. But in the course of my travels I like to take note of all kinds of remarkable events, so that later I may amuse people with my knowledge, and perhaps also learn a little myself. Among other things I am interested in all sorts of healing. In Antioch, when I was young, I once saw a famous Syrian magus who healed people in a wonderful manner; and in Egypt too there are places of pilgrimage where healing is done. So I would much like to meet some sick person whom that man cured, and learn something of his methods."

I pretended to have had a sudden idea. "But of course the most interesting thing of all would be to meet one of his disciples," I exclaimed. "Then I should gain firsthand information about him and about what he was really after."

Aristainos looked embarrassed and said, "Naturally they're now in hiding or have fled back to Galilee. His closest disciples numbered only twelve, so far as I know, and incidentally it was one of them who revealed his hiding place to the Council. They're all simple folk, fishermen from the Sea of Galilee and so on; except for a certain John, a young man of good family who has certainly studied, and speaks Greek. But then there was a customs man among them too—that sort of rabble, you understand. I hardly think you would have much to gain from them.

"But," he said hesitantly, "if you really are curious—though frankly I can't quite see why, when you could be leading a gay life in Jerusalem—there is a member of the Council called Nicodemus who could give you information. He is a pious searcher of the scriptures—a waiting, yearning man, if I may so describe him. There is no evil in him although he caused bad blood in the Council by defending Jesus. He is far too naïve a man to hold such a high position; and that was why he was not summoned to the night meeting of the Council, for it would have distressed him very much to have been of those who condemned the Nazarene to death."

"I have heard of him," I said. "Was it not he who took the king down from the cross and laid him in the sepulcher? He is said to have given a hundred pounds' weight of ointments for the enshrouding."

The word "king" jarred upon Aristainos, but at least he did not correct me as other Jews did. He admitted reluctantly, "You are well informed. It was a public demonstration on the part of Nicodemus and Joseph of Arimathea, but one must allow them that salve to their conscience. Joseph is merely an elder, but Nicodemus is one of the teachers of Israel and should have known better. Still, one should never judge a man's intentions from his appearance. It may be that by burying the Galilean those two are attempting to gather about them an opposition party within the Council, to whittle away the power of the high priest."

The idea delighted him, and he exclaimed, "I have no objection to that! Caiaphas' insolence has already begun to damage our commerce. He has put all trading in sacrificial beasts and the money changing of the temple into the hands of his countless kinsmen. You'll hardly believe it, but not even I have an exchange table in the forecourt under my own name. It may be that, in all innocence, Nicodemus is a really good politician. It is not seemly—it is not even lawful—for the forecourt of the temple to be made a rowdy market place. A certain degree of competition should be permitted in the case of money changing. All pious pilgrims would benefit if they were not forced to accept Caiaphas' rate of exchange for temple shekels."

His business affairs were of no interest to me. I said, "I would like to meet Nicodemus, but he would hardly be willing to receive *me,* since I am a Roman."

"But, my dear friend," exclaimed Aristainos, "that is a recommendation! A Jewish scholar regards it as an honor when any Roman citizen desires to gain knowledge of our doctrine. You can always feign piety. That will open all doors to you and commit you to nothing. I will gladly commend you to him, if you wish."

It was agreed that he should send word of me. The following evening I should be able to go and meet Nicodemus immediately after dark. I drew some money from Aristainos, but left the greater part in his keeping. He pressed me eagerly to employ one of his servants, who was an experienced guide and could open all the secret doors and delights of Jerusalem to me; but I said that I had taken certain vows since my dissolute winter in Alexandria. He swallowed that whole, expressed admiration for my will power, but regretted that I would miss so much.

We parted as friends. He came with me to his gate and would have given me a forerunner to clear my way through the city, but I did not wish to attract needless attention. Once again he assured me that I might come to him at any time if I found myself in difficulties. He is without doubt the most agreeable Jew I have met so far, yet for some reason I cannot feel unmixed friendship for him. His dispassionate pronouncements chilled me and revived my doubts, and that may account for my feeling of reserve.

When I returned to Antonia I learned that Claudia Procula

had sent for me several times. I hastened to her tower room. She had already gone to bed, but she put on a thin silk robe, threw a mantle over her shoulders and came out, attended by her lady in waiting, to talk to me. There was an alarming glitter in her eyes. The lines in her pale face had been smoothed out, and she appeared to be in a state of ecstasy.

Grasping my hands in both of hers she exclaimed, "Marcus, Marcus, he has risen from the dead! The king of the Jews has risen from the dead!"

I asked crossly, "Didn't the Proconsul tell you that his disciples came to the tomb last night and stole his body? There is an official record of the matter, attested by six legionaries."

Claudia Procula stamped and cried, "Do you suppose that Pontius believes in anything but his purse and his own advantage? But I have women friends in Jerusalem. Have you not heard how one of his followers went to the tomb at dawn—the woman from whom he drove out seven demons? The tomb was empty, except for an angel wearing robes that seemed made of light, and with a face as of fire."

"In that case," I said coarsely, "she must have got her demons back again." And I wondered, downcast, in what I had involved myself. Was I so crazy as to want to compete with raving women?

Claudia Procula was hurt and bitterly disappointed. "You too then, Marcus," she said reproachfully, with a sob. "I thought you were on his side, as I heard that you had been to the tomb and found it empty. Do you believe more in Pontius Pilate and his corruptible soldiers than in the evidence of your own eyes?"

I relented, for when she wept her rapt face took on a strange fire, and I would have liked to comfort her. But I realized the danger of confiding what I had seen to an overwrought woman. In my opinion, all the women's wild talk of resurrection, visions and angels merely served the cause of the Jewish Council and made everything more incredible than it need have been.

"Don't take it to heart so, Claudia," I begged. "You know I

have heard too much of the teaching of the cynics, and find it hard to believe in supernatural things. On the other hand, I have no wish to deny everything. Who is your witness and what is her name?"

"Her name is Mary," Claudia replied very eagerly, to convince me. "That is a common Jewish name, but she comes from Magdala by the Sea of Galilee. She is a lady of means, and a well-known breeder of doves. Her lofts produce thousands of unblemished doves every year for temple offerings. It is true that she won a bad name for herself after the demons had got her into their power, but when Jesus of Nazareth healed her she changed completely, and followed the teacher everywhere upon his wanderings. I met her when I visited a distinguished Jewish lady of my acquaintance, and she impressed me greatly by what she told me of her teacher."

"I should have to hear it from her own mouth to believe it," I said. "She may be just one of those fanatical dreamers who are bent on attracting attention at all costs. Do you think I might meet her somehow?"

"Is it wrong to have dreams?" Claudia Procula protested. "I have been so persecuted by dreams that I warned my husband against sentencing so devout a man. In the middle of the night I had word that he had been arrested, and people implored me to use influence with my husband so that he should not be convicted. But the dreams I had had earlier made a greater impact than this secret message. I still believe that my husband committed the most foolish act of his life in handing over that man to be crucified."

"Do you think I might meet this Mary of yours?" I persisted.

Claudia Procula became evasive. "It is not seemly for a Jewish woman to meet an unknown man, least of all a foreigner. I don't even know where she lives. I admit that she's an emotional woman, and a suspicious man like yourself might form a wrong impression of her if you were to meet. But that doesn't prevent me from believing her story." Nevertheless Claudia Procula's eagerness began to die down.

"But if by chance I should meet this Mary of Magdala," I said, "may I mention your name and assure her that she may speak freely and confidently of what she has seen?"

Claudia murmured that a man can't win a woman's trust as another woman can, and that anyhow no man can ever really understand a woman. However, reluctantly, she gave her consent. "But if you cause her the least trouble or unpleasantness," she said threateningly, "you will have to account for it to me."

With this our conversation ended, although Claudia Procula had obviously hoped to win me over as a fellow enthusiast and persuade me of the Jewish king's resurrection. In a way, I am bound to believe in it, after having seen the graveclothes lying untouched in the empty tomb. But I want to examine the whole matter in a rational way.

Fourth Letter

MARCUS TO TULLIA:

I continue my account and will mention everything in the order in which it happened.

Antonia is a cramped and gloomy fortress, and I had no wish to stay on there under constant guard. Moreover, the Proconsul was preparing to return to Caesarea, where his residence is. I gave him a lucky Egyptian scarab, and to Claudia Procula an Alexandrian looking glass, and I promised to pass through Caesarea on my return journey. This was at Pontius Pilate's request, for he did not want to let me leave Judea without questioning me. Claudia Procula too adjured me to tell her anything I might have heard about the risen man.

To the garrison commander I gave a handsome sum of money, so as to remain on good terms with him and to make sure of a refuge in the fortress, should I ever need it. But I have already noticed that no danger threatens me in Jerusalem as long as I respect the customs of the Jews and refrain from provoking them with my own.

For the centurion Adenabar I feel real friendship. On his advice I did not lodge at a large inn, but with an acquaintance of his, a Syrian trader near the Hasmonsan palace. I have been familiar with the customs and gods of the Syrians since my youth, and know that people of this race enjoy good food, keep their rooms clean and are honest in everything but money changing.

The merchant himself lives on the ground floor with his family, and carries his counter out into the street in front of his house every day. An outside staircase leads directly up onto the roof, so that I can come and go as I please and receive visitors unobserved. The advantage of this was stressed by both Adenabar and my landlord. His wife and daughter serve meals in my room and see that a jar of fresh water always hangs there. The sons vie with one another in running errands for me, buying wine and fruit and anything else I may need. This family, who are not well off, are glad to have me as a paying guest now that the feast is over and most visitors have left the city.

When I had settled into my new lodging I waited until the stars came out and then went down the outer stair to the street. Nicodemus' pottery is well enough known for me to find it easily. The gate was left ajar, and when I entered the courtyard I met a servant there in the darkness who asked softly, "Are you the man my master is waiting for?"

He led me up some stairs to the roof, and the starry sky above Judea was so brilliant that he did not need to light the way. On the roof an elderly man was seated upon cushions. He greeted me cordially, and asked, "Are you the God-seeker of whom Aristainos has told me?"

He invited me to sit beside him and at once started to tell me in a monotonus tone about the God of Israel. He began with the story of the creation of heaven and earth, and had got as far as saying that God had created man in his own image, from the dust of the earth, when I interrupted him impatiently.

"Master of Israel, I've heard all these things and read of them in Greek in your holy scriptures. I have come to you so that you might tell me of Jesus of Nazareth, the king of the Jews. This you must be aware of, since you receive me on your rooftop in the dark."

Nicodemus said in an unsteady voice, "His blood was upon my head and upon my people. I am full of pain and deadly fear on his account. That he became a teacher was God's doing, for no man could have performed the things he did unless he had been sent by God."

I said, "He was more than a teacher. I too tremble inwardly on his account, stranger though I am. You must surely know that he rose from his tomb, although you helped to swathe him and close the sepulcher before the Sabbath began."

Nicodemus raised his face to the starlight and cried in a voice of lamentation, "I know not what to believe."

Pointing to the sky I asked, "Was he the son of the stars of whom the prophets spoke?"

Nicodemus said, "I do not know, I understand nothing and I am no longer fit to be a Master of Israel. I was misled in the Council because they assured me that no prophet can come out of Galilee. That is true. Nothing is said of Galilee in the scriptures. But his mother, whom I have only just met, assures me that he was born in Bethlehem of Judea in the time of the wicked Herod. The scriptures show that a savior is to come from Bethlehem Ephratah. I have searched the scriptures without rest. Everything that was foretold of him has come about, even this: that no bone in his body shall be broken."

He began to recite the prophecies in a chanting voice, and translated them for me. When he had been doing this for some time, I grew impatient again and said, "It means nothing to me that the words of your prophets should have been fulfilled. For me the only question is whether or not he is risen. If he has come out of his tomb, then he is more than a king and his like has never lived in the world before. I ask you this without guile or treachery, for no one can harm him now. Answer me. My heart trembles within me with longing to know the truth."

Nicodemus confessed hesitantly, "I have heard that it is so, but I know not what to believe. Last night his disciples were assembled behind locked doors, for they fear persecution. At least, most of them came together, and all were much afraid. Then the crucified Jesus appeared among them and showed them the wounds in his hands and feet and in his side. He also breathed upon everyone in the room. Then he vanished as he had come. So I have been told, but it is very difficult to believe."

I trembled where I stood. "Tell me of his kingdom," I begged. "What did he teach about his kingdom?"

Nicodemus told me: "I went to see him secretly the first time he came to Jerusalem for the passover, and cleansed the temple. I cannot forget what he said to me then, although I did not understand it, and still do not. He said that no one may behold the kingdom unless he has been born again."

At once I remembered the teachings of the Orphics and Pythagoreans and philosophers who affirm that men are continually reborn, and may even become animals or plants according to the nature of their actions. I was filled with disappointment, for this is no new doctrine. But Nicodemus went on ingenuously, "I contradicted him and asked, 'How can a man be born again when he is old? He cannot return to his mother's womb and let himself be reborn.' Then Jesus gave me a key to his words and repeated it several times. 'He who is not born again of water and of the Spirit cannot enter the kingdom.' The part about the water I understand, for there are many who go out to the brothers in the desert to wait there in prayer, and who, after a time of testing, are baptized in their pool. John too came from the desert and baptized people with water, until Herod Antipas had him murdered."

I interrupted him, saying, "Those who become initiated into the mysteries of Isis, in Egypt, step without fear into deep water in a dark cave, but strong arms lift them to safety so that they do not drown. It is a symbolic initiation rite, and by no means new."

Nicodemus acknowledged this. "No, that is true; baptism with water is nothing new. But I asked him what he meant by being born of the Spirit. Jesus answered thus–these are his very words, and I impressed them on my memory–'That which is born of the flesh is flesh, and that which is born of the Spirit is spirit. The wind blows where it will; you hear the sound of it, but you cannot tell whence it comes and whither it goes: so is everyone that is born of the Spirit.' "

He was silent for a long time and I pondered his words. The stars of Judea sparkled in the sky, and through the darkness came a strong smell of damp clay and kilns. In a mysterious way this instruction forced its way into my heart, although I know only too well that my reason could not grasp it. At last I asked softly, "Is that all you know of his kingdom?"

Nicodemus reflected and said, "I heard from his disciples that before he began to teach he went out into the desert. There he watched and fasted for forty days and experienced all the false visions and revelations with which earthbound powers tempt a fasting man. The tempter took him up on a high mountain and showed him all the kingdoms of the earth and their glory, and promised him that he should rule over them if he would bow down before the tempter and thus renounce the task which he came into the world to fulfill. That temptation he overcame. Then angels came and served him in the wilderness. He returned to the world of men, began to teach and to perform miracles, and gathered disciples about him. That is what I know of his kingdom. It's not a human kingdom; therefore it was unjust and a crime to condemn him."

I was distressed by this talk of revelations and angels, since any highly strung person who had watched and fasted long enough can have hallucinations, but they vanish as soon as he eats and drinks and goes among people again. I asked Nicodemus impatiently, "Well, what sort of kingdom is it?"

Nicodemus lamented aloud, raised his hands and exclaimed, "How should I know? I have heard the sound of the wind. When

I met him I thought the kingdom had come on earth in his shape. He told me many other things. He even said that God had not sent his son into the world to condemn it, but that the world, through him, might be saved. But that is not what happened. He was simply nailed to a cross and died a dishonorable death. That is what I cannot fathom. Now that he is gone, the kingdom too is gone."

My heart said otherwise, but my reason forced me to remark ironically, "That is not much to give me, Master of Israel. The sound of a wind—and you yourself don't honestly believe that he is risen."

"I am no longer a Master of Israel," Nicodemus confessed humbly. "I am the least of the children of Israel, stricken down and wounded to the heart. But something I can give you. When the sower has sown his seed he tends it no longer. The seed sprouts, wind and rain drive forth the shoot, and the grain grows —though the sower sleep—until it is ripe for harvest. So it is with me; so it may be with you, if you are sincere. A seed has been sown in me, and it is sprouting. A seed may have been sown also in you, one day to be harvested. I can only wait in submission and confess how little I understand and how feeble is my faith."

"I'm far from being content to wait," I protested impatiently. "Do not you see that everything is still fresh in my memory? Each day carries something away with it into oblivion. Bring me to his disciples. He must have revealed the secret of his kingdom to them in a more intelligible way. I have a fire in my heart. I am eager to believe, so long as everything may be proved to me."

Nicodemus gave a deep sigh and said dissuasively, "His disciples—the eleven that are left—are frightened and bewildered and filled with disappointment. They are simple men, still young and foolish. When he was alive they argued among themselves about his teachings; they allotted amongst themselves high positions in the kingdom, and quarreled over them.

No matter what he said to them, they believed to the end in a kingdom on earth. Even that last evening, before he was arrested, he partook of the paschal lamb with them in the manner of the desert brothers, and told them that he would not drink wine again until he could do so with them in the new kingdom. I believe that it was because of that promise that he would not accept the pain-deadening wine which the women offered him before the crucifixion. But the promise encouraged the more childish of the disciples to believe that he would summon a legion of angels from heaven to help him, and would found a kingdom in which each of the disciples would rule over one of the tribes of Israel. From this you can see that his teachings have not yet ripened within them. They are ignorant men and know not what to think, although they were present at all his greatest works. They fear for their own lives and keep themselves in hiding. If you were to meet them now you would certainly be more bewildered by what they told you than they are themselves."

I couldn't understand this. "Then why did he choose only simple men to be his disciples?" I demanded. "If he was so great a miracle worker as they say, he could surely have chosen companions from among scholars as well."

"There you touch me at a tender spot," Nicodemus confessed. "You touch the core of my grief. It was not the wise men and scholars whom he called, but the poor, the simple, the oppressed. He is said to have spoken once to a great crowd of people, and said in so many words that it was the simple who were blessed, for theirs was the kingdom. For the learned and the rich he made everything too difficult. I might well have become one of his disciples, but then I should have had to resign from the Council—yes, and from my family too; sell my pottery works, and distribute the proceeds among the poor. Such were the stern conditions he imposed, making it impossible for men like us to follow him. Yet he had friends among rich and influential people, who helped him secretly. In fact he had information and connections which not even his disciples knew about, because he considered it unnecessary to tell them."

"Nevertheless, I should like to meet some of his real disciples," I said obstinately.

But Nicodemus said with firm dissuasion, "You're no Roman spy, that I can feel; but they would never believe you, being so frightened. Nor would you believe them when you saw what simple men they are. On the contrary, if they told you that they had beheld the risen son of God in a room where the door was locked, you would doubt them more than ever, and fancy that they had made up the whole story out of disappointment, and to save the rags of their self-esteem."

Nicodemus laughed sadly and said, "At first they wouldn't even believe the women who came back from the tomb saying that it was empty. One of them, who happened not to be present last night in their locked hiding place, refuses to believe what his own friends have told him. How then could you believe them?"

I did my best to persuade him to divulge the place where the king's disciples lay in hiding, or to bring me into touch with them in some other way, but it was clear that even now he did not quite trust me, for he flatly refused. When I saw that he began to regret having received me, I hastened to plead with him: "Advise me at least as to what I am to do, for I cannot endure to wait in idleness for something to happen."

He warned me, saying, "The sower has sown his seed. Should a grain have fallen in you, you would do wisely to wait in humility. But if you will, set forth into Galilee, where he himself so often walked, seek out the quiet ones and ask each of them what they have cherished of his teaching. Or speak to those whom he healed of sickness, and so convince yourself that none but the son of God could have wrought such miracles as those he performed during his lifetime."

I was not overjoyed at these proposals.

"How am I to recognize the quiet ones?" I asked. "Galilee is far from here, and I am a stranger."

Nicodemus hesitated, then gave me the password, saying, "Ask the Way as you go, but if anyone shakes his head and answers, 'There are many ways, and many false guides, and I don't want to lead you astray,' reply in your turn, 'There is but one Way; show it me, for I am quiet and humble of heart.' At that they will know you and trust you. And even were you to inform against them you could never harm them, for they keep the commandments and pay their tax and offend no one."

I said, "I thank you for your advice, and I will remember it. Yet he secretly performed some miracles in Jerusalem too. I would not like to leave the city yet, lest something should happen here."

Nicodemus was tiring of me now. He said, "Here you may meet the woman of ill-repute from whom he drove out the evil spirits. There is also a village called Bethany only a short distance from the city. Two sisters and a brother live there, with whom he used to stay. One of them he permitted to sit at his feet and listen to his teaching, though she was only a woman. The brother he raised from the dead, after he had lain in his tomb for four days and his body was said to be stinking. Go there and meet Lazarus. That's miracle enough for you. They will receive you if you bring them a greeting from me."

"Was he really dead?" I asked incredulously.

"Of course, of course," cried Nicodemus in irritation. "I know as well as you that there are trances resembling death. There are those who, amid wailing and playing of pipes, sit up on the bier, to the horror of their kinsfolk, and looking about them blinking. People are said to have come to their senses in the tomb, clawed their nails away, and shrieked until they suffocated because they couldn't roll aside the stone from the opening. Our law requires the corpse to be interred on the day of death, and that is how mistakes occur. I possess all the earthly knowledge I require, and can do without your advice."

He wrangled on: "What profit have you of anything if you start from preconceived doubt? What do you expect to gain from that? I can read your thoughts as you recall that he was a friend of the family. Easy enough for them to hit on something to convince the waverers, and lay the swooning Lazarus in the tomb, knowing that the teacher was on his way. But what could they hope to gain by that? Go and talk to them—to Lazarus and his two sisters—and decide for yourself whether or not they're telling the truth."

Of course Nicodemus was right. As I could get no more from him I thanked him and asked what I owed for his instruction. He flatly refused payment, saying contemptuously, "I'm no runaway circus artist who lives by teaching children to read, as is said to be customary in Rome. The masters of Israel do not teach for payment. He who desires to become a teacher must learn a trade, so that he may live by the work of his hands. Therefore I am a potter, like my father before me. But if you wish, give the money to the poor, and it may bring a blessing upon you."

He came down the stairs with me, and from the courtyard he led me into his reception room, so that by the light of the lamp in there I might see that—potter thought he might be—he was a man of consequence. He had at least that much vanity. I could see too that the room was the room of a rich man, full of costly things. Even his mantle was of the best material. But above all, I looked at his face, now that I could see it in the light. His eyes were nearsighted from reading, and his face—for all his gray beard—was childishly rounded. But his hands showed that he had not touched clay for many years, though he may have known his craft.

He too looked at me searchingly, so as to impress my appearance on his memory, and said, "I see no evil in your face. You have restless eyes, but they are not the eyes of a doubter or an evildoer. But you should let your beard grow, so that others too may see that you are a pious man."

I had come to that conclusion myself and had ceased to shave, but in two days my chin had not had time to produce more than black stubble.

Nicodemus came with me to the gate and barred it behind me himself. He no longer wished me to be seen by his servants. I stumbled over the worn paving stones until my eyes became accustomed to the darkness. Only at the corners of the big streets were any lights still burning, but I had carefully memorized my way and thought it would be easy to get back to my new lodging, although it was some distance from this lower part of the city. I reached the wall between the suburbs and the upper city without meeting anyone but a couple of Jewish watchmen. But at the archway itself a woman's voice greeted me shyly and asked, "What belongs to your peace, stranger?"

I started at the unexpected voice, but replied politely, "What belongs to your own peace, woman?"

The woman fell upon her knees before me in the street and said meekly, "I am your servant. Only command me and I will do what you wish."

I guessed her trade and said deprecatingly, "Go in peace. I want nothing of you."

But she was persistent; she seized the hem of my mantle and pleaded, "I am poor, and have no room to which I may take you, but there is a niche in the wall where no one will see us."

As is the fashion among Jewish women, she was so veiled and swathed in her garments that I could form no idea of her appearance or even of her age. But her poverty moved me. I remembered Nicodemus' injunction and gave her as many silver coins as I thought I owed for his teaching and advice.

At first she would not believe me when I repeated that I wanted nothing of her. But when she found that it was true she insisted upon kissing my feet, and exclaimed, "Never yet has anyone given me a present without requiring something in return. May the God of Israel bless you, though I am not fit to invoke a blessing upon anyone, and not even my money is acceptable to the temple coffers. But tell me your name that I may pray for you."

I did not want to give my name to a woman of her profession, and yet I was unwilling to wound her. So I said, "I am called Marcus, in the Roman manner. I'm a stranger in Jerusalem."

She said, "Your servant's name is Mary. But there are more Marys than seeds in a pomegranate, so I will tell you that I am Mary of Beret, the village of wells, that you may distinguish me from the other Marys who will certainly come the way of so liberal a man as yourself."

"I'm not at all liberal," I said, to be rid of her. "I have merely paid a debt and you owe me no thanks. Go in peace, and then I too may go in peace, and we need no longer think about each other."

She tried to make out my face in the darkness and said pleadingly, "You should not despise the prayers of the poor. It may be that one day I may do you a service when you least expect it."

"You owe me nothing," I repeated. "I ask no service of you. A way is all I seek, and that you can hardly show me."

She answered quickly, "Do you ask a way, stranger? But there are many ways and they lead men astray. I should only misguide you if I tried to set you on the path."

Her reply could have been no mere coincidence. Yet I was dashed by the thought that the quiet ones in the land plainly belonged to the most despised and rejected of people. Nevertheless, I tried to think of the mouse that gnawed the rope in which the lion was imprisoned, and said, "I have heard that there is only one way. And I too would gladly be quiet and humble of heart if I could."

She put out her hand and felt my face and the rough bristles on my chin. However humble I desired to be, her touch was distasteful to me. I must have started, for she recoiled at once and said sadly, "It's not the whole who require healing, but the sick. You took pity on me not for my own sake, but to pay a debt that oppressed you. You can hardly be so sick as to choose that way sincerely in your heart. But I've been sent to try you. If you had come with me to the hollow in the wall we should have parted from each other with evil thoughts. I give you hope, if you are inquiring about the Way in all sincerity."

"I am sincere and wish no one ill," I assured her. "All I want is to learn the truth about a number of things which you can hardly know of."

"Do not despise a woman's knowledge," she warned me. "In the kingdom a woman's intuition may carry more weight than a man's reason, even were I the most despised among the women of Israel. And my intuition tells me that these days are the days of waiting. In these days sister meets sister without despising her; brother meets brother without rebuking him. Therefore my heart is lighter than before, fallen woman though I am."

There was such happy expectation in her voice that I was compelled to believe that she did indeed possess some knowledge. "This evening I listened to one of the teachers of Israel," I said, "but he was an uncertain man of little faith, and his teaching left me cold. Could you, Mary of Beret, give me better instruction?"

As I said this I was assailed by a suspicion that this Mary might not be so bad a woman as she made out. She may really have been sent on my path to test me, for to reach my new lodging I was bound to pass through this gate. "What hope is it that you offer me?" I asked.

She asked, "Do you know where the Fountain Gate is?"

"No," I answered, "but I can easily find it."

"It leads to the Vale of Kidron and the road to Jericho," she explained. "That may be the way you seek. But if not, go to the Fountain Gate one day when your beard has grown, and look about you. You may see a man carrying a water jar from the spring. Follow him. If you speak to him, he may answer. If he does not, there is nothing I can do."

"Water carrying is no work for a man," I said incredulously. "It is the women who fetch water in Jerusalem, as everywhere else in the world."

"For that reason you will easily recognize him," said Mary of Beret. "But if he does not answer you, do not importune him, but return another day and try again. I can give you no other counsel."

"If your counsel is good and brings me the help I hope for," I said, "I shall once more be in your debt, Mary."

"On the contrary," she answered eagerly. "It is I who will be paying a debt if I can show anyone else the Way. But should the debt oppress you, give the money to the poor and forget me. In any event you need not seek me here by the hollow in the wall, for never again shall I return to this place."

We parted, and I had no idea of what she looked like, and I could never have recognized her in the light of day. But I thought I would know her cheerful voice if I heard it again.

I went back to my lodging, up the stairs to the roof and into my room. When I thought of all that had happened, the mysteriousness of the Jews annoyed me. Nicodemus must have known more than he had told me. I had the feeling that people had been watching me, and required something of me.

It may be that either the disciples of the risen king or Claudia Procula's friends suspect me of knowledge which they do not possess, but they dare not make themselves known to me, because I am a stranger. They have every reason to be cautious, since their teacher has been condemned, cast out and crucified.

The gardener whom I saw near the tomb haunts my mind as well. He said that he knew me, and I ought to have known him. Yet I do not intend to return and seek him in the garden, so sure am I that I should no longer find him there.

Fifth Letter

MARCUS TO TULLIA:

I will tell of my wayfaring to Bethany, and of what happened to me there.

My beard was growing. Having put on a simple tunic and a dirty traveling mantle I seemed to myself more like a robber than a cultured Roman. The Syrian gave me bread, salt fish and sour wine for my journey, and I set off through the city to the Fountain Gate. I passed the pool in the Vale of Kidron and followed the road alongside the dried-up stream. On the ridge to the left rose the city wall, and in the rocky slopes to my right were many tombs. Olive trees, gnarled with age, grew on the hillsides, and I passed a lofty height with a shady dark-green herb garden on its shoulder.

The air was fresh and warm and the sky cloudless. I met donkeys laden with firewood and charcoal, and country folk carrying baskets. I journeyed on, lighthearted, feeling that I was still young and strong. The pleasure of exercise dispelled the gloomy thoughts from my doubting mind and I felt open and receptive. It may be that I am really experiencing a time when the world is filled with expectancy, and no one quite knows what is to happen. A stranger like myself might come as near to the riddle as those who have lived with it. The earth did not seem to me like the old earth, nor heaven as it had been; I was seeing everything more clearly than before.

I saw Bethany from a long way off. The gable ends of the low houses had been newly whitewashed for the feast and shone through the trees. When I drew near the village I saw a man sitting in the shade of a fig tree. He sat so still in his earth-colored mantle that I started and stood still when I saw him.

"Peace be with you," I exclaimed. "Is this village called Bethany?"

He looked at me, and the eyes in his thin face were so glassy that at first I thought he was blind. He had not covered his head, and his hair was white, though his face, if sallow, was that of a young man.

"And with you be peace," he replied. "Have you lost the way, stranger?"

"There are many ways and many false guides," I said quickly, with rising hope. "Perhaps you can show me the right way."

"Was it Nicodemus who sent you?" he asked curtly. "If so, I am Lazarus. What do you want of me?"

He spoke in a blurred way, as if he had difficulty in moving his tongue. I stepped off the road and sat down at his side, though not close to him. I was glad to rest in the shadow of the fig tree and did my best not to stare at him too rudely, for it is the custom of the Jews to look at the ground when they meet a stranger. With them it is discourteous to look another person in the face.

He may have wondered that I did not start talking at once, for when we had sat silently for a time side by side, I fanning myself with the edge of my mantle—for I had walked myself into a sweat—he said, "You must surely know that the high priests are determined to kill me too. As you see, I have not gone into hiding, but live at home in my village. They're welcome to come and kill this body of mine if they can. I'm not afraid of them, nor of you. No one can kill me, for I can never die."

His grim words and glassy look alarmed me. I seemed to feel a chill breath from him. Therefore I exclaimed, "Are you out of your mind? How can any mortal assert that he will never die?"

He said, "Perhaps I am no longer a mortal. I have this body, certainly. I eat and drink and speak. But the world about me is no longer real to me. The loss of my body would be no loss at all."

There was something so singular about him that I believed him. "I've been told," said I, "that the man who was crucified as king of the Jews raised you from the dead. Is that true?"

He replied, mocking, "Why ask? Here I sit, as you see. I died the death of a mortal and lay enshrouded in my tomb for four days, until he came and ordered the stone to be removed from the entrance to the tomb and called to me, 'Lazarus, come forth!' It was as simple as that."

But he spoke of this without joy. Indeed there was a sneer in his voice. As I said nothing he went on: "It was all the fault of my sisters, and I can't forgive them for sending for him over and over again and making him return to Judea. If I hadn't sickened and died, he might not have come here at all and fallen into the hands of his enemies. He wept for me before he called me out of the tomb."

"I don't understand you," I protested. "Why, instead of rejoicing, do you reproach your sisters, seeing that he raised you from the dead and allowed you to return to life?"

Lazarus said, "I don't believe that anyone who has known death can feel joy again. He ought not to have wept for me."

He said also, "Jesus must have been the son of God—he who should come—although I was not so firmly persuaded of this as my sisters. I cannot understand why he should have loved me so much, for he had no reason."

We sat in silence, staring before us, and I did not know what further questions to put to him; he seemed to me so strange with his coldness and joylessness.

"He is more than Messiah," said Lazarus very decisively. "That is just what frightens me. He is more than anything the prophets could have foretold. I suppose you have heard that he rose up out of his tomb on the third day?"

"I have," I answered. "That is why I came to see you—to learn more about him."

"It is quite natural, plain and in every way understandable," said Lazarus. "What power could have kept him in the grave? I didn't need to go and see the empty tomb, as my sisters did. I can believe it without that. But, stranger, with all my heart and more fervently than anything else, I hope that never again in this life may he show himself to me. I could not bear to see him. No, no, not in this life. Not until his kingdom."

"What is his kingdom like?" I asked eagerly.

Lazarus looked at me with cold eyes and said, "Why not ask what the kingdom of death is like? I can tell you this: death is here and now and everywhere. That I know from experience. This world is the kingdom of death. So is your body. But in him, his kingdom came upon earth. Therefore his kingdom is here and now and everywhere."

Presently he bent his head and added, "But believe not what I say, for I may have misunderstood. It is all bewildering."

He said also, "Don't let my dejection depress you. The Way is the right one, of that I can assure you. If you continue upon is, you cannot go astray."

He stood up and shook the dust off his mantle. "You would like to meet my two sisters," he said. "I will bring you to them. Then if you will allow me, I shall go my way. It is hard for me to be in the company of people."

Indeed, he must have felt more dead than alive among others. It was difficult for him to move, too, just as if he had not full control of his limbs. I believe that he would have struck me as odd at once, had I met him first among other people without knowing who he was.

He did not take me to the village by the most direct way, but went before me up the hillside, and from there showed me the rock tomb from which Jesus of Nazareth had called him. His home was a well-kept farm. On the way he showed me a pair of donkeys at pasture, a vineyard, fruit trees, and fowls scratching near the house. It was as if he wanted to let me know, in country fashion, that he was not a man of absolutely no account. It was all so pleasant, serene and genuine that I found it hard to realize that I was walking beside a man who was convinced that he had been raised from the dead.

But for me this point is not conclusive. What matters is whether Jesus of Nazareth really is the son of God, and has risen from his tomb. If so, what was to prevent him from raising Lazarus also, during his lifetime? Thus I reflected, and as I did so, I wondered whether I really was the same Marcus who had studied in Rhodes, lived a night life in the hot streets of Rome, desperately loved another man's wife in the rose gardens of Baiae, and in Alexandria alternated between seeking out prophecies and drinking all night long in bad company.

What was this thing that had befallen me, and what Jewish sorcery had such power over me that here I wandered, dusty and sweaty, in a Jewish village among cackling hens, seeking proof of resurrection, miracles, and a God who allowed himself to be born in human shape, and then died and rose again that the world might be changed? For if this has happened, the world cannot remain as it is.

Accompanied by Lazarus, I looked into a large, dim room, of which the lower half contained jars and sacks and a manger, and the upper part a few pieces of furniture. But there were other rooms in the house.

Having called his sisters he led me to a stone bench in the yard and invited me to sit down. The sisters came out, covered their faces, as was the custom, and looked at the ground. Lazarus said, "This is my sister Martha, and this is Mary. Ask them what you like." Then he went away and appeared no more.

When I had greeted the women I said, "I should like to hear something of the teacher who I know lived here, and even raised your brother from the dead."

The women were shy of me and glanced at one another sideways, holding a fold of their mantles before their mouths. At last the elder one, Martha, summoned up courage and said, "He was the son of God. If you like, I can call the villagers together, for they were all there when he ordered the stone to be rolled away from the entrance and called our brother out, in a loud voice. Our brother came out with the graveclothes still swathed about him, and the sweat cloth over his face, so that everyone was struck dumb and trembled with horror. But he was our brother. We released him from the graveclothes and saw that he was alive. Later he ate and drank in the sight of everybody, and people watched him, gaping."

Mary said, "There is a man in the village who was blind and who received his sight again from him. Would you like to see him, so as to believe?"

"I have heard that he has healed the blind and made the lame to walk," I said. "Of that there are so many witnesses that I need not meet these. I would rather know something of his kingdom. What has he taught you about it?"

Mary told me this: "He knew beforehand that he was to die, and in what manner it had to be, although we didn't understand it then. When he had raised up our brother he withdrew into the wilderness, for there were far too many people swarming around him. But six days before the feast of the passover he came back to us. While he ate, I anointed his feet and wiped them with my hair, to do him as much honor as I could. Then he said that I had anointed him for his burial; so certain was he of his death. But why everything had to happen in this way and why he had to die so terrible a death is something that neither I nor my sister can understand."

Martha joined in: "How could we understand, being only women? They say that everything happened so that what was written might be fulfilled. My woman's reason does not tell me what good such fulfillment did, since he was who he was, and gave proof enough of it by his own works. But I suppose the scriptures had to be fulfilled in that cruel way so that all clever men might believe more readily. For it is man who has been given reason; in that respect women are lacking."

"But what did he say of himself and his kingdom?" I demanded impatiently.

Martha said, "You tell him, Mary, as you listened to him. I talk better about how to leaven bread and roast meat, harvest grapes and tend fig trees. I have no other learning. I needed no words to persuade me that he was more than a man."

Mary hesitated as to what she should say, and then began, "No man has ever spoken as he did. He spoke like someone with power. He said that he had come as a light into the world, so that no one who believed in him should remain in darkness."

"What light and what darkness?" I demanded.

Mary shook her head and said, "Ah indeed, how should you understand when you never heard him teach? He said this: 'He who sees me sees him who sent me.' He said also: 'I am the Way, the Truth and the Life.' "

I believed that at last I understood, and said, "When I seek the Way, then, I am seeking him."

Mary nodded eagerly and, turning her face up to mine, knelt down before me impulsively, with no more shyness. To make these things clearer to me, she asked: "Which do you think is the more difficult: to say to someone, 'Your sins are forgiven' or to call our brother Lazarus from the tomb where he had lain dead for four days and nights?"

I pondered her question, and said, "Both things are equally difficult and, by human reasoning, impossible. How could anyone forgive another his sins? Ultimately, all philosophy seeks to teach man to live rightly, to refrain from deliberately harming others, and to ripen to self-mastery before death. But man cannot help committing evil deeds. He can only see them afterwards for what they are, and resolve to be wiser next time. There, no one can help him. Each must answer for his own actions."

Yet even while I was speaking I felt the comfortlessness of all philosophy, for philosophy was no more able to free me from sorrow than the Orphic or Egyptian mysteries. Every now and then, without cause, I am seized by sorrow as with a sickness, so that life holds no more joy for me. Wine brings no relief then, nor does any bodily pleasure. It was this anguish that had driven me to seek among the prophecies for some meaning in my life. It was this anguish that had driven me from Alexandria to wander the roads of Judea.

Mary smiled disbelievingly, and said, "If you don't know what sin is you have no need of the Way, but will remain in the darkness. No man is without sin, not even the Pharisees."

Martha interjected angrily, "They, if any, are vile. They whitewash themselves like sepulchers, but inwardly they are who knows what. You are a remarkable man, stranger, not even to know what sin is."

"You Jews have your law," I said defensively. "From childhood you must learn your commandments, and you know when you break them."

"He didn't come to condemn us," Mary explained, as to a slow-witted person. "On the contrary, he came to deliver us from the domination of the law by showing that no one can be without sin. If a man does no more than speak a hasty word to his brother, he deserves perdition. But he condemned no one. Quite the contrary. To the most sinful he could say 'Your sins are forgiven.' Yes, there you are right. That is something that no man can say to another. But he said it. Does not that prove that he was more than a man?"

I sincerely wanted to understand, but could not. "I myself saw him suffer and die on the cross," I said. "He died a human death. Dirt and sweat ran from him in his agony, blood and water flowed from his side when a legionary thrust a spear through his heart. He did not step down from the cross. No angels came to punish his tormentors."

Mary clasped her hands to her face and wept. Martha looked at me reproachfully. It was heartless of me to remind them so vividly of their teacher's suffering. But I needed enlightenment.

At last Mary whispered, "He came into the world as a man and lived among us as a man. But he did things that no man can do. He forgave the sins of those who believed in him. He has even risen from the dead, so that we need mourn no more on his account. But all this is still a riddle which we cannot yet solve."

"You are trying to make me believe he was both man and God," I said. "But that is impossible. I might be able to conceive of a God who was everywhere, in everything that happened, and who was a part of each one of us. But God is a god and a man is a man."

Mary retorted, "You try in vain to confuse me. I know what I know, and sense what I sense. You too are aware of something, though you don't know what it is. Why else should you have come to us and asked about the way? How can you understand, if we don't? We only believe, since believe we must."

"You believe because you loved him," I returned bitterly. "Certainly he was a remarkable man and a great teacher. But it is hard for me to love him by hearsay alone."

"There is good will in you," Mary said, "or I would not listen to you or answer you. Therefore I will explain further. We have been allowed to learn the content of the law: Love God with all your heart and love your neighbor as yourself. In him we love God who sent him."

To me it was a startling idea that one could or ought to love God. Awe, fear and reverence I could understand, but not love. I shook my head. It was a doctrine that passed my understanding. Moreover, it seemed to me foolish to love one's neighbor as oneself, since there are both good and wicked people. So I asked slyly, "Who is my neighbor?"

Mary explained, "He taught that everyone is our neighbor, even the Samaritan, whom we children of Israel regard as unclean. The sun shines upon good and wicked alike. Evil must not be met with evil. If anyone strikes you upon one cheek, then turn to him your other cheek too."

I raised my hand protestingly and exclaimed, "That is enough! I have never heard a crazier teaching, and I realize that no human being could follow it. But you, you beautiful woman, you teach better than that master in Israel, Nicodemus."

Mary looked at the ground and let her hands fall. She said quietly, "Even on the cross he cried to his father, beseeching him to forgive those who were torturing him. So say those who were there and saw."

After a while she said humbly, "And do not call me beautiful. It only saddens me."

Martha protested, "Certainly my sister is beautiful. She has had many suitors. But since the death of our parents we three have all dwelt together under our brother's protection. That's how he showed such mercy in coming to us, and bringing Lazarus back to life. But for that we shouldn't have known what to do. At first we were afraid that the scribes would come here from the city and stone our brother. They threatened as much. But now they are not likely to come. Yet do what I will, I cannot help feeling anxious. He forbade this, but I cannot help it. I hate even to recall what I suffered when Jesus insisted on going to Jerusalem and letting them put him to death."

I was paying little attention to what she said, being disturbed by the irrational teaching which Mary had revealed to me, and which truly was not of this world. I had heard more than I could digest at one time. It would have been better to scoff at this doctrine and turn aside from so preposterous a way. I writhed at the mere thought of regarding the first half-wit or criminal I met as my neighbor, and of allowing myself to be insulted or assaulted without raising a finger in my defense.

But Mary said, "Let us not be troubled. And you, stranger, be not troubled either. Let us wait for what is still to come. He said that every hair of our head is numbered, and that not even a sparrow falls to the ground without his father knowing of it. Why then should we be anxious?"

Her words impressed me. In the same way as formerly, when doubting and yet wanting to believe, I had obeyed signs and omens, so now I was filled by a sense of certainty that I ought not to be so rebellious, so desirous of attaining truth in a twinkling. Perhaps in time everything will become clear to me, if only I am content to walk the way along which I am being led.

Therefore I rose, saying, "I have kept you from your occupations too long already. But I thank you both for listening to me so willingly, and for giving me an answer. Peace be with you."

Martha rose hastily and struck her hands together, crying, "Don't go yet. How could I let you go from here hungry and thirsty?"

Without heeding my protests she went in to prepare something to eat. Meanwhile I sat on the stone bench, plunged in thought, while Mary sat on the ground nearby. Neither of us spoke, yet our silence was not embarrassing, as is the silence of those who have nothing to say. On the contrary, Mary had said as much as I was able to receive. Part of it I had understood, and the rest may become clear to me one day; but nothing would have been gained by talking just then. Thus she was content to be seated near me; and from her presence I received an outflowing of serenity that put me in good heart.

Martha came back with bread spread with oil and seasoned with bitter seeds, vegetables chopped up with eggs, salt mutton and thick grape honey. When she had set it all out beside me on the stone bench, she poured water over my hands and blessed the food. But neither she nor her sister touched it, nor did

Lazarus come to eat with me. For all their kindness, I felt an outcast.

My walk to Bethany had not been long, yet I felt hungry on beholding the good food and I ate avidly, while Martha sat beside me, urging me to taste of everything and finish it all. I wondered whether they would throw away anything that I might leave, considering that it had been touched by a foreigner, and for politeness' sake I went on eating after I had had enough. At last I drank of the water that Martha had flavored with wine, and was overcome by a heavy drowsiness.

It was noon when I had finished, and Martha said considerately, "You must not think of returning to the city now, in the heat of the day. Stay and rest for a while, so that we may fulfill all that hospitality requires."

My exhaustion was immense, and I know not whether the spiritual or the physical weariness was the greater. When I tried to stand up and walk, my limbs felt so feeble and the two women's kindness was so refreshing that I had no wish to take my leave. The mere thought of it was pain. For a moment I fancied that Martha had mixed some narcotic in the wine, but why should she have done that? And it had had no bitter flavor.

"It is not far to Jerusalem," I said, "but if you will really allow me, I would gladly stay here for the noon rest. I like it so well here with you."

They both smiled mysteriously, as if they had known the truth of this better than I. For a moment their secret certainty gave them a singular look, as if they had been no longer just people, but something more. Yet I felt no fear of them.

They came with me into the inner courtyard, which was shaded by a roof of foliage. In my mood of drowsy unreality I noted that their farm was larger than I had thought. There were at least four buildings, put up at different times, enclosing a courtyard. The sisters pointed to a flight of steps outside the newest of the buildings, followed me and showed me their guest room on the roof. It was a small, cool room containing a low sleeping bench and a mat on the floor. The bed smelt of cinnamon. They said, "Lie down here and sleep your noontide sleep. He whom we have talked of often rested in this room. But when he had been alone and had rested, he would go up into the mountain to pray. He came and went here as he wished. Do the same."

There was a water jar and a linen cloth ready in that room. Heedless of my protests, Martha knelt before me, took off my sandals, washed my dusty feet and dried them with the linen cloth.

"Why do you do this?" I asked. "You are not my servant."

Martha looked at me with that same mysterious smile and said, "One day you may do someone else this same service, without being his servant. You see, to my eyes you appear wounded, sorrowful and full of anguish, even though outwardly your limbs are whole and sound and your head stored with diverse wisdom."

These words struck deep, for now as ever my knowledge is but a burning stab in my heart; all my questions circle skeptically round and round reality, and however greatly I may desire it I cannot bring myself to believe.

Mary said, "He did his disciples the same service on that last evening, when they were squabbling about which of them should be first in his kingdom."

Silently they went out, and as soon as they had gone I fell into a deep sleep on the cinnamon-scented bed in that good room of theirs. I awoke with a strong sense of being no longer alone; of there being someone near me, waiting for me to wake. The feeling was so strong that I lay with my eyes closed, trying to catch the breathing or movements of the stranger. But when I opened my eyes, I saw that the room was empty, and I alone. The depth of this disappointment caused walls and ceiling to waver before my eyes; they seemed so frail as to be on the point of collapsing. Again I closed my eyes and at once was aware of the same presence, and of being no longer alone in the room. I thought that I had known something of the kind inside his tomb. I was filled with peace.

I thought, It was in himself that his kingdom came on earth. Now that he has left his grave his kingdom too will remain on earth as long as he does. Perhaps it is the presence of his kingdom that I feel.

I slept again, but when I awoke for the second time I felt the whole weight and sluggishness of my body on the bed, smelled the bitter smell of my own sweat, and was aware of the sturdiness of the mud walls about me. My awakening was as heavy as lead, and I still had no wish to open my eyes, so dreary was it to awake once more to the world of the body.

When at last I felt strong enough to look about me and return to reality from the bliss of dreaming, I found that this time I was not alone. A woman was crouching motionless upon the mat, waiting for me to wake. She was clothed in a black mantle and had covered her head with a veil, so that at first I wondered whether she was a living person. I was not aware of any presence, nor had I heard her enter as I slept. I sat up on the edge of my bed, feeling the leaden weight of earth in every limb.

When the woman heard me moving she straightened her back and uncovered her face. She was very pale and no longer young. The experiences of a lifetime had worn away her former beauty, and yet a flame burned in her face. When she saw that I was wide awake she signed to me with one hand beneath her mantle to sit quietly, and began singing with guttural sounds in the sacred language of the Jews. Having half spoken and half chanted for a long time, she translated what she had said into Greek.

"All flesh is grass," she began, "and all its loveliness as the flower of the field. Grass withers, the flower fades, because the spirit of the Lord blows upon it. Grass withers, the flower fades, but the word of our God shall stand forever."

Then she said, "Truly our God is a hidden God."

She gazed at me with a spark in the depths of her black eyes, and I nodded to show that I understood. Yet her words still meant nothing to me. She went on: "And he said, 'It is a little thing for thee to be my servant, to raise up the tribes of Jacob and to bring back the scattered of Israel. I will also give thee to be a light to the heathen peoples, so that my salvation may reach to the end of the earth.' "

She resumed the sacred language of her interrupted chant, though hesitating now and then over the words as if she could not remember them all. Then she explained again in Greek: "That is what the prophet Isaiah foretold of him, and the quiet ones in the land have preserved the words in their memory; that he was the most despised, full of pains and grief, so despised that people hid their faces from him. He bore our griefs and laid our sorrows upon himself. He was wounded for our transgressions; he was punished that we might have peace. We all went astray, like sheep, each to his own way. But the Lord cast all our guilt upon him. When he was tormented he submitted, and opened not his mouth."

She shook her head. Tears began running down her cheeks but she went on still, in a broken voice, "He gave his soul in death and was accounted an evildoer, he bore the sins of many and prayed for the transgressors."

I had a dim recollection of having read something like this in Alexandria the winter before, with the Jewish scholar, but then the words had held no significance for me. The woman sat curled up on the floor, weeping and hiding her face in the black cloth so that I might not see her sorrow.

I said, "Yes, yes; I understand what you said. Thus it was foretold, and thus it came about—but what does it mean?"

The woman shook her head and answered behind the cloth, "We don't know yet; we don't understand. But there are no longer many ways, there is no longer each his own way—there is but one."

When she veiled her face I thought of that face, and said at last, "What belongs to your peace, woman? I seem to recognize you."

When she had dried her eyes on the cloth she uncovered her face again, tried to smile and answered, "And I recognize you. That is why I came here. When he was tortured on the cross you struck a scribe and thrust away those who were reviling him."

I couldn't help laughing. "No, no," I rejoined gently. "I struck no one. You are mistaken. There was indeed a scribe to whom I put a question, but he was insolent, so I appealed to the centurion and he drove off the mockers."

But the woman shook her head vehemently and declared, "I saw you strike a man who was jeering, because you were angry with him, although you are a foreigner, without share or part in the matter."

I saw no reason to argue with her; and besides, it had been so dark before the king's death that she might well have been mistaken. After a little while I said, "I'm sure I saw you there with his mother."

"Yes," she said, "I am Mary of Magdala. You have already heard of me. He drove the evil spirits out of me, and since then I have followed him. He allowed me to follow him, although people insulted him because of it."

Suddenly she threw up her head and looked at me, as if until then she had held herself in check, and asked, "Tell me! I have heard that you went to the tomb at the Governor's order and that you were the first Roman to see that he was risen. Tell me about this—testify to what you saw. No one believes me because I am only a woman."

I weighed my words carefully, not wanting to lie or to mislead her. "The earthquake had rolled the stone from the mouth of the tomb and the guards had fled. I entered the tomb with the centurion. We saw the graveclothes lying there, folded, and the sweat cloth separate from them, but there was no body in them. Seeing this, I believed; but then the Jews came and in their rage they tore open the linen. Yet I still believe he has risen. How this is possible I don't understand; such a thing has never happened before."

She listened reverently. I wanted to be impartial, so I added, "Of course, there have been and still are mysteries in different countries where it is the custom to bury a god, and for him to rise up again from the dead. But this is not real—only a sort of pious play-acting. You were at the tomb before us. Tell me what you saw. Did you notice the graveclothes?"

Mary of Magdala shook her head and explained, "It was still dark when I went to the sepulcher. I saw that the stone had gone and thought that someone had carried him away. But I dared not enter the tomb, and if I had I should have seen nothing because of the darkness. So I ran to the place where his closest disciples were in hiding and brought back Simon Peter, who is a big, strong fellow, and the young John to whom he had entrusted his mother. They ran as for their lives to the tomb, entered it, found it empty, but went away again quickly, being afraid of the Jews. I stayed behind and wept by the sepulcher, and a little later I looked inside. There was an angel there; he seemed clothed in light, with a face of fire, so that I was startled and began to tremble, and turned away when he spoke to me. But as I did so I saw *him* himself, although at first I didn't recognize him."

Her account differed from that of the guards. She looked at me apologetically, as if sensing that I doubted her, and explained, "It is not surprising that I should not have recognized him at first, for it never entered my head that it could be he. Not even his disciples recognized him at first, that time when he crossed the sea of Galilee and walked on the water to their boat. I took him for a stranger who had carried off the dead body. I reproached him for it and begged him earnestly to bring it back. Then he called me by my name and I saw who he was. He gave a message for the disciples, and I was so rapturously happy that I felt no ground under my feet as I sped away. But not one of them believed me."

I did not really believe her either. I just felt that she was the kind of woman who allowed herself to be carried away easily, and that she had confused the order of events when she narrated them. But I reverted to the main point and asked again, "Did you notice how the graveclothes were lying?"

She looked at me in surprise and shook her head. "How should I have noticed a thing like that? I was dazzled by the angel and had to turn away. And I was very frightened. The disciples didn't believe me though the women did. The disciples still fear for their lives and can think of nothing else."

She grew excited, as women will, and went on eagerly, "As you say, it must have been the earthquake that rolled the stone away from the tomb, though others are convinced that the angel did it. They also say that the same earthquake brought the steps of the sanctuary crashing down in the temple. Two of them never recognized him when he walked with them that same day on the road to Emmaus. They never recognized him, although he interpreted the scriptures to them, point by point, and told them why everything had to happen as it has happened. It wasn't until they reached the village in the evening and asked him in, when he took a loaf and gave them some of it, that they recognized him. But then he vanished before their eyes."

"You believe then," I said, and my tongue felt stiff, "that he is still here, coming and going as he likes and talking to anyone he chooses? And that some people recognize him, but others do not?"

"Just so," replied Mary of Magdala with conviction. "That is what I believe, and that is why I am waiting. Perhaps our hearts do not yet burn as they should; perhaps our understanding is too sluggish. Therefore he lets us wait until we ripen enough to comprehend the meaning of it all."

"Did you say he walked on the water?" I demanded, to remind myself of how impossible and irrational all this was.

Mary of Magdala looked at me confidently and declared, "He performed so many miracles that even a stone must have believed. Yet we still don't know what we are to think of him. Certainly it is written that his messenger is deaf and his servant blind, and it may be that we fulfill his purposes unawares."

"But why do you trust a foreigner like myself?" I asked. "You are a cultured woman, you speak Greek and know the prophets by heart in the sacred language of the Jews. I have also been told that you are a woman of means. Tell me something of yourself, so that I may understand you."

She said proudly, "I am not shy of foreigners. In my house I used to meet Greeks, Syrians and Romans—even members of the court. If he is indeed he, as I know and believe, his message is not to Israel alone but a light for the whole world, as it is written. For that reason, too, people laugh at me. When the demons attacked me I experienced much that those simple men do not understand. A sorcerer can cast a spell on the body of a person possessed, so that it lives in a basin of water and cries out when the sorcerer sticks a pin into water in another room. But *he* never wanted to exploit me as others had done; he only wanted to free me from the evil spirits when he found that I myself, with all my heart, desired to be rid of them. My face is as bare of my past life as a stone from which the rain has sluiced the living soil. Don't ask me of my past. Talk simply to me as I am now."

"As you wish," I said. "But you have not answered my question. Why do you trust *me?*"

Her face blazed once more and she exclaimed, "Because you took his part against the revilers at the crucifixion. Because you respected his suffering without knowing any more of him than what was written in mockery upon the cross. You defended him when his own people took fright and fled. There were no others there but we women and young John, who has no reason to fear, since his kinsmen are friends of the high priest. Even the agitators made bold to shout at the Romans on behalf of their comrades who were to die. But not a single voice was raised for him."

I saw then that she had converted her grudge against the disciples into friendship for me. After reflection I answered cautiously, "If I rightly understand you, you believe you know more about him than his own disciples have yet grasped, because you have been through a great deal in your life. But they mistrust you because you are a woman and easily influenced, and they don't believe in your visions; and so you want me as a witness."

Mary Magdalene interrupted me, crying, "Do you not understand even yet, you slow-witted man? He let even women come to him. He was good to Mary, the sister of Lazarus, and to Martha too. When he ate at the Pharisees' table he allowed a sinful woman to kneel by his couch, to wash his feet with her tears and dry them with her hair. This lost him his reputation with the Pharisees; they are ready to think any evil of him. But you shall hear more. He took pity on even a Samaritan woman once, by the well. And another woman who had been taken in adultery he saved from the hands of the scribes when they were going to invoke the law and stone her. Believe me, stranger, he understood women better than anyone else has ever done. Therefore I believe that we women understood and understand him better than his cowardly disciples."

Her voice broke; she was panting with wrath. Presently she went on: "Oh, they were high and mighty enough for a while, and healed the sick with his power. But when the day came to set off for Jerusalem on that last journey, as he wished, every one of them was full of excuses, although earlier they had been ready to quarrel among themselves over the thrones in his kingdom. He spoke to the people in parables, but to them he explained all things clearly. Yet even so they did not understand. Only Thomas, who has the clearest head of them all, had the sense to say, 'Well then, we will go too and die with him.' But do you suppose a single one of them did die, although they managed to get hold of two swords to defend him with? Two swords they found, though it is forbidden to obtain weapons secretly in Jerusalem. But did they defend him? That is my point."

She was talking with breathless vehemence, but calmed herself again and, after reflecting a little, admitted, "But of course he himself forbade them. He said, 'He who takes the sword shall perish by the sword.' But then again on the way to Jerusalem he told them, 'He who owns a cloak must sell it now and buy a sword.' I don't understand. He must have wanted to test them. Or else give them confidence in themselves. I don't know. At any rate, Simon Peter cut off the ear of one of the high priests' servants when they came by night to arrest him. And he put the ear back and healed it, so that nothing but a thin scar can be seen there now. Malcus' kinsfolk have told this story, though Malcus himself has been forbidden to speak of it.

"But let me empty out all my wrath," she continued. "Let me rail at those cowards. He kept watch alone, he knew his fate, he prayed. They say he sweat blood in his terrible anguish. Of them he asked nothing but that they should watch with him. And what did they do? Slept like logs in the garden! No, I cannot understand—I cannot forgive them! Were these the men to set fire to the temple? Why, they were too spineless even to slay the betrayer: he had to hang himself. I do not understand. I know not what he saw in them, or why he summoned them of all people to follow him."

So utterly feminine was she in her wayward censure that I wanted to laugh and stroke her cheek, to help her give vent to her despair in tears. But I dared not laugh, and could not touch her. I simply said once more, as discreetly as I might, "If it is so—if they really are afraid, and know not what to make of him, although he taught them—then no wonder that I, a stranger, should feel bewildered. But I believe not one of them is meant to die. Not yet, at least; not until his teaching has become clearer to them. Even the keenest human intelligence must be too slow to grasp such singular precepts all in a moment. These men are bound by all the Jewish prejudices to which they have been bred from childhood. Therefore I think it best for you not to appeal to me for evidence—or even mention me—in their presence. They would only despise me for being a Roman, just as you, no doubt, lost your reputation by consorting with foreigners."

She tossed her head sharply, but raising my hand in deprecation I made haste to explain. "No, on the contrary, as a Roman I understand you, Mary, certainly better than any Jew could ever understand you. In Rome women are free, and on an equal footing with men—yes, even superior to men, since a woman is always more cunning and in many ways more merciless than a man, and her thoughts are untrammeled by any logical consistency. So let us be friends, you Mary of Magdala and I, Marcus Manilianus of Rome. I respect you as a woman, and I respect you even more highly because he let you go with him. I can only assure you that I cannot but believe that he has risen, by what I myself have witnessed. And with your feminine sensibility you must have understood more of him than his disciples.

"Nevertheless," I went on, very warily, "I would willingly meet them some time, or at least some of them, to see what sort of people they are."

Mary of Magdala hesitated, but acknowledged reluctantly, "I am not on bad terms with them. I am bound to see that they get food and drink as long as they remain in hiding. They are ordinary fishermen. In their fear they do not know which way to turn, and then they quarrel until I have to step in; though perhaps you cannot understand this, since I spoke so bitterly of them just now. But of course there is much good in them; I admit that. They would like best to return to Galilee, but for the present they cannot make up their minds to anything. At gates and on the roads they are easy to recognize by their dialect.

By their faces, too, for that matter, for after living with him for two or three years they no longer look like ordinary fishermen. Perhaps you can't understand that, but if you ever meet any of them you will know what I mean."

Mary of Magdala was now warm in defense of these men, and assured me, "He must have had his reasons for choosing just these simple fellows to be his disciples. The only one of them who can have had any schooling is Levi; he was a customs official. But when I think of learned men, whether scribes or philosophers, I find it hard to believe that such people could grasp anything of his teaching. Believe me, a learned man might devote the whole of his life to the study of a single word of his, just as a scribe can brood for years over a single letter of the scriptures, or as a Greek may write a whole book about a place name in the *Odyssey*. And indeed I clearly remember his saying that these truths reveal themselves to simple people and babes and not to the wise."

I pondered her words. There might be something in them. A mind burdened with earlier erudition and an earlier way of thinking could hardly accept, without boggling, an utterly new and outrageous doctrine such as Mary had expounded to me. In the same way do I myself stumble at every step over former tenets; things that I have had to learn and have become used to thinking.

"Was that what he meant when he told Nicodemus that a man must be born again?" I asked, almost to myself.

"Nicodemus belongs to the quiet ones," said Mary of Magdala. "He is one of the devout who wait; he means well, but he knows the scriptures by heart, and whatever new thing he comes upon he has to compare it with them so as to understand it. No matter how much he were born again he would always remain a baby in swaddling bands—ones that were too tight!"

The thought of the baby made Mary smile. When I saw her white, stony face brighten so suddenly, and her eyes light up, I realized that in her day she had been an unusually beautiful woman. For even now, just because of that little smile, I had to own that she had great beauty. In a curious way she reminded me of the bright moon, and I remembered that she had made her fortune as a breeder of doves.

"You needn't wear soot-black," I said, without thinking. "Your colors are silver and green, Mary of Magdala; your flower is the violet, your wreath the myrtle. You don't deceive me."

She started, and said mockingly, "Are you playing the astrologer? Don't talk to me about earth forces. Even if I did wear silver and green again, the gods of earth have no longer any dominion over me. I have only to pronounce his name—Jesus Christ the son of God—for all evil to flee away and the powers fade to harmless shadows."

From her words I realized that she had been aware of her demons, and suffered during her bouts of possession. I regretted my chiding at once and I saw the smile fade from her face, leaving it as stony-hard as before. An uneasy spark still glowed in the depths of her eyes. Yet I could not resist adding, "Are you quite certain, Mary of Magdala, that you too do not compare all that is new with your earlier thoughts, so as to understand? Are you quite sure that you have done more than replace your old demons by a new and more powerful one?'"

She wrung her hands and rocked her body back and forth as if to subdue some pain, but she tried to look me straight in the eyes and declared, "I am sure, perfectly sure, that he was and is the light, the full and absolute light. He, the man; he, God." Yet compelled to betray the morbid suspicion that had consumed her, she persisted in her own defense and asseverated more for her own sake than for mine, "No, he is neither sorcerer nor demon, although he could walk on the water. If he had been no more than the mightiest of magicians I should certainly not have followed him, for I have had enough of witch-masters. And he never ordered me to follow him; he allowed me. That makes a difference, as you can see."

I was ashamed of my suspicions, yet I had felt bound to ask, for I wanted to achieve certainty, so far as anyone may achieve it by means of human inquiry. I saw that I had hurt her, and I begged her forgiveness as gracefully as I could. Then I came straight out with my request: "Mary of Magdala, lead me to his disciples, so that I may assure myself about them too."

Mary said evasively, "You cannot be ripe for that yet. Nor are they. We are all waiting. Wait patiently too."

But seeing my sincere desire she softened a little and said, "I don't believe you're a Roman spy. In your heart you are no traitor, I am a sufficiently good judge of character to know that. If you were, something very bad would happen to you—not through our power, but through the power of him who chose the disciples and whose will is to preserve them, as you yourself believed. Do you know where the Fountain Gate is?"

"I came that way," I said, smiling, "although it was a longer way round. I wanted to see the Fountain Gate."

"Then you know of the man who carries water," she said. "Be it so. One day perhaps when you are still and humble in your heart, he will show himself at the Fountan Gate. But I beg you to be in no hurry. Everything will come about in good time. If I didn't believe that I could not live."

I asked her whether she would return to Jerusalem with me, but Mary of Magdala preferred to stay alone for a while in the room where Jesus of Nazareth had often rested. She said, "Go when you please, and do not stay to give thanks if you see no one down there. We women know of your gratitude without that. Come and go as you wish. Yet I suspect that you know not for certain what you do want. I believe you may already be compelled to follow the one Way, even if unwilling. Peace be with you."

"And with you be peace," I returned; and something impelled me to add, "Peace be with you, woman. More than a beloved, more than a wife, more than a daughter, since he allowed you to follow him."

My words surely pleased her, for she remained crouching on

the floor, and when I had stood up she put out a hand and touched my foot as I was bending down for my sandal. It was a touch of such ineffable longing, of such groping for the unattainable, that it moved and shook me more than anything I had known. I would hardly even have understood it if in my recent dream I had not seen the kingdom descending upon the earth.

I no longer felt any grief as I went down the steps to the leaf-shaded courtyard. No one was to be seen, and the houses on all sides were silent. So I went my way without farewell, and when I came out to the stone bench I saw to my surprise that by Roman reckoning it was already the fifth hour. The shadow of the hill had stretched almost as far as the yard. I walked briskly back toward the city by the way I had come, so plunged in thought that I never looked about me. Again I passed the old olive trees on the hillside, now lit by the sun, though the road lay in cool shade. I passed the herb garden too, and now as evening came on there was a strong fragrance from all its medicinal plants.

I was first aroused from my thoughts by a monotonous tapping sound as I neared the gate. I saw a blind man crouching by the wayside, ceaselessly tapping his stick against a stone to attract the attention of passers-by. His eye sockets yawned emptily and his thin body was clothed in rags that were stiff with dirt. When he heard me pause he began whining in the piercing voice of the professional beggar: "I am blind, have pity!"

I remembered the bag of food which the Syrian's wife had given me and which I had not needed. Laying it in his gnarled hand I said quickly, "Peace be with you. Take this and eat, and keep the bag. I have no need of it." For when I approached him I smelled the appalling stench of his filth, and I preferred not to stay and empty the bag into his hands.

But he didn't even thank me. Instead he stretched out his hand and groped for his mantle, as he pleaded with me eagerly: "Evening is here, night is at hand and no one has come to fetch me from where I have sat all day. Have compassion, O compassionate, and lead me into the city. There I can find my own way, but here outside the wall I get lost and stumble over stones, and might fall into the ravine."

I was nauseated by the very thought of touching this horrible creature who could hardly have been called human any longer. I thanked my good fortune therefore that I had time to step aside, out of reach of his grasping hands, and I walked on hurriedly, trying not to listen to his professional wail as he called after me and began once more to strike a stone with his stick, as if to take revenge on it for his disappointment. In my mind I reviled him for his ingratitude; at least I had given him good food and a bag worth money.

But when I had gone about ten steps, I seemed to come up against a wall. I was forced to turn and look around. The hopes of the beggar revived and he whined, "Be merciful to a blind man, you who see. Lead me to the city and a blessing will come upon your head. When darkness falls, I grow cold, and dogs slink up and lick my sores."

I asked myself whether it was I who was blind or that stinking creature. To give him that food had not been particularly meritorious, since I didn't even need it. But I could really account it a good deed if I forced myself to touch him, feel his presence and lead him to the city gate. Yet the very notion was so repugnant that I retched.

I said reluctantly, "The ways are many, and so are false guides. How do you know that I shall not lead you astray and push you down into the ravine to be rid of you?"

The blind man started at my words, and was still, and the stick in his hand sank. "Peace be with you, peace be with you," he cried again, hopeful and afraid. "I trust you. How should I, who am blind, do other than trust him who leads me, since I cannot find the way myself?"

His words struck me to the heart. I had been blinded by my own fastidiousness. What could I myself do but hope that someone would lead me along the right road? I remembered the mysterious presence in my dream, that vanished when I opened my eyes. Resolutely I went up to the blind man, grasped his bony arm in both my hands, and raised him to his feet. Meekly he handed me his staff, meaning me to hold one end and lead him by it, so as not to soil myself by his touch. But I disliked the idea of leading him as one leads a beast by the bridle, and so I took his arm and began guiding him along the road. Nevertheless he still groped anxiously before him with the staff, for the Kidron road is no level Roman thoroughfare.

The going was slow, for he was so thin and frail that his knees sagged. To close one's hand about his arm was like grasping a a gnawed bone. I asked impatiently, "Why did they bring you so far from the gate when you can't take care of yourself?"

He lamented, "Ah, stranger, I am too feeble to hold my own at the gate. But in the days of my strength I used to beg in the road before the temple."

He was evidently proud of that memory, and repeated that he had begged near the temple, as if that had been a great honor. I marveled to myself how tough-fibered mankind is, so that even the most pitiable creature can find something to be proud of.

"I could hold my own by thrusting and hitting out with my staff, blind though I am," he boasted. "But when I grew weaker I had to taste bumps and bruises myself. At last they cuffed me away from the gate, so that I have no choice but to ask some merciful person to lead me out to a place by the wayside for the day. There are far too many beggars in the holy city, and many of them are very strong."

He fingered a corner of my mantle, and said, "There is fine stuff in your mantle, stranger. You smell good. You must be rich. Why do you wander about outside the walls at night with no companion? Why does no one run before you to clear the way?"

I owed him no explanation; yet I said, "It has become necessary for me to find my own way." Then the whim took me to ask him, "And you—have *you* heard of the king of the Jews, Jesus of Nazareth, who was crucified? What do you think of him?"

The beggar grew so angry that he began to tremble, and shaking his staff he cried, "Yes, I have heard enough about that man. They were right to crucify him."

I was much astonished. "But I have heard that he was a good and merciful man," I said. "He healed the sick, and to those who toiled heavily and hard he desired to give peace."

"Oh, indeed—peace!'" the blind man repeated with a sneer. "He wanted to overthrow and destroy everything, even the temple. A malicious troublemaker, that's what he was, and a man of ill-will. You shall hear. By the pool of Bethesda there lay a well-known lame beggar on his bed, and now and then he let someone jostle him down into the water to arouse the necessary pity. No one has been cured at that pool within the memory of man, however much the water may bubble now and then. But the place is outside the Sheep Gate, and the shady colonnade is a good place to beg in. And then, what should that Jesus do but come along and ask him, Do you want to be well? The lame man gave a crooked sort of answer, saying that there was always someone else who got down to the water before him when it bubbled. Then the Nazarene told him to stand up, take his bed and go his way."

"And he was cured?" I asked incredulously.

"Certainly he was cured; he picked up his bed and went," answered the blind man. "That Galilean has a most dreadful power. So the fellow lost a good livelihood, which he had carried on for thirty-eight years. Now in his old age he will have to keep himself by working, having no lawful reason to beg."

The blind man grew yet more embittered. "And to cap everything, it was the Sabbath. The poor fellow ran straight into trouble because he was carrying his bed, and there was squabbling with the priests. And as if that wasn't enough, Jesus met him again, in the temple, and warned him against sinning any more, lest worse befall him. Then in self-defense the man accused Jesus to the priests, testifying that he had healed him and expressly told him to carry his bed, although it was the Sabbath. But what could the priests do? All his followers were around him. He blasphemed and proclaimed far and wide that he had power to break the Sabbath and work on the Sabbath, like his father. Yes, yes, he made himself God's equal. Of course he had to hang on the cross."

But from my silence the blind man realized that I was not of the same opinion, so he continued, "What would become of the world if the temple were torn down? Where would the maimed get alms if there were no more rich sinners to atone for their sins by giving to the poor?"

He thumped his staff on the ground and gloated, "Even I was able to go with the crowd and shout 'Crucify him, crucify him!' The Roman wasn't sure what judgment to give, since he doesn't know our laws, or perhaps likes to see people desecrating our temple or blaspheming against God. All we beggars who have any standing are dependent on the temple and the guardians of the peace. For this reason we were hastily summoned together from our places by the temple and the gates, to go with the rest and shout 'This is the truth!' I was there too, and called for Barabbas. Barabbas was an innocent man compared to Jesus; he had done no worse than kill a Roman."

I said in horror, "I do not understand you. How deeply rooted must your wickedness be that you can boast of such a thing? He might have had power to heal you too, if you had believed in him."

The blind man turned his eye sockets to me, grinning crookedly and showing the stumps of his teeth.

"Who do you think you are, and what do you think you know? You must be impure and defiled, being a foreigner," he whined. "You had better lead me by my staff so that I need not touch you. The God of Israel would blow you to ashes with one breath if I cursed you. But if you belong to the followers of that man Jesus, may worms devour you alive."

He hissed out his hatred at me until I smelled the stink of his breath, and he clutched my mantle so that I could not pull myself free.

"You are a simple one," he sneered, pointing at his eye sockets. "Not even God himself could make eyes grow again once they've been poked out. I would not even want my sight restored, for that matter, for what is there in the world for anyone like me to look at?"

I could have got away by striking him, but I could not bring myself to lift a hand against him. "Calm yourself, sinless one," was all I said. "We are nearly at the gate. There I shall leave you, so as to defile your purity no longer."

"If only I were stronger," he sighed, staring at me with his empty eye sockets. "I will show you something, stranger." Suddenly, with an unexpected hold, he wound his arm around my neck from behind and drove his sharp knee into my back. I felt his free hand groping for my purse. Indeed if he had been stronger I should have been in a serious fix, unable even to shout for help; as it was, it was not difficult to wrest his repulsive arm to one side and free myself from his robber-grip.

He said, panting, "This is my advice to you, stranger. Let this be a lesson to you. Reflect before you listen to the request of anyone unkown to you, and don't lead beggars along unfamiliar roads. Had I been stronger I would have had you in my power, and whistled up companions to help me. You would have lost your fine mantle and your purse. Had I been wicked, I would have pressed my thumbs into your eyes so that you could not have recognized me, to bear witness against me. And yes, yes! If you'd been a Roman I would gladly have killed you."

"Thank you for your warning,'" I said ironically. "How do you know that I am not a Roman?"

The beggar answered, "No Roman would ever have under

taken to lead me as you did, you who know little of the world's evil. I should have had a kick from him or a whiplash across my face. No mercy can be expected from a Roman. All they want to do is to build roads and aqueducts and see that measures keep their measure and weights their weight."

We had reached the pools near the gate. I asked, "Have you yourself met the lame man you talked of? Does he really feel resentment toward his healer?"

"No, I haven't," the blind man admitted. "I just repeat what I have heard. But why did he heal only that man, and a few others? Why did he not cure us all? Why should one receive grace and another remain in darkness forever? You must agree that we have reason to speak ill of him."

"You will have heard too," I remarked, "that he, King Jesus, stepped out of his tomb on the third day."

The beggar shook with laughter. "Women's gossip," he hissed. "And you, a grown man, believe it!" But his laughter was as much sobbing as sneering. "His disciples stole him from the tomb; that's clear," he said, "so as to cheat the people to the end. God exists. That I know. But here on earth there are no powers except money and clenched fists."

He felt fiercely in front of him along the roadside with his staff, hit it against a stone, which he bent down to pick up. "Here is a stone," he shouted, shaking it before my eyes. "Do you imagine that it will turn into bread? No more can the world change and become different. It is a world of hatred and murder and whoring, a world of greed and revenge. The God of Israel is a god of vengeance. The Romans will suffer for it one day, but at least it won't be that Galilean's doing."

I went strangely tense, and my limbs turned cold. "Jesus of Nazareth," I said. "If you are or were more than the king of the Jews, if you are in your kingdom and your kingdom is still here, turn this stone to bread and I will believe in you."

My words made the beggar put his staff under his arm and begin rolling the stone between his hands to feel it. The stone yielded to his fingers. Suspiciously, he blew dust from it, raised it to his nose and smelled it. Still more incredulously he pinched off a piece, put it in his mouth, tasted, chewed and swallowed. "This is not bread, but a cheese," he said, and railed at me for my stupidity.

I too had to pick out a piece of the white interior of the stone and taste it. It was indeed a hard, ball-shaped country cheese. It must have fallen off some load, and become so covered in dust from the road that at first sight it looked like a stone.

The beggar sucked at a piece and asked suspiciously, "Are you a magician? Did you turn that stone into cheese in my hand by invoking the Nazarene's name?"

"Cheese or bread, it is at least food for man," I said. "If he was able to turn a stone into cheese in your hand when I asked him to do it in his own name, then you too must believe that he is risen."

But as I was saying this I began to have doubts in my own mind as to whether, without being aware of it, I had noticed something unusual about the stone which the blind man had happened to hit by the roadside. In itself that was an amazing coincidence, yet there are stranger ones that that.

The blind man was more practical. He quickly slipped the cheese into the food bag I had given him as if he were afraid that I might take it from him, and then began poking with his staff at the other stones beside the road, and knelt and felt them with his hands. The stones were stones, round lumps just like the cheese, and stones they remained. After a time he ceased his search.

We had come along a road that sloped gently upward toward the wall from the Vale of Kidron. Thus we were standing in the shadow of the city, but behind us the crest of the somber hill was bathed in red by the setting sun. I looked about me for fear of phantoms and prayed aloud, "Jesus Christ, son of God, have mercy on my unbelief."

At that moment a dazzling light shone upon me, and suddenly it felt unreal to be standing where I stood. The reality within me seemed plainer than the massive city wall before my eyes. For the briefest instant, as in my sleep in Lazarus' house, this reality was as true as—yes, even truer than—the reality of the ground and stones. But the blind man saw nothing; he merely pleaded in a woeful tone, "Don't call upon that man, don't shout his name, if he is really risen. His blood is upon my head too."

The brightness faded as quickly as it had come. My sight was still dazzled, and I raised my arms as if to cling to the sweet buoyancy I had felt. The shadow of the wall fell over me again, even more somberly than before, and I returned to earth with heavy limbs. When I looked across the valley to the steep, sunlit hill, my reason told me that something flashing up there had cast a brightness over me, just as with a mirror one may make a fleck of light play in the midst of shadow.

Nevertheless there lingered within me an exultant certainty that he was real and that his kingdom existed. This secret certainty was stronger than my reason, so that I truly desired to believe. I thought, Why am I in such a hurry? Why do I want everything at once, and completely?

Joyfully I grasped the beggar by the arm and said encouragingly, "Bestir yourself. A few paces more and we are at the gate."

But the blind man resisted me, tore himself free and complained, "The road is steep here. Where are you taking me? You're not going to lead me to the precipice and push me over, to avenge the man I helped to send to the cross?"

I answered, "It is not much I know of him, but I don't believe he rose again to be avenged. No, that is certain.'"

We reached the gateway. The guards knew the blind man and greeted him with a few gibes, and a question as to how much he had managed to grab for himself during the day. Probably they would have searched him and taken their share if I had not been with him. They asked no questions of me, since my oiled hair and the stuff of my tassel-less cloak were evidence enough.

The beggar was reassured by the familiar voices of the guards; he felt the walls of the archway with his staff, broke suddenly free and hurried ahead, for here he knew the way. Beside the gate there was a little open space, and by its walls some maimed and crippled mendicants were still sitting, holding out their hands and begging alms in monotonous voices. But for the most part the evening activities of the city were ceasing, and we were met by the smell of cooking fires, freshly baked bread, garlic and hot oil.

When the blind man had gone a few paces ahead of me, he began brandishing his staff and calling upon his fellow beggars. "Israelites!" he cried. "The man following me has led me here, and I can bear witness of him. He is possessed. He changed a stone to cheese in my hand by invoking the name of the crucified Jesus. Pick up stones and stone him to death. He must be one of that accursed man's disciples, and will bring evil upon us."

He bent down and caught hold of a lump of fresh dung, which he threw toward the sound of my steps so accurately that it hit me and dirtied my mantle. Seeing this, the other beggars hastened to grab him and hold him fast, begged my pardon on his account and warned him, saying, "Are you out of your mind as well? This is a rich foreigner. How could he be a disciple of the Nazarene's? He is no Galilean; we can see that from his face."

They wailed in chorus, stretched out their hands to me and displayed their infirmities. I distributed a fistful of coins among them, then took off my dirty cloak, wrapped it around the blind man, laughing aloud and saying, "Here is the mantle you fingered so greedily. Use it for your comfort some night when you have to stay by the roadside and shiver because no one will lead you home."

The blind man shook his fist at the others, yelling, "Now do you believe he's possessed? Why, if I hit him on one cheek, I swear he'd turn the other one. He's mad enough for it."

His words made me laugh more than ever. Perhaps the teaching of Jesus of Nazareth was not so impossible to follow as I had thought. When I tried to return this fellow good for evil, my own satisfaction merely increased. I had the feeling that only thus could I get the better of his malice. To strike him or report him to the guards would have been merely to vanquish one evil with another.

The other beggars joined obsequiously in my laughter and told their companion, "He's not possessed, just tipsy, can't you see? Only a tipsy man would take off his cloak and give it to you; only a tipsy man would think of guiding you, and only a raving drunk would roar with laughter when you insulted him."

In a way they were right. A superhuman intoxication hummed in my head, made me laugh aloud and dimmed my sight so that I was not in the least disconcerted by the glances I met as I walked through the city clad only in my tunic. Anything else might have been staged beforehand, but not the hard cheese which the blind man's staff touched among all those other similar round stones.

The Syrian trader's wife struck her hands together when she saw me coming back half clad, and the Syrian himself was startled, thinking that I had fallen among robbers. But when I just laughed, went to my room for money and sent him out to buy a new mantle, he grew calmer and thought like the others that I was drunk and had gambled away my garment. With many apologies he returned some time later bringing a good woolen mantle with little tassels at the corners. It was of fine Judean wool, he told me; he pinched the stuff and rolled it between his fingers to display its quality and the excellence of the dye. He also assured me that he had beaten down the price for me to a reasonable sum.

At last he said, "This is a Jewish cloak. To find you a Roman one I should have had to go all the way to the forum and pay many times the price. You can cut off the tassels if you like, but there's nothing to prevent you keeping them, now that you've grown a beard. For my part, I too fear and revere the God of Israel and go to the forecourt now and then to drop a coin in his sacrificial coffer, to secure good business."

He looked at me with a crafty smile in his black eyes and gave me back what was left of the money, counting it out carefully. I offered him a reward for his service, but he raised his hands in deprecation and said, "I need nothing from you, for the clothes dealer has already paid me a commission on the business. You're in a far too generous mood to go out again tonight. Rest in your room, rather, and sleep your head clear, but first eat some of the good soup that my wife has made. She has put plenty of onions in it, and herbs that will save you a headache in the morning."

As I did not immediately start to go upstairs, he shook his head in concern, threw out his hands and cried, "Well, well, I'm only thinking of your own good. If you insist, I can send the boy out for another measure of sweet wine, but after that you must drink no more. And don't trip on the stairs tonight, or you might break your neck."

When I tried to defend myself and to explain, with a stuttering tongue, that I was perfectly sober, he held up his hands in great distress and went on, "Your face is red and your eyes are shiny; but as you will, as you will. I will send for a young woman who keeps company with foreigners. But she cannot come before dark, lest she lose her reputation in our quarter of the town. Have patience until then. She will keep you in bed and calm you so that you have peace to sleep yourself sober. She can neither play nor sing, certainly, but she is healthy and well grown and will certainly send you to sleep without lullabies."

He was so firmly convinced that he knew what was wrong with me that it was all I could do to dissuade him. To please him I went to bed, and considerately he came up too, to cover me with my new mantle. Presently his daughter brought me a steaming bowl of strongly spiced soup and stayed to watch me eat, tittering shyly with her hand before her mouth. The soup scalded my tongue, yet its heat only seemed to increase my light-headed elation.

The girl also replenished my water jar, but when she had gone I could stay in bed no longer. On tiptoe I stole up to the roof, and as the stars came out I sat wrapped in my new mantle, listening to the quieting of the city and breathing in the cooling air. Now and then a light puff of wind brushed my hot face, and in my happy state I felt as if an unseen hand had stroked my cheek. Time quivered in me, the dust of earth quivered in me, but something else persuaded me for the first time in my life that I was more than ashes and shadow. This knowledge made me still.

"You risen son of God," I prayed in the darkness, "erase all vain learning from my head. Take me to your kingdom. Lead me into the only Way. I must be mad, ill, bewitched by you. But I believe that you are more than anything that has ever existed in the world."

I awoke, cold and stiff, with the blaring of the temple trumpets. The sun shone upon the eastern ridge, but the city still lay in a hazy dawn twilight, and the morning star hung bright over the horizon. My head had cleared. Shivering, I wound the woolen cloak more tightly about me and crept back to my room and my bed. I tried to feel ashamed of my night thoughts, but I was not ashamed. Rather, I felt as if a cool light yet dwelt in me although the fever had passed.

For this reason I have let my beard grow and stayed in my

room, to think over carefully and to write down what befell me that day. When I have finished writing I mean to return to the Fountain Gate. I feel an inward assurance that everything that has happened to me and is still to happen has a purpose. This certainly gives me security. Whatever mad things I may have written, I do not blush for a single word.

Sixth Letter

MARCUS GREETS TULLIA:

In greeting you, I greet a curious alien past. Even the hot nights of Rome I recall as having happened to someone else rather than to me. One short year divides us, yet that year has been longer than others. These last few days alone have seemed like years to me. I have been carried farther from you, and have changed. I am another Marcus. You wouldn't understand me now. When I think of you, I see your willful mouth drawn into a mocking smile as I tell you what has happened to me.

You live amongst all that I too used to think important. You pay attention to those who greet you, and the manner of their greeting. You are careful in choosing jewelry to wear at a party, for your friends' pleasure, your enviers' indignation and your enemies' resentment. You swathe the thin silk of your gown closely about your smooth body, and you scrutinize your figure in the polished marble panel in the wall. Then you deliver a pinprick to the slave girl who is clumsy in dressing your hair. Lastly you raise your beaker of wine with a weary smile, pretend to listen to the reading of some philosopher or historian, are charmed by the latest song favorite, let your sandal dangle from your toe so that the man reclining beside you at the table is certain to note the slenderness and whiteness of your little foot. Slim and slight though you are, you have strength and stamina. Your thirst for pleasure can keep you awake night after night in sultry Rome. In company with others you taste, abstractedly and fastidiously, of birds' tongues, snails and delicacies from the sea, which you would just as soon not eat. But if you have exhausted yourself with your lover you find no difficulty in devouring an underdone steak in the middle of the night, to renew your forces for the tireless game.

Thus I see your shadow, Tullia. No longer full of life but as in polished black stone, and your shadow does not tantalize my senses as it did last winter in Alexandria, when in vain I strove to forget you. Something else now fills my mind, through no act of my own. You would no longer recognize me, Tullia. Perhaps I should not recognize you.

So I believe that it's rather to myself that I write these letters, even though it is you I greet in them. I write to search into myself and into all that has befallen me, according to the precepts of my good tutor in Rhodes, who used to urge me to write of such things as my own eyes had seen and my ears heard, and not merely of what other men had written in other words. No, I no longer write just to pass the time and dispel my boredom. You are no longer near me as I write; you withdraw ever farther. That does not sadden me, Tullia; I do not feel that I have lost anything. Not even your body binds me any longer; I am too full of other things.

Bearded, in simple sandals and the dyed Jewish mantle, I walked at dusk back to the Fountain Gate. I have not tended my nails, and not even pumice stone would remove the ink from the fingers of my right hand. I who am used to sweating-rooms and hot water have been washing in cold, for when I went to the men's baths at the gymnasium I was stared at because of my beard. I have not even rubbed depilatory ointment into my armpits. My body is the hairy body of a barbarian; but I don't mind, and don't even think it matters. I want to melt into my surroundings, so that men may trust me, even if later I return to the old ways in which I was brought up.

For I do not love this city, whose people have invoked his blood upon their heads. When the women of Jerusalem wept over him as he staggered under the lash to the mount of the cross, he is reported to have said that they would do better to weep for themselves and for their children. And I cannot but feel foreboding when I behold the temple, whose sacred veil was ripped from top to bottom by the earthquake, and where the stairway lost several steps at the second tremor. That is omen enough.

I was thinking of all this on my way to the Fountain Gate. People were still thronging the streets of the bazaar, every language in the world echoed in front of the booths, camel bells jingled and donkeys brayed. I admit that the sacred city of the Jews is as much a capital as any other, but I do not like it here.

Only a couple of beggars remained by the gate, but they didn't recognize me, and I saw no sign of the blind man. A group of women came in through the archway with water jars on their heads, gossiping with animation. They never troubled to draw a fold of their mantles to their mouths on my account; I was unimportant.

The sky turned dark blue. Dusk deepened. Three stars were already shimmering when the guards trust a torch of pitch into the holder beneath the arch and lit it. I was disappointed, yet prepared for disappointment, prepared to come here day after day until I received a sign. I was already thinking of returning to my lodging, but lingered still. It made no difference where I was.

Then a man with a water pitcher appeared in the gateway. He carried it on his shoulder, steadying it less skillfully than the women, and walked slowly and cautiously so as not to stumble in the half-darkness. Not until he had disappeared into a street that led steeply uphill did I follow him. The steep street turned into a series of shallow steps. I could hear his tread and his labored breathing under the weight of the jar as I walked a few paces behind him.

The way was long. He turned aside into winding alleys but did not increase his pace. We kept climbing up into the upper city, but I noticed that he was not choosing the shortest way to his destination. In a lonely place he set the pitcher down upon the ground, steadied it with his hand and waited. I went up to him and stood beside him without speaking. We stood there by the wall for a long time until he had stopped panting. Then at last he turned to me, greeted me, and asked, "Have you lost your way?"

"And with you be peace," I said. "There are many ways and many false guides."

"There are only two ways," he replied knowingly. "The way to life and the way to death."

"For me there remains only one," I rejoined. "I cannot find it of my own strength, but I hope and trust that someone will guide me."

Without replying he raised the pitcher to his shoulder again and went on. I walked beside him and he did not forbid me. Presently, I suggested, "The steps are steep. May I help you? Else you will get out of breath again."

He said, "It's not the weight of the jar that makes me breathless, but fear. I believe no good will come of this." But he let me take the pitcher on my shoulder. It didn't seem very heavy. He walked ahead and warned me of uneven places where I might have stumbled, for the alley was dirty and smelt of urine. I soiled my sandals.

But the house we stopped at, after climbing high into the upper city through a gate in the old wall, was large and of the better sort. In the starlight I could discern no more than its outline, but my companion rapped on the door, which was at once opened by a serving-woman. She did not greet me, but took the jar from me without hesitation and showed such evident respect for the man with me that I knew he must be more than a servant.

He led me into a quiet court where trees were growing. There I was met by a youth of about fifteen. "Peace be with you," he said shyly. "My father and my uncle have retired, but allow me to take you to the upper room. Do you care to wash your hands?"

Without waiting for my answer, the serving-woman poured water copiously over my hands from the very pitcher I had carried, as if to show that after all there was no lack of water here. The boy handed me a linen towel and said, "My name is Mark."

As I dried my hands he went on eagerly, full of his own importance. "I was with the master the night they came and arrested him. I dashed out of bed in just my tunic and ran to warn him, for I knew he meant to spend the night in the garden of Gethsemane. They grabbed me, too, so that my tunic was torn and remained in their hands. I had to run off naked, with the rest."

"Don't talk so much, Mark," my companion warned him. But he himself was just as full of hidden excitement, now that he was safely in the courtyard and could master his fear. "My name is Nathaniel," he said. "Why should I make a secret of it? I met him on the road to Emmaus, the day he left his tomb."

"But you didn't recognize him at first," Mark blurted out. Nathaniel laid a hand on the back of Mark's neck to quiet him. Mark seized my hand trustingly in his hot one, and I could feel that he had never done any manual work to speak of. He led me up some steps to a gallery that ran along the roof, and from there to the upper room of the house.

This was a big room faintly lit by a single lamp, so that the corners lay in darkness. When I stepped in I saw that two men were awaiting me there. They stood hand in hand, quite silent in the half-darkness, and one of them I recognized. It was the handsome John, whom I had seen with the women on the mount of the cross. The other man was older, his brow was furrowed and his eyes were searching and suspicious.

"Peace be with you," I said.

But they made no reply. At length John turned with a questioning look to the older man, as if urging him to speak. But the man's eyes remained just as suspicious as he looked me up and down. The silence became oppressive. Then at last Nathaniel said apologetically, "He followed the water jar."

"I seek the only way," I assured them, dreading lest they should dismiss me from mistrust.

There were several couches around a large table; the room was obviously the banquet hall of a well-to-do house. When the suspicious man had scrutinized me sufficiently, he waved his hand. "Nathaniel, Mark, you may go," he said, "but stand guard in the courtyard."

When they had left he turned the big key in the lock of the door and said, "Peace be with you, stranger. What do you want of us? I fear the way you seek is too narrow for you."

But John broke in on his words, and reproached him. "Thomas, why must you always begin by doubting everyone and every thing?" To me, he said confidingly, "Whoever seeks shall find, and to him who knocks the door shall be opened. We have heard that you're quiet and humble of heart. You have knocked with devotion; therefore we have opened the door."

He invited me to sit, and sat down opposite me, looking at me with the spring-clear gaze of a dreamer.

After a moment's hesitation Thomas sat too, and said, "I am one of the twelve of whom you've heard. He chose and called us to be his messengers, and we followed him. John is the youngest of us. I have to curb his rashness.

"You must not reproach us for being overcautious," he went on. "No doubt you know that the authorities are fabricating charges against us. They say we have conspired together to set fire to the temple as a sign to the people. They say we murdered that one of us who betrayed him. Why should I not admit that we have disputed about you? It was I who warned the others most earnestly against you, except for Peter, who wouldn't even hear you mentioned because you're a foreigner. But Mary Magdalene spoke in your favor."

"I know you," said John. "I saw you standing by the cross, and noticed that you didn't listen to those who abused him."

"I know you too, and have heard of you," I said. It was hard not to stare at him, for I had never seen so beautiful a face on any young man before. It was as candid as if no evil thought could ever have come near it. Yet this beauty was not lifeless, as in a sculpture; his was a living, burning face, from which emanated serenity and warmth.

"Well, and what is it you want of us?" asked Thomas again, in a surly voice.

His opposition made me wary. It was as if he were jealously trying to guard a secret which the messengers possessed in common, and which did not concern outsiders. "I wanted only to ask you to show me the Way," I answered humbly.

Thomas looked unwillingly at John and then said, "Before he was arrested he told us that there were many dwelling places in his father's house. He said that he would go and prepare a place for us there; he must have meant us twelve, although afterwards Judas failed him. And he said, 'You know the way where I am now going.' "

He rubbed his furrowed forehead and looked perplexed. "I said at the time that we had no idea of where he was going, so how could we know the way? Now you come, foreigner, and ask me the way although I don't know it myself."

John reminded him, "Thomas, Thomas, he answered you. He told you that he himself was the Way—that was it—the Way and the Truth. You can't say you don't know it."

But Thomas sprang up in desperation, pounded the flat of his hand with his fist and cried, "But what does that mean? I don't understand. Explain it."

John would gladly have explained, as I could see, but dared not because of me. I reflected, and then joined in the conversation, saying, "On the third day he rose from his tomb."

"Yes, indeed," said John. "Mary Magdalene came and told us that the stone had been rolled away. We rushed to the place, Peter and I, and saw that the sepulcher was empty."

"Yes, yes," Thomas observed ironically. "Mary Magdalene saw angels and a gardener who was a ghost."

"A gardener?" I asked with an inward tremor.

"Women's twaddle," Thomas went on, without noticing the interruption. "Like Nathaniel and that other one on the road to Emmaus. They didn't even recognize him."

John said with conviction, "Here in this very room he revealed himself to us that same evening, when we were sitting behind locked doors and were all afraid. He was here with us and spoke to us, and made us a promise which I hardly dare so much as think of, far less speak of to a stranger. But I can assure you that he was here among us, alive, and that afterwards he disappeared as quickly as he had come. And we believed."

"Quite so," Thomas said with a sneer. "You were as bemused as Nathaniel and that other man, to say nothing of Mary. I wasn't there, and I don't believe in visions of that sort. I shan't believe it until I see the nail holes in his hands and put my finger in them. Nothing less than that will make me believe. This is my last word, though I should drop dead this minute."

The young John was so greatly distressed by his words and doubts that he turned away his head. But he made no protest. It seemed to me that Thomas's suspicions during the past few days had affected even the faith of the eyewitnesses, so that secretly they too began to doubt what they had all seen together.

A strange joy seized me, and I said resolutely, "I do not need to see to believe. I understand that he has risen again and is still on earth. Why, I do not know, but I am waiting. In these days something has been happening which has never happened before, and we have certainly not seen the end of it."

But Thomas said derisively, "You're not even one of the children of Israel, though you seem to have had the tassels of a proselyte stitched to the corners of your cloak. I can't see why you should persist in spying on us like this. I mistrust your purpose. You needn't think I don't know of your having been the Governor's guest in Antonia. You're trying to lure us into a trap so that we too may end on the beam of a cross or be stoned in a pit."

He wrung his gnarled fingers, stared anxiously before him and went on, "I don't know whether you've seen what stoning is like. I have, and I don't want to experience it myself. At least not now, when he is dead, be his tomb empty or not."

"Then why do you stay in Jerusalem?" I demanded in his own brusque tone. "Why don't you leave and go back to your own place quietly, without any fuss? What are you waiting for?"

He lowered his eyes, as if all his days he had been accustomed to bowing to a voice of command. Fingering a fold of his mantle he answered defensively, "I cannot set off alone. But in my opinion, we're wasting time. The most sensible thing to do would be to go into the desert for a while and then return home, each to his own place. But here we twist and turn, argue irresolutely and can come to no agreement."

John looked at him with his spring-clear gaze and reminded him, "You have no longer any home, once he has chosen you. You laid down your tools and followed him. He who looks back after setting his hand to the plough is not fit for his kingdom. That's what he said. No, Thomas, we can't go back to our former life."

"What is his kingdom like?" I asked quickly.

But Thomas shook his head with a look of mockery and said, "At least it cannot be as we believed it, stranger."

Again he struck the palm of his hand with his fist and exclaimed in impotent fury, "Wasn't I, too, ready to exchange my cloak for a sword and to die with him and for him? God be merciful to us, but he, the son of man, had power and strength to make what he would of the world. Yet he let himself be nailed to the cross, mute as a lamb, leaving us in such a predicament that we don't know what to believe or where to turn.'"

He resumed, "When a person is stoned, blood runs from his mouth; blood and mucus run from his nose; he screams and weeps and all his filth escapes into his clothes before he yields up his spirit. Why should we incur that fate, now that he has gone and has forsaken us?"

John gently touched his shoulder and said with conviction, "When the hour came we were all as weak as each other. But remember that he promised to send us a defender."

Thomas gave him an angry nudge, as if he had blurted out some secret, and went on, to put me off the scent. "That's easy for you to say, John. You know little of life. You were your father's favorite son and had authority over older men at his fishery. It was for the sake of the laborers and the oppressed that I followed him when he called me. But what pleasure any of the down-trodden could take in his lunatic death is beyond my understanding. All he did was to call down the derision of the Council and the Romans upon himself and us."

But he failed to lure me from the trail. I asked John curiously, "What was that you said of a defender?"

John gave me a candid look and admitted, "I didn't understand that myself and still don't, but I trust in his promise. Something will happen to us, as you said yourself. That is why we linger in Jerusalem."

They both looked at me, and their faces were as different from each other as any two human faces could be. Yet in them both there was something of the same nature, some similarity, some link, for all Thomas's bitter words. When they ceased speaking it was as if I had been irrevocably excluded from their fellowship. I thought of what Mary Magdalene had said about these chosen messengers, and understood what she meant. I believe that even I would have been able to distinguish these faces amid a crowd of others. Now that I had met them, I thought I might also recognize those messengers who distrusted me and did not want to meet me.

When they had been silent long enough for me to understand that despite John's good will I was an outsider, I said awkardly, "I wish you well. I am not a Jew and thus not circumcised, and I don't intend to be. But I've heard it said that he had compassion even on Samaritans, whom the Jews condemn. He is also said to have healed the servant of a garrison commander in Galilee, because the Roman believed in his strength. I too believe in his power and strength; I believe he lives still and will yet come to us. If it should be so, I beg you not to leave me out in the darkness. Surely I should do him no harm. How could anyone harm a man who has risen from his tomb and who comes and goes through locked doors? I don't want to harm you either; on the contrary, I will help you if I can. I live in the house of the Syrian trader near the Hasmoneans' palace. I am well-off and am willing to help you with money too, if need be."

"Prove that," said Thomas, holding out his calloused hand.

But John said deprecatingly, "We're in no need of that sort of help—at least, not for the present. My own family is well-to-do, and Matthew has money, and the master has rich sympathizers who paid for our lodging when we traveled, being unable to follow him in any other way. No, we need neither bread nor clothes, but only such things as he alone can give us. If he returns I will not forget you, but the secrets which he has entrusted to us I naturally cannot reveal to a stranger."

Thomas said warningly, "I suspect it was a mistake to listen to Mary. This stranger's curiosity bodes no good."

Turning to me, he went on threateningly: "You must know that when we walked with him we had power to heal the sick—ay, and even to drive out evil spirits. And though just now our powers may be at their weakest, you would be wise to beware of us. It was we whom he chose to be about him. It was we who admitted certain people to see him, and excluded others as we thought fit. And if one of us twelve could be a betrayer, how deeply then should we not mistrust every stranger!"

"I fear neither you nor your power," I said. "I never heard of his using his power to strike even his adversary, much less any who patiently seek him."

"Ah, you know it all, don't you!" said Thomas. "But he cursed a fig tree once so that it withered away before our eyes, and all because it bore only leaves and he found no fruit on it. It wasn't even the season for figs."

But John said, "We never knew quite what he meant by that. It must have been a parable that we didn't understand."

"It was to the people he spoke in parables," Thomas objected. "To us he talked openly. But if we failed to understand then, how should we now? So it would be better to leave here without more delay."

I was growing weary of his objections and threats. "Be it as you will," I said. "I am sorry if I have troubled you both at a time when other things weigh so heavily on your minds. As for me, I have come from Alexandria in search of the ruler of the world, whose birth is foretold in many different prophecies. Such prophecies are current among other races besides the Jews. The sign has been noted both in Rome and Greece. And it is in Jesus of Nazareth, who was crucified as king of the Jews and whose death I myself witnessed, that I have found the ruler of the world. His kingdom is different from what I expected and different, it seems, from what you expected. But his resurrection has convinced me of its existence."

Yet when I had said this, my eyes smarted with tears of disappointment; I turned away my head and looked with blurred gaze at the great banquet hall, whose corners were hidden in darkness. For a brief moment I was aware of the same presence as in Lazarus' guest room. But this was no dream. On the contrary I was wide awake and susceptible to impressions. I was filled with a desire to call upon him and take his name, as when the stone had been turned into cheese in the blind man's hand.

But some dread withheld me from doing so in this room and in the presence of these two men. No, I dared not speak his name. I said humbly, "Peace be with you," and turned to leave.

Thomas walked a few paces ahead of me to unlock the door, but when he had turned the big wooden key and grasped the handle, the door would not open. He shook it and turned the key once more, but in vain. "This door has warped and jammed,'" he said angrily.

"Don't force it or you'll break the lock," said John, coming up to help him. But John could not work the lock either. They were both surprised and looked at me reprovingly, as if it had been my fault. So I went over to them and tried. I have no great experience of wooden locks and wooden keys, but the key turned obediently and the door was easy to open. Cool night air wafted toward me; above the garden I saw a sky of stars, and one star flew in a golden streak across the heavens, like a sign. The sticking door and the shooting star I took as a token that he himself, their king, would not shut me out of his kingdom as these his messengers wished to do. But they saw no omen. Thomas simply turned and twisted the key in the lock, muttering to himself that he being a poor man was unaccustomed to keys, for he had nothing worth locking up.

They both remained in the room as I went down the steps. In the courtyard young Mark met me and asked considerately, "Can you find your way to your lodging, stranger? The second watch of the night has already begun."

I said, "Don't concern yourself about me or my welfare. It's true that Nathaniel led me here by detours and winding alleys until he was breathless from fear, so that I shouldn't know where I was; all the same I think I can get back to the city. I go first through the wall and then downhill, and I can take my bearings from the stars. Once I find the theatre and the forum, I know my way."

But Mark said eagerly, "Father and Uncle asked me to be your host this evening. I offered you no refreshment, because our Lord's messengers wouldn't eat with you, since you're a Roman. But allow me to show hospitality at least by walking back with you to your lodging."

I protested, smiling. "You're young, and youth needs sleep. As it is, you've had to sit up on my account."

"On evenings like this one can't sleep," said Mark. "Wait; I will fetch my mantle."

The sleepy serving-woman grumbled at him by the gate, but Mark laughed, patted her cheeks and slipped out through the gateway with me. I saw that he had brought a stick weighted with lead at one end: no very pleasant discovery, even though I had no fear of a half-grown boy.

He guided me confidently straight down the hill, and evidently had no intention of misleading me to prevent my getting home. In dark places he took my hand and led me, lest I should stumble. I believe he wanted very much to talk but did not like to as I was silent.

At length I felt bound to say, "You knew him then, this Jesus of Nazareth?"

Marcus pressed my hand hard and replied, "Yes indeed I knew him. I was there to arrange and serve the meal when he and his messengers ate the paschal lamb a day early, according to the custom of the holy ones of the desert. That was his last evening. But before that I saw him and greeted him as the Son of David when he came riding into Jerusalem on a donkey."

He bragged a little: "Father had got a donkey for him; it was waiting at a certain place for his disciples to find. On that day the people spread their clothes on the road before him, waved palm branches and shouted Hosanna. Father and Uncle let him use the upper room without charge."

I was curious, and asked, "Who is your father? How could he show sympathy with Jesus without fear of the authorities?"

Mark's face clouded and he said softly, "Father won't have his name mentioned in connection with these matters. But he belongs to the quiet ones, although he is rich, and I believe the quiet ones had asked him to protect the king. But Jesus didn't want to endanger my father or his household by letting himself be arrested at our place, and so he went to Gethsemane for the night. But Judas, the betrayer, knew the room; so they came to us first, with burning torches and clashing weapons, and banged on the door. That was when I jumped out of bed and ran to warn him."

He explained, "Father can always defend himself before the Council by telling them that he lets the upper room regularly for parties and weddings and such things. And no one has ever molested him, for he has friends among the men in authority. They may know perfectly well that the Galileans are in the habit of gathering in that room after dark, but they don't want to stir up more trouble and attract attention by trying to stop them. They are oppressed enough already by their guilt in murdering the son of God in so terrible a way."

"Was he the son of God?" I asked, to test the boy.

Mark answered sincerely, "Of course he was the son of God, and his anointed. Nobody but one sent by God coud do what he did. And besides, he has come out of his tomb and is alive, although he was dead. My Uncle Nathaniel has even eaten with him since then. Dead bodies, and spirits without bodies, cannot eat. So of course he is alive."

In my heart I liked his straightforward boyish faith, yet my reason made me say ironically, "Clearly you are not yet burdened with learning, since you're so ready to believe all you hear."

The boy defended himself. "I can read and write Greek and a little Latin besides. Father has business affairs in Cyprus and even as far away as Rome. I am not as ignorant as you think. Remember that I have seen him several times, and heard him speak. Once when he came home to us he laid his hands on my head. For you it must be harder to believe, since you only saw him die, I have heard. But I saw him in the days of his strength and power."

We had reached the wall that divides the upper city from the lower, and I paused at the gate where I had met Mary of Beret. "I can find my way from here," I said. But I did not move, nor did Mark seem willing to leave me. Another star fell across the sky, and we both saw it.

"Even the stars are full of unease in these times," I remarked. "Something is happening. Perhaps the days of his power are only now beginning, but in a way we can't yet comprehend."

Mark did not take his leave or turn homeward. Shyly he fingered his mantle and poked at the ground with his stick.

"But," I said, "I am surprised that Nathaniel didn't recognize him at once, and Mary Magdalene only when he called her by name."

"They couldn't expect to," returned Mark in their defense. "Even while he was alive he took on many aspects; they changed with his mood. It's hard to explain. It was as if he had everybody's face. All who believed in him thought that he resembled someone they had once loved. It was difficult to look him in the face. His gaze was too grave. I often saw old men lower their eyes after meeting his."

"You may be right," I said. "I saw his suffering on the cross, knowing nothing about him. But I couldn't look at him. I should never be able to describe his appearance. True, it was fairly dark. I thought it was out of respect for his agony that I avoided looking at him very closely; yet perhaps I could not have done so even had I wished. And I am not surprised, seeing that he was the son of God. Even his guards acknowledged that, when the earth shook at the moment of his death.

"But," I continued, giving vent to my bitterness, "however he may have chosen his messengers, they are ignorant men, and it doesn't seem to me that they have the right to prevent others from seeking their teacher. That is wrong, and ill-done of them. I believe as you do. They exaggerate their fear so as to keep his mystery to themselves. They would hardly be in danger of further persecution even if they left their hiding place."

Mark pondered, and then said, "I think you're wrong. They may be ignorant men, yet there's something about them that other people lack. I believe *they* dared look him in the face and took no harm. At least John did. It was John he loved most. Don't be too hard on them, stranger."

But I heard the smile in his voice as he went on. "Though I must say, they're not always easy. I believe Father's tired of them too, because of their quarrels and hot tempers. Peter especially—the biggest of them—is headstrong, and bickers with the women; and yet, it's they who feed the men and keep them hidden. Big and strong though he is, he's very childish. In any case, Galileans in general are different from us of Jerusalem. They don't grasp the subtleties of the scriptures as the masters of Israel do. They're country folk, and see things in a practical, literal way."

Presently he added, "It's true that they're curt with strangers; not even while he was alive did they let just anyone come to him. Someone else besides you has sought them out, but they refused to see him because they didn't consider him a child of Israel."

This made me curious. "Tell me about it," I said.

"Have you heard how he sank to the ground on the way, when the arm of the cross he had to carry became too heavy for him?" said Mark. "The Romans caught hold of a man coming into the city from the fields, and forced him to carry the cross. They took him for an ordinary laborer, but he is a great landowner and respected in the synagogue of the libertines. At first he was going to complain of such treatment, but then he changed his mind. He knew nothing of what was happening; he is from Cyrene, and avoids having anything to do with politics. But when he found out, and learned whose cross he had been carrying, he was filled with distress and wanted to learn more of Jesus from his disciples. Yet Peter distrusted even him. Besides, it was just at the time that the disciples were most frightened. He never went back to ask them again about the Way. It might be worth your while to find him and talk to him. Jesus may have said something important to him on the road, since he was so troubled afterwards."

"Where can I find him?" I asked.

"He is called Simon of Cyrene," said Mark. "Ask in the libertines' synagogue; they're sure to know him there."

"What sort of a synagogue is that?"

"They read the scriptures in Greek," Mark explained. "It was founded by liberated slaves who returned from Rome as rich men. Immigrants from Alexandria and Cyrene support it too, for as a rule they have so little of the Hebrew in them that they no longer understand the language of our fathers. It's a wealthy, broad-minded synagogue which doesn't lay overheavy burdens on its supporters. I think you would be well received there if you should care to hear the scriptures read in Greek some Sabbath."

This was advice I valued. "I thank you, Mark," I said. "I was shut out, and bidden to seek the Way by myself. Perhaps this man Simon is seeking it as well. It's easier for two to search than for one. Peace be with you."

"And with you too be peace, O friend of the Governor," he returned meaningly. "If anyone asks, you will be able to tell them that there is no dangerous conspiracy here."

"I am my own friend, and have no others," I replied, irritated that this youth should so pointedly convey his suspicion that I might pass on what information I had gleaned to the Romans. "Were anyone to ask me, I could at any rate affirm that the two I met tonight are neither incendiaries nor disturbers of the peace. But I don't believe anyone will ask me anything. And in any case, Pontius Pilate is the man who above all others wants to forget this whole matter as quickly as possible."

"Peace be with you," said Mark again, and we parted, and nothing more befell me that night.

I did not need to go to the synagogue of the libertines to find Simon of Cyrene. My landlord, Karanthes the Syrian, said at once when I asked him about this man, "Give yourself no trouble over this; wait a moment and I'll tell you all you want to know about him."

Calling his son to take his place at the counter, he vanished into the alleyway, and I had barely time to quench my thirst, seated there on his threshold, before he was back again. He began, "Yes, well, that man Simon has made money in Cyrene in his day, and when he moved here some years ago he bought a number of fields, vineyards, and olive groves near the city. He has interests in other towns of Judea as well. He lives in the Greek style. They say he even attends the theatre and the gymnasium bathhouse, although he wears a beard; and he's not regarded as an orthodox Jew. Some declare that he's not even circumcised, but he's too rich for anyone to inquire into that. At least he observes the law and keeps the Sabbath holy. He seems to have been involved in a shameful business the other day, when the Romans dragged him out of the crowd to carry the cross of that agitator they crucified. The disgrace of it has so preyed on his mind that he has shut himself up in his house and speaks to no one."

He explained to me exactly how to find Simon's place, and then asked with a sly smile, "What do you want of him? Are you thinking of investing in land or raising a loan? If so, I know many better men you could turn to, and I don't recommend Simon at all; it seems he goes about gathering dry branches for firewood and hardly eats anything but bread and green vegetables."

His information sounded contradictory to me, and I was curious to meet Simon of Cyrene. But my landlord assailed me with questions as to what I wanted the man for, and I believe he had my interests at heart; so at last I said reluctantly, "I want to meet him on account of that very incident you mentioned, to ask him what he knows of Jesus of Nazareth, since he carried the cross for him."

Karanthes was much upset, and tugging at my mantle he said warningly, "Don't talk so loud about unpleasant matters!"

But I said, "You've treated me well, and I don't want to conceal anything from you. I have reason to believe that the Jews' crucified king was the most remarkable man who has ever lived, and that he was the son of God. I'm as good as convinced that he left his tomb on the third day, and that he's still alive, although he was dead. Therefore I want to find out all about him, including whatever Simon of Cyrene may know."

My Syrian landlord answered with tears in his voice, "Alas, and woe upon you! What misfortunes have I brought upon my household and my livelihood by receiving you into my guestroom? If you weren't a friend of Adenabar the centurion, I would be wise to gather up all your belongings forthwith and throw you out of my house. Things like this are spoken of in whispers within four walls and not in the street, where anyone may hear. In any case one should never put faith in the tales of cranks and the visions of crazy women. Certainly I know and have heard rumors of what you allude to, but believe me, you would do best to keep away from such things or the Jews will soon be hurling stones at your head. You can't yet have grasped that for the Jews, religion is politics and politics religion, and nothing they do is altogether divorced from their fath; their God is ever-vigilant and keeps watch upon them day and night to see that they conduct themselves as his law prescribes. So in these matters it is best to walk on tiptoe and hold one's tongue, especially when one is a foreigner."

"I am a Roman citizen," I said. "No Jew can harm me. I am not under their jurisdiction. If they were to charge me with anything concerning their religion, not even the Proconsul would dare to sit in judgment over me; I should be sent to Rome to appear before Caesar."

"But they say that Caesar doesn't live in Rome any more; that he is away on an island somewhere," said Karanthes innocently. "In his place is another who rules; a crafty, rapacious man who handles the bribes."

Now it was my turn to grab my landlord, clap my hand over his mouth and look about me in a fright lest someone should have heard him.

"Had you said that in Rome," I told him, "you would have talked the head from your body."

Calmly Karanthes loosened my hand from his mouth and said, "There, you see? In Rome do as the Romans do, but in Jerusalem as the Jews do. Here the name of the crucified man is just as inflammable and dangerous as the name of that other man in Rome."

He hesitated a moment, looked about him, and then squatted down beside me to whisper in my ear as I sat there on his threshold, wrapped in my dyed Jewish mantle.

"Rumors are rumors," he whispered, "but only afterwards did we lesser people and foreigners fully realize from how great a disaster we were saved by the swift action of the Jewish Council. You see, at passover time we were all living on the brink of a volcano without knowing it. The people had already proclaimed him king and son of David, and it's said that he had secret support from a congregation and conspiracy in the desert, called the quiet ones. It seems they meant to set fire to the temple during the feast, as a sign to the people, overthrow the Council and set up an administration of workpeople and small farmers. As you can imagine, this would have been a really welcome opportunity for the Romans to interfere. The Governor had already mustered a whole legion in readiness, from all the garrisons, and he himself lodged in Antonia; for he dared not stay in Herod's palace as he usually does. But when the rioters lost their leader, they had to creep back underground again.'"

"I don't believe you," I said. "According to all I've heard, his kingdom is not of this world at all."

"Yes, well, rumors are only rumors," remarked Karanthes placidly. "But there must be something behind such persistent and consistent stories. There's no smoke without fire. What do *you* think?"

"I believe that the Council and the priests and the scribes spread that kind of rumor themselves, so as to justify a brutal murder," I said firmly. "He wasn't like that. I've heard that he told people if they were struck on one cheek to turn the other, and that one should never repay evil with evil. And that I believe is the only way to free oneself from the power of evil, which leads merely to revenge and fresh revenge and revenge again."

"Then he has only himself to blame," said Karanthes in a matter-of-fact tone. "Anyone who works here on earth and performs actions and proclaims doctrines must submit to this world's laws. He may have been exploited by others for their own ends; it's possible, for no one has heard anything but good of the man himself. But the only possible course for the Jewish Council to take was to draw their conclusions according to the facts, and their political common sense. It is not seemly to heal the sick and raise the dead in order to lead folk astray, or to proclaim that one is the son of their God. So far as we know, their God has no son and can never have one. That is just where he differs from other gods. Such things make for political disturbance. And in a revolt it is always the hotheads who seize power, not the sober ones. I'm sure that my shop would have been in flames and my daughter lying in the gutter with a broken head and spread legs as soon as the disturbance had begun, and before I had even had time to hail the new king."

I pondered his warning and all I had heard and experienced. Then I said reflectively, "I believe that his revolt begins inside people, not outside them. This is where it differs from all others. But how that is to come about I still don't know."

Karanthes raised his hands in resignation and said, "One can see you're not married. Do as you please, but don't say I didn't warn you."

So I went to the house of Simon of Cyrene. It lay in a narrow alley and was outwardly no different from other houses in the city. But the door was locked although it was the middle of the day. When I had been knocking on it for a time, a serving-woman came, opened it a crack, and quickly covered her head at the sight of me. I greeted her and asked for her master, but she said defensively, "My master is sick and keeps to a darkened room; he does not wish to see anyone."

I told her my name, mentioned Aristainos the banker as my reference, and said at last, "I am sure your master will see me, for I want to speak with him on the very matter that is weighing upon his mind."

The servant let me in and went to fetch her master. I noticed that behind its shabby façade the whole house had been rebuilt in the Greek style. The large atrium had an opening in the roof and a rain-water basin in the floor, which was decorated with mosaic figures—flowers, fishes and birds—although Jewish law forbids such images. Along the walls were bronze objects and Greek vases as in any other cultured home. Presently a Greek slave came in, carrying a scroll under his arm. He was dressed in an elegantly pleated linen mantle, and had gray hair. His eyes were red-rimmed, as if from much reading in bad light. He greeted me in the Roman manner and made me sit down and wait.

"What is that you're reading?" I asked.

Putting the scroll behind his back, he answered, "It's just a book by a Jewish prophet. I'm tutor to my master's sons, Rufus and Alexander, though my master is a simple man who doesn't care for poetry."

"Allow me to guess what it is," I said with a smile. "I read the same myself in Alexandria, and recently I have heard some of it recited. Is it not the book of Isaiah the prophet?"

The slave was startled; he glanced at the roll in his hand and then at me, and asked, "Are you a seer or a magician that you know what I've been reading to my master?"

"I'm by no means a magician," I answered. "I know a little

of astronomy, thanks to my foster father Manilius. You will hardly have heard of his work *Astronomica.*"

He said, "I haven't, but I know that the Romans borrow everything from us Greeks, translate it into their language and publish it as their own."

The gray-haired slave was evidently tender of his dignity. I asked, "What do you think of the Jewish prophet?"

He answered, "I'm a Greek. These pretentious Jewish obscurities bore me. I read the book aloud to my master, but think my own thoughts meanwhile. The tortoise can beat Achilles, as has been proved. As a slave I have assumed the role of the tortoise. I never attempt to circumvent Aesop and Homer, as do the Jews."

Simon of Cyrene entered, and I looked at him closely. He had tossed a ragged mantle, gray with age, over his shoulders; his beard was unkempt, and he had the big hands of a tiller of the soil. He was a powerfully built, middle-aged man, and his face was deeply browned by the sun. He sat down on the red-covered master's chair and waved the slave impatiently away.

Without greeting me he demanded curtly, "What is your business, Roman? What do you want of me?"

I looked about me, fearing eavesdroppers. Then I replied, simply and straightforwardly, "I have heard that you grieve deeply on account of Jesus of Nazareth, and that you have tried to meet his disciples but they rejected you. I too seek the Way. Help me if you can."

With his head on one side, he stared suspiciously at me under his bushy eyebrows and denied this, saying, "I seek no way. Who told you that? I found my own way many years ago, and so far it has served me well."

I observed him carefully, and noted that he carried his head like a slave and had a slave's suspicious look. Involuntarily I glanced at his ankle to find the indelible mark of the shackle, but his eyes followed the direction of mine and he hastily drew his feet in under the marble bench. At the same time he struck a little metal disk with a wooden hammer, to summon his servant.

"You have sharp eyes," he said reluctantly. "Yes, I was a slave, but received my freedom more than ten years ago, and made my fortune in Cyrene in grain dealing before coming here to Jerusalem, where my great-grandfather once lived. I have two sons, and I want no one to look down at them because of my origins. But I was born a slave, and my father, and my grandfather before him. That sets its mark on a man, even if no one notices it. I have my place in the synagogue and at the theatre, my sons have Greek tutors and I live in a civilized way, as you see. Perhaps one day I shall be able to purchase Roman citizenship for my sons."

The servant entered, bearing a silver tray; he offered me a gold beaker and filled it with dark wine from a dusty jar. On the tray were honey cakes, and beside them a barley loaf gray with ashes. Simon of Cyrene took an earthenware beaker from the tray and was given water. He broke a piece of the bread, blew the ash off it, and drank the water. I can't deny that this surprised me.

"It may be that I too am weary of honey cakes," I said. "If you will allow me, I will taste your barley bread. But your wine I won't despise, since you have broken a seal on my account. Water would have been just as welcome, since from what I see it is water from the spring."

"I get this from a good spring far from here," said Simon of Cyrene. "Such a spring as I used to dream of as a boy, when I toiled under the glaring sun in the fields of Africa. I used to dream too of barley bread like this, for our slave bread was made of chaff and shelled corn, peas and African oats. When I grew rich I drank wine for a time, until I discovered that I didn't like it. I ate honey bread and roast gazelle and spiced sauces, until I found out that pure bread and fresh vegetables were more to my taste and kept my body healthy. I have experienced many things: more than you can guess, Roman."

Yet he spoke of this in no embittered way, but quite as a matter of course.

"It was a long time before I fully grasped that I was free," he said, "and could enjoy the things I really like. My bed is still the hard sleeping bench of a slave, for soft down pillows make my back ache. I know very well that people laugh at me when, after having seen to my land and paid my laborers their daily wage, I gather twigs in my mantle and carry them home. I blame no one for wastefulness, but to be wasteful myself affords me no pleasure at all. As a boy I was flogged nearly to death for knowing no better than to collect dung and dry thistles from another man's land, as fuel for my mother's fire. For this reason I delight in gathering good fuel on my own land, and carrying it home to my own house in my own mantle."

He went on to say, "I may be a stern master, for I tolerate no idleness among my workpeople; but I have never forbidden an olive gatherer to climb down from the tree and say his prayers. What I like best is to walk about my estate, gird up my mantle and work among the rest with my own hands."

It seemed as if he wanted to avoid the subject I had introduced, for he continued, "That is the way I have found for myself. In my slave's mind I have thought much about human freedom, so I never force my own kind of freedom and my own pleasures on others, but let them live in their own way. Perhaps it was childish of me to move back to Jerusalem, but from the stories my mother and father told me I knew that this is the promised land. They told me of the God of Israel too, or as much of him as they knew, although we slaves had neither synagogue nor teachers. Neither I nor even my father was circumcised as the law requires, so little did we know of the covenant between God and the people of Israel. Of the grain trade I know all there is to know, and would certainly have done well in Rome. But the grain that is shipped here for free distribution is tainted with blood, as the weals on my own back testify. A man yearns for the tales of his fathers, and the God of his fathers, and for a people of his own. I should never have made a Roman, and I see no point in increasing wealth for its own sake. I have enough for myself and for my sons, and I've invested my money prudently, duly considering every kind of risk. Now I ask no more than to live rightly, to revere and worship God and obey the commandments, without harming anyone else, and to delight in things that give me delight. The way I have found, you see, is very simple."

"I respect your way," I said. "In you there is none of the boasting and insolence that make rich freedmen in Rome so insufferable. They will pay any sum to be invited to a senator's house or to address a man of title by his first name. Their manner of life excites nothing but ridicule. It's understandable that you should have followed your tastes and adapted your house to the Greek style, and that you should show me your golden cups. But you're not the slave of your possessions, as I realize from what you say."

Simon of Cyrene threw out his hands.

"That's what I've striven for," he said. "I want to be as free as it is possible for any man to be. Even were I to lose all I possess—for no one can avoid misfortune—I shouldn't lose much, being content with little. That little gives me more joy than any abundance."

"Why then," I asked, "has your encounter with the Nazarene so disturbed you that you hide in a dark room, behind locked doors, and refuse to see anyone?"

Sighing heavily he wiped his forehead with his hand and avoided my eye. "What do you know of him?" he demanded.

"I came here from Alexandria really to pass the time, and to see the holy city of the Jews at the feast of the passover," I replied. "I stopped and looked at the crucified man just as the sky darkened. I watched him suffer and die. On the third day after that I saw that his tomb was empty and that he had risen. Since then, I've never been rid of him. I heard that you carried his cross for some part of the way, and I can see that you haven't been rid of him either. Why is this? Did he say anything special to you?"

Simon of Cyrene pressed his fists together and answered, "No, he said nothing at all; that's what troubles me. He said nothing, he merely looked at me. I know nothing about him." Simon went on to tell me, "I never meddle in politics, and I obey the commandments of the law as my synagogue prescribes. The other two were robbers, you could see that. I was on my way home from the fields, and I stopped to watch. Just at that moment he fell beneath the weight of his cross, and he couldn't get up again. By then I was jammed in by the crowd. A merciful woman bent and wiped the blood and sweat from his face with her own sweat cloth; but he couldn't get to his feet, although the Romans kicked him with their iron-shod boots. The centurion looked about him and pointed to me, in the arbitrary way the Romans have. There must be something of the slave in me still, for I obeyed and they laid the cross upon my back. He looked at me then, and struggled up onto his trembling legs. I made no protest, but carried his cross all the way to the hill. If I had lodged a complaint the centurion would have been severely reprimanded, but I was unwilling to stir up unnecessary trouble with the Romans. I stayed while they stretched him out and forced his arms down with their knees. The provost marshal of the legion drove the nails through his wrists. Then he looked at me again, and I turned away, fled back to the city and shut myself up here."

He rubbed his face with both hands, shook his matted head and went on. "You could hardly understand. I have seen many men crucified. I have even seen slaves mocking their own companions who'd been nailed up for killing a foreman in anger or setting fire to a field. I would not have thought I could be so strongly affected by the sight of suffering. But he looked at me. I felt dizzy, and so I fled, for I was afraid the earth would give beneath my feet.

"How am I to explain it to you," he cried in despair, "when

I don't understand it myself? When he was lying there on the ground looking at me, his face swollen from blows and the crown of thorn twigs on his head, nothing was of any value to me any more. People oughtn't to look at one like that. I went into a dark room and drew my mantle over my head, and dared not run out into the courtyard even when the ground shook and a wall split. Next day I broke the Sabbath and walked far, and sought out his disciples, but they would not listen to me. Afterwards it was said in the city that the disciples had made the Roman guards drunk and carried his body away by stealth, to deceive the people. But something tells me that this is not true. A man who can look at a person as he looked at me can rise from the tomb by his own strength. *You* explain to *me* who he was and what he wants."

"So far as I've understood," I replied cautiously, "he brought his own kingdom with him on to the earth. His kingdom is still with us. I seek the way to it, and I hoped he might have said something to you which would have guided me."

"If he only had," Simon of Cyrene lamented. "He may have thought me unworthy, seeing that I accepted his cross so unwillingly. But now, since he looked at me, even fresh spring water tastes musty, and good bread sticks in my throat. Ay, even my sons have become strangers to me, so that I no longer rejoice when I see them. And strangers they are in any case, for I wanted to give them a different upbringing from my own. Yet formerly I took delight in seeing how well they behaved, and how they could read and debate with their teachers on matters of which I neither have nor desire knowledge, my own experience sufficing me. But in this matter my experience is no help to me. I have been robbed of joy, and might just as well go back to the slaves' quarters and have a ring forged around my ankle."

"Have you heard of the quiet ones in the land, who were awaiting him?" I asked at length.

"Why else do you suppose I have the prophet Isaiah's book

read aloud to me?" Simon of Cyrene asked bitterly. "There has been so great a demand for it these last days that I had to pay five times the price for a Greek scroll. But there's no help for me here. Don't talk to me of the quiet ones in the land. I know that they recognize one another by greetings and secret signs, but I refuse to get mixed up in politics. I'm a libertine and want no other position."

"But," said I, "they can hardly be striving for any political goal. At least not any longer. I think they believe that God has been born on earth in human shape, that he walked among them, and suffered, and that he has risen again to fulfill what was written and in some inconceivable way to open his kingdom to them. But there is still no one who knows how all this is to be explained."

Simon of Cyrene heaved up his broad shoulders and shook himself, as if to rid himself of an invisible burden. "On these shoulders of mine, then, I have borne God's cross," he said, horror in his voice. "I won't deny it, or contradict you. My heart tells me that you speak the truth. He looked at me twice."

With agony he went on, "I had heard of a new teacher who had given great offense, but I could never have connected him with that bloodstained man, crowned with thorns, reeling away to be crucified. It wasn't until we were up on the hill and someone read the inscription to me—for I can't read—that I realized that this was the same Jesus of whom I'd heard. But I'd never believed more than half of what was told of him. Life has taught me to be incredulous. I didn't care much about the miracles he did, either; but in Jericho there is a chief tax collector named Zaccheus. This Zaccheus climbed up into a sycamore tree for a better view of the new teacher, and it seems that Jesus called him down and visited him in his house, although he's a publican. When Jesus had gone, they say, Zaccheus shared out half his possessions among the poor, and paid back fourfold all that he had wrongly extorted. After confessing to his misdemeanors he was charged, but acquitted, on the score of insanity, and removed from office. Now, I can well understand that anyone possessing that power can command a lame man to rise up and walk, but it's an incomparably greater miracle to make a rich man distribute half his property among the poor. Such things just don't happen. It's impossible. Even the judges saw that Zaccheus was out of his head. I should really like to meet him sometime and hear from his own lips what it was that Jesus said to him, and how he could have lost his wits to such a degree."

If my Roman common sense has helped me in no other way, it has at least made me practical, Greek philosophy notwithstanding.

"You're right," I said. "Let's start for Jericho at once and meet this Zaccheus. He may have learned something from him which is of greater value than all the possessions in the world. Such a secret is well worth searching out. You said yourself he had only to look at you to deprive everything else of its value."

But Simon of Cyrene demurred. "Jericho is a long day's journey from here, even if we hurry. Today is the eve of the Sabbath, and in any case I would rather not leave Jerusalem just now. If he really has risen, then his kingdom that you speak of so eagerly is nearest to us here. That's only common sense."

I knew he was right. Not even Jesus' own messengers wanted to leave Jerusalem, but were waiting here for something to happen.

I said, "We have this in common, that we're both outsiders who by chance have witnessed these events. Yet I no longer believe in chance; I begin to suspect that you and I were specially led to find his Way. In any case, we have both got a thorn in our hearts and shall know no peace until we see daylight in these things."

Simon of Cyrene answered bitterly, "I had daylight and a way. But I'm no longer free, only struggling like a fish in the net. I never wanted eternal life, such as the Pharisees believe they can obtain by obeying the law to the uttermost letter.

I've seen far too many slaves breathe their last, to believe in another life. I hold rather with the Sadducees, who have no such hopes. In our synagogue we don't argue about these things. Our teachers have sat at the feet of the sages of Alexandria. I believe a little in sorcery, both harmful and useful, for I'm bound to believe what I see with my own eyes. By giving alms and obeying the law within reasonable and wholesome limits, I comfort my mind, having seen how full the world is of cruelty and heartlessness. But I do not believe that by good actions I can purchase eternal life. A deceiver can surely not bribe God, though he should have a trumpet blown before him when he distributes alms. I don't believe there's any life after death—not even a shadow-existence such as Greeks and Romans imagine—nor that one may be born again as a cock; for in Cyrene they tried to force even that belief upon me. There were dogs there that chased runaway slaves and were fed on slaves' flesh."

He plunged among his memories and went on. "People came all the way from Rome to the great farming estates in Africa to learn how economically and practically the labor was organized, how cheaply slaves can be fed, and how they are bred by mating strong slaves with strong women. But of what profit is it to sit and recall old times? It no longer helps me to rejoice in my freedom."

His strong wine had mounted to my head without my noticing it, and I said smugly, "Simon of Cyrene, I do not despise you, freedman though you are. I am indeed a Roman citizen, and have even the right to wear a gold ring on my thumb; but in Rhodes I learned not to attach importance to the privileges of birth, but rather to distinguish myself by my own achievements. However, I never distinguished myself to any great extent, having cultivated thought rather than action. I have never even considered slaves and the slave system except to reflect that slaves present awkward problems for their owners, and that a prosperous man is never at peace for the menials that swarm about him day and night. In this way a comfort-loving person becomes the slave of his own slaves. But you've opened my eyes to the fact that a slave is a human being too, much like myself, even though he be branded on the forehead, and perhaps castrated if his vicious disposition needs curbing. Simon of Cyrene, you are my neighbor, and I would like to love you as myself if I could. That was something that the risen man taught. No doubt I'm better educated than you, but in these new things my learning is of no value. I feel that I've been tossed into an entirely new world, where I must learn everything from the beginning. Therefore in all sincerity I would like to be your friend, widely though we differ in rank and standing."

But my words hurt Simon's pride, which among freedmen is more sensitive than in others. He thumped his earthenware mug on the arm of his chair so that water from it splashed into my eyes, and exclaimed, "For shame, Roman! Your thumb ring I cast into the gutter, and I make water on your philosophy. Those are but the vanities of idle people, and they grow not a single ear of corn. The same is true of this curiosity of yours: all you want is to have some story to tell which will mark you out from other men. Crafty vanity shows in your sparse beard, and the tassels of your mantle. You're like an actor who seeks a new part at all costs because he has failed in all the others."

A few days earlier I would have flung my wine in his face, railed at him and rushed from the house. But his biting words dispelled my tipsiness, so that I fell silent and began pondering what he had said. Could he really be right in thus condemning me? It was from natural curiosity alone that I had started upon this way, but the farther I have followed it, the more clearly do I see that I am vitally concerned in it and am changing with every step I take.

"Forgive my boasting," I said. I, a citizen, actually stooped to beg the pardon of an uneducated freedman! "As men we are equal in this matter. I'm in no way exceptional. They say that on the last evening he knelt down and washed the feet of his disciples to teach them humility. I'm mad enough to kneel down willingly and wash your feet if you will, Simon of Cyrene."

"I wash my own feet, and need no servant to do it for me," Simon snapped. Then he added, more mildly, "Don't be offended by what I say. Since he looked at me he has become a matter of life and death to me."

As a sign that he regarded me as a friend, Simon touched my forehead, shoulder and breast, and his touch was not distasteful.

"Perhaps you've been guided to me at just the right moment," he said. "The boys' Greek tutor has been reading the scriptures to me, yawning incessantly; and I myself grasped no more of them than he. I was just thinking of leaving my house in search of a scribe who could interpret the prophecies to me. Probably he would have split every word in two and explained everything first by the letter and then symbolically, and after that compared this scripture with others, and I should have been none the wiser. You see, since he looked at me I know that this teaching is not a written doctrine, but a kind of life."

Simon looked about him and asked, "What has happened? I feel a great relief, and am free of my fear."

It was as if a cloud had glided away above the open roof of the atrium, for all at once everything brightened. At that moment a tall man came in and walked, wrapped in his mantle, across the room toward the inner part of the house as if he had not noticed us at all. Simon of Cyrene called after him, "Is that you, Eleazar? Has anything happened out in the fields?"

He stood up and said, "That is my bailiff, Eleazar. I expect someone has broken his arm, or a donkey has fallen down the well, and I am needed."

He followed the man, while I stayed seated, wondering where I could have seen the stranger before; for there was something familiar about him. I couldn't help laughing when it struck me that he reminded me most of my old teacher in Rhodes. It seemed to me that he was slightly bald in just the same way, and had he been dressed in the Greek fashion the likeness would have been quite striking. But I knew that my teacher had been dead for many years, and I was saddened, as I reflected on how receptive and open to good I had been at *that* time.

Presently Simon of Cyrene returned and said with annoyance, "I don't know where Eleazar can have got to. Perhaps he went out through the courtyard when he didn't find me in my room." He struck the metal disk with the hammer, and when the servant appeared he said, "Go and fetch me Eleazar. He passed through this room just now, but never saw me because I was sitting in shadow."

The servant said in surprise, "I haven't seen Eleazar today." But he went to look for him, then came back to say, "No, no, you must have been mistaken. Eleazar isn't here and the gate is locked."

Simon of Cyrene went to see for himself. I heard him talking angrily to a serving-woman, walking from room to room, and shoving things aside. It was a long time before he returned and said, "There's no one here. The servant swears she hasn't opened the gate since you came, and no one in the house has seen Eleazar."

I said in amusement, "Well, I thought he was my late teacher from Rhodes. Lucky that he has left tracks on the stone floor, or we should both believe that we'd seen a ghost."

I pointed to the prints of bare feet on the polished floor. Simon of Cyrene bent to look at them, and said absently, "Eleazar seems to have hurt his foot."

He touched a footprint with his finger and picked up a speck of blood on it. I fell on my knees and stared at the marks. A cold shudder ran through me from head to foot as I raised my eyes to his and stammered, "Now I see why his disciples didn't immediately recognize him."

But Simon of Cyrene didn't understand; he snapped irascibly, "My house is ill-guarded indeed if people can run in and out here when the gate's shut."

"Did you really not recognize him?" I asked.

Simon of Cyrene insisted stubbornly, "That was Eleazar, my bailiff."

Raising my hands I exclaimed, "No, no; these footprints are holy ones and your house is blessed. He who has risen has passed by and allowed us to see him because we seek his Way so eagerly."

Simon's brown face turned gray, but he protested with vehemence, "That was Eleazar; I saw him and recognized him. I won't have you frightening me like this."

"Believe what you like," I returned. "I know what I think. There was something about him that was familiar to both of us, since we have both seen him. But how could we have known at once that it was he? Mary Magdalene didn't recognize him either until he spoke her name."

"What *is* it you're trying to make me swallow?" demanded Simon of Cyrene suspiciously. "I've seen a sorcerer call up spirits, but his spirits were images on illuminated smoke, and they moved with the smoke. No spirit leaves footprints on the floor."

"He's not just a spirit," I said. "Do you still not understand? He came out of his tomb and still lives among us, coming and going as he chooses. Even through locked doors."

But Simon's slave-reasoning would not yield, "I can believe that he rose again, because of the way he looked at me," he said. "But I can't see why he should show himself to you and me. We're not his disciples; we never knew him in his lifetime. You're an uncircumcised Roman and I'm an ex-slave. Why should the king show himself to us?"

"His kingdom was close to us before he showed himself," I said. "Didn't you notice how light it grew just before he came? You felt a sense of relief, you told me, and so did I. I still feel in a cheerful mood. Why should we marvel at his purposes, though we are outsiders? By showing himself to us he must surely have meant that we too have the right to seek his way as best we can."

"If that was he I will hand over my property to my sons and

follow him wherever he chooses," Simon said, "but it was not; it was Eleazar." Nevertheless he began bitterly bewailing his fate, clenching his great fists and sighing, "Why should this happen to me? Could he have found no younger man to gather into his net? This is just how misfortune comes upon a man, suddenly, when he least expects it. What ill-luck brought me into his Way just when I was hoping to spend my days in contentment with what I have?"

From this I saw that he did believe, albeit against his will. I said cheeringly, "Simon, my brother, be sure that he can give you incomparably more than you've had hitherto. But if the Way seems to you too hard, don't follow him; stay as you are. I don't believe he would force anyone to follow him who in his innermost heart had not already prepared himself for the Way."

At that moment there came a violent knocking at the gate, and we both started. We heard the squeal of the lock and the opening of the gate, and then the voice of the servant woman, arguing. Past her and into the room rushed a short man with a large head, wringing his hands and crying, "Where is he? Where have you hidden him? When I saw him come in here I tethered my donkey to the ring in the wall and waited patiently, but he has not yet come out. I want to see him."

"Of whom do you speak, stranger?" asked Simon. "There is no one here but my guest, and we have been conversing together for a long time."

The comical little man came over and peered shortsightedly up at me, and then said, "This is not the man I'm looking for." He was expensively and elaborately dressed for a Jew, and if I am not mistaken he wore a mantle of Milesian wool.

"Whom do you seek, then?" asked Simon again. "And why do you force your way so shamelessly into my house?"

"It matters not to you whom I seek," the little man retorted mysteriously. "It was a man who passed me on the road. I didn't recognize him until he was some way ahead, but he didn't stop or hear me when I called. And although I urged on my donkey as hard as I could he reached the city before me, and I saw him come in here."

At that moment there was another knock at the door, and in walked a countryman with a frank, sunburnt face. Simon of Cyrene sighed with relief at the sight of him and exclaimed, "There you are, Eleazar! Why did you pass through here just now without a word, and where did you go?"

But Eleazar answered in surprise, "I've not been here at all; I come now straight from the fields to hear what troubles you, master, for you have not been out there yourself for many days. The footsteps of the master refresh the soil, and I know not which way to turn without you there to direct me. Surely you are not sick?"

I was staring at his feet. They were bare, and seemed to me red with blood. Pointing to them, I said, "Have you hurt your feet?"

Eleazar glanced at them in embarrassment and replied, "No. That is the dye we use to mark the sacrificial lambs, and I haven't washed, for I came with all speed to my master so that he may tell me how things are done in Cyrene, and bellow in my ear. For unless he does so, I cannot order the tasks to please him."

The little man looked from one to another of us, and losing his temper he shouted, crimson in the face, "Are you making a fool of me? Why do you talk of fields and lambs when I ask you quietly and calmly where you have hidden him?"

I said in reproof, "You fly at us like a fighting cock, little man. My name is Marcus and I'm a Roman citizen; our host is Simon of Cyrene and this man is his bailiff, Eleazar. Who may you be, and how dare you burst into a strange house as if you'd lost your wits?"

Haughtily he replied, "I am Zaccheus of Jericho, once chief among the publicans. Don't mock my stature, for I'm no contemptible man in my own city—at least, not in Roman eyes."

I clapped my hands in astonishment, and Simon of Cyrene

exclaimed, "I have heard of you, Zaccheus. We were speaking of you but now. What wind has blown you hither? Were it not the Sabbath tomorrow we would have journeyed to Jericho to find you."

Zaccheus glowered at us suspiciously, but I added my own assurance: "That is true. You then are the man who at the command of Jesus of Nazareth gave half your proprety to the poor, and made fourfold restitution to those you had fleeced."

Zaccheus said, "It was no command. Of my own free will I distributed what I had wrongfully acquired. But what do you, a Roman, know of him?"

Eleazar rubbed his foot on the floor uncomfortably and said, "My master seems in good health, and I do not wish to listen to things that addle the brain and sicken the stomach."

"Don't be afraid," I said. "But explain to us why you, a poor man, should fear to hear the Nazarene's name."

Eleazar shifted his feet, stared at the floor and said, "His burden would have been light and his yoke pleasant to bear. He promised us peace if we would come to him. But anyone who promises good things—things that are better than before—laborers, herdsmen and ploughmen, is brought before the judges. So they crucified him too, and I want to hear no more of him."

"No, no!" cried Zaccheus eagerly. "You quite mistake his teaching. He came to find those who had gone astray, and he called even me a child of Abraham, although he knew me for a greedy, merciless man. Nor did he make a mock of my appearance but called me by name and bade me come down from the tree which I had climbed so as to see him, and he was then my guest."

"And his kingdom is not of this world," I put in as my contribution.

"But when he spoke we believed that his kingdom would soon be revealed," said Zaccheus. "I did not go to Jerusalem with the others for the passover, since I am a sinner and no gift of mine is accepted in the temple. It was only from those who returned after the feast that I learned in what a terrible way he had been murdered, and now I no longer know what to think or believe. I was filled with restlessness, and at last I mounted my donkey to ride to Jerusalem and gain particular information as to everything that has happened. But on the highway near Jerusalem he passed me."

"Who?" demanded Simon of Cyrene.

Zaccheus reddened again, looked at the floor and twisted his hands. "He himself passed me," he whispered. "Don't *you* tell me that I'm out of my wits. I was just weary from my journey, being far from robust; my donkey was going slowly too, with drooping head. Only when he had gone on ahead of me did I feel that a force had passed by, and when I looked attentively at him I recognized him."

"Did you really see him enter my house?" asked Simon sharply.

"He could have vanished nowhere else," Zaccheus assured him. "I had heard it said in Jericho that he had risen from the dead, but that I didn't believe, for such a thing has never happened before. But when I realized that it was he, I dared not shout aloud after him, nor did I want to attract attention by knocking immediately, for fear of exposing him to some danger. But now, be mericful and admit me to him, so that I may bow down before him and hail him as Messiah."

When Eleazar heard the word Messiah, he swore coarsely and cried, "Don't speak that word! He healed the sick and raised the dead, he rode like a king into Jerusalem, and with a scourge he cleansed the sanctuary. But his strength was not enough to crush the Council, though many a man had shod his staff with iron, and we were only waiting for a sign to follow him. Well and good; we have had our sign and we believe it; he was crucified between two thieves, and let no one talk to me of a Messiah again as long as I live. I believe of my own free will and shall not be misled again. My children shall know that there is no Messiah and never will be."

"So you knew him too, Eleazar," said Simon of Cyrene reproachfully. "Why did you never tell me about him while there was yet time?"

By now Eleazar was exasperated, and without weighing his words he exclaimed, "You were the last person I could tell; you, a rich man, and so miserly that you gather firewood from the ground so that widows and the fatherless can find none for themselves. The rich would have had no place in his kingdom; they were the ones we should have swept from his path first of all, and then shared out fields and vineyards and olive groves among the people. It is true that some said one thing of him and some another, but I believe that the children of light would have returned to Jerusalem to lead us. But John the Baptist was beheaded and Jesus of Nazareth was nailed to the cross. The rich and powerful and those learned in the law have in all ages murdered the prophets of our people. And now I can no longer endure the gall in me, but spew it up on your floor, master. You know how things are done in Cyrene, but I have learned through bitter experience how they are done in Jerusalem and Judea."

When he had finished speaking, Simon of Cyrene said in a faint voice, "If I have offended against you so grossly, and have really deprived widows and fatherless of their dry twigs, then strike me. I deserve it."

But Eleazar did not strike him. On the contrary, he repented of his spitefulness and hung his head and declared, "No, no, my words were unjust. You're a good master—the best master one could find nowadays. On the contrary, you take care of widows and the fatherless, and you never keep too close and petty a reckoning of your sheaves and olive baskets. Many live solely on the crumbs that fall from your table. It is just that I am bitter and my heart black on Jesus of Nazareth's account. He showed his power and promised so much, but he left us with empty hands."

"They are not empty," I said, "for he has given us something greater and stronger than anything that has ever been known in the world before."

I pointed to the footprints, which had so faded that one could barely discern them in the sunlight. Simon of Cyrene now told the others what had happened to us and of the figure we had seen. At last he suggested, "Zaccheus, go, and take Eleazar with you, since you still don't believe me and suspect that we have hidden him. Search all the rooms and corners in my house, look in the cellars and sheds and on the roof, leave no place unexamined, and so remove all shadow of doubt that he has vanished from my house in the same manner as he entered it. Then come back, that we may discuss the matter and decide what to do."

The doubtful expression in Zaccheus' eyes showed that he did not altogether believe Simon of Cyrene. But he agreed to the proposal and said, "It was not for nothing that I was promoted to be chief among the publicans. If I had a customs officer's crowbar I should be sure to find all the secret places in your house. If I can't find him, no one else can, and then I shall half believe that he is no longer here."

Impatiently Simon bade him ask the servants for all the crowbars he needed. Followed by Eleazar, Zaccheus went into the inner part of the house with the jerky gait of a crippled man, and began a thorough search. Simon and I were silent for a long time, in an atmosphere of constraint.

At last I said, "As we talked of Zaccheus, he came. That may be a sign."

Simon had no time to answer, for just at that moment we heard a great clamor and noise from the street outside, and once more we heard the servant open the door and begin wrangling with a crowd of people. Then in perplexity she came to Simon, sighed and said, "I know not what to be at, or what's happening in your house. There is a mob of beggars out there, all excited and saying they have heard that you, Simon of Cyrene, are this day going to distribute food and drink to all the poor and wretched folk of Jerusalem."

Simon clutched his head in both hands and cried, "Do I dream or wake? There's no gathering of guests in my house today." Turning to me, he said reproachfully, "What a sorcerer —what a malignant sorcerer you must be! This is all your doing, and I haven't a clear thought left in my head."

He hurried to the door and I went with him, and when he opened it we saw that the narrow alley outside was crammed with maimed, wounded, possessed people; with emaciated, withered women and children who with their eyes swarming with flies held out their leather-dry hands to Simon. They all shouted flattery and praise, and blessed him in the name of the God of Israel. Vainly Simon attempted to discover the source of the rumor that he was to give a banquet; but none of the beggars could give a plain answer to that question, and at each end of the alley one could see more of the wretches, limping or crawling and making all the haste they could toward his house.

Then Simon of Cyrene gave in, and summoning his servants he said to them, "Admit all these poor creatures to my courtyard, but keep them in order and see that they steal nothing. Bake bread and carry out to them everything eatable in the house, and distribute it so that each one gets a share. Mix wine for them too, from the great jars. But admit only those who got here first, no more. The courtyard will hold no more, in any case."

To me he said, "I can but thank him who created heaven and earth that my two boys Alexander and Rufus are on a visit to my farm in Kiriath and will stay there over the Sabbath, for these unhappy folk might infect them with their diseases and their dirt, though for myself I care naught."

He went to make sure that the servants were obeying him and bringing out all there was to eat in the house, without stinting oil, flour, honey or dried fruit; and that they also opened the jars of salt fish and served the sharp sauces. When he saw that over seventy beggars had crawled into the courtyard and sat down, he realized that his stores would not suffice to feed them all, and sent out servants to buy bread and grain.

When the beggars were let into the courtyard they looked timidly about at the Greek columns and kept silence, so as to give no offense. Zaccheus now returned, after searching every room and cellar, poking into every sack and rummaging in the charcoal store. He was dusty, floury and sooty from head to foot; he panted violently, wiped his face with his sweat cloth, which made him dirtier than ever, and said to Simon in an accusing tone, "You're a cunning fellow. So this is how you've cheated me. Among all these it was easy enough for the man you were hiding to get away unobserved."

Simon sighed. "If you who knew him do not believe me, who then could put faith in what we have to tell and what we ourselves have seen? He showed himself to you on the road, and to us in my house. God be merciful to me! After all that has befallen me today, I truly believe that he is risen to disturb the world as he has disturbed my house. Therefore I beg you to tell us about him and about what he taught, so that we may understand what it is he requires of us."

With his own hands he fetched water, and as he placated Zaccheus I washed his head and Eleazar his feet, and Simon fetched him a clean mantle.

When Zaccheus saw how eagerly we all three waited upon him so as to hear the word of eternal life, he grew calmer and said soberly, "He confided no secrets to me, if that's what you think; what he said in my home he said for all to hear. When he came to Jericho he restored the sight of a blind man who believed him to be the son of David. But to me he said, 'The son of man has come to find and save the lost.' He said also that in his kingdom there is more joy over a sinner who repents than over ninety-nine good people who need no repentance."

Simon of Cyrene said at once, "That is unfair. What joy is there for a person who does his best to live rightly, if his lord passes by without even wanting to speak to him? How can a sinner be more pleasing to him than a good man?"

But Zaccheus raised his hands warningly and continued, "He called me by name and was a guest in my house, although I am a sinful and despised man. When he called, all my bitterness left me, though throughout my life it had been a prison to me because of my dropsical head and my maimed body, so that I never thought good of anyone, only evil. If he could accept me —he, the king of Israel and the son of David—and forgive me my sins, then I no longer needed the approval and favor of men. This was so great a deliverance that for pure joy I shared out half my estate among the poor; but I suppose neither of you can understand that."

Simon of Cyrene admitted, "No, that's not easy for us to understand, but no doubt your injustice and evil dealings were already so great that you feared that the day of discovery might be near. So then you reformed and atoned for your actions in the best way you could, so as to preserve at least part of your property."

But Zaccheus answered cheerfully, "You don't hurt my feelings by that; on the contrary, I admire your good sense. I myself have learned to be equally suspicious of people's motives and actions. I know what happened to me in his presence. But at home in my house he told a puzzling story which I don't fully understand even yet. It was about an eminent man who journeyed to a far country to receive the dignity of a king, but was to return home again afterwards. Before leaving he summoned his ten servants and entrusted ten minae to their care, bidding them do business with them on his behalf while he was away. But his countrymen hated him and sent word to him that they would not have him for their king. When he had become king and returned home, he called the servants and ordered them to give account of what each of them had earned for him. The first servant told him proudly that his mina had brought in ten minae. The king said, 'Well done, good servant; since you have been faithful in the smallest thing you may choose ten cities to govern.' "

I could not help breaking in, so disappointed was I, to ask, "Was he really only speaking of money? I thought you might know something of eternal life."

Zaccheus said, "I was only a tax collector. He must have thought that I would most easily understand a parable about money."

Simon of Cyerene concurred: "We Jews best understand everything to do with money—better than you, a Roman trained by a Greek philosopher. Ten minae is really a large sum, though they may have been only of silver, not of gold. And much depends upon how long their master was away. No one could honestly increase one mina to ten in a short time; luck and cunning would be necessary as well."

Zaccheus inquired, "Am I to go on with my story or not? Another servant had increased his mina fivefold, and he was given five cities to rule over. But the last servant had with him the mina he had been given, and he had knotted it up in a cloth, fearing that he might lose the money somehow if he began to do business with it. To excuse himself, he said, 'I was afraid of you, for you are a stern man, and take what you haven't gathered and reap where you haven't sown.' Then the king said, 'I judge you from your own words, you bad servant. You knew that I am a stern man and take what I haven't gathered and reap where I haven't sown. Why did you not give my money to a trustworthy banker to handle, if your dared not act on my behalf yourself? Then at least I would have had my mina back with interest.' He ordered the others to take the one mina away from the servant and give it to the one who had ten. But the others said, 'He has ten minae already.' "

I put my hand over my mouth so as not to say what I thought of this long and boring story, but Zaccheus, looking at us triumphantly, raised his hand and said, "Listen carefully to this, and remember it, for this is what he taught. The king replied: 'I tell you that to every man that has shall be given, but from him that has not, what little he has shall be taken away'; and finally he commanded his enemies to be brought before him—those who would not have him as king—and had them put to death."

Both Simon of Cyrene and I pondered this mysterious story. At length I said dejectedly, "I don't understand the meaning of it, but it is wrong and unjust."

Zaccheus admitted: "Nor do I understand it, but it has disturbed me ever since I heard that he was dead. Now I can only think that he compared himself to the man whom his countrymen hated and who journeyed to his own kingdom which is not of this world, to receive the dignity of king. Surely he means to return one day and require account of all to whom he entrusted a mina, to see what each of us has made of it."

I asked, "Are you sure you remember the story accurately, just as he told it?"

Zaccheus declared, "At least I believe I remember the pith of it. Many others heard it and can bear me out. Some say he spoke of talents and some say there were only three servants, but what he taught they all remember in the same way, just because it was so startling and unexpected and unfair."

He reflected, and then said, "I don't believe that it was money he meant; it must have been something else. He himself warned people against collecting goods which moth and rust consume, and said it was better to lay up treasures in his kingdom."

Simon of Cyrene suddenly remembered something, and gave an order: "Go at once to the sheds and storehouses, gather together what you find there of wool and linen, and distribute it among the poor people now eating in my courtyard." Then once more he stared somberly before him.

Eleazar hesitated, rubbed his feet on the floor and said, "You can do what you will with your own belongings, master, but surely I may first take a new mantle and body garment for myself; I would be glad of something for the children too, and for my wife."

Simon thrust his hands between his knees, rocked himself to and fro where he sat, and said, "Do as you like, and the rest of you may take what you want as well. Plunder me—seize all that I have gathered together during my life. Take this ragged mantle off me too, if it is of service to anyone."

Zaccheus, disconcerted, said, "Don't go to extremes, Simon. Moderation is needful both in taking and giving. Otherwise you are acting rightly, for he said: 'What you do to these least and smallest, you do to me.' This is the Way."

Suddenly he became uneasy, and springing up he said, "How is it with my donkey, I wonder, which I tied to your wall? The street was packed with beggars, and someone may have untethered the beast in the hurly-burly and taken it away."

Then he calmed himself, sat down again and said, "Never mind; I'll do no less than you in what concerns the kingdom, Simon. If anyone has stolen the donkey, it's because he needs it more than I do, and I've no intention of running after him and bringing him to trial. Let him keep it."

Simon went on breathing heavily and rocking to and fro, but then he began to smile, saying, "All this has taken a great deal out of me. It's as if someone were nipping piece after piece off me with pincers when I hear those insolent beggars guzzling and squabbling among themselves for the best bits. I'm sure they are trampling bread and salt fish underfoot in their greed. But I must just get used to it, if it is what he wants."

"Do you really believe," I asked in amazement, "that having vanished from your house he wanted to test you, and revealed himself to some beggar to tell him that you were giving a feast?"

"I believe what I believe," retorted Simon angrily. "But if he is fooling me I shall fool him, and we shall see which of us laughs best."

He led the way into the courtyard. There we saw the beggars

squatting in orderly fashion on the ground, dividing the food amongst themselves. They were not squabbling at all; on the contrary, they offered one another the best pieces, just as if they were indeed guests at a banquet. Food was put into the hands of the blind, and handed around to all those who could not reach the dishes.

Meanwhile Eleazar brought armfuls of woolen blankets and linen cloths and placed them between the pillars. From the glowing charcoal rose the aroma of roast meat, and the servants baked barley bread and wheaten rolls and caraway-spiced oil cakes as fast as they could. But the woman doorkeeper wept aloud, and the boys' Greek tutor fled to the roof and refused to come down.

The joy and good order among the beggars so irritated Simon of Cyrene that he yelled, "Eat and drink till you burst your bellies, and take away with you whatever is left over. But know that I, Simon of Cyrene, do not offer you a single crumb of it. The host of this banquet is Jesus of Nazareth, who was crucified by your Council. May he bless your food, that it may bring you life and not death. I cannot force myself to bless it, for the gall rises in my throat with a bitter taste."

The beggars thought he was joking and looked at him innocently, and some tried to laugh. This annoyed Simon of Cyrene more than ever, and he yelled even louder, "Jesus of Nazareth, the son of God, invites you to accept all these things, for he has risen from the dead and his Kingdom remains with us so long as he walks among us, coming and going as he pleases—even through locked doors if need be."

The beggars were frightened now and glanced at one another, but the boldest of them laughed loud and shouted, "Blessed be you, Simon of Cyrene, among all the men of Israel. But why do you give us only sour wine, when from your talk we can hear you have been reveling in sweet wine with your distinguished guests?"

Beside himself with rage, Simon of Cyrene called to the servants, "Open the small jars too, and mix that wine in the largest mixing vessel so they may believe that Jesus of Nazareth, the son of God, performs miracles even after death."

The servants did as he ordered, but to save what could be saved they began to vie with the beggars in drinking, and Eleazar drank too. Meanwhile Simon of Cyrene fetched a pot of costly spikenard ointment, knocked the neck off it and shouted, "All this filth, and the putrid stench and the flies in your eyes and on your sores offend me. I know that smell all too well. It's like lying in the dark in a slave's hovel again, with a chain round my leg. Anoint your heads and faces with this, for it has a fragrance which princes might envy you."

And indeed a delicious fragrance overspread the whole courtyard when he opened the little pot. He wandered about smearing the ointment on the beggars' hair with his thumb, and altogether behaving as if he had taken leave of his senses, now roaring with laughter, now swearing frightful oaths. But when he reached a certain boy, who was eating ravenously, he dropped the pot, knelt down beside him and in a perfectly sane voice ordered, "Fetch me my fine-tooth comb so that I may comb the lice from the hair of this child."

When he had been given the comb he actually began to comb out the lice from the grimy boy's matted hair, and kill them, and did it as deftly as if this revolting task had been his all his life. The boy's head was scabby with the bites of the vermin and he cried out when Simon combed it, but he was in such a hurry to fill his belly that he had no time to resist.

The beggars became nervous, and whispered to one another, "Simon of Cyrene has gone out of his mind over Jesus of Nazareth. And no wonder, after the way the Romans insulted him by forcing him to carry the cross of the blasphemer. We would do well to eat and drink quickly and accept what he gives us and then go, before he begins to demand it all back again."

Their elders said, "Rich men have been known to let uninvited beggars come to their feasts, when heated with wine, and then turn angry and trample upon them to make them render back what they have eaten and drunk. Let us therefore make haste."

They looked askance and in fear at Simon of Cyrene, but he was so deeply engrossed in cleansing the lad's head from vermin that he heard nothing of what they said. When he had combed it thoroughly, he dragged the child over to the pool, tore his rags off him and washed him all over, impervious to his screams. The rest of the ointment he used on the boy's head, breast and feet, and then chose from among his son's clothes a body garment, mantle and red sandals, dressed him in them and said, "Now you smell and are clad like the son of a prince. May he punch me on the nose if you are not grand enough for his kingdom."

The beggars grabbed the clothes which Eleazar was distributing among them and began warily stealing toward the gate, watching for a chance to snatch the lad away from the clutches of the raving Simon. But Simon saw their purpose and cried, "Don't go yet, O guests of Jesus of Nazareth! Each one of you must have a gift from him."

He called to me and Zaccheus, and we helped him to unfasten the many locks of an iron-bound chest. Out of this he took a sealed leather bag, then ran back to the courtyard, broke the seal and began to distribute silver coins among the beggars, who all stretched forth their hands. To some he gave one drachma and to some four, while others received a ten-drachma piece; for he dealt the money out at random, without looking to see what each man received.

The beggars began grumbling and saying, "Why did he get so much and I so little?"

But Simon of Cyrene said, "Blame Jesus of Nazareth for that. He takes what he has not gathered and reaps what he has not sown." And again he grasped the bag, and gave even more to those whom he had given most; but when he started taking back money from those who had received the smallest coins, the beggars considered the time had come to leave and they fled through the gate, taking the boy with them.

Simon of Cyrene wiped the sweat from his face, jingled the moneybag in wonder and said, "Such a thing has never happened to me before. Should I take this as a sign and a precept? For I still have half of it left in the bag, although I was ready and willing to give it all away."

I urged him, "Put the money back in the chest while you may, and lock it. Next comb your beard lest lice should have got into it, and bid the servants clear up. I don't know whether you've been foolish or clever in what you have done, but at least I'm sure the beggars will be content, and that they're hardly likely to bother you again for a long time."

Zaccheus was sitting beside Eleazar on the edge of the great mixing vessel; he laughed gaily and called, "Roman, come here! Bring a cup and dip up some wine for yourself. There's plenty left at the bottom, and so dear a wine must not be allowed to stand and spoil."

He drank and cried, "Blessed be the vine harvest in the name of him who died and rose again to make ready a kingdom for us all. All three of us have seen him, and you, Eleazar, have at least seen his footprints on the stone floor, so you are bound to believe us who are more than you, a mere ploughman and herdsman."

Tenderly he wound his arm around Eleazar's neck, kissed him, and explained, "Take no offense, for it is only in this world that I'm your superior; in his kingdom it may be you who will take precedence. He said that there the first shall be last and the last first."

Eleazar struggled and broke free and said reproachfully, "You're all in a ravishment, my master Simon most of all. But I too am enraptured after receiving new clothes and distributing so many costly things among folk who are destitute. At any rate the wine has gone to my head, for I am unused to strong wine."

But Simon of Cyrene felt his own head and said, "Peace be with you all. I am weary unto death and shall now retire to my darkened room and lie down. For many nights I have been unable to sleep, and have lain awake worrying over Jesus of Nazareth. Now I feel that I have found peace, and I believe I shall sleep all through the Sabbath."

Unsteadily he walked away to his room and we did not follow him, for both Zaccheus and I realized that sleep was the best thing for him in his present state. Yet he remembered the claims of hospitality, for turning he looked back at us with tousled hair, blinked and said, "I hope that all this is only a bad dream; I shall be sure of that when I wake and see you no more. But you, my dream-Zaccheus, stay the night here in my guest room if you will. Eleazar shall sleep himself sober and then go home and keep the Sabbath before three stars appear. But to you, Roman, I know not what to say, for you must certainly be a dream and I shall not be seeing you again."

Eleazar obeyed; he went over into the shadow of the colonnade, lay down on the ground and wrapped his mantle around his head. Zaccheus and I remained standing where we were and scrutinized each other closely. No longer did his face seem to me that of a repulsive dwarf; his eyes shone and his cheeks were flushed with wine, just like those of an ordinary man.

He asked me whether I knew anything of the disciples whom Jesus had chosen as his messengers. I told him what I knew and what Mary Magdalene had seen and how Jesus had revealed himself, through locked doors, to some of the disciples in the upper room. I told him that I had met Thomas and John, and confessed frankly that they had not trusted me or been willing to receive me. At last I said, "My heart burns within me. If I went and told them of this they would never believe me, but you they might believe, for they know you. They might then more readily trust us and confide their secret to us, for they must know more than we do and be acquainted also with his mysteries, although they refuse to reveal them to outsiders."

Zaccheus said confidently, "I will visit them. Matthew at any rate trusts me, for he too is an ex-publican. He and I understand each other, and he may be able to put in a word for me with the rest."

"Do that," I replied. "I have no longer any wish to go there, and anyway I cannot force myself upon them." I described the room where I had met Thomas and John. He thought he knew the house and its owner, but would not mention his name to me.

"Go in peace to your dwelling and await word from me," said Zaccheus.

Thus we parted, and I went to my room marveling greatly at all that had befallen me at the house of Simon of Cyrene.

Seventh Letter

MARCUS TO TULLIA:

I am still writing to you, Tullia, as if to greet you. My good tutor in Rhodes taught me to appreciate the deceptiveness of memory, by which we readily confuse and alter things in retrospect, and forget the order of events. Even those who have witnessed the same event retain different impressions of it, and describe it differently, each according to the aspect which most aroused his curiosity. I write now to remind *myself* how, and in what order, these things have occurred.

I began writing on the eve of the Sabbath, when the temple gates closed with a rumble that could be heard across the city to the most distant valleys. During the Sabbath itself I still stayed in my room and wrote, for the Jews like foreigners too to respect that day and not run about the streets. They themselves attend their synagogues in feast-day dress to pray and hear the scriptures, and the steps they may take are restricted to a set number. I have heard that in the temple their priests make double sacrifice, but this is not reckoned as a breach of the Sabbath.

Before sunset and the end of the feast, the centurion Adena

bar came to greet me. He had left his helmet at home and put on a Syrian mantle so as not to attract attention in the streets. With a great yawn he said, "What belongs to your peace? Are you yet alive? I have not seen you these many days. There is no more tedious day than the Jewish Sabbath, for we may not so much as march out to the circus on exercise for fear lest the sound of our footsteps offend the Jews. Give me a drop of wine, for in Antonia they keep it locked up today. If they did not, the legionaries would brawl from sheer boredom or go down into the city, drunk, and annoy the Jews by showing them the ear of a pig."

My Syrian landlord looked after me well. To keep me quiet and in a good humor he had brought me a jar of Galilean wine, which he prizes as the wholesomest of all wines. It seems not to be too heady, nor does it upset the stomach; and there is no need to mix resin with it to make it keep, provided one drinks it before it has time to turn sour.

Adenabar drank of it avidly, wiped his mouth, regarded me attentively and said, "Upon my soul, you've changed so much that no one would know you from a Hellenized Jew. You're growing a beard, there is ink on your fingers, and a look in your eyes that I don't like. Surely it can't be just the imageless god of the Jews that has bemused you? That often happens to foreigners who come here merely to see the temple, and then start brooding over things that no ordinary brain can stand. Only Jewish heads are equal to it, for Jews have been accustomed to their God since childhood, and by the time they're twelve years old they're so steeped in their faith that they no longer need their parents' help in blessing bread or leading in prayer."

"Adenabar, my friend," I said, "you and I together have experienced certain things. Therefore I confess to you that I am indeed bemused. I'm not even ashamed of it."

But he interrupted me swiftly. "Address me by my Roman name, for I feel more Roman in mind than ever before. My

Roman name is Petronius. Under that name I sign the quaestor's receipt for my pay, and receive my written orders—when anyone troubles to jot those orders down on a wax tablet. You see, I now have hopes of a whole cohort and a posting to Gaul or Spain, or perhaps even to Rome itself. So I'm trying to improve my Latin, and accustom myself to my Roman name."

Again he looked at me searchingly, as if trying to estimate how unhinged I really was, and how far he might venture to confide in me.

"To me you're Abenabar," I told him. "I don't despise you for your Syrian birth. I myself no longer feel a foreigner, even among the Jews; I am trying to learn about their customs and beliefs. But I wonder they don't send you out on guard duty in the desert, or somewhere within range of Scythian arrows. You'd lose your life sooner then, so that what you know would no longer be an embarrassment to anyone."

"What I know? Are you raving? Are you quite out of your mind, or have you been at this good wine ever since this morning?" Adenebar asked, in mild reproof. "But you're right in this: I do feel of considerably greater consequence than before. And don't talk about the desert, for that dazzles a man and makes the most hardened of us see visions." Looking at me askance, with a sly smile, he went on, "You must have heard that Jerusalem has become a bad place for sensible people. Do you remember the earthquake we had one morning? They are saying that the graves of many holy men opened then—that those precious corpses walked away, and have already appeared to crowds of Jews."

"I know of only one who has risen," I said, "and you know who that is. They are inducing you, through promotion and a foreign posting, to hold your tongue about him. It's not as easy to silence a centurion as it is a common legionary."

Abenabar stared at me in feigned bewilderment and replied, "I've no idea what you're talking about. But do you remember the legionary Longinus? Whenever he picks up his spear now it behaves very queerly. During exercises he can't throw it straight. It has already wounded him in the foot, and once when he was at target practice with the sack of hay, it slipped from his grasp and nearly transfixed me, although I was standing behind him. But there's nothing wrong with the spear; the fault lies in Longinus himself. I threw his spear myself, as an example to the rest who refused to touch it, and hit the sack perfectly at forty paces. And Longinus can handle any other spear, but not his own."

"You evidently mean the spear that he drove into the side of the son of God," I remarked.

Adenabar shook himself, as if to rid his person of vermin, and protested, "Never call that man the son of God—it sounds terrible to me. But the provost marshal has grown so stiff in the arms that he can't even lift the scourge. It's all he can do to carry food to his mouth, and that only by making a real effort with both hands. The surgeon in Antonia can find nothing the matter with him, and suspects him of malingering so as to get his plot of land a little earlier and live comfortably in the veterans' town. He has only another two years of his twenty-year service to run. He has been flogged, for according to army surgery, flogging cures many aches and pains that don't appear on the surface. But he took it like an old legionary, with a bit of leather between his teeth, and his arms regained none of their strength. I think he'll be invalided out with rheumatism; that is a lawful complaint in the legion. We officers suffer from it even more than the men when we have to exchange our comfortable garrison duty for lying on hard ground in the cold and wet.

"But," Adenabar ended reflectively, "I can't remember that the Nazarene cursed any of us. On the contrary, he cried out to his father from the cross, asking him to forgive us because we didn't know what we were doing. I thought he was delirious, though, for his father wasn't there."

I said irritably, "I can't see what all this has to do with Longinus and the provost marshal of the legion."

"I believe we were all thoroughly frightened by the Nazarene," said Adenabar. "He was no ordinary man. And when those who had been there heard that he had risen again they were even more frightened; for soldiers will believe any rumor that breaks into their monotonous life. And the wilder the rumor the more readily do they believe it. Now it has come to such a pitch that if a child falls from the wall during the night, or an old oil jar cracks and leaks over the floor, the whole garrison gets on its legs and calls upon all the gods for help.

"But it's said that the Jews in the city are having just as much trouble," he went on. "No one dares sleep by himself these days. Children wake in the night and say that some stranger has been bending over them and touching them. Others say that they've been roused by something warm dripping into their faces, yet when they light the lamp they can see nothing. There's a report that even members of the Council wash their hands continually, and busy themselves with all kinds of purification according to the strictest letter of the law—even the Sadducees, who are not usually so particular in these matters. But nothing evil has happened to me; I have not even had bad dreams. How is it with you?"

"With me?" I answered. "I'm looking for a way."

Adenabar stared at me oddly. He had drunk half the wine in the jar, without troubling to mix water with it; yet I could detect no sign of drunkenness in him. "I've heard it said," he began warily, "that there are many ways and many false guides. How can you, a Roman citizen, believe that you can find the Way, when the Jews themselves are not sure of it?"

I was greatly surprised at these words, and cried, "You don't mean to tell me that you know the quiet ones in the land and are also seeking the Way?"

Adenabar burst into loud laughter, slapped his knees and

shouted, "Ha, you fell into the trap! Never believe I don't know what you've been about these last days. I have friends in the city, too—more than you have."

Grave once more, he declared, "I think the Romans make a great mistake in keeping the same legion here in this country year after year. Elsewhere, this principle is well enough; the men get to know the land where they keep order, and the inhabitants make friends with them and teach them their ways and customs. After twenty years' service every legionary is given a piece of land in the same country, marries a local woman, and teaches Roman ways to those about him. But this is not so in Judea and in Jerusalem. The longer a foreigner lives here, the more he begins to fear the Jewish god, or else detest the Jews to the point of mania. Believe it or not, there are even Roman officers, especially in the smaller garrisons, who have been secretly converted to the Jewish faith and allowed themselves to be circumcised. But not I, be sure of that! It's out of sheer curiosity that I've learned something of the different ways that are followed by the Jews; not in order to spy upon them, but to understand them better and avoid falling into the clutches of their terrible God."

"At the cross, you yourself acknowledged him to be the son of God," I reminded him. "You entered his tomb with me and saw his graveclothes lying untouched after he had risen."

"True enough," Adenabar admitted. Suddenly he flung the earthenware beaker to the floor so that it shattered to pieces, sprang up with face distorted, and yelled, "Cursed be that Jewish king! Cursed be all this city of sorcery where there's not even an image to smash! It's a queer thing if one may not take a single life. Innocent people have been crucified before without rising up and haunting the place. That Nazarene is undermining discipline."

"I've come to the conclusion," I said, "that for some reason incomprehensible to us he *wanted* everything to come about as it has. One day we may understand why, for his kingdom is still with us on earth. No doubt that's why shields fall in the fortress: it's a sign that he requires something of us Romans, as well. But you need have no fear of him. He taught that evil is not to be repaid with evil. 'If anyone should strike you on one cheek, turn the other to him.' And other things of that kind, which are against all reason."

Adenabar was not startled by what I said, but owned, "I too have heard such things about his teaching, so I believe him to be a harmless man and am not afraid of him, though of course it would be disagreeable to meet him if he really is still walking about the city. My hair would probably stand on end if he suddenly appeared and spoke to me. But he reveals himself to no one who is uncircumcised, so I heard; only to his disciples and to the women who came with him from Galilee."

His wily words fired me so that I abandoned caution and told him of the apparition I had seen in Simon of Cyrene's house, of how I thought I had beheld the risen man in the shape of a gardener the very day he came out of his tomb. Adenabar shook his head pityingly and said, "You must have led a most dissolute life in Alexandria, and certainly studied more than your head could stand. The climate here doesn't suit you. You would do well to leave this place without delay. Fortunately for you, I'm your friend and won't inform against you, so long as you promise to be calm and patient."

In a burst of anger I exclaimed, "I have been suspected enough of spying for the Romans. I am loth to suspect anyone myself, or I might fancy you'd been sent to warn me against meddling in Jewish affairs."

Adenabar avoided my eyes, looking somewhat ashamed, rubbed his hands together between his knees and confessed, "To be frank with you, the garrison commander did hint that I was welcome to come along and hear what belongs to your peace, for on no account does he want any friend of the Proconsul to become embroiled with the Jews. I think he might like to know what you've discovered about this odd conspiracy of theirs. But of course he can't have you spied upon, since you're a citizen and are said to carry a letter of recommendation from so exalted a source that I daren't even name it. Nor do I mean to pass on what I've heard in friendly conversation. At most I might say that you are disturbed in your mind, as most people are these days. But on the subject of apparitions and visions I shall be dumb. He's a stern man and doesn't believe in those things. I should only make myself ridiculous and risk my promotion by reporting such tales."

He wiped his forehead, looked up at the ceiling and remarked, "I thought just now your roof was leaking, for I seemed to feel a drop or two on my face. This cheap Galilean wine is stronger than I thought. Shall we make a pact? Will you bring a reconciliation between the Nazarene and me, if you ever meet him and he will listen to you? I cannot run after him myself, because of my rank, as you may understand, but I must be at peace with him."

He began busily scratching himself, looked about and remarked, "There ought not to be any vermin here. I would never have recommended this place to you had I known that things start crawling over one as soon as one sits down."

As he clawed himself I too began to feel an itching on my skin, and every hair of my body seemed on end. I shuddered. "There are no vermin here; the room is perfectly clean," I said. "I believe someone is coming to see us."

Adenabar quickly stood up, wrapped his mantle around him and said, "If that is the case, I'll go my way. We've had our talk, and the wine is nearly finished."

But he had no time to leave, for we heard the voice of the Syrian landlord below, and then steps on the stairs. Adenabar backed against the wall and stuck out two fingers for protection. In stepped Zaccheus of the large head, dragging with him a man whose face was hidden under his mantle. "Peace be with you, Zaccheus," I said. "I have kept to my room all this time, eagerly awaiting word from you."

"Peace with you also, Roman," returned Zaccheus with marked coolness. He seemed quite to have forgotten how he had flung his arms about my neck and kissed me, after Simon of Cyrene's wine had gone to his head. But the man with him recoiled a step at the sight of Adenabar, and asked, "Who is that?"

My landlord had politely attended them to my door, and now said, "That is only a centurion from Antonia and a good friend of mine, for all his rank. Do not fear him. He understands Jews and will defile you no more than do I or my house, now that you're in it."

The stranger gave Zaccheus a box on the ear and cried, "So it was treachery after all, and you've led me into a trap—you Judas Iscariot, and worse!" He turned to flee, but I reached him first, seized his arm and held him back; for I thought it wrong of him to strike the crippled Zaccheus.

Zaccheus rubbed his cheek, stared at Adenabar and me in a startled way and declared, "Had I known this I would never have brought you here. The Roman is craftier than I would have thought. Strike me on the other cheek too; I deserve it."

Adenabar surveyed both Zaccheus and his companion and said, "I believe I recognize you, Jew, by your face and your look of guilt. Why else should you have been so scared at the sight of a Roman centurion? I suppose you're not one of the companions of that Jewish king we crucified the other day? You certainly talk like a Galilean."

Zaccheus, anxiously speaking on his friend's behalf, asserted, "No, no, you're quite mistaken, sir! He is a publican and tax-gatherer just like me. Both of us are true friends of Rome, as are all those children of Israel who love peace and good order."

But the stranger said, "Heap no more sins upon your conscience, Zaccheus. Neither of us is any friend of Rome. It is true that I have been a publican, but I have repented of my deeds and that sin has been forgiven me."

I dropped his arm hastily and rubbed my hand, which was

burning like fire. "Peace be with you," I said. "I believe I know who you are, and you must not fear the centurion, for he means you no harm. On the contrary, he desires to be reconciled with your lord, if that is in any way possible."

Then the stranger drew himself up, and looking me and Adenabar in the face he said, "I am not ashamed of my Lord's name, for he who denies him denies also his kingdom. I am Matthew, one of the twelve whom he chose, and not even death has power over me, for he will give me eternal life in his kingdom. You Romans he will hurl into outer darkness, where there is wailing and gnashing of teeth."

This was something new to me, and I exclaimed in surprise, "I did not know he spoke such harsh words! But peace be with you, however this may be, and blessed be this room where you have been pleased to set your foot, you messenger of the king. Sit down, and you too, Zaccheus, and tell us of your Lord, for I burn with the desire to know more of him."

Matthew sat down cautiously, and Zaccheus squeezed himself almost into his lap in alarm. Matthew glared in an ugly way at Adenabar and said, "I suppose your legionaries have surrounded the house now that it is dusk. I could never have believed a Roman would think of so treacherous a trap."

Adenabar was offended and answered vehemently, "You, Galilean, should not blame us Romans for all evils. Not even the Proconsul himself desired to condemn your teacher; it was the Jews who compelled him to it. I have no quarrel with you or your king, and as far as I am concerned you may slink away anywhere you like. The Jewish Council might have something to say to you, but not the Romans."

No doubt Matthew was ashamed of his fear, for when he realized that he was safe and that no one sought his life he became boastful, as Jews will, and said, "I would not have called upon you, Roman, if I had not heard far too much about you. Without knowledge of the law and the prophets you, an uncircumcised, pretend to be in search of the Way; you mislead foolish women and spy upon our secrets. I can only suppose that you are possessed by an evil spirit, or are a sorcerer, since you were able to persuade even John to answer your questions. Leave us in peace, go your own ways and don't meddle in matters of which you can understand nothing. This was what I came to tell you, so that you may no longer trouble bewildered women."

His words wounded me sorely. Within me I felt a deep ill-will toward him, and would have liked most to quarrel with him; but I was forced to look at his face. In his features and eyes and in the wrinkles of his brow I discerned the same unexplained something which distinguished him from other people and marked him as one of the king's disciples. It was assuredly true that he knew and understood these things better than I could ever do. Therefore I answered him humbly:

"I won't contradict you. I simply believed that his Way would be open to all who desired to seek it in simplicity, with a humble heart. I believed that the door would open to me too if I knocked upon it with fervor. At least explain to me why he made himself known to me in the house of Simon of Cyrene."

Zaccheus looked imploringly at Matthew, but Matthew's face hardened and he replied, "Our master came to seek the lost of Israel. That was why he called me too, the day he sat at my toll table in Capernaum. I stood up at once and followed him. For his sake I left my house and my property—yes, and my family too. Zaccheus also was a lost child of Israel, and even Simon of Cyrene belongs to a Greek synagogue and carried the cross for him. We might possibly understand if he had shown himself to both of them, but never can we believe that he would appear to an uncircumcised Roman. So we have talked the matter over among ourselves. Little faith though we can put in the visions of flurried women, we place even less in a Roman. You may be a sorcerer and a magician, and desire to acquire our knowledge for your own dark purposes. You may be the man spoken of by a blind beggar of this city: the man who changed a stone into bread by the wrongful use of our teacher's name. You hoodwinked Simon of Cyrene and Zaccheus. Everything that happened in Simon's house when you were there resembled sorcery, and was not like the kingdom at all."

Zaccheus nodded and agreed: "Quite so! I was confused and frightened by all that I had heard. He conjured in such a way that Simon of Cyrene saw the wraith of his servant Eleazar whilst Eleazar was still on his way to the city; then he persuaded Simon to give us strong wine, so that we were utterly befuddled. I would rather believe you, Matthew, whom I know, than a Roman whom I do not know."

Turning to me he went on, "Simon of Cyrene too has thought better of it and will have no more to do with you, since you do not belong to the lost children of Israel. He bears you no ill-will, although your witchcraft has involved him in considerable financial loss. But it would be well for you not to seek his company any more, for indeed there are too many false guides in the world."

I think Matthew sensed my dejection and respected my humility when I did not gainsay them, but turned my head away to hide my tears; for he relented, saying, "Try to understand us, Roman. I am far from wishing to impute evil intentions to you, and would rather put the best construction on everything. Perhaps you are not a sorcerer; perhaps some powerful demon has gained possession of you and makes you abuse the name of our crucified master, though you know neither him nor the secret of his kingdom. But I must give you stern warning, for it was upon us alone, his chosen, that he bestowed power and strength to heal the sick and cast out evil spirits in his name. We failed the test, I confess, and because of our little faith that strength went from us; but we know that in due time it will return. Until then we can do no more than watch and pray and await his kingdom."

With a look of reproof he raised his hand against me so that I felt his strength, though he himself disclaimed it. He was sitting at some distance from me, and never touched me, yet it was as if he had struck me a violent blow.

"I bid you and your errors depart from us!" he said. "And here I can best quote his own words, for he warned us, saying, 'Do not give what is holy to the dogs.' He came not to overthrow the law and the prophets, but to fulfill them. He forbade us to go among heathen or even into the cities of Samaria. How then may we reveal his Way and his Truth to you, who are a Roman?"

His words did not wound me, although in the coarse manner of the Jews he called me "dog." So profound was my dejection that I said, "I thought his teaching was altogether different; yet I must believe you since he called you to be his messenger. In your eyes, then, I may be no more than a dog—but even dogs are tolerated in their master's house; they hear his voice and obey him. Let me cite to you that king of Israel who said that a live dog is better than a dead lion. Do you begrudge me a live dog's place at the gates of the kingdom?"

At this Adenabar, who until now had sat silent, jumped up, made the sign of the horn with two fingers and cried, "Are you, a citizen of Rome, so demented as to beg for a dog kennel near the king of the Jews? Truly you are the one who has been betwitched and had his vision distorted, and the mystery of the risen man is more terrible than I thought."

Zaccheus huddled against Matthew, but Adenabar dared not so much as touch them. On the contrary, as soon as he was calmer he raised his hands in entreaty and explained, "I am a soldier and a centurion, and did not wittingly commit a crime against your king in obeying the order I'd been given, and keeping watch at his crucifixion. But if you will reconcile me with him, I will gladly wash my hands in the Jewish fashion, or burn my old clothes, or scrape leaven from cracks in the walls, or whatever form of purification you may prescribe. I do not want to quarrel with your lord, nor have I any designs on his kingdom; I would prefer to go my own way in peace."

I believe that Matthew was glad to find that he and the other disciples had nothing more to fear from the Romans, at least so far as Adenabar was concerned. He said, "I have heard that when he was on the cross he forgave you Romans because you knew not what you were doing. I did not hear it myself, but for my part you may go in peace."

Adenabar said vehemently, "No, no; I may not have known what I did, but even if I had known, as a soldier I could have done naught else. Therefore your words bring comfort, and I believe that your master too seeks no quarrel with me."

But Matthew turned to me again, wiped his eyes and said wearily, "I know not what to think of you. Your humility speaks in your favor, and you don't talk like a man possessed."

He raised his hand sharply, and in argument with himself went on, "Yet on no account can I acknowledge you as my brother, since you are a heathen and a Roman, and eat what is unclean. Had you been a proselyte at least . . . but those tassels on your mantle do not make you a child of Israel."

Zaccheus too smote his gaunt breast and said, "No, he does not belong to the lost children of Israel as I did. Jesus himself called me a child of Israel, but this man is uncircumcised. How could he be gathered to Abraham's bosom?"

I reminded him, "Only yesterday your words had a different ring; you even laid your arm about my neck and gave me the kiss of brotherhood." Yet as I said this I was much aware of how dependent both these Jews were on their covenant with the God of Israel, rejecting all those who remained outside it. Zaccheus became ugly again in my eyes.

He replied, "I was tired after my journey, and still bewildered by all that I had heard of events in Jerusalem. Moreover, you tempted me to drink of that strong wine. I knew not what I was doing; but now I understand things better."

Adenabar said to me in derision, "In your place I should

need less to convince me. You've been struck first on one cheek, then on the other; and the more you turn your head, the harder are you hit. Stop this nonsense and face facts: it was not for your sake that their king rose from the dead."

Yet, although I had already bidden farewell to my hopes, I said stubbornly, "My head is my own, and I'll turn it as I choose. None but Caesar has the right to deprive me of it. Go in peace now, Adenabar, since you have no longer any reason to fear."

Adenabar said reluctantly, "I won't leave you defenseless with these two."

Taking Matthew by the hand, Zaccheus said, "No, no; it is we who will go. Remain alone together, Romans; our way is not yours."

But I wouldn't let them go. I went out with Adenabar, heedless of his warning; then returned, and so humbled myself as to fall on my knees before the implacable publican and plead, "Have pity on me, you who are called his chosen! Wherein is your doctrine so extraordinary, if it allows you to offer friendship to your brothers alone? We Romans do as much. I believed his teaching to be compassionate: but your heart must be of stone if you can reject me thus. The rich man tosses scraps to dogs from his abundant table even though he despise them. Therefore teach me."

Matthew had been calmed by Adenabar's departure; he sat down again, and suddenly—abandoning all opposition—he hid his face in his hands, so that I realized that his agony was now greater than mine. His voice had changed when he said, "Try to understand me, and don't reproach me for lacking compassion. That breaks my heart, and my heart is broken already. We are like sheep scattered by a pack of wolves. Even if we could seek refuge with one another when danger threatens, we are all astray now that our lord is gone. Ah, Roman, why must you torment me? We know not what to do beyond steadfastly defending what is left to us. We quarrel even amongst ourselves, and wound each other with words; for Peter says one thing and John another, and not all of us can yet believe in his resurrection, and comprehend it. You seek your way to us in sheep's clothing, but how can we be sure you're not a wolf? Grapes are not to be harvested from thorns. How are we to believe any good of a Roman?"

He wrung his hands, and spoke out: "He bade us love our enemies and pray for those who persecute us—but how can any man do that? And he said, too, 'If your eye cause you to offend, pluck it out and throw it away; if your hand cause you to offend, cut it off and throw it away.' As long as he was with us we believed him, but when he went the strength in us went too, and we no longer know where we are. How should we distinguish between true and feigned understanding in another, when we ourselves have not yet attained understanding?"

"But," said I in despair, "he must surely have taught you to pray in the right way, and made a covenant with you, and given you a mystery through which you may keep in touch with him, for he was more than just a man."

Zaccheus tapped Matthew warningly on the shoulder, saying, "You see? There he goes nosing after your secrets, of which I too have no knowledge. He's crafty, for all his innocent looks. He made me drunk, to coax out of me what the Messiah confided to me in my own house."

But Matthew was not angry. On the contrary, he seemed to have grown calmer and to have thought over what I had said, and he replied, "You are right, stranger. He did indeed teach us the right prayer and seal a pact with us. But I cannot teach you what he gave to us alone."

It was as if he had become more mildly disposed toward me, and his whole nature was suddenly filled with gentleness. Smiling like a child, he pressed the palms of his hands together and said, "He knew why he called us. In each of us he must have seen something he needed for the building of his kingdom, although we didn't understand that at the time. For my part

I, being a customs officer, can read and write—in Greek too—do difficult sums and use various kinds of weights and measures. Thus in my mind I continue to measure and weigh very carefully all that is said and done. Having no new measure I must use the old one: that of Moses and the prophets and the holy scriptures. And with that one the heathen cannot be measured. No, it won't work, try as one may. And my heart is heavy still, because these very qualities of mine—for which he must have chosen me—caused me to take one of his sayings especially to heart: 'With what measure you mete it shall be measured to you again.' I have an idea that he has given us an altogether new measure, but I still don't know what it is. So I have to keep turning back to the old ones, which I learned as a child."

These words struck deep and I remembered my good tutor in Rhodes, who taught me that man is the measure for everything. For this reason, mistrust and error have hitherto been my only yardstick for life and the world. This doctrine has made me as tolerant of others' failings as of my own, and I can judge no one over-severely. I have contented myself with aiming at the middle way—the way of balance—having found it as great a struggle to live up to the rigors of Stoic virtue as to pursue a life of unbridled pleasure.

But in a flash I understood what Matthew was saying, and sensed that Jesus of Nazareth was indeed introducing a new kind of measure into the world. He had walked the earth as a man and as God's son, and returned from the grave to bear witness to his divine origin. Had the new measure been introduced by a human being it would have been just one more human scale among many, subject to dispute and doubt; but coming from him it is not to be conceived of by reason, or quarreled about: it is the one true measure, and could save a man if he made it his own.

What manner of measure is this? How should I know, when his own messengers can only guess at its nature? Is it perhaps for Jews alone, who regard themselves as God's chosen people and therefore hold aloof from all others? Yet it was these who rejected their king.

Matthew may have read my thoughts, for he said, "We grope in darkness between old and new, and still do not apprehend his kingdom. We thought he had chosen us twelve to rule over the twelve tribes of Israel. Through Messiah, Israel is to rule all the peoples of the world. We can't ignore the prophets, and all that is written. Here is a contradiction too terrifying for us to understand. When he cleansed the temple he called it his father's house. How could we reject a covenant entered into by God with Abraham and Moses? All Israel would be divided. Therefore we cannot open his way to outsiders and heathen. We might as well eat what is unclean. Go your way, tempter."

Zaccheus said, "I have served the Romans and learned to know them. Therefore my deliverance was sweet. It was a glorious thing to return to Abraham's bosom from my straying. Torment us no longer. We have enough to endure without that."

Noting his self-satisfaction, I remembered my own pride and said, "Be it as you will. I have made myself a dog before you. Now I see that you both suffer from Jewish avarice. You want to keep everyone else out, although you yourselves don't yet understand what has happened. Nor do I. Yet what I do understand is this: if God is born on earth as a man, if he suffers and dies as a man, and then rises from the dead, it concerns every human being in all the earth, and not just you Jews alone. Therefore I mean to go on trying to solve his riddle and to seek him—if not with you, then alone. Depart in peace."

Matthew stood up to go, and Zaccheus did the same, with a hostile glance at me. But Matthew was not hostile. Rubbing his forehead he said, "Your thought is too unreasonable for me to understand. How would it be possible? Could the God of Israel so extend his power to all nations that no one would fall into perdition? No, no. He said himself that many are called but few are chosen."

He began vigorously wiping his face and passing his hands down his body as if to brush off spiders' webs, and cried aloud, "No, no! This is error and possession! He warned us, saying that by no means all who acknowledge him as their lord shall enter his kingdom. I remember his own words very plainly: 'Many shall say to me in that day: Lord, Lord, have we not prophesied in your name and driven out evil spirits and done many deeds of power? And I shall say to them: I have never known you; away out of my sight, you lawless!' Those words condemn you too, whatever you may be able to achieve by the abuse of his name in your conjurations. You will harm only yourself by this, not us whom he knew and knows."

Matthew's words made me tremble with fear, for I remembered the time when I had met the blind man on the road and tested the power of his name, and how the stone had been transformed into a cheese in the beggar's hand. But I had meant no harm by it. Therefore I trusted that Jesus of Nazareth would forgive my action, even if his disciples did not. But I understood now that I must not abuse the power of his name, as I did not know him as his chosen did.

I therefore said humbly, "I confess I don't know him enough. I have no right to use his name. But you have given me much to think about, and Jesus of Nazareth is plainly less gentle and merciful than I thought if he requires me to pluck an eye from my head or cut off a hand to follow him. Are you sure you rightly understood him?"

Matthew gave no direct answer to this question, but said, "I do not believe my Lord requires anything of you, since you are outside it all, and lost. I don't believe you can win any place in his kingdom unless you first acknowledge the God and the law of Abraham, Isaac and Jacob. Only then could you begin to seek his way."

He wrapped his mantle about him, covered his head and went out and down the dark stairs. Zaccheus followed him, and neither of them wished me peace. When they had gone I threw myself on my bed, desolate and wishing I were dead. I grasped my head in both hands and asked myself who I was and how I had fallen into this predicament. It seemed as if it would be better for me to leave this haunted city, where nothing happens as it does elsewhere, and where a God without image rules. People shun me and look over their shoulders at me because I am a Roman. The incomprehensible kingdom of Jesus of Nazareth is not for me. But if I gathered up my belongings and went to Roman Caesarea, I could seek distraction in theatre and circus, wager on chariot races, and find delights enough and to spare.

As I was thinking this I beheld a vivid picture of myself in years to come. I saw myself from outside. I saw a fat body and a bloated face. I had grown bald and lost several teeth, and with a babbling tongue I was repeating a story which I had already told a thousand times. My tunic was stained with wine and vomit, and I was surrounded by flute players and by girls who tried in vain to stimulate my jaded senses to enjoyment. This was my future if I now gave up and returned to seek the middle way. After that, the flames of the funeral pyre, ashes, and shadows.

I did not rebel against this vision, though it was uglier and more repulsive than my philosophy had led me to believe. I could imagine submitting to it, but it held no charms. I have an alternative. It has brought me from Alexandria to Joppa, and thence to the mount of the crucifixion near Jerusalem, and on to an empty sepulcher. That truth none can take from me. Slowly the thought returned to me that none of this has befallen me without purpose, and that I am still helping in my own way to bear witness to something which the world has never before seen.

His kingdom remains on earth since his resurrection. In

my comfortless solitude in the darkness of this haunted city I felt as if that kingdom were somewhere quite close to me—as if it were no further off than a touch, a step, an inward trembling. I was seized by an indescribable temptation to call aloud upon Jesus of Nazareth, the son of God; but shut out as I was I dared not invoke his mighty name.

Nevertheless I seemed to have attained to some inner clarity, and my new perception so much surprised me that I sat up in bed. Had his disciples not rejected me, but received me into their circle, instructed me, and tried in every way to convince me of his miracles and his resurrection, I should certainly have felt doubts; I should have tried to entrap them by my questioning, and lead them on to contradict themselves. But their surly opposition only stiffened my faith in the reality of the kingdom and the resurrection of Jesus of Nazareth, so that I no longer doubt these most incredible of truths. The disciples have experienced too much at once to be able to digest it all. In comparison with them I have received only a tiny fragment; yet what I have had I believe in. My life and philosophy have so ripened me that I can accept a new yardstick. Man as the universal measure no longer satisfies me, and no yoke of Jewish law and custom binds me to the past.

At that moment the oil in my lamp gave out, the flame flared up, turned blue and died, and there was a smell of burning. But I felt no fear of the dark or of loneliness, as sometimes happens when a lamp is suddenly extinguished. There was darkness outside me, but on closing my eyes I knew that light prevailed within; and this was something I had never known before. It was as if I had had another, inner pair of eyes. These eyes beheld a clear light, while those behind my eyelids saw only darkness. I remembered the gardener I had met, and his words soughed through my thoughts: "I know my own and my own know me."

Humble and trembling I said aloud, still with my eyes closed, "I dare not say that I know you, but with all my heart

I desire to know you and wish that you might know me, and not turn me away."

When I had said this a stillness entered into me, and with it the simple knowledge that all is happening to me as it must happen, and that I can gain nothing without patience. I must be content to submit and to wait. Time stood still; the whole circle of the world stopped too, and waited.

I was roused from this rapture by a hand on my shoulder. I started and opened my eyes. I was still sitting on the edge of my bed, and it was my Syrian landlord who had entered the room with a lighted lamp in his hand, and was now touching my shoulder.

Setting down the lamp beside him he squatted before me on the floor, shook his head in concern, caught at his beard, felt his earrings and said, "What ails you? Are you ill? Why do you mutter to yourself in the dark? It's a bad sign. I fear that your Jewish guests have bewitched you, so that you're no longer yourself."

These anxious words of his restored me to reality and to the room in which I sat. But I didn't resent his coming. On the contrary I laughed, patted his head and answered, "No, I'm not ill, but in better health than ever before; for now at last I see that a simple life is better than a muddled one. I'm no longer beset by uneasy thoughts, and my Jewish guests left me to my own peace and will have nothing more to do with me. Have no fear on my account, for I am healed of my diseases."

Karanthes was reassured by my manifest joy, but complained, "The smaller Jew reviled my doorway, and they left behind them such disturbance that the children cry in their sleep, and when I try to sleep myself I feel as if I were lying in the rain. So I come to see how you are, and have brought another lamp so that you need not feel distressed by the darkness."

I assured him that I was not afraid of the dark, and said, "I have a feeling that I shall never be afraid of it again, and that even in solitude I shall never be quite alone. The world is a captious, wayward place, and I shall no longer try to understand it with my reason. In the hour of my deepest dejection, when I was as dead as that oil-less lamp, joy burst into flower: I feel jubilant beyond measure, and I'd like to pull your beard to give you that same gladness."

Karanthes suggested, "Build yourself a house, plant trees, take a wife and beget children, and your joy will be complete. Only then will you know that you're alive."

"All in good time," I answered. "I believe the time has not yet come for me to do as you propose."

I didn't want to make him uncomfortable by talking any more about Jesus of Nazareth. I told him that I was very hungry, for while I'd been writing I'd had no appetite. This gave him more pleasure than anything I could have said; we went downstairs while his family slept, and having brought out bread, olives and salad we ate together, and drank wine enough to make Karanthes giggle.

Eighth Letter

MARCUS TO TULLIA:

My simple joy continued. I believe it rose from the relief of no longer feeling impelled to torment myself with vain thoughts, or to suffer inquisitive envy because others may possibly experience things in which I have no share.

When I had written all I had to write I went out and wandered through the alleys of Jerusalem, watching the coppersmiths at work, and the weavers and potters. I engaged a guide to show me the palace of the Hasmoneans, and climbed the towers of Herod's palace, including one ancient tower inhabited now only by bats. I visited the temple forecourt and passed some time in the forum, and I also went out of the city to survey it from the neighboring heights. Here in Jerusalem all goes on as if nothing had happened. I believe that within a week most of the inhabitants had forgotten Jesus of Nazareth and his frightful death, and wanted to hear no more of him.

I was wearying of this Jewish city, whose customs are foreign to me. No longer could I see anything remarkable even in its temple, which has so phenomenal a renown. In truth all great cities are alike; customs alone vary. The celebrated temples resemble each other though their sacrifices and ceremonies differ. Their one common characteristic is the amassing of money in some way or other. If the Jews in their temple forecourt sell sacred texts in decorative cases for binding on arm or forehead, this seems to me little different from the Ephesians' way of offering amulets and statuettes of Artemis for sale to travelers and foreigners.

The other evening at dusk when I was on my way home through the darkening alley, my landlord Karanthes saw me from afar and same hurrying as if he had been waiting for me. Smiling slyly and rubbing his hands he told me: "Someone has been asking for you and is awaiting your return."

I was happily surprised, and asked, "Who can it be? I have no friends in the city. Why are you so mysterious?"

Karanthes could contain himself no longer, but burst out laughing and cried, "Ah, how glad I am that you're well again in every way and living like a human being! I am far from curious about your ways and paths, but to avoid malicious tongues I have asked her to remain in your room. She is sitting there modestly on the floor with her mantle wrapped about her feet. You might have found a better one, of course, but everyone to his taste. At least she is well grown, and her eyes are beautiful."

I could not think what woman could be waiting for me. I hurried up to my room but I did not recognize my visitor, though she meekly uncovered her face when I came in and looked at me as if she knew me. I had only met her in the dark before, and it was by her voice that I recognized her as she said, "I have surely done wrong in forcing myself upon you, and I would not hazard your reputation if you're tender of it. A woman of my sort ought not to betray knowledge by day of a man she has spoken to at night, but I have something to tell you which will certainly surprise you."

I said, "Mary of Beret. I know you, but I never knew your face was so beautiful and your eyes so bright. And I have no fear for my reputation. On the contrary, I am glad you're here, though I cannot understand how you found me."

"Don't speak of my face and my eyes," she begged, "for they are my curse. But the city is smaller than you think. There are already many who know of you and of your obstinate curiosity about things that don't concern you. You met the man with the water jar, then, although you had less profit by him than you'd hoped."

I fancied she had come to claim a reward for her advice, and said at once, "Yes, of course, and I must owe you something."

She shook her head quickly and said, "No, no, you owe nothing. On the contrary it is I who am in debt to you, and that is why I have come here uninvited."

I looked at her, unable to imagine what she could want of me. Her face seemed to show that she was younger than I had thought, and it was a round, pretty, Jewish face from which one could never have guessed her profession.

By the door Karanthes coughed discreetly behind his hand to attract my attention, for inquisitively as a magpie he had followed me in. "Supper is ready," he said, "but of course the food can wait if you would prefer to keep company with your friend first. Say the word and I will bring water and clean towels, and no doubt you'll know how to make sure that she has not rummaged through your belongings and hidden anything away in her clothes."

Mary of Beret flushed and looked at the floor, ashamed. I said quickly, "You quite mistake me, my dear landlord, for our intentions are not what you suppose. Let your wife or your daughter bring the food, or serve it yourself, whichever you prefer, for I am hungry and shall eat with my guest."

Mary of Beret raised her hands in horror and cried, "No, no; it is not fitting that a man should eat with a woman, or at least not with a woman like myself. But allow me to serve you at your meal. Afterwards I will gladly eat what you leave."

Karanthes looked at her benevolently and said with approval,

"I see that you're a sensible, well-brought-up girl. This man from Rome is not yet sufficiently conversant with the customs of the country. My wife would rather die than offer you food, and I cannot allow my innocent daughter to see what she ought not to see. But it's quite another matter if you will go down with lowered eyes to fetch the food, serve it like a servant and eat what is left."

He explained to me, "You know I'm not a prejudiced man, but there's a limit to everything. If she had come here in a litter, dressed in fine linen or gold-embroidered silk, with jewels about her neck and dripping with fragrant salves, I would have regarded it as an honor to serve her with my own hands; yet at the same time I would have sighed with anxiety on your account. This sensible girl knows her place and will do you no harm."

He bade the girl go with him, and soon she returned carrying my supper. She had girded up her mantle about her waist in the manner of a serving-woman, so that her legs were bare to the knee. Eagerly she led me by the hand onto the roof, poured water over my hands and dried them with a clean towel. When I had seated myself she took the lid from an earthenware pot, set a loaf before me and said, "Eat, Roman, and the eyes of your servant shall rejoice at every mouthful you take. Ah, if I might be your servant, and serve you always!"

But her eyes were on the loaf as I broke off a piece of it, and so I drew her down to sit at my side, dipped the bread into the spiced sauce and put it into her mouth, so that she was obliged to eat with me despite her protests. Not until she had refused three times would she consent to dip her hand into the dish and help herself.

When we had finished she pressed her head against my arm, kissed my hand and said, "You are as they described you to me, and as I imagined you, after speaking to you in the dark by the old gate. You treat a woman as your equal, though with us she is valued less than a donkey or a draught animal. Here when a girl is born the father tears his clothes and won't even look at the child or say a kind word to his wife."

Staring before her she went on, "A woman's life in a country village is wretched, and a pretty girl is married off to some old man who owns more fields and vineyards than most. Vanity was my downfall. I gazed at my reflection in my water jar and foolishly went into the fields with the first stranger who gave me pretty ribbons and beads and whispered false promises in my ear. So short and simple is my story that I need tell you no more, for I believe you can guess the rest. I should have been little worse off than my sisters, while young, if I had lived in another land. But even as an outcast, an accursed, I am a daughter of Israel, and my sin so preys upon me that I would give anything to be pure again. But the God of Israel is a God of wrath, and in his eyes a women defiled is worth no more than a dog or a corpse."

I said comfortingly, "Mary of Beret, you surely can't be more sinful than many others who are forced to live in this world in your way."

She looked at me with dark eyes, shook her head slightly and said, "You don't understand what I mean. What consolation is it for me to think that there are many more sinful than I, when I know myself and am aware that inwardly I am all foulness and anguish? There was one who would have helped me. He did not condemn even an adulteress, but was merciful and saved her from stoning. He blessed all children, even girls, and there was no sin in him. But I never dared approach him; I saw him only from a distance. In any case his followers would most likely have kept me away from him. With his power he healed many whose bodies were sick, and surely he would have shown me compassion too, for my heart is sick and I'm ashamed of myself and of my life."

"I know whom you mean," I said.

Mary of Beret nodded. "Yes, yes. But the devout and learned who are without sin crucified him. Afterwards he rose from the dead and has shown himself to his followers. I have heard that from a sure source, unbelievable though it may sound; and I've heard that you know of it too, although you're a foreigner and an outcast. This is why I've come to you."

Suddenly she burst out weeping, threw herself down before me, embraced my knees and cried, "I entreat you, take me with you and we will travel to Galilee together and seek him. All who were able have left the city today to walk to Galilee. Women too. He appeared to his disciples late last night and promised to be there before them. There they will meet him. Perhaps I too might meet him if you're willing to take me with you."

I shook her roughly by the shoulders, raised her up to sit again and said eagerly, "Stop weeping and crying out so wildly and tell me what you know, so that we may take counsel together what to do."

When Mary found me so ready to listen to her, she wiped the tears from her eyes, calmed herself and began her story:

"You have met that rich woman, the breeder of doves, who went with him. She understands you and knows that you're steadfastly seeking the new way. But she was strictly forbidden to meet you again because you're not a child of Israel. It was she who advised me to find you, because she could not take me with herself, and because you, as a Roman, are as despised as I. She said that it is the teacher who best knows who shall be allowed to listen to his voice. In the evening the eleven were assembled in the upper room, and Jesus joined them there, passing through locked doors; and he stood in the midst of them just as on that first evening after he had risen from the tomb. You know about that. He assured them that he was of flesh and blood, and allowed Thomas to touch his wounds; so that now they all believe in his resurrection. They didn't tell the women all that he had said, but at once began to make ready for their journey. He had told them earlier that he would go before them into Galilee. They left the city in twos and threes, and the guards did not molest them. The women too have gone. He has healed some, and Simon of Cyrene has set off as well. They all believe they will meet him in Galilee."

I pondered her account, and thought it sounded credible; for why should this Mary make up such a story? And I could safely take it that Mary Magdalene still wished me well, though she dared not meet me again because of the disciples.

"But why Galilee in particular?" I asked. "And what is to happen there?"

Mary of Beret shook her head and said, "That I don't know—and why should I? Isn't it enough that he told the eleven to go there? They were so eager to start that the first of them set off this morning as soon as the gates were opened."

Shyly she touched my knee and entreated, "Make ready also to leave Jerusalem, and let me be your servant and come with you, for there is no one else who will have me in his company and I can't make the journey to Galilee alone. I have no money for the hire of attendants, and without companions I would fall into the hand of legionaries and robbers."

I was very willing to believe what she said, and it was certainly not her intention to deceive me. Her own eagerness was the best proof of that. But she was telling me only what she had heard at second hand, and in these perplexed days many rumors that were spread from mouth to mouth might become garbled and misleading. I felt therefore that I must have this tale confirmed from some other source.

I told her to have patience, and explained, "We can't dash away now, at night; and anyhow I have no mind to plunge headlong into an adventure of this kind. Let us be prudent and sleep on the matter. Tomorrow, if I can get information from elsewhere which bears out what you have told me, I will plan the journey, choose the road and the resting places, and so equip ourselves that we may reach Galilee as easily and speedily as possible. There we can look about us and think over what we're to do."

But Mary lamented, "I have waited all day as it is, and my heart is so impatient that I can scarcely close my eyes. Why can't we set off as we are, without bag or baggage, and sleep in the dwellings of the quiet ones in the land, or out in the fields, now that the nights are no longer so cold? In this way our journey will cause you no needless expense."

I laughed at her innocence and said, "I think I'm a more experienced traveler than you. Sometimes the cheapest way is more expensive in the end; if one falls sick, for instance, or is set upon and beaten by vagabonds. Leave me to arrange the journey, and in Galilee you in your turn can advise me where we should go."

She said, "I know only Capernaum by the Sea of Galilee. He lived and taught there. That is where we should make for if we hear nothing more of him on the way."

"Go in peace then," I said, "and come again tomorrow at noon."

But Mary of Beret must have feared that I would abandon her, for she said quickly that she had nowhere to go and asked to be allowed to sleep on the roof near my door, or in a corner of my room. It seemed to me that I might just as well accustom myself to her society at once, since I should have to travel with her and stay the night at the same places. She didn't disturb me, but lay still on a mat in her corner all night, wrapped in her mantle.

In the morning, when the horns had sounded, she recited her prayer aloud in the Jewish manner, but apart from that she tried her best to be quiet and not disturb my morning occupations. Bidding her wait in my room I went down to my landlord, who was already setting up his stall at the door.

"Karanthes," I said, "the time has come for me to leave Jerusalem and continue my journey. That girl is still up in my room and I shall take her with me. I've not forgotten what you said last night. Therefore buy her new clothes and dress her decently from head to foot; and supply her also with a suitable quantity of jewelry, so that no one may despise her or consider her too vulgar a companion for me. But don't overdo your purchases, for I would not have her too conspicuous."

My Syrian landlord struck his hands together in astonishment and cried, "I do not know that you're acting wisely, but no doubt you know your own business best. You can find girls like that in any town, and that would save you her traveling expenses. Apart from that, you are behaving more sensibly now than when you were meddling in Jewish politics, of which you know nothing."

He never asked where I was going, being far too busy considering how to comply with my request in a manner advantageous to us both. I went straight to my banker Aristainos, whom I found hard at work with abacus and letters of credit. He greeted me with a cry of pleasure, looked me up and down and said, "You seem to have taken my advice more thoroughly than I would have expected. Your beard is longer than mine already, and to judge by your mantle tassels you're at least a gate-proselyte. Have you found out what you wanted, and are you satisfied?"

I admitted cautiously, "Yes, I've found out even more than I wanted to know, and I'm so well satisfied that I've had enough of Jerusalem. People have been praising the beauty of Galilee, and of Herod Antipas' new city Tiberias, on the Sea of Galilee. It seems that at the hot springs there one may restore one's health, attend theatres and circuses, and live entirely in the Greek manner without giving offense."

Aristainos' face took on a queer expression and he avoided my eye. So I added hastily, "I believe I overstrained both mind and body last winter in Alexandria. I long for baths and massage and a little Greek drama to steady my wits after all I've learned and heard."

Aristainos smiled and remarked, "You've evidently fallen into the clutches of some glib tout of Herod's. Herod has sunk a great deal of money into the building of Tiberias, from a desire to make it as modern and Greek a city as possible, and he hopes that travelers and seekers of health will be tempted to squander their money in those most free-and-easy surroundings. Will you go through Samaria, or take the pilgrim route east of Jordan?"

"I've come to ask you advice about all that," I told him. "I should like a little money to take with me, and a draft on some business friend of yours in Tiberias. To tell you the truth, I've found an agreeable girl to accompany me on my journey. In Baiae I learned that any youngish man does well to take his own provisions to bathing resorts, or he may be unfortunate."

Aristainos' smile was now sardonic. "As a banker I'm just your servant," he said, "and I've neither the right nor the wish to be inquisitive. But does my memory fail me, or have you already had enough of the teachings of the crucified Jesus of Nazareth?"

I felt an invincible repugnance to lying to him; so as he continued to look at me searchingly, I chose my words and said, "Yes, I have indeed heard many remarkable things about him. I may make a few inquiries in Galilee too, if I have time. I can't deny that since his death there has been a ghostly sort of atmosphere about this sacred city of yours. I've been thinking about him a great deal."

Aristainos pondered, eyed me askance and remarked, "Your sudden inclination to go to Galilee is surprising. I've heard that many from the city set off in that direction yesterday. Among the common people it is rumored that miracles are happening there. I know that you're too enlightened a man to keep company with fishermen and carpenters; nevertheless it does seem a coincidence.

"We may speak frankly," he went on. "I've reason to believe that our Supreme Council was wearying of the Galileans who accompanied that man, and of the rumors spread by them and their women. The common people are ready to believe any lunacy. It's hard to suppress rumors and even harder to accuse anyone on the basis of rumor alone, because then everybody says at once that there can be no smoke without fire. A crucifixion suffices as a warning and an example to the people, and to persecute his disciples would be to make too much of the matter. Better that he should be forgotten. And so I believe that our leaders have conveyed a hint, indirectly, to the Galileans that they will be molested no further so long as they shake the dust of this city from their feet. They're welcome to return to Galilee, which lies under the jurisdiction of Herod Antipas. He can deal with them as he thinks fit; and I fancy that at home among their own people, where everyone knows them, they'll be harmless. No one is a prophet in his own country. I'm explaining all this to you lest you should gain any wrong impressions, including such ideas as no sensible person would trouble to clothe in words."

As I sat in his splendid room, surrounded by strong walls, doors and bolts, his matter-of-fact remarks were to me like earth strewn over glowing embers to extinguish them.

"If these things are as insignificant as you say, you're remarkably well informed about them," I commented sourly. "I too can be frank. I've heard it said that he has risen from the dead and revealed himself to his disciples, and has promised to go before them into Galilee."

Aristainos twitched at a seam in his mantle as if moved to rend his clothes. But quickly regaining his self-command he smiled a wry smile and said, "It was accursed folly to give those crafty disciples of his the chance to steal his body from the tomb during the earthquake. It enables them to tell any kind of wild story. Of course, they can impose a tale like that on their secret adherents and so put their flight from Jerusalem in a favorable light. I might understand you if you'd been bewitched by the scriptures, or if you were a Hebrew soured by waiting for the Messiah. But you're a Roman and philosopher. A dead man does not rise from his grave. Such a thing has never happened and never can happen."

"Why then are you so heated and upset, O man of sense?" I asked. "I understand, of course, that you're attached to your house, your money and your business, and that you're bound to do your utmost to preserve things as they are. I on the other hand am free to come and go as I will, and even to think such thoughts as you dare not think. I am now leaving in order to bathe in the hot springs of Tiberias, and it is no concern of yours whether in secret I may be hoping at the same time to hear of—or even see—something that has never happened before."

Surveying his little beard and his well-cared-for complexion and hands, I was filled with repugance for him and his world. I remembered the sisters of Lazarus, and Mary Magdalene; even Mary of Beret seemed dearer to me for her hopes than this man, who was chained by his money and his gains. He had no hope. That was why he so firmly denied hope to others.

He must have guessed my thoughts, for he at once altered his demeanor, threw out his hands and said, "You must forgive me. Of course you know your own business best. I realize that in your heart you are a poet, and therefore inclined to think about things which a businessman dismisses from his mind. And you will certainly never let yourself be cheated by swindlers, or believe in stories without evidence. How will you travel? I can offer you an experienced caravan guide and camels or donkeys; also, an excellent tent with all equipment, so that you may be independent of inns and avoid their dirt, vermin and dubious company. It would be wisest to hire a couple of Syrian legionaries to attend you; then you need fear nothing either by day or night. This all costs money, of course, but you can well afford it."

I myself had contemplated something of the kind, and that was why I had applied to Aristainos. I understood his willingness too, for a caravan of this sort would be most profitable to him. But then one of his agents would be watching my every step and would afterwards report everything that I had done. Next, for his own advantage, he would pass on to the authorities anything that they might want to know about me. Therefore I hesitated.

"I really meant to travel on my own," I told him. "Not once have I visited the gymnasium here and I hope that a slightly more arduous journey will drive the slackness from my body. But I must also insure that the woman who is to come with me is comfortable."

"Quite so," he assented eagerly. "Even minor inconveniences can make a young woman irritable and capricious. Nor would you like to see her white skin covered with red bites. Allow me to make her a little present while you think it over."

He went out, and returned with a fine Greek hand mirror adorned on the back with a skillfully drawn satyr embracing a refractory nymph. It was a beautifully polished, valuable mirror and I was unwilling to incur an obligation to him by accepting it. But he pressed it into my hand saying, "Do not fear; this is no magic mirror. It will merely help your friend to entertain thoughts pleasing to yourself, if she first looks at her own reflection and then at the ardent satyr. There are said to be mirrors that slay the person who looks into them. As a man of sense I find this hard to believe, but it is always best to be cautious. Therefore I hope with all my heart that you may meet with no such mirror on your journey, and see things that no man ought to see."

He gave me no time to reflect on the meaning of his words, but began counting on his fingers; he told me that I should need a maid for my companion, a cook, a servant for myself, a pack-ass driver and a tent pitcher, and said at last, "I think twelve people will be enough and a retinue of that size will attract no attention, being exactly suited to one of your rank."

I saw in my mind's eye a train of babbling, squabbling, shouting, singing attendants whom I should be quite incapable of keeping in order. The mere thought of this set me against the plan, and I said, "Expense does not trouble me, but my most precious luxury is solitude. Make some better suggestion, and take back your mirror. The unseemly drawing is amusing, but I hardly think it would enhance my position with the Jews."

He took the mirror without protest and said, "Now I know. There's a certain Nathan who has taken service with me from time to time. His only fault is that he never speaks, but he is a thoroughly reliable man and he knows Judea, Decapolis, Samaria and Galilee equally well. When I fetched the mirror I saw him sitting out in the courtyard. That means he is looking for work. I have nothing else for him just now, and I do not want him hanging about there for days on end, for his silence annoys my servants. I know he has taken caravans as far as Damascus. Explain to him where you are going and how you wish to travel, and he will arrange everything in the best way. You may safely hand him your purse and he will see to payment at the inns. He doesn't wear out his tongue in bargaining, nor does he pay what is asked; only what he himself thinks reasonable. In this way he receives no commission from the innkeepers, certainly, but he is content with his wages."

"I would like to meet such a man," I said, wondering whether this was some wily idea of Aristainos'. But he laughed at my misgivings and showed me to the courtyard where Nathan was sitting. He was a sunburnt man, barefooted, dressed in a dirty white mantle, and his hair was cut short. When he looked into my face his eyes seemed to me the most melancholy I had ever seen; yet for some reason I felt immediate confidence in him.

I asked Aristainos to explain my purpose to Nathan, but he threw up his hands laughing and went back to his room to tell his bookkeeper to count journey money into a purse for me and make out an order on his business friend in Tiberias. It was as if he wanted to wash his hands of the whole affair, and when I looked at Nathan again I realized that at least this was no spy I had before me.

I said, "You are Nathan and I am Marcus, a Roman. I am

going to travel to Tiberias with a woman, and I desire to do this in as simple and inconspicuous a way as possible. I can pay you the wages you ask, and you shall have charge of my purse on the journey."

He glanced at my face and then at my feet, as if judging whether I could walk, but replied only with a nod. Yet I seemed to detect a certain surprise in his face.

"I think three or four donkeys will be enough," I went on. "My companion and I need sleeping mats and cooking pots. Get what you think needful, and come at noon to the house of Karanthes the trader."

He nodded once more and let a twig from which he had peeled half the bark fall to the ground. Seeing that it fell bark-upward, he nodded a third time. He was indeed no talker. After all Aristainos' questioning I was pleased that this man should ask me nothing. I went indoors again to take my leave of the banker, who gave me a businesslike account of my money and told the bookkeeper to hand me the purse and the draft.

"May your journey be a happy one," he said. "When you come back we shall meet again."

I returned to the courtyard and handed the purse to Nathan. He weighed it in his hand and fastened it to his girdle, reflected for a little, glanced at the sun and then went his way without more ado. Both our agreement and his behavior were so utterly unlike all oriental bargaining that it was with great wonder that I stood looking after him. Nevertheless I had a feeling that he would not deceive me.

I now set off up to the city within the walls, where on that dark night I had followed the man with the water jar. I went ever higher among the bewildering alleyways and steps, and after searching for a while I found the gate in the old wall through which we had passed. Firmly though I had resolved never again to trouble the messengers who had turned me away, I wanted if possible to assure myself that they had left the city.

I seemed to recognize the great house that I had visited. The heavy gate stood ajar, but I saw no one stirring in the courtyard, and suddenly I felt an unaccountable fear and dared not enter. Hesitantly I walked past, then turned and went by it again. Yet I could not go in. Even had I wanted to I should not have been able.

After long indecision I turned away, annoyed and scolding myself for my lack of courage. I was surprised to note how deserted this quarter was, for I had met only two or three people. Near the wall I became aware of a montonous knocking. A beggar was sitting there trying to attract my attention by tapping his stick on a stone, but he was too proud to ask for anything.

I had found it wisest not to distribute alms among the beggars, for they only limped after me and I could never be rid of them. But this beggar, who had lost his feet, just looked at me without a word, and stopped tapping when he saw that I had noticed him. I felt bound to pause and throw a coin on the ground before him.

He picked it up without thanks, and asked, "What do you seek, stranger? Sitting footless here in my place I see a great deal—and some things that not all would like to see."

"Then give me a sign if you can," I begged him.

"Preparations for a journey and hasty departure are the only signs I know of," said the beggar. "Even men who do not willingly show their faces by day have begun to move. As far as I know they are fishermen and they were no doubt in a hurry to get back to their nets. Does that sign suit you?"

"It suits me better than you know," I answered, and was glad, and threw him another coin. He picked it up absentmindedly and stared at me, as if to make out who I might be. Then he asked suddenly, "Did you not lead a blind man home one evening and give him your own mantle at the Fountain Gate? If so, I would advise you too to buy a net and follow the others. It may be that a great catch awaits you."

I felt a lump in my throat and my heart quaked. "Who bade you tell me this?" I asked.

But the footless beggar shook his head and said, "No one bade me tell you. I said it from sheer bitterness, for if I still had my feet I would go to Galilee today. It is like a song and a shout of rejoicing: To Galilee, to Galilee! But I cannot follow it."

"You do not talk like a beggar," I remarked.

"I have not always been one," he answered proudly. "I know the scriptures, and sitting footless in the dirt of the street I find it easy to believe and grasp things which the hale and hearty cannot comprehend. For this madness of mine I have been struck on the mouth before now, and I would do better to hold my tongue, but I couldn't resist the temptation when I saw you straying so timidly around that house, which I too have been watching."

"To Galilee, then," I said. "You strengthen my hope."

"To Galilee, then," he repeated devoutly. "And if you meet him, ask him to bless us also, the least of his brothers, who are struck on the mouth by the wise."

Plunged in thought I went down again to the outer city, but as I approached the house of Karanthes the Syrian my feet grew impatient; a sweet fever of expectancy warmed my mind and within me there rang out like a song and a shout of jubilation: *To Galilee, to Galilee!* I could think of nothing else.

I could not go straight upstairs, however; I had to sit down to wait on the front doorstep, for my landlord's wife and daughter were up in my room helping Mary to dress. Karanthes explained, "Women are women, and they could not resist the temptation to look more closely at the beautiful clothes and cheap jewelry. Thanks to these my wife is now persuaded that Mary of Beret is no wicked woman, but rather an innocent girl whom you mean to rescue and make respectable."

I had no time to reply, for his wife and daughter now called to me from above and with gay chatter invited me to come up and survey the bride. Amazed at their altered frame of mind I obeyed, and was yet more astonished at the sight of Mary. In her new clothes she looked even younger than she had the evening before. She wore an embroidered sash about her waist and a band across her brow, a necklace of colored stones, and large rings in her ears; yes, and an anklet. Flushed with delight she cried out her greeting and said, "Why do you dress me like a rich man's daughter at a feast? I am washed and combed and anointed, and have a veil with which to hide my face on the journey, and a mantle to wrap around me to protect my clothes from the dust."

She tried the veil, wrapped the mantle around her and showed herself from every side so that all her ornaments jingled. Her childish pleasure touched me, for it was as if she had stripped off her evil past with her old clothes. Karanthes too came to look at her as if she were the work of his hands, and he felt every piece of stuff and every trinket. He made me do so too, naming the price of each item as if to impress Mary with the amount I had spent on so simple a girl. Mary's face was overshadowed as she listened, her joy faded and she began to look at me with misgiving.

I thanked Karanthes for his trouble and spoke cordially to his wife and daughter, until all three of them perceived that their presence was superfluous and went away, tittering behind their hands. When Mary and I were alone, she stared at me in fright and withdrew with her back to the wall as if seeking protection.

"What is it that you want of me?" she asked. "A thing like this has only happened to me once since I ran away from my village to the city. An old woman found me in the street and put strange clothes on me. I thought she meant it kindly until I discovered what sort of house hers was. She beat me when I could not serve her guests in the way they wanted, and it was three days before I managed to escape. I thought you were different, and I have prayed for you because you're kind to me and didn't touch me last night, although I was much afraid you would. But now I mistrust your purpose. I wasn't beautiful enough for you when I was poor and unkempt."

I couldn't help laughing, and I comforted her: "Have no fear; I seek no earthly kingdom, for in that case I might as well stay with you here in Jerusalem. I've experienced enough to know that all earthly desire is but a glowing pit in which there is no breath of coolness, but which grows hotter the deeper one goes. Therefore I desire only that other kingdom, which still lingers among us on earth. That is what I am going to Galilee to seek, with you."

But my kind words did not please her. Tears welled up in her dark eyes; she stamped on the floor, snatched off her necklace and brow-band, flung them away and cried, "Now I see why you wouldn't even trouble to choose the jewelry yourself, but let others do it. Your indifference wounds me. I don't want ornaments that you didn't choose yourself—and yet I have never had such beautiful ones."

It was so hard for her to renounce the finery that she wept all the more bitterly, stamped with both feet and sobbed, "Don't you see that the simplest necklace of seeds and kernels, threaded by you, would have been dearer to me than these costly things?"

Now I became angry too; I stamped in my turn and commanded her, "Cease this howling at once, Mary of Beret! I cannot imagine what makes you behave so badly. What will the people below think of me—of both of us—when they hear all this thumping and bawling? A weeping woman is as ugly as a sack, and I don't see how I can take you with me to Galilee if you misinterpret my kindness in so wounding a manner."

This frightened Mary. She stopped crying at once, wiped her eyes and hugged me, kissed me on the corners of my mouth and begged me prettily: "Forgive my foolishness. I will try to be better if you will only take me with you."

Her caress was like that of a naughty but repentant child, and mollified me at once. Stroking her cheek I said, "Then keep your trinkets, so that the guards along the road may respect you as my lady companion. Later I can surely find an opportunity to string you a necklace of berries and kernels if you like that better; though we're no longer children."

We were indeed no longer children, but at that moment I was filled with the longing to be a child again at heart, so that I should know no more lust or wickedness but be able to delight in every day as it came. I did not know what awaited me in Galilee; I might be making this troublesome journey for nothing. But I wanted to enjoy the journey itself, and my hope. I wanted to enjoy my mere expectancy.

Karanthes called up to me that the donkeys had arrived. I saw by the sun that it was noon. Eagerly I ran down and Mary of Beret followed. In the alley before the house I beheld four sturdy donkeys, two of them saddled with sleeping mats. The third was laden with two hampers, and on the fourth sat a poorly clad woman who dared not so much as raise her eyes from the neck of her mount. Nathan greeted me respectfully but in silence, merely glancing at the sun to point out that he had come at the hour stated.

"Who is that woman? I want no such person with me," I said indignantly. But Nathan made no reply and looked away, as if the matter in no way concerned him. Karanthes went up and spoke to the woman, and returned, tugging uncertainly at his beard.

"Her name is Susanna," he said. "She says that Nathan has promised to bring her as your servant, for she wishes to return to her home in Galilee and is unable to walk so far. Therefore she sits ready on her donkey, and desires no payment if she may come too. I understand that she has been ill since the feast of the passover, and her companions left her behind when they returned home."

The woman sat there as before, not daring to look at me. Understandably I was angered, and cried, "We need no servant; we wait upon one another. I cannot begin to carry all the sick people of Jerusalem to Galilee."

Nathan gave me an inquiring look, and seeing that I was in earnest he shrugged his shoulders, threw out his hands, unfastened my purse from his belt, cast it on the ground before me and walked away down the alley, careless of the donkeys. The woman lamented, but remained stubbornly seated.

I realized that my departure would be further delayed if I were compelled to find another guide, who incidentally might be untrustworthy. Wrath boiled up in me, but I swallowed it down, called Nathan back, bade him fasten the purse to his belt again, and said bitterly, "I bow to the inevitable. Do as you please, so long as we may set forth before any more people gather to gape at us."

I hastened indoors, settled my debt to Karanthes, gave him more than he asked, and said, "Keep for me the things I have left here, for I shall be returning to Jerusalem."

Karanthes thanked me profusely and said with a nod of conviction, "Quite so, quite so. I am sure you will be back very soon."

Inquisitive people gathered round the donkeys while Nathan skillfully loaded the baskets with what I desired to take. The men felt the animals' legs and examined their teeth, and the women commiserated with the sick Susanna, who sat hunched upon her mount without daring to exchange a word with anyone. Even beggars collected, to stretch out their hands and wish us luck upon our journey, and Nathan distributed such alms from my purse as he thought reasonable, lest they bring harm upon us by their curses. Thus considerable clamor had broken out in the traders' alley before Mary and I could mount our donkeys at last, and Nathan take his place at the head of the procession. So far as I was concerned he might as well have tied a sack over my head, for he uttered not one word as to the route by which he meant to lead us into Galilee, nor the inns at which we should stay.

At first, however, he took us through the outer city to the market place that stank of salt fish, by the Fish Gate, and through this gate out of the city. The guards knew him and wanted to search the baskets on the pack animal, but when I shouted to them that I was a Roman they at once abstained, and stood watching us for a long time after we had passed. To my surprise, Nathan now followed the road that ran along the wall up to the Antonia fortress, and halted the donkeys in front of the archway. When Susanna saw the legionaries on guard at the gate she began wailing again, and hid her face against her donkey's neck. In vain I urged Nathan to go on; he merely signed to me that I must enter the fortress. I now suspected that he was dumb, for never yet had I heard him utter a word. Yet, surveying his short hair I also wondered whether he might have taken a vow of silence.

Reluctantly I went through the archway, and the guards did not stop me, odd though I looked with my beard and my striped mantle. At that very moment, as if I had called him, the garrison commander came down from the tower.

I went up to him, greeted him with raised arm and said, "I'm on my way to Tiberias to take the baths. My guide considered that I ought to take my leave of you and ask advice for my journey. I am traveling simply, without other following than two women."

He asked, "Do you go through Samaria or along the Jordan?"

I was ashamed to confess that I did not know, and so I answered, "Whichever way you think best."

The gloomy, rheumatic man fingered his upper lip and explained, "The Samaritans are a malignant people, and cause much annoyance to simple wayfarers. But Jordan is still in flood. You might have trouble at the fords, and at night you might hear the roaring of lions in the scrub. Of course if you desire it, I will give you a couple of legionaries to attend you, if you will pay them and find occasion to mention my helpfulness to the Procurator."

Evidently he was not enthusiastic about diminishing his garrison even temporarily by two men. So I replied, "No, no.

I am traveling in a land in which Rome keeps the peace, and I have nothing to fear."

"In that case I will give you a sword to be your companion," he said with relief. "As a Roman citizen you're entitled to travel with a sword, yet to be on the safe side you shall have a written permit, since you're so oddly dressed and have let your beard grow untrimmed."

I went in therefore, drew sword and shoulder strap from the quartermaster, and bought my permit from the secretary so that the commandant might benefit in a suitable manner by my departure. He then accompanied me cordially across the courtyard to the gate, but tried in vain to conceal his smile when I girded my sword over my Jewish mantle.

Nathan did not smile, but he nodded in satisfaction as he urged the donkeys forward once more. We were now skirting the temple area, and crossing the Kidron we joined the road which wound around the Mount of Olives, and which I already knew as far as Bethany. When the city was out of sight I dismounted and continued on foot. In Bethany I called to Nathan to stop, and made for Lazarus' house.

After I'd been calling for some time, he came walking from his garden and returned my greeting. I asked after his sisters, and he said, "My sisters have gone to Galilee."

I asked, "Why did you not go with them?"

He shook his head and replied, "I have no reason to go to Galilee."

"But I've been told that he, your lord, has gone there before them and awaits them there."

Lazarus said coldly, "What has that to do with me? I tend my garden and remain near my tomb."

He spoke in a horribly blurred manner, his eyes were somber, and it was as if he had been brooding over some riddle which he could not explain to any stranger. I felt a chill in his presence and regretted having turned aside to greet him.

"Peace be with you," I said in farewell.

"Peace!" he repeated derisively. "If you knew what peace meant you would hardly wish it for me."

He drew his yellowish hand across his brow and continued, "I have pain in my head and my thoughts won't hold together. I was afraid when I heard you call my name. It always frightens me now to hear anyone call me. I will give you a parable. If you and I were pin points, or even smaller, and everything around us was the size of a pin point, we should still believe we were as big as we are now, for we should have only each other to compare ourselves with. To me the world and everything around me has become as small as a pin point. Why did he consent to be born, to die and to rise again in this pin-point world? That is something I cannot understand."

I could not help thinking that his brain must have undergone some deterioration during the days he had lain dead in his grave, and that he could no longer think in the same way as other people. I turned away in silence and returned to the road. Nathan looked at me searchingly, a certain wonder in his face such as I had seen there before. But he said nothing. We continued on our way.

The road ran down into a valley and crossed a watercourse. We walked along the hillsides and halted only once to water the donkeys at a well. Nathan's was no sulky silence; on the contrary I felt full confidence in him as a guide. Nor did I any longer bear a grudge against the sick woman, for she rode last and was as unobtrusive as she could be. Indeed, when the shadows began to lengthen I grew concerned for her, and wondered how far her strength would sustain her. Nathan urged on the animals incessantly, walking with long, tireless strides as if he had been in as great a hurry as ourselves. I saw that he avoided Samaria and followed the route of the Galilean pilgrims, who went by way of Jericho when traveling to and from the temple at the great Jewish feasts.

Not until the first stars appeared did we stop in a little village where Nathan led the donkeys into the enclosed courtyard of a modest inn. Here we had to attend to our own wants. Quickly and deftly Nathan unloaded the animals and carried our sleeping mats into an empty, dung-smelling but clean room. Susanna hastened to kindle a fire in the yard and made a clatter with the cooking pots to show that she meant to be useful and prepare our meal.

She mixed pieces of mutton with her pottage and left it to steep; then fetched water and insisted on washing my feet. She washed Mary's feet too, and treated her with all respect. When the food was ready she served first me and then Mary. I felt comfortable and content.

I called out a genial invitation to Nathan and Susanna: "I know not whether I'm offending against your laws, but after all we are traveling together and shall sleep in the same room. You'll be eating the food that I am eating, so sit here and eat with us."

They washed their hands, squatted down and ate. Nathan broke the bread, blessed it in the Jewish manner and handed me a piece, but paid no attention to the women. He ate sparingly, and did not touch the meat; while eating he stared before him, plunged in his own thoughts, and I did not try to talk to him. Having looked to the donkeys again he wrapped himself in his mantle, covered his head and lay down by the threshold to sleep, as if hinting that we would all do well to rest. But when Susanna had finished her meal she threw herself down and tried to kiss my feet, in thanks to me for taking her under my protection.

I said, "You must thank Nathan and not me. I only hope that the journey will not be too tiring for you, so that you fall sick again."

She protested, "No, no! Galilean women are as tough as leather. My sickness was chiefly sorrow, but I shall get well again for joy at coming home again to my country on the shores of Gennesar."

Next morning Nathan roused us before sunrise and had us on

our way so quickly that I found myself sitting on my donkey, shivering sleepily in the morning chill and gnawing at a piece of bread, while the red sun was still climbing above the hills. But gradually as the sunlight brightened and grew warmer I was filled with joy. The blue heights, the vineyards and the silver-gray olive trees on the slopes were beautiful to see. I believe we were all filled with the same joy, for suddenly and to my great astonishment Nathan lifted up a harsh voice and began singing a Hebrew song.

I looked questioningly at Mary, but she just shook her head to show that she did not understand the words. There was something both jubilant and solemn in Nathan's rising and falling chant. When he ended it I got off my donkey and waited for Susanna to come up. At my question she looked at me trustfully and explained, "That is a wayfaring song: 'The Lord is my keeper, the Lord is thy shade upon thy right hand. The sun shall not smite thee by day nor the moon by night. The Lord shall preserve thee from all evil; he shall preserve thy soul. The Lord holdeth his hand over thy going out and thy coming in, now and forever more.' "

I did not properly understand her country speech, so she began crooning the same words in her own language, swaying her body; and suddenly to my surprise she burst into tears. I touched her shoulder consolingly, saying, "Don't weep, Susanna; tell me what troubles you, and perhaps I can help you."

She answered, "No, no; I weep for joy, because from the deepest sorrow and as it were from the very jaws of death I have come up again into the light of day."

I could not but feel uneasy at having brought two mentally unhinged companions with me on my journey; yet I smiled, for by any reasonable standards I myself was a mad Roman, hastening without pause or rest in search of a resurrected Jewish king.

Toward noon we came down into the valley of the Jordan, and beheld wide, fertile fields and the gray walls of Jericho before us. The air grew blazing hot, but every now and then a breeze brought us the light yet pungent scent of the palm groves which are the wealth of Jericho.

Here spring was further advanced than in Jerusalem, and we saw people already harvesting wheat with sickles. Nathan did not lead us into the city, but along cattle tracks that skirted the walls, and at midday we rested in the shade of those walls near a spring, and let the donkeys graze. Nathan went a little apart from us to pray, and turned with uplifted arms toward Jerusalem, so that Mary too remembered the day prayer and Susanna murmured something piously to herself. This divided them from me, for I am accustomed to praying merely as custom requires, at sacrifices and at the festivals of places where I may be staying; and that kind of prayer, I believe, is of no effect. I simply comply with the customs and manners of different countries so as not to be conspicuous. Now I was filled with a sort of envy, and I wanted to ask them to teach me their prayers. But they were Jews, and regarded themselves as God's chosen people; and so I suspected that Nathan and Susanna would refuse such a request. Mary's praying seemed to me little more than a childish habit, and had nothing to offer me.

During our halt we ate bread, onions and cheese. I drank only water. When I offered Nathan wine he said nothing, but pointed to his short hair, and I realized that he was bound by some kind of vow. Yet he looked at me so cordially that I asked him, "Have you made a vow of silence too?"

He answered, "Where words are many, sin in not lacking." But he smiled conciliatingly as he said this.

After that he had no patience to rest any longer, but urged us to hurry on. We returned to the highroad and saw, far across the plain, the flooded Jordan. Our journey was now so hot and sweaty that each of us had enough to do to endure it for himself. Besides this, both we and the donkeys were set upon by stinging flies, which I fancy came from the oxen that were drawing wheat sheaves to the threshing floors.

When evening came we had a long day's march behind us

and were all weary, thirsty and stiff. We spent the night in a village that had a spring of running water, that we might wash ourselves properly. I had already noticed that Nathan seemed to be avoiding the inns of towns, where we might have lodged more comfortably and been served with ready-cooked food. But when he bent his searching gaze on me, I felt no displeasure. Indeed, my body enjoyed this simple life after the enervating days in Jerusalem.

Mary, tiring of idleness, kilted up her mantle and helped Susanna make a fire and prepare the meal. I heard them chattering eagerly together as women will, while I watched the stars come out.

When we had eaten, Mary moved her sleeping mat close to mine and began whispering in my ear: "That Susanna is an ignorant woman, and one might almost think that she was weak in the head. But I suspect that she belongs to the quiet ones in the land and knows something of the crucified Jesus, although she's afraid of us, and will not give herself away."

I sat up quickly. Nathan had already covered his head and lain down to rest by the threshold, but Susanna, still on her knees, was murmuring her prayer. I could not resist the temptation and whispered to her, "Tell me how you pray, so that I may learn a good way to do it."

Susanna raised her hand deprecatingly and protested, "I'm an ignorant woman. I don't know the law. I can't pray as one ought to pray. You'd only laugh if I taught you my prayer."

I assured her, "I won't laugh, for I want to be quiet and humble of heart."

Mary said, "Your prayer is new. I never heard anyone pray in that way before."

Timidly, yet mindful of the gratitude she owed me, Susanna taught us the prayer, first explaining, "I learned it because it is easy to remember and I have been told that it may replace all other prayers, for nothing remains to be added to it. I pray thus: Our father who art in heaven, thy name be hallowed, may thy kingdom come to us and thy will be done on earth as it is done in heaven. Give us every day the bread we need. And forgive us our debts as we forgive them who are in debt to us. And lead us not into temptation, but free us from evil. In truth."

I asked her to repeat the prayer and realized that it was a simple one and easy to learn. I said it aloud to myself, thinking about each phrase, and found that indeed it required no additions, for all that a simple person can need is expressed in it. It was not the subtle prayer of a scholar, but it gave me enough to think of to spare Susanna further questions.

The next night we had to spend near some flooded scrub. Somewhere far to the north, snow was melting on the hill where the waters of Jordan rose. The inundation had driven the wild animals from their lairs, although the tributaries of the Jordan were almost dried up. As the stars came out I heard jackals yapping uneasily in the hills, and a little later we heard the echo of a roaring like distant thunder. It was a noise I recognized, although I had never heard it in the wilderness before but only in Rome, at night, within the walls of the circus. The donkeys began to tremble, and we had to bring them into the room where we were sleeping on a raised part of the floor. Mary had never heard the roar of lions before and she pressed closer to me, begging me in a quavering voice to put my arms around her, stifling though the night was.

Nathan soothed the donkeys, barred the door and sat with his back against it, listening tensely. Susanna could not sleep either; so I took the opportunity to ask her, "From whom did you learn the prayer you taught me last night?"

In the distance the lion roared again, and the frail mud walls of the house seemed to shake. Susanna clapped a hand to her mouth in a fright and said, "You mustn't ask me such things."

But Nathan opened his mouth and said to my astonishment, "Tell him; have no fear of him."

Susanna looked about her uneasily in the wavering light of the earthenware lamp, and then began:

"It was Jesus of Nazareth, the man they crucified in Jerusalem, who taught his disciples that prayer, and he also taught it to us women who walked with him in Galilee. He said it was enough, and that we needed no other prayers."

I cried in surprise, "Surely you would not lie to me! Did you really walk with him in Galilee?"

Susanna answered, "I am not at all a clever woman, and couldn't lie even if I wanted to. Five sparrows are sold for two farthings, and yet God has not forgotten one of them. All my life I had been greedy for money and possessions and would not even allow myself proper food. When all the others went to see the new prophet I went too, thinking that there I might get something free. In the temple nothing is given free. I listened to his teaching and made nothing of it, but then he spoke to the people and looked straight at me as he said, 'Beware of covetousness, for a man's life doesn't depend on the amount of his possessions.' This was down by the lake. I thought he really knew who I was and had heard of my avarice. But then he told of a rich man who had fertile fields and pulled down his barns to build new and bigger ones, for now that he had saved so much he meant to take his ease for many years. But God said to that man, 'You fool! Tonight your soul will be required of you, and who then will get everything that you've collected? So it is with the man who stores up treasures for himself, but none in the kingdom!' "

She drew a deep breath and went on. "I was angry with him and went home again, but I couldn't forget his words, and at last they were like a boil throbbing inside me. I went to hear him again. He was speaking then about the ravens that God feeds and the meadow flowers that neither toil nor spin. He forbade his disciples to seek food and drink and ordered them to seek the kingdom, saying that then they would gain everything else as well. I pitied him very much, although he was said to have fed a great crowd of people with only a few loaves and fishes. But one can't do that every day. I had no wish to share out my money among lazy, good-for-nothing paupers, but I sold the stuffs I had woven, left my fields to the care of a steward and went with Jesus to support him and his disciples for as long as the money lasted. For it seemed to me that the miracle worker would soon starve to death if no one fed him. There were some other women who were doing the same thing, from compassion; he was such an unpractical man."

Susanna sighed at the recollection of her wanderings with Jesus' followers, and continued her story. "I wouldn't say a word against him. I'm telling of this just to show that he didn't understand much about this world's affairs. And so we women had to look after him; and I must say too that his disciples fished now and then to bring in something. It was said in Nazareth that he was not a particularly good carpenter, although he had learned the trade under his father. He could make yokes and ploughs, but not a good wheel. Besides, he was far too trusting; he gave Judas Iscariot the purse to look after, and I'm sure it was sometimes lighter than it should have been—you could see that in the man's eyes. I'm not saying I understood what the Nazarene taught; not even his disciples always did that; but somehow just to be near him was good. So I didn't leave him and return home, although I sometimes wanted to. Knowingly and purposely, though without cause, he made many pious men his enemies, and I couldn't bear that he should allow a woman like that dove seller from Magdala to go along with him."

Mary now broke in, exclaiming, "Mary Magdalene is a compassionate woman and wiser than you, you ugly country hag in your sackcloth."

Susanna flared up in anger: "If you take her part I know what sort of a woman you must be, and why you are in such a hurry to jump into that Roman's arms every night. It's very true that I am only an ugly country hag and wear sackcloth, but I can both spin and weave, and bake and cook and clean out the corners; and I've followed the plough in my time too, when I didn't want to waste money on hiring a lad. In any case, Jesus of Nazareth was altogether too good for this world, being thoughtless and credulous by nature. He worked miracles and healed the sick without so much as finding out if they were worthy of such grace. One had only to touch his mantle to be healed of all pains. He seemed to me like a careless child let out alone into a wicked world. If only he'd been willing to listen to good advice he would never have gone to Jerusalem for the passover. But he was stubborn and thought he understood the things of this world too, better than other people. That was why everything turned out as it did."

Susanna was now vehement, and had begun to scold Jesus of Nazareth as if he'd been a naughty boy. But then, recalling everything that had happened, she burst into tears, saying, "All that I have left of him is this sacking I wear and the prayer he taught us. When he was dead we flapped away in all directions like a flock of sparrows. I was sick with horror when I fled from the crucifixion. For days I couldn't swallow a morsel of food. I just lay in a cave below the temple, hoping that no one would recognize me. Then at last I met this Nathan in his white clothes, who has cut his hair short for his sake. He gave me to understand that Jesus had risen from the dead and gone before us into Galilee."

Susanna clapped her hand to her mouth and stared at Nathan, as if afraid of having said too much in her loquacity. But Nathan said, "The talking of women is like the crackling of dry twigs under the pot. I knew that the kingdom was near, but Jesus I never knew. I cut my hair when I heard that he had risen from the tomb, for if that is so he is the son of God: he for whom we have waited."

Susanna said, "But I knew him, and well too, for it was I who washed his clothes. He was human, knowing both hunger and thirst, and at times he wearied of his disciples and of the hard hearts of the people. But he must have risen from the dead, if that is what is said, and I am not at all surprised. On the contrary, I weep for joy on his account and hope that all this evil may be turned to good. Perhaps he will really establish a kingdom in Galilee if we will only be patient, and if we have angels to fight for him. Otherwise nothing can come of it. Nevertheless, morning, noon, and night I repeat the prayer he taught us. For me it is enough, since he said so."

Her words made a deep impression on Mary who, half doubting, asked her, "Did you indeed wash his clothes?"

Susanna boasted, "Who else would have got them white enough? Your Mary Magdalene can never have stood at the washtub in all her life. Salome had enough with her own boys' things, and Johanna kept servants. That woman would have had herself carried in a litter after Jesus if she'd dared. But she learned to walk on her own feet."

No longer able to master my wonder I asked, "Why was it you followed him, and sacrificed your property, since you didn't approve of his behavior or his disciples or the others who went with him?"

Susanna looked at me in equal surprise and explained, "He was like a lamb among wolves. Who else would have fed him and tended him? Even his own mother thought he was crazed. And the Nazarenes led him once to the brink of a cliff to hurl him over it, but in the end they dared not."

"Then you loved him?" I asked.

Susanna wriggled in irritation and said crossly, "What should a dried-up old carcass like me know of love? But the world is full of lazy good-for-nothings, greedy priests, heartless tax collectors and other treachery. A countrywoman only has to show herself in a town for the very hair to be stolen from her head. I pitied him, for he was innocent and knew nothing of evil."

Pressing the palms of her hands together she added in a

low voice, as if ashamed of what she was saying, "Besides, he had the words of eternal life."

"What do you mean by that?" I asked.

But Susanna made a gesture of impatience. "I don't know. He just had. I didn't understand the words; I just believed."

"And do you still?" I persisted.

"I don't know," she replied, impatient still. "When blood and the sweat of agony poured off him on the cross, I believed no longer and fled, for I couldn't endure to watch his sufferings. Therefore it may be I fell sick from disappointment afterwards, fancying that I had squandered my possessions to no purpose. Though not quite that, either. I was sick chiefly from his sufferings, for he had deserved no such death, even though he may have said hard things about the scribes and Pharisees. He said no worse than any countryman who knows them and who may have had to destroy his friut crops or throw away his vegetables through ignorance of the law. But now all must surely be well again, and I believe in him if only I may meet him just once more and hear his voice."

Reason compelled me to doubt her, in that stifling mud hut. The donkeys stirred restlessly at the manger and outside, the lion was roaring. It seemed to me that Susanna was making herself out to be more foolish than she was, and was slyly withholding from me the most important part of what she knew. If she had spent long hours in the company of Jesus of Nazareth, seen his miracles, heard him speak to the people and picked up a little here and there of what he taught his chosen disciples, she must also have found out such things as were not intended for all to hear.

"His wisdom," I said again. "Do you really remember nothing else of his secret teaching?"

Susanna looked at me still more disapprovingly, and explained, "Wisdom cannot be taught to women and children. That was why I couldn't endure Mary Magdalene, who was forever sitting at his feet imagining that she understood everything, while the rest of us were doing useful work. There were enough and to spare of that sort, I can tell you; for it was not twelve we had to feed and look after but sometimes as many as seventy. For me, his wisdom was himself. For me he was the bread of life, as he said. I don't know what he meant by that, but I believed him when he said it."

I could only shake my head at her simplicity, and I ceased to question her. Yet while the clay lamp was still flickering, Susanna felt a need to convince me; and she pondered so strenuously over this that she plucked at her fingers and rocked to and fro for a while before explaining, "His father in heaven is also mine. And he let children come to him and said that to those who are like children his kingdom is open. That saying I understood. I understood that my task as a child was not to puzzle my head over my father's purposes but to realize that he knows best about everything. That is the only secret I have learned."

During that restless night I had no sleep, and the muffled roarings reminded me so vividly of Rome that sometimes between sleeping and waking I fancied myself back there, and expected to wake on a purple cushion amid the fragrance of rose essence, exhausted by passion. This dream was like an oppressive nightmare; yet as soon as I awoke, with a start, I was filled with an equally oppressive sense of futility. Here I lay, bearded, unkempt and smelling of sweat, in a dirty mud hut among donkeys and Jews, fancying that hereby I should attain to something that was contrary to all reason. In Rome I should have had my hair curled and arranged the folds of my mantle in precisely the correct manner. I should have passed my time in reading, or listening to some interesting court case, or doing something else, waiting only for the hour when I might see Tullia again.

There the thoughts I entertained today would have been as much derided amid the simple luxury of the freedman as in the cultured society of the intelligentsia, where it is good form to believe in nothing. And I would have been among the loudest laughers.

Nevertheless, those same frivolous women and clever young men queued up at the door of whichever stargazer, witch master or sibyl happened to be fashionable at the moment, and paid large sums for lucky talismans. They laughed at this themselves, skeptical of their own superstition, yet at the same time hoping that there might be something in it. Everything is a gamble. Fortune is capricious and the chances of winning uncertain; but it is better to play than to abstain and be content with emptiness.

Was I still gambling, here by the Jordan, doubting in my innermost heart but thinking it better to go on and take a chance than to leave it alone? What did I expect to win, when all was said and done? It may be no more that a mirage, this kingdom which I imagine still lingers on this earth and to which I hope to find the way. Imprisoned by these painful thoughts I felt a repugnance for Mary, breathing there at my side; for stubborn Susanna and silent Nathan. What had I, a Roman, to do with them?

I repeated in my mind the prayer that Susanna had taught me. It was the first of the Nazarene's secrets that had been disclosed to me. The magic power of some hidden wisdom might possibly be bound up with it; yet however I turned those phrases about in my mind, the prayer remained what it was: a formula for the submission of simple people, something to repeat to oneself humbly, and so cast away one's cares and win peace of mind. I was not childlike enough to feel that it helped me.

That night we all slept badly, and in the morning were sleepy and quarrelsome. Mary of Beret took it into her head to demand that we should turn up into the hills and take the road through Samaria. She had no wish to run into some lion that had been driven from the thickets by the flooded river. Susanna went through her cooking pots and food bags again and again, insisting that she had lost something, thus delaying our departure. Even Nathan seemed uneasy and looked warily about him, and the hornet-plagued donkeys were so restive that we had to hold on to them the whole time.

Exasperated by Mary's chatter, Nathan at last appealed to the scriptures and said, "There is a way which seemeth right unto a man, but the ends thereof are the ways of death." Pointing to the sword hanging at my side he set off resolutely, as if to show that we might do as we chose, but that he at least meant to go forward as had originally been planned.

Mary lamented, "You men will come off lightly, but I'm the youngest here. The lion is a wise beast and always chooses the tenderest flesh. So I have heard."

Susanna snapped, "If Jesus of Nazareth went this way, surely we can follow him. If you're afraid, I can ride ahead and chase the lion off; it won't touch me, that's certain."

I remarked irritably that none of us knew which way Jesus of Nazareth had taken into Galilee, if indeed there was any truth in the story at all. It might well be an ingenious tale spread by the Council in Jerusalem to induce the Galileans to leave the city. I had no desire to encounter a lion with nothing but a sword, even though at the circus I had seen a well-trained man make such an attempt and escape with his life. But Nathan knew the roads and their perils, and in my opinion it was wisest to do as he said.

So we continued on our journey in a prickly mood. At the flooded ford we had to gird up our clothes and drag the refractory donkeys after us. No sooner had we crossed than we fell right into the arms of some legionaries, who greeted us with glad shouts at the sight of Mary. Because of my sword they pulled me off my donkey at once, threw me on the ground and would most likely have slain me had I not shrieked at them in both Greek and Latin that I was a citizen. Despite my permit to bear arms they searched all our baggage, also—for the sport of it—Mary's clothing, and they would certainly have dragged her into the bushes if I had not been a Roman.

Their lack of discipline was accounted for when I discovered that they were not a road patrol, nor were they taking part in any maneuvers: their leader had made up his mind to bring down a lion, and lay in ambush with a few archers on a knoll, toward which these legionaries were to drive the lion with clamor and clattering of shields. This was no agreeable task even though the lion, to all appearances, was no longer in the neighborhood; so they had drunk wine to stiffen their valor.

This violent episode was so unpleasant and upsetting that I could easily put myself in the Jews' place, and understand why they so bitterly hated the Romans. My ill-humor was exacerbated to wrath, and when at last I encountered the centurion who was so desirous of a lion skin, up on the knoll, I let him and his men know what I thought of them, and threatened to report their misconduct to the Procurator.

This was an error on my part, for the scar-faced centurion eyed me malignantly and asked what sort of man I was to be wearing a Jewish mantle and traveling in Jewish company. He said accusingly, "Don't tell me you belong to the mob that has been passing along here by the dozens on their way to the Sea of Tiberias. This is no season of pilgrimage but of harvest. Those wayfarers were up to no good."

I had to mollify him and apologize for my impetuousness. Then I asked what people these were whom he had seen. But he had seen none at all himself, for the Jews traveled by night and tried to circumvent the usual check-points and tollhouses. He was only repeating what he had heard. He warned me in a condescending tone, "Take care you don't fall into their hands, for all Galileans are fanatics. Theirs is a thickly populated country and troublemakers keep pouring in from the desert. Only a year or two back we had an agitator who proclaimed a Jewish kingdom and baptized men with witchcraft in the Jordan to make them invulnerable in battle. The Jewish Tetrarch of Galilee was compelled to behead him in the end to show that not even he was invincible. But some of his followers may still be about."

Presumably he regarded me as a man of no standing, for he dismissed me abruptly, as if he had done me a favor.

When we resumed our arduous journey, Mary of Beret regarded me with a patronizing air and remarked, "You seem not to be a person of much consequence among your own countrymen, since a sweaty, scarred centurion may treat you so arrogantly."

"Would I be greater in your eyes if I wore a helmet on my head and nailed boots on my feet?" I demanded acidly.

Mary tossed her head and replied, "Legionaries at least know what they want. Since you're a Roman you might travel as a Roman and take advantage of what privileges you have. Then I would not need to blush for your hairy legs and bearded cheeks when you speak to another Roman."

I stared at her, unable to believe my ears. I longed to cut a switch and give her a hiding. With an unsteady voice I asked her, "Who can that girl have been who promised to bless me all her days if I would only take her with me—yes, and sleep out in the open fields if need were? Just who do you think you are?"

But Mary tossed her head again and said in reproof, "I could never have believed that you of all people would throw back in my face anything that I happened to confide to you about my life. I have been unfortunate, but if I meet the risen Nazarene and he forgives my sins and cleanses me, you will no longer be able to reproach me with my past. Tell me what horrible sins you yourself hope to atone for by making yourself so meek in your search for a new way."

I don't believe she truly meant what she said, but was only giving vent to her resentment at the vexations of this day. I made no reply. She dropped back beside Susanna; I heard them both wrangling shrilly with each other, and then uniting in rage against Nathan and me.

That evening the sun set terrifyingly red behind the mountains of Samaria; for a moment the air of the valley had a ghostly glimmer, and the Jordan, roaring by in its deep furrow, darkened before our eyes. This strange sight made everything unreal and drove away my evil thoughts. I recalled how the air had darkened as the king of the Jews writhed in agony on the cross, and how at the moment of his death the earth had trembled. By his resurrection he had proved that his kingdom was real. In despising my traveling companions, in accounting myself better than they and nursing a grudge against a foolish girl, I was merely removing myself from that kingdom.

So, when we had washed ourselves at the inn, I went over to Mary and said, "I forgive you your wicked, ungrateful words, and forget them."

But at this Mary grew angrier than ever; her eyes darkened and she answered hotly, "Do *you* forgive *me,* having hurt me so deeply and then turned your back on me the whole day? Truly in my heart I was ready to forgive you and say a kind word to you, since you're a man and one can expect no better of you, as Susanna says too. But I will not have you pretending to forgive me before I forgive you."

Nathan, hearing all this, raised his eyes to heaven and spread out his hands in a gesture of despair. His resignation made me yield too, so that I no longer felt any anger. "Let it be as you will, Mary of Beret," I said. "Forgive me, and I readily acknowledge that I have nothing to forgive you, so long as we may be good friends again."

But Mary planted her fists on her round hips and called acidly to Susanna, "Come here and look and find out whether this is really a man or just one of those Roman geldings I've heard about."

Susanna tittered behind her hand as she gathered rushes and dung for the fire, and I could no longer control myself. The blood rushed to my head and I gave Mary a slap on the cheek that could be heard a long way off. Hardly had I struck her than I repented of it and would have given anything not to have done it. Mary began to sob, breathed in through her nose many times and rubbed her smarting cheek. I would have begged her forgiveness, but Nathan raised his hand in warning. Presently Mary cast her eyes down, and coming up to me on tiptoe said, "You did right to strike me. I've been teasing you on purpose all day. It shows that at least you like me better than the donkey that you've been forever patting on the neck. Kiss me now to show me that you truly forgive me my ill-nature."

Shyly she put her arms around my neck and I kissed her once and once more, to show that all was again well between us. In fact I found it pleasant after my rage to hold her in my arms and kiss her, and so I kissed her a third time. Then Mary pushed me away, but with her hands still on my shoulders she looked at me intently and asked, "Would you kiss Susanna like that if she had hurt you and then begged your forgiveness?"

I looked at Susanna's leathery old face and compared her dry mouth with Mary's soft lips, and realized that Mary had led me into a trap. Therefore I ran to Susanna, took her by the elbows, raised her to her feet and said, "If I have hurt you in any way, then kiss me in token of forgiveness."

Susanna said pityingly, "Oh you poor man, to let a giddy-headed girl play with you like that! But Mary isn't bad at heart."

She wiped her mouth shyly with the back of her hand and kissed me, with an amused glance at Mary. Mary looked dashed, then rebuked Susanna, saying, "How can you, a child of Israel, go and kiss an uncircumcised Roman? I may do so, for I am a sinner anyway, but you have defiled yourself."

Susanna said defensively, "I have no great knowledge of the law, but I've already eaten from the same dish as he. I know that in his heart he is the child of the same father as I am, Roman though he may be."

Her words moved me and she repelled me no longer, though she smelled powerfully of garlic, which she was in the habit of chewing by way of refreshment while sitting on her donkey. I said, "Susanna, if he himself allowed you to wash his clothes, then you have shown me a great favor in kissing me."

But when we had eaten I drew Mary aside into a dark corner and asked her bluntly, "I suppose you are trying to seduce me into sinning with you? In no other way can I explain your conduct. Yet it was to save you from sin that I brought you with me."

Mary breathed into my ear, "You have treated me better than other men. I cannot make myself out, but your indifference wounds me. At least then I should know that I do mean something to you."

"A body is a body," I said bitterly. "You wouldn't have to coax me long to make me fall. I'm bound by no vows and have sworn no fidelity. But then we might as well return at once to Jerusalem."

Mary sighed. "Life is strange, and I am much afraid of Jesus of Nazareth. But I believe that only he can make me clean and untouched again, and I've been assured that he was not stern even to the greatest sinners if they repented of their sins and believed in him. But if I were to sin with you, I don't believe I should feel any remorse afterwards. On the contrary, it seems to me it could only do me good. That shows how steeped in sin I am, for certainly no innocent girl would feel like that. Yet no human being can avoid sin. When Mary Magdalene was comforting me about my sins she told me he'd said that a man who does no more than look at a woman with desire commits adultery with her in his heart. In this the Nazarene makes quite impossible demands which no one can fulfill."

"Mary of Beret," I said appealingly. "Have we not trouble enough with our bodies on this arduous journey, without tormenting ourselves with sinful thoughts? Tonight you shall not turn any lion into a pretext for lying close to me. It would only inflame us both."

Mary sighed even more deeply, and then said, "I won't trouble you or tempt you any more, so long as you admit and promise that you would gladly sin with me if you dared."

I snapped my answer: "As you will. In my heart I have already done so. Be content with that."

Pressing my hand against her hot cheek she whispered, "How I wish that I was a virgin and without sin." But she plagued me no more and did not lie down to sleep beside me.

I thought to myself that she could know little of the kingdom to which she sought the way, but that after all one could not expect great knowledge from her. And I began wondering what Nathan desired of Jesus of Nazareth, since he had cut his hair short to please him. Did I too perhaps wish for something which, measured by the measure of the kingdom, was as childish as Mary's hope?

Next day we left the winding furrow of the Jordan. When we had turned from the caravan route and come up onto the slopes of the hills, we saw the Sea of Tiberias billowing before us. A fresh wind blew in our faces, the waters foamed white, and far away on the other side we could just make out a snowy mountaintop against the sky. We followed the western shore of the lake and reached the hot springs by evening. A little farther on rose the arcades of the city of Herod Antipas. The wholesome smell of sulphur came to meet us, for the waters of the springs were led into many basins and pools, and the Tetrarch had caused a bath establishment to be built around them. Along the shore were villas in the Greek style and a few fishermen's huts. Comprised in the bath buildings were inns for both Greeks and Jews.

I had had enough of the hardships of travel, so I put up at the comfortable Greek inn with Mary; but Nathan took the donkeys and Susanna to the Jewish one. I felt it prudent not to appear in their company here in Galilee, since Jesus' disciples mistrusted me, and it seemed to me best that Susanna should find out what was happening. I relied on her to pass on to me anything that she might learn, since I had done her the great service of bringing her to Galilee. Nathan I knew well enough to let him keep my purse and see to the donkeys. I thought too that this was the best way of attaching him to me. Their intention was to go on next day to Capernaum where Jesus of Nazareth had worked, on the northern shore of the Sea of Galilee. It was a short day's journey from Tiberias. So far as Susanna knew, Jesus had never been in Tiberias.

Next day I woke at dawn, and limped a little in climbing to the roof. After the close valley of the Jordan the air of Galilee was fresh to breathe; the lake lay like glass, streaked with the fire of sunrise, and I smelled the aromatic fragrance of the myrtle bushes. I seemed to see everything about me more clearly and sharply than ever before and could distinguish every scent, yet as if I had been disembodied. It was an intoxication, and I reveled in it until I felt the chills of ague and noticed that one foot was swollen.

In the afternoon I was already shivering with fever, my leg was swollen to the knee, with a red streak that started from a chafed place on my heel. The Greek physician attached to the baths lanced the boil with his knife and gave me blood-cooling drinks. For a fortnight I lay sick at the inn, thinking I should die. But Mary of Beret nursed me, and I believe that the hot, sulphurous waters of the springs helped to cure me. For days I could keep no food down, and when I began to recover I felt limp and feeble. The physician warned me against overstraining my foot, and so I passed the time in recording my whole journey from Jerusalem. No word had come from either Nathan or Susanna.

Ninth Letter

Marcus to Tullia:

After my recovery I felt exhausted and depressed. I could not escape the idea that my unexpected and dangerous illness was a warning to me not to meddle in mysteries that did not concern me. I stayed in my room, shunning the society of other guests though the famous baths of Tiberias were visited by people of many countries. Most of them were rich persons in search of cures for the ills born of wealth and soft living, though there were also a few Roman officers among them who were suffering from the effects of camp life.

I had massage, and even summoned a barber to dress my hair in the Greek manner. I let him trim my beard, too, and pluck out my body hairs, since all these things were now a matter of indifference to me. I may have behaved like a sulky child, for I had been sincere in my search and did not think I had deserved such punishment as this. I thought of you too, Tullia, now and then, in a diflerent way from when I had been in Jerusalem and longed for you, from defiance. With the simple-minded Mary I was merely bored, for after nursing me so faithfully and restoring me to health she became excessively self-satisfied and looked upon me as her own property.

Then one day there was a great stir in the place, and Mary hurried to bring me word that the wife of Pontius Pilate the Procurator had arrived from Caesarea to bathe in the hot springs. From the roof I beheld her litter and her suite. Herod had supplemented her escort of legionaries by his own red-mantled horsemen, who attended her all the way from the Galilean border. A summer palace by the baths had been prepared for her, with a private pool in the garden.

It's true that I knew Claudia Procula to be delicate and nervous, as are many women who are aware of advancing age, even though they may not admit it to themselves. No doubt she was in need of these health-giving baths, and the spring climate of the Sea of Galilee is certainly the freshest and best in the whole of the east Mediterranean region. The envoys of Herod Antipas send many visitors from Damascus—even from Antioch—to Tiberias. Nevertheless, I wondered whether there might be any other reasons for Claudia Procula's unexpected arrival.

After two days I could no longer master my curiosity but wrote a message to her on a double wax tablet, asking whether I might wait upon her. The servant soon returned, and told me that Claudia Procula had been amazed and delighted by my letter. I was to come immediately, as I was.

Because of my bad heel I had myself carried through the gardens as far as the arcade. There I stepped from my litter and limped in with my stick. The favor shown me attracted a great deal of attention and many guests came to watch my arrival. Earlier, Claudia Procula had let it be known that by reason of her ill-health she desired neither visitors nor marks of honor.

But the servants ushered me straight into a cool, sunny room where Claudia Procula was reclining on a couch with purple cushions. She was strikingly pale, and dull of eye. Beside her, in a respectful attitude, sat an expensively dressed Jewish woman of about her own age.

Claudia stretched forth both her slender hands to me, gave a cry of delight, and said, "Oh, Marcus, how glad I am to see a familiar and understanding person! What has been happening to you? What is the matter with your foot? I'm ill too, and sleepless, and when I do sleep I have nightmares, and I have pains in both stomach and liver."

To her companion she explained, "This is the young man I told you of. A friend of my childhood, Marcus Mezentius Manilianus. His father was the most eminent astronomer that Rome has ever had. He is related to the Maecenas family too, and so can claim descent from the Etruscans who in their day vied with Aeneas himself. I last saw him in Jerusalem at the passover, but I never expected to meet him here."

I let her prattle on, even though she did not keep strictly to the truth but exaggerated considerably. Yet if for some reason she wished to present everything in the best light and exalt me in the eyes of her companion, why should I object? Turning then to me she indicated the other woman and said, "This good woman is Johanna, wife of Herod Antipas' quaestor. I met her in Jerusalem and she has promised to keep me company as long as I remain here. I have complete trust in her."

The woman smiled and looked at me searchingly. She had a fat, flabby face, but her eyes showed her to be no fool; she was experienced in life.

"Greeting, Marcus Mezentius," she said. "But why do you, a Roman, wear a beard and dress like a child of Israel?"

"One adopts the customs of the country," I said easily. "I'm a philosopher and like to learn the ways and traditions of different places. And truth to tell, I feel a deep reverence for the God of Israel and his law, insofar as it does not prevent me from acknowledging the genius of Caesar."

Claudia Procula now noticed my clothes for the first time, and cried, "Why truly, you are much changed, and I hardly think my husband would approve of that dress." She chattered on with animation, talked of Pontius Pilate's health and cares, and offered me good wine, pastries and fruit; then at last she dismissed her servants and said, "Johanna, make sure that no one has stayed to listen to us. I will not tolerate eavesdroppers."

Johanna performed her task in an experienced manner, for having cast a casual glance into the anteroom, she wandered apparently at random around the room feeling at the hangings, and at last leaned out of the window. Claudia Procula beckoned me nearer, lowered her voice and asked, "Do you still remember Jesus of Nazareth, who was crucified in Jerusalem?"

I glanced at Johanna and hesitated; then replied, "Yes, I remember him, and he has obsessed my thoughts. I would have liked to hear more of him, but his disciples are suspicious people and disapprove of strangers."

Claudia Procula said, "The disciples have returned to Galilee and to their former occupations. Most of them are fishermen here on this lake."

"Yes," I said. "When I left Jerusalem I heard a rumor that they had gone from there. Many others are said to have followed them into Galilee. But will they not be persecuted here?"

Johanna put in eagerly, "No, no. Here no one will persecute them any more. Able advisers have persuaded the prince Herod that he would gain nothing by it. In fact, he is afraid of them and prefers to ignore them. He made a political error in beheading John the Baptist. Now he won't even hear the word prophet."

Claudia Procula explained, "You must remember that I did all in my power to prevent my husband from harming that holy man!"

"Why torment yourself with an old story?" I returned slyly. "Innocent men have been executed before now. The world is what it is. We cannot alter it. Forget him and nurse your health. That is why you're here."

Claudia Procula replied vehemently, "You don't understand what all this is about. The world is not what it was. Jesus of Nazareth rose from his tomb, though you did not believe it then. He has revealed himself to his own. Whether or not you believe it, he is here."

Johanna, in a fright, pressed her hand over her lady's mouth and warned her: "You know not what you say, *domina!*"

I looked at her attentively, remembering that Susanna had mentioned that very name, and made a bold guess: "I know your face, noble Johanna. You were with Jesus of Nazareth while he was alive; you cannot deny it."

Johanna stared at me in fear, and acknowledged, "I don't deny it at all and will never deny it. For his sake I left home and husband, and followed him until forced to return because of my husband's position. But how can you know anything of that?"

I felt tired and downcast, and unwilling to pretend any longer. "I know and I believe that he has risen from the dead," I said. "And therefore I believe also that he is the son of God. But what this implies I don't know. Nothing else like this has ever happened before. I wanted to seek his kingdom, but his own people did not know me and would not receive me. But hearing that he had gone before them into Galilee, I followed after them, hoping to find him here.

"But," I continued bitterly, "as soon as I arrived I got blood poisoning in my foot so that I couldn't move. That must be a sign that he will have nothing to do with me. But confess frankly, Claudia, that it is on his account that you too have come to Galilee."

Both women looked in profound astonishment first at each other and then at me. Then together they exclaimed, and asked, "Do you, a Roman and a philosopher, really believe that he has risen from the dead and come to Galilee?"

"I believe it because I must," I answered, still with bitterness. I was just then filled with a violent desire to unburden my heart, and I told them how I had visited Lazarus and met Mary Magdalene, and how the messengers Thomas and John had turned me away, and what had happened at the house of Simon of Cyrene, and how Matthew and Zaccheus had come to me and with menaces refused me even the right to utter the name of Jesus of Nazareth.

Johanna said, "That was wrong of them. I myself remember a time when a man who never even knew him healed a sick person in his name. The disciples forbade the man to do it; but then Jesus himself rebuked his disciples and said that at least that man would never speak ill of him. I don't understand why you shouldn't use his name, if you believe in him."

I told them too how I had brought Susanna with me from Jerusalem. "Do you know the old woman?" I asked Johanna.

Johanna, concealing her contempt with difficulty, replied, "Of course I know the quarrelsome old chatterbox. She's an ignorant rustic without knowledge of the law. Yet Jesus allowed even her to follow him."

Claudia Procula looked at me with surprise and misgivings, and said, "You are indeed changed, Marcus, since the Rome days. You seem to have forgotten even your Tullia for the sake of the Nazarene. Don't think I don't know of her. Roman gossip comes as far as Caesarea. I find it hard to understand what it is you're really seeking from Jesus of Nazareth."

"What do you seek?" I retorted irritably.

Claudia shrugged her now somewhat bony shoulders and said, "I'm a woman and have the right to dream. I know that if I met him, he would cure my sleeplessness and all my other ills. But above all, of course, I'm curious to see a prophet who has been crucified and has risen again from his grave."

I said, "I have lost all curiosity—all desire to dream. I seek only his kingdom, while it remains on earth. I've been told that he has the words of eternal life. But that's all the same to me. Tell me now whether he has indeed come to Galilee and revealed himself here to his own."

Johanna's face darkened as she said, "I am not sure. He confided the secret of his kingdom to his disciples, but to others and to us women he spoke only in parables. No doubt it was that we saw, yet did not see—heard and did not hear. The disciples keep themselves to themselves and don't tell the women anything. For this reason Mary is angry with them and has gone home to Magdala. All I know is that some days ago seven of them went out fishing in the morning, and came back with their nets full to bursting. Something had happened to make them exult and laugh for joy, but they wouldn't say what it was."

I said, "I'm surprised that those ignorant fishermen should now be at odds with Mary Magdalene, who has spent so much money on their account. At least one might have expected that they would have informed a lady of such high standing as yourself as to what is going on. I suspect that it is thanks to you that they're safe from persecution here."

"They're ungrateful folk," said Johanna. Then, trying to be fair, she added, "They must be guarding some secret which has been entrusted to them. But why did he choose *them?*"

Claudia Procula observed haughtily, "I at least, as wife of the Procurator of Judea, might expect the fellows to recognize my rank and tell their master that I wish to meet him. I have shown the greatest possible good will in requesting such a thing of such people. Besides, they might benefit secretly by my favor."

I could not refrain from saying, "Claudia, I believe you only imperfectly understand what his kingdom is. He is no sorcerer or impostor. Try to understand: he is the son of God."

Claudia, offended, snapped, "Don't forget that I myself am related to Ceasar and used often to dine at his table in the days when he lived in Rome."

Johanna threw out her hands as if signing to me, and said, "I'm only a woman, and Israel denies that women have souls.

Yet he allowed us to go with him, and in my heart I perceive something of his kingdom. His disciples still quarrel among themselves about whether and when he will found a kingdom in Israel. But Israel has rejected him and crucified him and invoked his blood upon its head. After that deed, Israel can no longer be God's chosen people—that much my common sense tells me."

I was beginning to weary of this profitless conversation, and Claudia Procula had dwindled in my estimation. Impatiently I asked, "Be that as it may, how are we to meet him?"

Johanna answered, "I don't know. We can only wait. I've waited and waited, and nothing has happened. Perhaps he has forgotten us woman. It frightens me too that you should have had a bad foot from the moment you arrived, so that you can't stir from the spot to look for him."

"I'm almost well again now," I said. "In a boat or a litter I could go anywhere. But my heart is heavy and I don't want to force myself upon him. I don't believe anyone can, for that matter. I imagine he appears only to those of his own choice. If need be, I will resign myself to the belief that I'm unworthy to behold him."

Claudia Procula remarked with a sneer, "How can you be so feeble? I'm impatient to see him; the baths alone will hardly cure my sleeplessness. If I were a man I should do something. But I have to think of my position."

Johanna pondered, and then, addressing me, suggested, "You could take a boat to Magdala and meet Mary. It is impossible on my husband's account for me to visit her, for in spite of everything she is a woman of evil reputation. For the same reason we can't invite her here to meet Claudia Procula, even in secret. Go to her, and ask her what we're to do. Explain that of course I'm no more ashamed of her company now than I was when we were wayfaring together; but that at present I have to consider my husband's position at court. This is a complicated matter which perhaps you can't altogether grasp, being a man; but as a woman she will understand it perfectly well."

Noting my hesitation she smiled wickedly and said, "You're a gay young Roman. You may safely visit her; no one will wonder at that. In her day she was possessed by seven demons, and even now her reputation throughout Galilee remains consistent with that, although she has turned over a new leaf—I think."

I began to feel that I had nothing to gain by joining in these feminine quarrels. I promised at all events to think over the proposal, and after that we chatted for a while about everyday things. Claudia Procula asked whether I would accompany her to the city to watch the races a little later, when her health was improved. Herod Antipas is proud of his city and of the race course and the theatre he has built, and Claudia felt bound to comply in some degree with what was expected of one in her position. She then dismissed me, and we promised to let each other know without delay if either of us heard anything of Jesus of Nazareth. Claudia also promised to invite me to dine with her soon.

On my way back to the inn I noticed a Sidonian trader who had sat himself down in the shady arcade and was unrolling fabrics from his staff. I stopped and bought a gold-embroidered silken cloth which I sent at once as a present to Claudia Procula.

Mary of Beret had been impatiently awaiting me, and had certainly seen me haggling with the curly-bearded Sidonian. She must have thought I had bought something for her, for after vainly waiting for a time she began nagging, and said, "I see you can walk perfectly well now, so long as it's to do something you like. You keep me in here behind the curtains as if you were ashamed of my company, although no one here knows any more of me than that I've been nursing you and caring for you while you lay at death's door. I would like to meet a few people too, and talk to other women in these lovely gardens, listen to music and be rowed out onto the lake beneath an awning. But you never give a thought to me—only to yourself and your own comforts."

I was filled with deep dejection when I thought of the fervor with which we had left Jerusalem and of how today all our hopes seemed to be running out into the sand. Claudia Procula had spoken of Jesus of Nazareth in a very different way during those guilt-laden days in Jerusalem when the earth shook. Johanna her companion also was surely different now from what she had been when she walked with Jesus of Nazareth without a thought of her home or her husband's exalted position as keeper of Herod Antipas' moneybags. Here among marble arcades and gardens, where gentle flute music sounded from the myrtle groves amid the sulphurous smell of the hot springs, everything seemed to have reverted to the days of old, and all this luxury and comfort left no room for the supernatural.

I said, "Mary of Beret, do you not remember why we came here?"

Mary tossed her head, stared at me with round eyes and said reproachfully, "I remember better than you, and am eagerly awaiting word from Nathan or Susanna. There is nothing else I can do. In the meantime why should I not enjoy the things here that are new to me?"

"Everything here belongs only to this world," I said. "One tires more quickly of this kind of society and surroundings than of anything else. I would gladly exchange it all for even a distant glimpse of the risen man."

"Of course, of course," Mary assented impatiently. "I too. But why should I not enjoy myself while I wait? I am like a poor country girl who has come into a Syrian toyshop on her first visit to the town. I don't imagine I shall ever have all these things myself—I'm not such a fool. But why shouldn't I look and touch?"

I did not understand her and was bored by her arguing. "You shall," I promised her stiffly, longing to be rid of her.

"Tomorrow I will hire a boat and we will go to Magdala. I have heard that the rich dove breeder has left her companions and returned to her own house. We will call upon her."

Mary of Beret was far from pleased at my promise. "Mary Magdalene is a hotheaded woman," she grumbled. "It is true that she was the only one who was kind to me, and spoke to me as to a human being and convinced me that Jesus of Nazareth was a king; yet I'm afraid of her."

"Why?" I asked in surprise. "It was she who first sent you into my path by the gate in the old wall, and put those words into your mouth."

"She might require me to do something that I don't want to do any more, now that you have taken me under your protection," explained Mary. "Her will is stronger than mine, so that when she gives an order I have no will at all."

"But what order of hers are you afraid of?" I asked.

Mary complained, "She dresses in black. She might tell me to take off these beautiful clothes that you've given me and wear the sackcloth of a penitent. She might order me to leave you, now that you've brought me to Galilee. That's what I'm afraid of."

"Mary of Beret," I exclaimed, "what is it you're really hoping for, and imagining about me?"

"I hope for nothing and imagine nothing," she cried with equal vehemence, and a fierce toss of her head. "Do not think it. I just want to live in your company, one day at a time. You sang another tune a few days ago when you lay burning with fever and tossing in your bed, and I moistened your cracked lips and you begged and prayed me to keep my hand on your forehead, and wanted me to hold your hand all night while you slept. But don't fancy that I'm imagining anything on that account—oh no. These days have been good days and among the best of my whole life. I would not like them to come to an end before they must. But do what you like, of course. It's evident that we shall not do as *I* like."

I saw that it was now high time to be rid of her. The longer she stayed with me, the more firmly she bound me to her day by day, so that I became quite needlessly accustomed to her presence. The same thing happens to a man who thoughtlessly acquires a slave or a dog, and becomes attached to the dog or dependent on the slave.

Next day, therefore, I hired a fishing boat and two rowers, and we set off across the bright billows of the Sea of Galilee towards Magdala. From vanity Mary of Beret tried to shade her face from the sun, for at the inn she had done as the other women of the place and diligently anointed her face with cucumber juice to remove her sunburn. During the journey on donkeyback she had never given a thought to such a thing.

I chatted to the oarsmen so as to accustom myself to the Galilean spech. They were surly men and gave curt answers to my questions. As we rowed past Tiberias it was plain that they shunned this fair, new Greek city which Herod Antipas founded only a few years ago, and on which he has spent a great deal. To pass it the more swiftly they tried to hoist the sail, but the wind was unfavorable and changeable, and they at last had to resign themselves to rowing.

I remembered that Jesus of Nazareth was said to have walked on the waters of this lake. Here in the bright sunshine, with the hills hanging in brown and blue haze on the further side, with the wind blowing freshly and the water splashing, the story seemed incredible. I was possessed by the melancholy idea that I was chasing a mirage, a dream, or a tale invented by superstitious fishermen. Now, after my illness, an immeasurable time seemed to have elapsed since the days in Jerusalem. It was as if Jesus of Nazareth had never existed.

To bring myself back to reality I asked the men, "Did you ever see Jesus of Nazareth in the days when he taught the people on the shores of this lake?"

They glanced at one another, rested on their oars and asked suspiciously, "Why do you wish to know that, stranger?"

"I was in Jerusalem when he was crucified," I explained. "To my mind he didn't deserve such a disgraceful fate."

The fishermen said, "You can understand it; he was a Galilean, and we Galileans are despised in Jerusalem. But it was his own fault for delivering himself into the hands of greedy priests and sanctimonious Pharisees."

"Did you ever see him?" I asked again.

They hesitated and looked at each other; then their racial pride triumphed and they declared, "Certainly we did, and many times. Once there were five thousand of us listening to him. He fed us all on five barley loaves and two fishes, and we were filled. Indeed, there were twelve baskets of food left over. That was the kind of man he was."

"What did he speak of? Do you remember what he taught?" I asked eagerly.

But they were ill-at-ease and said, "It is not fitting for simple men like us to repeat what he said. We should only draw the wrath of the authorities upon us."

I encouraged them: "Tell me at least something of what you remember. I'm only a traveling foreigner; I will tell no tales."

They said, "Remember then that it was he who said it, not we." Then with one voice they continued: "Blessed are the poor, for theirs is the kingdom. Blessed are the quiet ones, for they shall inherit the earth. Blessed are they who are persecuted and mocked. Blessed are you, for great is your reward in heaven. No one can serve two masters. Grieve not. It is harder for a rich man to enter the kingdom than for a camel to go through the eye of a needle."

I had the impression that they had often recalled these words among themselves and adopted what they best liked of the Nazarene's teaching. They remembered no more of it, or were unwilling to repeat it, and there was an unmistakable look of gloating pleasure in their eyes when they looked at my good clothes and my cushion.

"What more do you remember of him?" I asked.

They answered, "He was a good fisherman. He could point out a shoal of fish, though others might have cast their nets in vain all night. Once they came ashore laden to the gunwales when others returned from the lake empty-handed. He could cow the winds, and flatten great waves in a short time. They say he healed the sick, too, although we never cared about that, for we have never been ill. What surprised us most was that he came from inland, from Nazareth, and yet had such good knowledge of water and wind and the movements of fish."

I could get no more out of them, ask as I would. They only grew suspicious. At last I remarked, "In Jerusalem it was said that he rose up from his tomb and walked back to Galilee. Have you heard anything of this?"

They pulled harder at their oars, and answered only after a pause. "Women's gossip. No dead man leaves his grave. He was a man as we are, even though he did teach and perform miracles. You won't get us to fall into that trap however cleverly you choose your words."

After that they would say nothing more, except, "These are stories from the Capernaum side. We are fishermen of Tiberias."

Magdala is a large fishing village with thousands of inhabitants. From a long way off we smelled the stench of the fish salteries coming to us across the water. When the boatmen had jumped overboard and hauled the craft up onto the beach I paid them and sent them home. Not until I had limped through the village, supported by Mary and my stick, did I let her ask where Mary Magdalene lived. She was well known. A large group of buildings, away from the town toward the dove cleft, was pointed out to me at once. A vegetable grower on his way home from a visit to the village readily offered to let me ride his donkey when he noticed that I was limping. He smiled in a curious way when speaking of Mary Magdalene, but said humbly and appreciatively, "She is a clever and very rich woman. She has many dove catchers in her service, and in her big lofts she raises doves herself for the temple. She owns an herb garden and shares in the salteries. She travels a great deal, but is said to have recently returned home."

Glancing at me sideways he remarked with a friendly grin, "She's not as young as she was. They say she has altered her way of life and gives alms to the poor. But you must know your own business best."

I had started this journey without expecting anything from it at all, but as I approached her house, sitting between two empty vegetable baskets on the donkey's back, I was seized with an unexpected longing to behold her white face again. I remembered her as I had seen her in Lazarus' guest room, and it seemed to me that I had never before longed to see any woman in just this way. The owner of the donkey saw my expression and said, "You seem to be like all the others. The nearer you come to her house, the more impatiently you hurry on. I don't want to go near it, so forgive me if I leave you here at the fork."

He continued on his way, urging on his donkey so as to increase his distance from the house as quickly as he could. Mary of Beret sighed, and said warningly, "No good will come of this. Let us turn back. The sun hurts my eyes, however much I cover my head. I am sweaty all over and can hardly breathe."

But I limped boldly in through the gate, and in the middle of the great courtyard I saw a woman dressed in black feeding the doves. A cloud of doves flapped about her; some sat on her shoulders, others swung on her hands. When she caught sight of us she threw her grain on the ground, rubbed her hands together and came to meet us, baring her face. Surprised but pleased she greeted Mary and me, and exclaimed, "I felt that someone was on the way, but I had no idea it was you, Marcus the Roman, and you, Mary of Beret."

"Peace be with you, Mary Magdalene," I said, and looked at her lined, white face, and her eyes, which were filled with such joy that I could have thrown myself on the ground and embraced her knees.

She warded off the doves that still fluttered about her head, and showed us across the court into a garden and to a summer-house that she had had built there. First of all she fetched water with her own hands and knelt before me to wash my feet, heedless of my protests. The touch of her hands felt soothing and sweet to my injured foot. Mary's feet too she washed, though Mary of Beret tried to push her away, holding one hand to her mouth and tittering. Then, having given us fresh spring water to drink, she dismissed Mary with the words, "Go and look at the dovecotes and at my house, and trouble us no longer, foolish girl."

Mary of Beret almost ran off, as if relieved to get away. Mary Magdalene looked after her, shaking her head, then turned to me and asked, "What have you done to that girl? Was it you who gave her those gaudy clothes? I think a demon lurks in her eyes, though she was meek and penitent enough in Jerusalem."

I defended myself: "I believe I have done her no harm. I haven't so much as touched her, if that's what you mean. She nursed me faithfully in Tiberias when I lay there sick with my bad foot."

Mary Magdalene said, "When a man does something for a woman with the best possible intentions he often harms her more than he knows. You're no fit guardian for such a girl, Marcus. You had better part company with her."

"She seeks Jesus of Nazareth as I do," I replied, and unburdened my heart by telling her of our departure from Jerusalem, of how Susanna and Nathan had left me in the lurch and how, in Tiberias, I had met Johanna in Claudia Procula's rooms. Mary Magdalene nodded as I told my story, and I saw a hard smile overspread her white face.

"I know the greedy Susanna and the haughty Johanna," she

said shortly. "There must have been scales over my eyes during the time when we walked together like sisters; I saw only Jesus. You have seen enough of his disciples to know the kind of men they are, and how tight-fistedly they guard the secret of the kingdom. Probably, like me, you're wondering by now of what kind of material he expected to build his kingdom. I returned home to wait, having had enough of the company of stubborn men and the mutual envy of the women. I know that he walked before us into Galilee, but it wouldn't surprise me if he never wanted to see any of us again. Perhaps he is as disappointed in us as we are in each other, in our hearts. I left the fishermen to their fishing, and his mother too has gone home to her own place in Nazareth."

She pressed her hands together, rocked her shoulders in pain and lamented, "Why am I only human, and a woman at that, and so obstinately hardhearted, now that he's no longer with us? His kingdom is slipping away from me. Woe upon me, who am so feeble in faith that I no longer fully trust in him!"

She looked about her in horror, as if she had discerned the presence of lurking figures, and cried, "He is the light of the world. When he is absent, darkness steals about me though the sun shines. I'm afraid lest the evil spirits return to me. But if they come I will live no longer. I would rather hang myself. I have suffered enough already."

Her anguish oppressed me like a stone in my breast. Yet I tried to console her, and told her of Johanna's belief that Jesus had appeared to the disciples when they were out fishing one morning.

"I've heard of that," Mary said curtly. "But those rustics were most likely just pleased at having caught a hundred and fifty big fish. The net was so full that they had to haul it right to the beach so as not to tear it. If they really had met our teacher, why should they not have told of it, to comfort others?"

It was as if she bore a grudge in her heart against the disciples and would be envious of them if Jesus really had revealed himself to them in Galilee, and not to her. In a way I could understand this, for it was she who had first hastened to the tomb at dawn, and she to whom Jesus had shown himself for the first time after his resurrection.

"Mary Magdalene," I said, "don't yield to despair. If he has returned to Galilee, then his kingdom is near. Perhaps I have no part in it, and perhaps he will turn me away as his disciples did. But I am sure that you will meet him again, if he is in Galilee."

Mary gave me a proud glance from her dark eyes and said, "Do you comfort me, Roman, when his own give me no comfort?"

Yet her face began to shine as if the sun were shedding light upon it, although we were sitting in the shade of her summer house. She touched my hand, and her touch was again full of strength as she asked, "Do you really believe that? Surely I do too, though my heart is rebellious because I cannot bring myself sufficiently to revere the disciples whom he has chosen. I am a wicked, worthless woman not to accept his will. Teach me what humility is, Roman. I deserve it."

"Tell me rather whether you think he will receive me into his kingdom, although I am a Roman," I said dejectedly.

Mary Magdalene replied in the same contemptuous tone as Johanna: "The disciples are still expecting him to build a new kingdom in Israel. For me he is the light of the world. Why should it not concern you as closely as the children of Israel, if you believe him to be the Christ? His kingdom is eternal life, and no earthly realm."

Her words made my heart quake with dread. "What is eternal life?" I asked.

Mary Magdalene shook her head. "I don't know," she confessed. "I suppose he is the only one who does know. That was not the kind of knowledge he taught when he walked hereabouts; he taught people how they should live for his kingdom. I am not sufficiently humble or childlike in my heart to understand what eternal life is. I only know that it is in him and with him. And there is nothing else I need to know."

I pondered what she had said. "How shall I live, then?" I asked. "Is it not enough to try to be quiet and humble of heart?"

"Love your neighbor as yourself," said Mary Magdalene. "Do to others what you would like them to do to you." Suddenly she clapped her hands to her face and burst out sobbing. "How should I teach you when I myself have betrayed his teaching? We were all like brothers and sisters when we walked with him. He has been away from us but a very short time, and already I've begun to hate and envy my brothers and sisters in my heart. Perhaps he has sent you to me so that I might escape from my wickedness and be humble."

All at once she touched my bad foot, held her hand on the half-healed boil and prayed aloud, "Jesus Christ, son of God, have mercy on me a sinner. If it be your will, let this foot be well again as if it had never felt pain."

She looked up, fixed her eyes on me in breathless expectation and said, "If he wills this, it is a sign. Throw away your stick and walk."

I stood up, let the stick fall and walked a few steps. I did not limp, and felt no pain in my foot. At first I wondered, then turned back to my place and explained, "May this be the sign you prayed for. I need no sign from him, for I believe already. To be honest, my foot is well again, and new skin has grown where the boil was. I suppose I was limping from sheer habit, since the Greek physician who lanced it warned me so sternly not to strain my foot."

But Mary Magdalene smiled, picked up my stick from the ground and asked, "Shall I take back my prayer and let you limp again?"

I answered hastily, "No, don't do that. I should be sure to limp all my life if you called upon him for that."

My words startled Mary Magdalene, and looking around as if she had been caught doing some forbidden thing, she said hurriedly, "No, no, we can wish no evil to another with his help; we harm only ourselves then. And one cannot curse in his name—only bless."

She smiled radiantly and stared before her and through me as if she saw something invisible to me. At the same time she bent my stick between her hands, and to my boundless astonishment I saw that it seemed as supple as a withy, although it was a perfectly stiff staff of hard oak. I could only stare, unable to believe my eyes, until she woke from her thoughts, felt my eyes upon her and looked at me.

"What are you staring at?" she asked, and she stopped bending the stick.

I raised both hands in warning, and whispered, "Bend the stick again as you were doing just now."

She tried, putting forth all her strength, but the stick no longer gave by a hairsbreadth. I took it from her, and it was the same stiff hard stick I had leaned on when I limped. The conjuring trick hadn't been performed deliberately, for she had been sitting plunged in thought, unseeing, and could not make out why I was so greatly excited. I went into no explanations, but preferred to think that this pliancy of hard wood was a gentle sign to me, because I had not believed that my foot was healed by the power of Jesus of Nazareth's name. Why it happened I could not imagine, since in fact I had not wished for anything. But hope was kindled in my heart once more.

Nor was it witchcraft that made me see the stick bend, for I felt none of the rigidity one knows when a sorcerer performs his tricks. On the contrary, everything about me felt pleasant and fresh and light. Therefore I said, "Mary Magdalene, you fortunate woman! He is your Lord, and you must not be impatient. When you call upon him he is with you even though you don't see him. How this can be I don't understand, but so I believe. You are indeed blessed among women."

We were both filled with new hope when we left the summerhouse. Mary Magdalene showed me her garden and her dovecotes, and told me how the birds were caught in the cleft nearby, and how as a young girl she had climbed its lofty steeps without fear of robbers and without dizziness.

We entered her house. It was full of fine rugs and costly furniture, but she said she had destroyed her Greek vases and sculptures after being delivered from the power of the demons, because the law of Israel forbids the faithful to make images and likenesses of man or beast. From this she went on to relate how Jesus, when—as so often—plunged in thought, would take a stick and draw in the sand. But he always erased with his foot what hc had drawn or written before Mary or anyone else could see what it was. She told me other things about Jesus of Nazareth whenever she happened to think of them, as we wandered through her great house.

She had bidden her servants prepare a meal for us, but having asked me to recline at her table she did not keep me company there. She said, "Allow me to follow the custom of my country and serve you while you eat." She also summoned Mary of Beret to wait upon me, told her to pour water over my hands and smilingly instructed her as to how a man was best served at table. She herself mixed wine for me to drink. It was a light Galilean white wine which went to my head like a breeze. After the salt and sweet mouthfuls that introduced the meal, she offered me fried fish and then pieces of dove in rosemary sauce; and I know not when I last tasted such well-cooked and delicious food.

Not until I was replete and could not have swallowed another morsel would she consent to sit on the mat at my feet and eat, and allow Mary to eat too. She had mellowed and brightened, and her face was lit by a lovely smile. Regarding her through the fine gauze of the wine I realized that she must indeed have been one of the most beautiful and alluring women in the land. Even Marv of Beret was encouraged by her kindness, and at last ventured to say, "When you smile as you are smiling now, Mary Magdalene, I can well believe that many men have journeyed all the way from Damascus and Alexandria on your account, and that with the help of their gifts you were able to build your great house and fine furniture. But how is it done? Teach me the way to acquire such astonishing presents in return for something for which the camel drivers of Jerusalem pay only a few farthings."

Mary Magdalene's face darkened at once, and she said, "Don't ask me of such things. But be assured that no woman can learn without instruction. Only a woman possessed by an evil spirit, or by many, can achieve it. Yet at the same time that demon so torments and consumes that woman that she seems to go with a noose perpetually about her throat. She is satisfied with nothing and enjoys nothing, and at last she hates herself even more than the men, and the men more than anything else."

Mary of Beret shot her an incredulous sideways glance, tilted her head and said doubtfully, "I expect what you say is true. Yet I would choose the demon if he could make me wonderful in the eyes of men."

Mary Magdalene slapped her across the mouth and said, "Be silent, foolish girl! You know not what you say."

Mary of Beret was frightened, and burst out weeping. Mary Magdalene breathed hard, sprinkled water round about herself and said, "I don't ask your pardon for striking you; it was not from anger I did it, but for your own good. I hope that someone would do the same for me if ever I said anything as witless as you did. A demon can force you to live in tombs and eat garbage; no chains can bind you and not the strongest men can hold you when the demon rages in you. And I know not which demons are the worse: those that gnaw at the body or those that wear away the soul until only emptiness remains.

"You have saddened me," she went on, "but I bear you no grudge on that account. No doubt it was necessary that you should remind me of my past. Beneath the surface of my body nothing remained but a skeleton gnawed clean, and with me as their instrument the demons drove many men to destruction. My sin was measureless, yet it was forgiven me. You should pray, 'Lead us not into temptation but deliver us from evil.' Instead, you pray in your heart, 'Lead me into temptation and drive me into the arms of evil.' I can see that, in your eyes and your mouth, and your feet which you rub so impatiently on the floor. Do you no longer remember who it was in Jerusalem who promised to be content with salt fish and a piece of barley bread for the rest of her life, if only she might be rescued from her misery? For this reason I set you in the path of this Roman, but instead of casting your eyes upon the ground in thankfulness, you're trying to set snares for his feet."

Mary of Beret sobbed in her fright and dared not look at me. In my heart I could not help pitying her, but Mary Magdalene stared at her with somberly furrowed brow.

"Think carefully what it is you want," she said. "Do you want temptation, sin and evil that will destroy you, or do you want a simple straightforward life?"

Mary of Beret looked up and declared fervently, "I want to have my sins forgiven like you, and I want to be cleansed so that I may be pure and untouched once more. Don't make me tell you what I would like then. But might it not come true if I pray devoutly?"

Mary Magdalene said in a persuasive tone, "I understand you better than you think and I read your simple mind. Trust me, I have more experience than you. Take off those gaudy clothes and stay with me, for your own good. I will teach you to catch doves and to sweep evil thoughts from your mind. Perhaps Jesus of Nazareth will have compassion on you, should he ever show himself to me."

But Mary of Beret wept even more bitterly than before, clung to my knees and cried, "This is just what I was afraid of, Marcus, and you mustn't leave me in her hands. She will make me her day laborer or sell me as a slave. She has a terrible reputation, though you don't know of it."

Mary Magdalene shook her head and declared, "If you were more experienced you would understand that you must now part from Marcus, for a time. Otherwise your Roman will grow thoroughly tired of you and send you shamefully away. How do you know but that with me you may not learn something that will make you more pleasing in his eyes?"

I could only sigh with relief that Mary Magdalene should so tactfully seek to relieve me of a burden that was becoming intolerable. Mary of Beret hugged my knees and wetted my mantle with her tears, but when she had wept for a while she grew quiet and resigned herself to her fate. Mary Magdalene sent her to wash her face and put on new clothes, and said when she had gone, "I have a responsibility toward that girl. She is still so young that her heart turns as readily to good as to evil. Such a girl is too great a temptation for a man. It says well for you that you have withstood the test and not yielded. Mary of Beret in her simplicity is one of the least among us. If you were to seduce her it would be better for someone to hang a millstone around your neck and drop you into the sea."

"I have had no intention of seducing her," I said in an injured tone. "On the contrary it was she who in her childishness tried to seduce me. If I had not fallen sick I might have taken her from sheer boredom when Susanna and Nathan left me in the lurch. But this way is best. Look after her, and that will leave me freer to search for Jesus of Nazareth."

Mary Magdalene remarked, "I don't believe Susanna has deceived you. She is too simple-minded for that. She may be lingering in Capernaum in the same bewilderment as everyone else because nothing is happening. But allow me to ask what you desire of life, Marcus Mezentius."

Her question made me feel humble of heart; I thought about my life, and began to tell her of it: "I have been fortunate. When I was young I learned foreign languages in Antioch and was educated at the school of rhetoric in Rhodes. My highest aim was an official position as secretary to some Governor in the east, or a sojourn in Rome as domestic philosopher to some uncultured rich man. In reality I was embittered by my failure to enter the cavalry when I came to Rome, although otherwise I had no inclination for soldiering. Through a certain will I acquired the right to wear a thumb ring, but by then that distinction meant nothing to me. In fact I rather despise it, and keep the ring in my purse. As soon as I was able to acquire everything I wanted, I found that scarcely any of it had any real value. After that I was blinded by desire, until I was compelled to flee from Rome for fear of being murdered. What do I desire of life? I can't answer that question. I can only ask myself what power it was that made me leave Alexandria for Jerusalem and what power halted me before the cross of the king of the Jews when the whole world was darkened.

"By a fortunate chance, it became possible during my early manhood to attain to everything which I had so hotly and vainly longed for in youth," I went on. "Friendship, success, worldly pleasures. I could even have won power had I desired it, but that sort of craving I have never understood. Soon I had only the taste of ashes in my mouth. After immoderate pleasures I was beyond consolation. But I do know that I have no wish to live as a bloated, burnt-out old man in Rome, thinking old thoughts and eternally telling worn-out anecdotes like an imbecile. That is the only future I can see for myself if I return to Rome. I should be beheaded anyway, for as you may know, a *coup d'état* is expected there soon. Then everyone will be asked on whose side he has stood. I have enough respect for Caesar's genius not to meddle in the intrigues of a bloodthirsty, low-born man. I would rather be quiet and humble of heart."

"What do you hope for from Jesus of Nazareth?" asked Mary Magdalene.

"I have sensed his kingdom," I said, "and it is not just dreams and poetry, like Vergil's kingdom of death; it's as real as the world we live in. Yes, when I think of him, his reality blends with this one in a confusing way. Mary Magdalene, I'm happy to be living in these days, just for the sake of knowing that he is in Galilee. No, I neither ask nor wish for anything from him but what he himself chooses to give me. For his kingdom cannot be just an ordinary earthly realm, but something new which I don't yet comprehend. Otherwise there would be no sense in anything, for kingdoms have been founded since the beginning of the world and all have gone under, even Alexander's. Probably only Rome will endure. For that reason alone his kingdom cannot be an earthly one."

We spoke further on other matters until Mary of Beret returned to us. She had washed her face, combed her hair smooth, and put on a white mantle, and her feet were bare. Like this she looked so touchingly young that my heart softened toward her and I could think no more ill of her. That our parting might not be too sorrowful, I decided to return to Tiberias that same day. Mary Magdalene promised to let me know at once if she heard anything of importance, and bade me greet Johanna and Claudia Procula from her.

I walked back to the village of Magdala and my foot gave me no more trouble at all, so that for a moment I considered walking all the way to Tiberias by the shore road. But down by the beach I met the two fishermen who had brought us to Magdala; they had evidently waited for me, for they were in no hurry and I had paid them well. The sky was now overcast and the wind had freshened so that the waves of the lake foamed white. They stood observing the sky and the black clouds hanging up among the hills above the dove cleft, and they said, "The Sea of Galilee is treacherous. A sudden squall can drive a boat offcourse and swamp it. Can you swim, lord?"

I told them that in my youth I had won a wager by swimming from Rhodes to the mainland, undaunted by currents; but they had never heard of Rhodes and so could not appreciate the feat. It's true that a boat followed me all the way and that I was in no real danger. But I had been spurred on less by the wager than by my infatuation for a teasing girl who had promised to crown me with a garland if I won it. So I put forth my uttermost strength in that swim, though when the wager was won, I no longer felt attracted to the girl.

I stretched myself out now on the cushions in the stern of the boat and watched the clouds race over the sky, while the fishermen girded up their mantles, shoved off and grasped their oars. I realized that they knew I had visited Mary Magdalene. How could such a thing remain a secret in a fishing village where everyone must have known everyone else and a stranger would be observed with curiosity? Nor were they surprised that I had left Mary of Beret, but laughingly exchanged a few jests with one another.

"What do you mean by those words?" I demanded.

"Nothing bad. Nothing bad at all," they assured me. "Just that the lady dove catcher seems to have gone back to her old ways. How much did she pay you for the girl?"

I owed them no explanations, but being hurt on Mary Magdalene's account I said, "She allowed the girl to stay with her out of pure kindness, to learn her trade."

Both men roared with laughter, saying, "Of course, of course; the girl will certainly learn a trade. Mary has taught many girls to play upon heathen instruments, dance lewd dances and catch doves—but what kind of doves we won't, for decency's sake, mention."

Before I could reply to them I heard the howl of a squall, the boat heeled over, the waves rose steeply and a foaming sea hurled water into the boat, soaking my cushions. I had time to say, "That's a warning to you for your wicked words," but then we were all three kept busy trimming the boat, which scudded like a chip before the stiff wind toward the opposite shore. If we had continued on our true course we should have been swamped in an instant.

Both these blockheads wanted to step the mast and hoist sail, but I forbade them sternly, for we carried no ballast.

Lightning flashed among the thunderclouds that rolled out from behind the hills, and the day darkened. We bailed for our lives but could not prevent the boat from filling, and soon we were rolling and pitching and drifting nearer the eastern shore, with water to the gunwales. Drenched and frightened the fishermen gave me menacing looks and said, "We took a curse aboard when we took you, you Roman heathen. We have made ourselves guilty of a godless action in helping you to carry an Israelite girl to a house of joy. But we did not know your purpose."

I clung fast to the boat's edge where I sat up to the neck in water, and flung back my answer: "It is you who have brought a curse upon yourselves by speaking ill of Mary Magdalene."

The water was not very cold, yet we were chilled through by the time the wind dropped enough for us to bail out the boat and bring her ashore at the mouth of a dried-up stream. The level strip of beach was narrower and bleaker than that of the western side, and the mountains rose steeply in front of us. The wind was still blowing strongly and the waves rushed so violently in upon the shore that the fishermen were loth to put out again in that headwind, even though they believed it would drop toward evening.

Dusk began to fall and we were cold, though we wrung out our clothes as well as we could. A little way off, where the low beach ended at the foot of the hills, we spied a modest shed with a glimmering fire in front of it. I proposed that we should go there and dry our clothes, but the men hesitated and said, "We're on the wrong shore. Luckily we have no nets with us, or we should be fined for unlawful fishing. Robbers and criminals flee here too, from Galilee. And lepers live in the caves."

They had flint and iron with them, but the storm had soaked all the dry rushes on the beach so that we had no kindling. I started toward the shed and after further hesitation both men unwillingly followed me. When I came closer I saw a man sitting before the fire. He threw an armful of twigs on it so that it blazed up. I smelled grilled fish and freshly baked bread. Beside the hut a throwing net was hung out to dry.

"Peace be with you," I said in greeting to the solitary fisherman. "We were caught in the storm. Will you allow us to dry our clothes by your fire?"

He willingly made room, and I took off my clothes and spread them out to dry over a stick. I saw that he had heated some flat stones and baked bread upon them, while on embers at the bottom of a pit he was grilling two big fish. The sixth hour had already passed and the shore was swiftly darkening in the shadows of the hills, although we could still see light glowing over the houses and arcades of Tiberias on the western side.

I looked more closely at the fisherman and found him to be a man with clear-cut features and a gentle, simple appearance; a man of whom one need have no fear. He greeted my two rowers kindly too, and showed them a place by the fire. They felt his net and asked what sort of catch he had made. He answered shyly that he hoped the storm would drive a shoal into the bay where the stream ran out, and that he meant to try his luck there next morning.

Without explicit invitation to us, he took up a loaf, blessed it, broke off a piece for each of us and took one himself. He had sour wine, too, some of which he poured into a wooden bowl carved from the root of a vine, blessed that also and passed it around so that all four of us drank from it in turn. He had cooked the fish well, but having no salt, had seasoned it with chives and bitter herbs. We sat in silence and ate. I noticed that now and then my companions cast a suspicious look at the man who sat looking at the ground and smiling to himself as if enjoying every mouthful. When he had eaten he picked up a little stick, apparently to mask his shyness, and began abstractedly drawing in the sand with it.

While we ate, our clothes began steaming in the heat of the fire and were soon dry. The stiffness left my limbs, warmth returned to my body and I felt comfortable and well content. I was overcome by drowsiness as I sat there, and could hardly keep my eyes open. I looked with gratitude at the friendly man who without a word had so hospitably shared his meal with us. I noted his scarred hands and feet and seemed to detect something feverish and haggard in his face, as if he had been suffering from some illness and had withdrawn into solitude to recover. But I did not want to seem inquisitive, since the fishermen asked him no further questions. Without even noticing it I fell asleep, naked as I was by the fire, and just as I dropped off I felt him covering me with my dry clothes.

I dreamed then, and awoke and sat up with tears pouring from my eyes. The two fishermen were sound asleep beside me, snoring gently. The tears ran hot and smarting down my cheeks, and an unspeakable sense of desolation filled me after my dream. The fire had gone out. From the stars and moon I saw that it was already the third watch of the night. The lake shone before me, level and smooth as a mirror. But there were only three of us; the fourth man had gone. Seeing this I felt a great dread. I threw on my clothes and sprang up, and it was with relief I saw that he had only gone down to the water's edge and was looking out over the lake. I wrapped my mantle around me, went quickly over to him and stood beside him.

"What are you looking at?" I asked.

He didn't turn, but answered, "I saw the heavens opening and the glory of my father, and I longed to go home to my father."

I noticed that I had addressed him in Greek and that he answered in Greek. From this and from his words the thought struck me that he might be one of John the Baptist's disciples, and had fled from Herod's persecution to this side of the lake to live in solitude by fishing.

I said, "I too seek the kingdom. I was awakened by tears of longing. Show me where the Way lies."

He said, "There is only one Way. Whatever you do to the least of these, you do to me."

He said further, "I do not give as the world gives. But be not sad or afraid. The spirit of truth shall come after me, but the world cannot receive him for it cannot see him and does not know him. But if you know him, he will stay with you and be in you. I forsake no one."

My heart turned to water within me, tears blurred my sight and I raised my hands awkwardly but dared not touch him. "You don't speak as men speak," I whispered. "You speak as one having power."

He said, "To me is given all power in heaven and on earth."

Only now did he turn to me. In the light of the stars and moon I saw his sweet, grave smile as he looked at me. His gaze undressed me, just as if one garment after another were falling from my body and I was becoming more and more naked. There was nothing disagreeable about this feeling; it was a deliverance.

When he had looked at me he pointed across the lake and said, "Over there in the Tetrarch's city, in the Greek theatre, a girl is weeping because she has lost her brother and has no one to turn to. What was it you dreamed?"

"I saw a white horse," I remembered.

"Be it so," he returned. "Soon you will see a chariot race. Wager a sum of money on the white team. Then find the girl and give her your winnings."

"How, in so big a city, shall I find a girl who has lost her brother?" I asked. "And how much shall I wager?"

He smiled again, but now his smile was so sorrowful that it cut me to the heart. "Ah, Marcus, you ask so much so needlessly," he said in reproof.

But I didn't understand his warning. I merely asked in astonishment, "How do you know my name? Do I know you? It does seems to me that I have seen you somewhere."

He shook his head and said, "Is it not enough that I know you?"

I saw that he wanted to conceal his own identity, and became more convinced that he was one of the quiet ones in the land whose mind had been clouded by brooding on his faith, and by solitude. Why else should he have boasted that he possessed all power in heaven and on earth? Yet he might have the gift of prophecy. Therefore I resolved to remember his hint. But he said further, "Oh, you man! You see and yet see not. You hear and hear not. But one day, Marcus, you will remember. Then you will die for my name's sake, that my name may be glorified, through you, as my father's name has been glorified through me."

"What evil is this that you foretell?" I said in horror, not at all grasping what he meant. I thought perhaps he couldn't speak Greek properly and that I had misunderstood him.

He sighed heavily and let his mantle suddenly drop from his shoulders so that he was naked to the waist. He was so poor that he had not even a body garment. Turning away from me he said, "Touch my back."

I stretched out my hand, passed it over his back and felt the weals of the scourge. He sighed again and put his hand to his side. Following it with my own I felt a deep scar. He seemed indeed to have been persecuted and ill-treated, so it was not surprising that he should be a little queer in the head. Silently I cursed these Jews who tortured each other like this for the sake of their faith; for there was no evil in this man, whatever he said. Filled with a strong compassion, I said to him, "Tell me your name at least. Perhaps I might help you, so that you may no longer be persecuted."

He said, "If you acknowledge me before men when the time comes, I will acknowledge you before my father."

"But your name," I said again, "and who is your father, you strange man, since you so brag of him?"

He made no answer, but wrapped his mantle about him again and began to walk along the shore as if he had no more to say to me. He made so singular an impression, flesh and blood though I had proved him to be, that I dared not follow him and trouble him with further questions. After hesitating for a time I returned to the shed and lay down again to rest. I fell asleep at once, and had no dreams.

I woke up to sunshine and the flash of water. The hill on the other side shimmered gold beyond the dreamlike arcades of Tiberias, and all was as fresh and lovely to my eyes as if I had awakened renewed, in a new world. Both fishermen were already on their feet; they stood with hands clasped and prayed: "Hear me, Israel."

But the solitary fisherman was gone, and his net too. He had set out the remains of the supper as if for us. We ate avidly but did not talk. When we had finished we returned to the mouth of the stream, shoved out the boat and climbed aboard. I looked about for the fisherman but he was nowhere to be seen, although in the evening he had told us that he meant to cast his net just here in the morning. I could not even see any footprints.

The men began rowing with powerful strokes. The boat shot forward as if through a disk of glass, which reflected the hills and streaks of fire from the rising sun. I still felt the same lightness and freedom as if I had taken off many layers of superfluous clothes. But the more I thought about the night's happenings, the more I doubted, and wondered whether after all I had just had an unusually vivid dream. How could a hermit on the Sea of Galilee know Greek?

The men pulled rhythmically and strongly, keeping their eyes fixed ahead without once glancing behind them, as if wishful to get away from the strange shore as soon as possible. But I did look back to see if I could spy a solitary figure somewhere on the beach. In vain. At last I asked, "Who was that man we spent the night with? Did you know him?"

The fishermen answered, "You're too inquisitive, Roman. We were on the wrong shore."

But one of them added after a while, "He may have been someone we've seen before—perhaps someone who has spoken to the people. He must have been scourged and driven from Galilee; it doesn't take much for that to happen. John lost his head for daring to forbid the Tetrarch to marry his brother's wife."

The other joined in: "There was something in his face that put one in mind of Jesus of Nazareth. Had it not been impossible I would have taken him for the Master. But as I remember Jesus he was taller and graver and not so gentle in his manner as this man. It may have been one of his relatives or companions who has gone into hiding."

The fantastic thought struck down in me like a thunderbolt and shook me to my very core. "Put about at once!" I cried, and leaped to my feet. They would not take me seriously until I threatened to throw myself into the water and swim ashore. Reluctantly they turned the boat and rowed back. The prow had not touched bottom before I jumped into the water and ran to the shed. There were the ashes of the fire and the hole in the ground, just as when we had left the place, but no one was to be seen. I ran like a madman along the beach in both directions, looking in vain for footprints, until the fishermen seized me and forced me back to the boat.

There I covered my head and rebuked myself for my foolishness in not recognizing Jesus of Nazareth, if it had indeed been he. Then again I doubted, reflecting that this man had been a living man like myself. I had felt him with my own hands, and had perceived nothing divine in him whatever, as I understood divinity. Perhaps it is something as simple as the bread he gave us and the wine that we had drunk. Who am I to prescribe in what manner and in what form the son of God shall reveal himself to men?

I was filled with torturing uncertainty, and knew not what to believe. Therefore I went word for word through what he had said to me, and what I had asked him. At last I thrust these thoughts aside, reflecting that I should know soon enough whether or not I would be watching a chariot race in Tiberias.

Yet I could not help rebuking the two fishermen bitterly, and I said to them, "I told you myself that the Nazarene rose from the tomb on the third day. If you really thought you recognized him, why did you not speak to him and ask him whether he was the man?"

They looked at each other in mutual understanding and asked in their turn, "Why should we have spoken to him? If he had required something of us, he would have spoken to us. And we feared him."

They said further, "We shall not mention this meeting to anyone, and nor must you. If he really was Jesus of Nazareth, which is hard to believe, he has good reason to seek solitude and hide from the Romans."

This I could not deny, but I protested, "If it is he, what has he to fear in all the world? In Jerusalem he showed himself to his disciples when they were gathered together behind locked doors."

Both men laughed sourly and said, "Stranger, you mustn't believe every word the Galileans tell you. We're emotional people with a lively imagination."

When I was back in my familiar room in the comfortable Greek inn I was deeply relieved to be alone again, able to think in peace and spend my days as I chose. Mary of Beret had dogged me everywhere. Not until I was rid of her, thanks to Mary Magdalene, did I perceive how greatly she had distracted me.

In the peace of my room I relapsed again into thoughts of what had befallen me by the lake; yet as I sat thus the peace of the room became desolate and I began to feel restless and irritable. In these comfortable surroundings, where the most important thing for those who dwelt here was to make time pass and compare diseases and diets, I no longer felt it possible that I had met Jesus of Nazareth. The excitements and terrors of the storm must have given me some sort of nightmare mingled with reality. Even the fishermen had amused themselves by teasing me. If he had been Jesus of Nazareth and had wanted to reveal himself to me, surely he would have spoken openly, and made himself known.

My unease became so oppressive that I couldn't sit still, but had to pace up and down my room with tears in my eyes, unable to enjoy my solitude any longer. At last I sent word to Claudia Procula that I had returned, only to have her reply that she had no time to receive me. The servant told me that she was entertaining distinguished guests from the court of Herod Antipas.

Not until the next day did Claudia Procula send a servant to me with an invitation to dine with her. I was not the only guest; Herod Antipas' Roman adviser was also there, Johanna's husband Kusas and Herod's own physician, whom Herod had sent to examine Claudia Procula. This free-thinking Jew had studied medicine on the island of Kos, and was so completely Hellenized that he seemed more Grecian than any Greek. Before the meal and Claudia Procula's arrival we were offered diluted wine with sweet and sour dainties to nibble at, in the hall of the palace. The members of the Tetrarch's court tried to ensnare me with all kinds of questions. But I confined myself to praising the medicinal baths, and in evidence showed my foot which had healed so quickly from the blood poisoning.

Claudia Procula allowed Johanna to attend the meal too, although her husband obviously disapproved. Yet Johanna was very silent. Claudia Procula was pale, and complained that she was still sleepless, although wearied by her baths. Whenever she did sleep she had nothing but nightmares, and a servant had to rouse her because she wailed in her sleep.

"And Marcus," she said, turning to me. "You could never guess in what a dilemma I find myself, poor, weak, sick woman that I am. My husband warned me of it when I wanted to come here, but I would never have dreamt my position would be so difficult, for I have always been retiring and have refrained from taking part in politics. Tetrarch Herod is far too kind. He wants to organize some big races in my honor, to show his friendship for Pontius Pilate. But I am loth to attract needless attention. It seemed to me more than enough that he should have sent his red-cloaked horsemen to meet me at the border."

She threw a markedly malevolent glance at the courtiers and said, "You see, the plan is that his beautiful wife Herodias and myself should sit side by side in the Tetrarch's box and receive the people's acclaim together. But I don't even know Herodias. I've also heard that according to Jewish law his marriage is illegal."

The members of the court threw up their hands as if to ward off this insult, but I noticed that at least the big-bearded Kusas looked worried. Having nothing to lose, and being independent of the Tetrarch's favor, I answered candidly, as I saw it was what Claudia Procula wanted: "We're all friends here. The fox is a clever animal, and I have heard that Herod Antipas is flattered by being called the fox. His purpose is that you, the most eminent Roman lady in these countries and a kinswoman of Caesar's, should show your approval of this marriage, which has made such bad blood that even a prophet has been executed because of it. I can imagine the thunderous applause that will be aroused among the emotional Galileans by your public appearance at the circus, where they will have the opportunity of demonstrating their love both for the Romans and for the Tetrarch's lady. I suppose a couple of cohorts will be needed to maintain some sort of order, and all spectators will have to be searched at the gates to make sure they have nothing they might throw at you."

Claudia Procula said quickly, "Of course I have nothing personal against the Lady Herodias, but if I patronize the races and sit next to her, and this provokes demonstrations, my husband in Caesarea will hardly be able to determine whether these demonstrations are aimed at the Romans or merely at the princess. I have heard that people refuse even to salute her, but withdraw from the streets and turn their backs when she appears."

The Roman adviser explained, "Should the people demonstrate one can always stress that the uproar is aimed at Rome. Then the Tetrarch will have the opportunity of castigating his people soundly. The princess would greatly approve of that."

"But my husband would not," Claudia Procula objected. "Pontius Pilate is a moderate man and does his best to avoid unnecessary disturbance. This is certainly a matter which concerns the Tetrarch, and not him, but we cannot know which version of it will be relayed to Rome. It was as well you took my part, Marcus, for I have already decided that the most I can do is to accept the invitation as a private person. In that case I will have a box to myself, although naturally after the contests I am prepared to salute the princess and be friends with her. I am not bigoted, and such an attitude would indeed not become my position as wife to the Procurator of Judea."

"I never knew the Galileans were interested in racing," I remarked, to give the conversation a less dangerous turn.

"The fishermen and peasants know nothing of horses," the physician explained scornfully. "But the circus and the theatre are the best means of spreading culture and vanquishing prejudice. We no longer live in the days when the people fled into Egypt and wandered in the desert. Teams travel about and compete in different countries. One is coming here now from Idumea, and another from the cavalry in Caesarea. A fine team is expected from Damascus, and the Arab tribal chiefs are quite mad about racing. No personal grudge would deter them from taking part."

Kusas remarked, "Racing is well calculated to allay hatred. The Arabs are indignant because the Tetrarch's former wife was an Arab, and had to flee back to her father's tent."

"A strange country," I observed dryly, "if racing can reconcile different nations. In Rome they fight for their colors with stones and cudgels, both before and after the contests."

The Roman adviser explained, "It is a sign of education when people crack each other's skulls and beat each other black and blue, over horses and drivers. Religious disturbances are a different matter. But we may hope to enjoy some years of peace again, now that we're rid of that king whom your husband, Claudia, was so prompt to crucify in Jerusalem."

"You mean Jesus of Nazareth," I said. "Don't you know that he has risen again and has returned to Galilee?"

I said this in the same tone in which I had previously been speaking, so that they might think I was joking. But everyone started and scowled, until Kusas said, "The Galileans are superstitious folk. Bless me, even the Tetrarch believed, when he heard of Jesus, that it was that camel's-hair prophet he'd executed who had risen from the dead. But let us speak openly. I didn't think that this unpleasant rumor could have reached the ears of a chance traveler."

The Hellenized physician began speaking, with lively gesticulation: "Since hearing of this I have thought about it a great deal, and also questioned some of those who saw him die. His bones were not broken, although they were in a hurry to get him down from the cross. Blood is said to have run from his side, too, when a soldier drove a spear into him to see if he was dead. The art of medicine holds that a dead body cannot bleed. Suppose he had been given a sleeping draught, or was in a coma, or heavily drugged. Why else should his disciples have stolen his body from the tomb? They may have managed to revive him, and he may be really hiding somewhere in the caves. He was after all an accomplished magician."

The Roman adviser said sharply, "A man whom Rome crucifies does not revive. That is a serious accusation you're making against Pontius Pilate. Be careful what you say."

"I happened by chance to arrive at Jerusalem just as he was dying, and saw it," I said. "Therefore this thing interests me particularly. I can testify that he really died on the cross. And even if he had been only unconscious, he could never have survived the spear-thrust in his heart. I saw it myself."

But the physician was fond of his theory, and objected, "It is hard for a layman to be sure that death has occurred. For that an experienced doctor is needed." He began describing some cases he had known, until Claudia Procula put her hands to her ears and exclaimed, "Cease talking of such horrible things, or I shall be dreaming of ghosts again tonight."

The physician was abashed; he turned to me and by way of changing the subject he asked, "Is it true that Mary Magdalene has abandoned her former profession, as they say?"

A glacial silence followed. He looked around in surprise and asked, "Have I said something indiscreet? Is this something we may not speak of? But why? There are indeed at least a million people in Galilee, but it's still a small country. By this lake, at any rate, everyone knows the comings and goings of everyone else. In her day Mary Magdalene was the most celebrated attraction in these parts, and at night strings of litters were carried to her house from Tiberias, by torchlight. I heard that you had been to see her, to give her charge of the girl you brought with you from Jerusalem. What is the matter with that?"

When I did not answer he went on unconcernedly, "But many people believe her to be a dangerous woman. In her youth they say some Samaritan magician roamed the country with her and conjured up spirits with her help. But to a sensible physician there is nothing very strange in such things."

Kusas said reluctantly, "My wife knows her, though naturally she never sees her now. Jesus of Nazareth cured her and she no longer practices witchcraft, but distributes alms and lives a simple life. In general I'm of the opinion that Jesus of Nazareth did more good than harm. He was neither an agitator nor a blasphemer, though he was convicted of blasphemy. My wife Johanna accompanied him for a time, in fulfillment of a vow, for he had cured a relative of ours of the ague; and she had nothing bad to tell of him."

Raising his voice he struck the palm of his hand with his fist and said vehemently, "And no harm would have come to him if he had not had the notion of going to Jerusalem. Time after time Pharisees came here to question him, so as to concoct some charge against him, but they never succeeded. It is anyway a wicked waste of the people's wealth to send tithes from the country to the temple. So far as I can understand, Jesus of Nazareth said that God could be worshiped only in spirit and in truth. The Supreme Council naturally suspected that the revenues would diminish because of that saying. But it is madness for a smallholder to have to pay one tithe to the temple and another to the Tetrarch, land tax and toll to the Romans, and on top of that road tax, salt tax and market tax. It's only a question of time before the peasants lose their fields and orchards from inability to pay their dues. The result will be crowds of vagrants, general unrest and discontent and hatred of all by all, as has already happened in Judea, where the rich are merging small properties into large farming estates. I assured the Tetrarch many times that he had nothing to fear from Jesus."

The Roman adviser was on the point of making some remark, but Claudia Procula was before him and said with emphasis, "I agree with you, Kusas. Jesus of Nazareth was a good and devout man, and Pontius Pilate would never have condemned him if the Jews had not forced his hand."

After dinner Claudia Procula complained of a headache and withdrew to her own rooms. The physician followed her considerately to mix a soothing drink for her. Kusas rose too to confer with his wife about household matters, as he said. But the Roman adviser and I remained lying alone at the table, and emptied a cup of wine together. He drank robustly, and tried to pump me about news from Rome. He would have liked to know more of the influence of Sejanus, but I was careful not to say too much. I explained that it was a whole year since I had been in Rome, and after that he lost interest in me. I asked him in my turn about the court and the Tetrarch. He burst out laughing and said, "I would at any rate advise you not to call him 'fox' in public. All descendants of Herod the Great are revengeful and tender of their dignity. It's true they're all unusually gifted and dissolute, but at least they're loyal to Rome, since they have Rome to thank for their position. It's only that their kinship is so involved that it is safest not to inquire into it too closely. Herod the Great was grandfather to this Herodias and father to Herod Antipas. The Jews have therefore every reason to deplore that marriage. Fortunately a Tetrarch may obey his own laws, or an attorney would have a hard time of it at his court. In questions of crimes against life I have the right of veto, but naturally I'm not such a fool as to use it. All I am trying to do is to amass a little capital by means of my good position. And Tiberias is not such a bad town for people like us. What do you say to getting drunk and going out to have a look round the city? I can show you how pleasantly one can arrange one's life even among Jews, as long as one has the sense not to meddle in things that don't concern one."

When I excused myself on the grounds of my foot he changed his tone and said defensively, "Of course I have informants in different towns, and the legion maintains small garrisons here and there. I see to it that no arms are smuggled into the country, and that the Tetrarch does not lay up too large a stock of them. I also keep an eye on his foreign affairs. Fortunately he has annoyed the Arabs, and Persia is too far away for a petty prince like him. I am well thought of in Rome."

I asked how he had managed to avoid the infection of Jewish religion in a country swarming with prophets and holy men. He waved both his hands and said with conviction, "I stick no fingers in that wasp's nest. We have set up Caesar's image, of course, and sacrifice to it in spite of Tiberius' modest deprecation, but naturally we don't force the people to do so. These folk are still so uncivilized that even men about the court slink out of the theatre if we arrange a performance. We cannot dream of letting any condemned man be really slain on the stage, as in Alexandria; in the tragedies we have recourse to the usual bladders filled with blood. The Jews won't even watch amusing scurrilities. Oscan farces are not to be thought of."

I remembered something, and asked whether any troupe of actors was visiting Tiberias at the moment. He shook his head and answered, "Not so far as I know. Unless the Tetrarch himself pays for a performance it is difficult to persuade any of the inhabitants here to do so. Interest in the theatre does not enhance one's popular reputation as it does among the people of cultured countries."

He now decided to go and Kusas went with him. I took respectful leave of them outside in the courtyard as they stepped into their litters, for I lost nothing by being polite to these two influential men. Herod's physician availed himself of the opportunity to make a tour of the baths to snatch a fat patient or two from his colleagues, to swell his purse. As soon as they had gone, Claudia Procula summoned me, and holding her head with both hands asked me in a faint voice, "Did Mary Magdalene know anything fresh? What message did she give you?"

"She is waiting," I answered. "No one seems to know any more than we do."

Johanna said, "I have had word that in the interior of the country, in the Nain region, a man believed to be Jesus has been going about. But he disappeared again before the quiet ones were able to find him."

Claudia Procula complained, "Willingly and devoutly I made a troublesome journey to give him the chance to cure me and so gain renown after his resurrection. Why does he not appear to me? There is nothing to prevent him, since he can pass through locked doors if he likes. I shouldn't even be frightened, I have such ghastly nightmares every night. I'm getting tired of waiting; these sulphur-smelling baths weary me, and I don't know what to wear for the races. For all his good qualities Pontius

Pilate is closefisted, having grown up in modest circumstances. His mother was originally a barbarian woman from the northernmost part of Britain, where they eat peat."

"I gave Kusas a hint of your worries," Johanna said. "He realizes that the Tetrarch owes you a silken gown at least, if you really will honor his contests with your presence."

"If he tries to palm off any of Herodias' rags on me, I shall take it as an insult," said Claudia Procula fiercely. "I hope you made that clear. I don't care to accept any gift from a Jewish harlot. Whatever I have must come from the Tetrarch's foreign treasury."

She turned to me and explained, "You know better than anyone, Marcus, that I'm not vain—just a saddened woman who prefers retirement to public life. But if I consent to appear publicly, for Rome's sake alone I must dress as befits my husband's position. However, these are matters that no man can really understand, whatever he may say."

"No, indeed, I do not properly understand," I admitted. "It is as if these races were more important to you than Jesus of Nazareth, for whose sake you came here. At this very moment the risen son of God is building up an invisible kingdom about us: yet you're more concerned about what to wear, to amuse Arab chiefs and rich horse breeders."

"I have enough of invisible things every night in my dreams," said Claudia Procula crossly. "I experience then all the marvels of the underworld; I can't move a limb or even call for help, although I feel I'm breathing my last. As the moon waxes my evil increases, so that I fear for my reason."

Depressed, and heated with wine, I returned to the Greek inn. In the road against a garden wall sat an old woman dressed in sackcloth, her head covered so that I did not know who she was. But she had been waiting for me. She greeted me by name and said softly, "I'll go on ahead, down to the beach. Follow me, but don't let anyone see you."

She started ahead and I followed a little way behind. She

led me to a lonely part of the shore where no one could see us or hear what we said to each other. Only then did she uncover her face and I saw that it was Susanna. But she did not smile or greet me joyfully. On the contrary she breathed heavily and sighed and wrung her hands as if suffering bitter pangs of conscience, and did not know how to begin. I rebuked her sternly for her desertion and asked where Nathan was, and my donkeys, and my purse too. She groaned more bitterly than ever and said, "I have certainly not deserted you, nor has Nathan, and nothing has been lost. On the contrary, Nathan is using the donkeys to carry sand and clay to the new customs house in Capernaum, so as not to waste the time for which you're paying him. He will give strict account of everything. While you rest here the donkeys are working for you and adding good money to your riches. But indeed I know not whether I do right or wrong in revealing secrets to you, and I should certainly never have sought you out if you hadn't kissed me on the mouth in spite of my being such an old bag of bones and having not many teeth left, though many Galilean women of my age have perfectly sound teeth. I can't make out why that should be."

"Don't stand there prattling of your teeth," I scolded her, "but tell me at once if you have heard anything of Jesus of Nazareth."

Susanna said, "Yes, yes indeed. By all means. Anyone can scold. I may tell you that Jesus of Nazareth appeared long ago to some of the disciples by the lake, and ate with them and made Simon Peter their leader. I understand he has appointed Peter to be the shepherd who is henceforth to feed his lambs. But may a demon fly away with me if Peter will ever consent to feed you like a lamb or keep watch over you, who are no child of Israel, and not even circumcised. I can't understand why he chose Peter, of all men, as leader—Peter who denied him before even the cock crew. Certainly Peter is the biggest and strongest of them, but he is too quick-tempered to counsel others."

"Did they themselves confide this to you?" I asked dubiously.

Susanna, with her hands between her knees, signed and mourned: "Oh, how tender my feet are. I could never have walked all the way from Capernaum, but I was allowed to ride in the boat of the tax gatherers to the heathen in Tiberias. I am only a simple old woman, and no one tells me anything. But there is nothing wrong with my hearing, and someone has to clean the fish and salt it down in jars, and wash the men's clothes and cook for them. In that way one picks up one thing and another—perhaps more than one is meant to at times, for they all believe me to be too feeble-witted to understand anything. I am so weak and tired and I long so for Jesus that I can't sleep. Sometimes I go down at night to the shore, to pray. If I happen to hear something then that is not meant for my ears, that is not my fault but rather God's will, for it could hardly happen against his will, if these disciples are really such holy men as they believe—for they positively swell with pride because Jesus has shown himself to them many times already, always to a group, now here, now there, and has taught them a little. But Peter and James and John stand first in his favor; they have something like fire in their faces, so that one can see them in the dark without a lantern.

"Nathan's an honest man," Susanna went on. "He has even made a vow, and a man is always a man, so I believe more in him than in my own woman's wits. He says I owe you a message since you so generously brought me with you from Jerusalem to Galilee, although the holy ones had forsaken you; so for me you were the good Samaritan whom Jesus used to take as an example when he taught; and a Roman seems to me no worse than a Samaritan, for the Samaritans scorn the temple and serve God on their own mountain and celebrate the passover according to their own ideas. But the Romans know nothing at all about anything and so are innocent—except you, of course."

Thus she poured out her fear and anguish in a flood of speech until at last I had to interrupt her and ask, "So Jesus of Nazareth, then, is the Messiah, and the son of God, and is risen?"

"Indeed he is risen, and walks in Galilee and has appeared to many people," said Susanna, and burst into tears. "May he forgive me if I have done wrong and wickedly now, and betrayed him to you. But surely you mean him no harm?"

"But why has he not shown himself to Mary Magdalene or Johanna or you?" I asked in surprise.

"My lord, we are only women," said Susanna, genuinely astonished. "Why shoud he reveal himself to us?" She put her hand to her mouth, unable to repress a titter at such a silly idea. But she was soon grave again, and continued, "The sons of Zebedee must have said something to their mother Salome, for Salome is such a selfish and ambitious woman that the boys would not dare to keep it from her. But at least Salome has told no other women anything yet. I know one thing for certain: word has gone out throughout Galilee to them who believed in him and whom the disciples trust. Among them are the seventy whom he once sent out to proclaim his name, but there are many other quiet ones as well. The message has gone from mouth to mouth and village to village: The Lord is risen, keep yourselves in readiness. The time is accomplished: he remains only forty days on earth. But before he leaves it he will call all his own to his mountain to say farewell to them. Or at least I know not whether it is he himself who has summoned them, or his disciples."

"His mountain?" I said. "What mountain is that?"

But Susanna shook her head and declared, "I don't know, but I believe his faithful and the quiet ones know. There are many hills to which he used to withdraw to pray, both near Capernaum and on the other side of the lake, but I think this one must be in the middle of Galilee and near roads, so that those who have received the message can assemble there quickly, without attracting attention, when word comes. There is also talk of a medicine of immortality, but I don't know whether he has given anything of this kind to his disciples, or whether he means to give it to all his people on the mountain."

"Susanna," I said, "I know not how to thank you for your loyalty. May he bless you for your goodness in not leaving me in the dark. I will go with them to the mountain when the time comes, though they should slay me. Ask Nathan to hold the donkeys in readiness, and to keep one for you too, if the others won't take you."

Susanna said gaily, "Yes, indeed; I had thought the same, and I bless you, Roman, who are more merciful than his own people. My heart has been gnawed by the fear that they will all suddenly spring up and go, leaving me behind on lame feet so that never again should I see my Lord. But now you promise not to leave me behind even if the others do."

We further discussed whether I should journey to Capernaum so as to be near the disciples, but Susanna feared lest they should recognize me too soon and mistrust me. The main road into Galilee runs through Tiberias, however, and she thought it best that I should stay quietly where I am and wait for Nathan or her. She also believed that so many people will be gathering together on the mountain, and from so many directions, that they won't all know each other. When the time comes it may be possible to ask one's way to the place in the manner of the quiet ones, even if the disciples should vanish from Capernaum by night, and make their way across the hills.

We parted from each other with these promises and hopes. Susanna went back along the shore without having eaten or drunk, although I would gladly have treated her to whatever she wanted. She was afraid that someone might see us together and report it to Jesus' disciples.

So hope entered my heart and stilled it, and my unease left me. Inwardly I prayed the prayer that Susanna had taught me, and I believe there is no earthly honor or mark of favor, no success or wisdom that I would not gladly exchange for Jesus of Nazareth's kingdom, if he would open it to me. I examined my mind to its depths, and I believe it is not immortality or eternal life that I desire. I wish only that he would look at me and acknowledge me as one of his own.

For some days since meeting Susanna I have occupied myself solely in recording what has happened.

Tenth Letter

Marcus greets Tullia once more:

In my heart I know that I have long ago departed from you, Tullia. I know that nothing of what I've written can convince you. If you were to read it you would only jeer at me and think that the Jews had addled my brains. Yet I am consumed by the strange notion that one day I might look at you, and that in that hour your clothes would drop from you and your body itself be merely a superfluous garment; that I should then see your soul and bring you to believe as I myself believe. I think it would mean abstention from much that you value and find pleasant in this life. But if I could look at you thus, none of that would mean anything to you any more, and so you would be renouncing only unnecessary things. But the idea is surely futile. Such belief is possible only if one has experienced and seen these things for oneself. And there are many who do not believe, even when they've seen them with their own eyes.

But I will relate what happened next. On the day before the races Claudia Procula sent me a message, telling me as if it were a mark of supreme favor that she would take me into her box and that I might sit behind her. When I arrived at her rooms she had dressed herself in purple silk, which was perhaps thoughtless. But she could always point out that she was a distant kinswoman of Caesar's. Her hair was splendidly dressed and she wore a costly diadem on her brow. For me she had provided Roman clothes and a toga, and a barber was waiting to shave me and curl my hair.

"It is high time you left off this Jewish nonsense and appeared like a Roman among the barbarians," said Claudia.

I reminded her of the utter confusion of dress prevailing among the visitors to the baths, and of how even the Roman adviser had let his beard grow and adopted the Oriental fashion of dress, so as not to make needless parade of his Roman nationality at the court. But at last I was obliged to give my real reason:

"Don't be offended, Claudia, but I have no desire to go to the races. On the contrary, I want to be ready to leave at any moment, for I've reason to think that the followers of Jesus of Nazareth will soon be gathering to meet him. I hope to get word of this in good time, so that I may follow the disciples at a distance and find the meeting place."

Claudia Procula said sharply, "That is no news to me. Johanna knows of it already. If I were younger and this were Rome and I had enough reliable protectors who could hold their tongues, I might be tempted into this adventure too, and go to the mountains in disguise. It *is* on a mountain that they're to meet, is it not?"

I asked in astonishment, "Why did Johanna say nothing of this to me? Doesn't she trust me?"

"I believe she was told to be silent," remarked Claudia casually. "But she has promised to speak to Jesus of Nazareth about me. Jesus is known to have healed sick people from a distance. Or perhaps he will give Johanna a piece of stuff which he has held against his body. So you are not needed there at all, Marcus. Be a Roman again, and come to your senses. These races are the greatest event of the year in all Galilee and the neighboring lands."

I stared at her, unable to believe my ears. "So you exchange God's son for a chariot race," I said reproachfully.

"There's a time for everything," was Claudia's excuse. "The baths have done me good, and I'm no longer as crazed in my wits as you. Seriously, I believe you've lost all sense of proportion."

"Claudia Procula," I said sternly, "your husband condemned him to the cross, however thoroughly he may have washed his hands of it afterward. Are you not afraid?"

Claudia Procula threw out her hands: "But Marcus, I did all I could to save him. He must surely know that, or at least he will come to know it. Besides, Johanna explained to me very particularly that these things had to be, to justify the holy scriptures of the Jews. So in fact he should be grateful to Pontius Pilate who, under pressure from the Jews, helped to fulfill the holy scriptures. Certainly the Jews' philosophy is obscure and complicated, but I can well believe that Johanna is right. Besides, Johanna is coming to the races too, even though it may delay her arrival at the mountain. So you can see what an important event this is."

I could do nothing with her; but I would not let the barber shave off my beard. He merely cut it shorter, and waxed it, and said it was now in the style affected by the Herodians.

Herod Antipas' circus is no vast building. I believe it would not hold as many as thirty thousand spectators. At any rate it was crammed full of a yelling, excited crowd. There must have been more foreigners than Galileans on the benches.

Herod had caused a gallery to be erected for Claudia Procula opposite his own on the other side of the arena, and the rails of it were hung with rich carpets. Everything showed that he wanted to keep on good terms with Pontius Pilate, for Claudia's box was only one step lower than his own. He had also installed boxes for the Arab chiefs and other visiting dignitaries, and the members of his court had received appropriate instructions; for when Claudia appeared with her suite she was hailed with mighty shouts of acclaim from all sides. The people joined in, to give vent to their excitement.

We saw Herodias and her young daughter enter Herod's box. She was magnificently dressed, so far as one could see from the opposite side of the arena. At least Claudia Procula sighed and said that that ambitious whore might have done her and Rome the courtesy of dressing a thought less pretentiously. She too was greeted by loud cheers from different quarters, but the people did not join in these, and the foreigners soon fell silent when they saw that the cheerers were cuffed and beaten and menaced in various ways. With that Herodias had to be content and take her place. Lastly Herod Antipas appeared, throwing wide his arms in glad greeting to all. As if to demonstrate their disapproval of his wife, his people acclaimed him by rising, cheering and stamping their feet.

Into the arena there now came a troop of gladiators, who fought in twos and in groups; but their weapons were blunted and no blood flowed. Because of the Jewish law Herod dared not allow any condemned criminals to fight in the ring. His horsemen then displayed many feats of skill, until the people began stamping and demanding that the racing teams should appear.

The chariots were indeed splendid and the horses superb as one team after another circled the arena in the introductory parade. Bookmakers with their great wax tablets now began moving among the benches to take wagers. Herod Antipas' own coal-black team seemed the favorite. By no means all the teams were thus matched in color, for the barbarian drivers had chosen their horses according to their own judgment from among those in their masters' stables. The colors to wager on were seen only on the chariots and in the livery of the charioteers. The bookmakers were also shouting of an Idumean and a Syrian team, neither of which bore a color.

The last one to drive in was that of an Arab prince, whose horses were snow white. But the preceding chariots had already formed the usual exasperating jam at the entrance, and the mettlesome white horses were brought to their knees when their driver was forced to rein them in just as they were about to sweep round at full gallop on their parade lap. This was so bad an omen that many people laughed. The charioteer lost his temper and gave his team a flick of the whip; and this of course made them more restive than ever.

At an orthodox, safe chariot race, of the kind appreciated by experts because it allows of reasoned wagering, and because the excitement mounts with each succeeding contest, the teams are usually matched in pairs, and each pair circles the arena several times. Losing teams retire from the tournament, and the last race is run off between the remaining two. But the barbarians here love speed and noise, and to my amazement all the teams lined up together, in an order determined by lot. I heard that they were to run forty laps. I pitied the horses, of which many must inevitably break their legs, and was tolerably sure that a contest of this sort would cost some man his life.

But on beholding the rearing white team I remembered what the solitary fisherman had told me, and wondered whether I really dared stake money on it. When I inquired about it I was told that it had been one of the favorites, but that because of the bad omen no one would back it. In grueling races such as this, powerful horses and quick-witted drivers may well triumph over swifter teams, if luck is with them.

Claudia Procula threw up her arm and cried, "Herod's team!" The gleaming black horses and their dark-skinned driver did indeed inspire confidence. The color was red, however, for no sensible person would put money on black. Claudia turned to me half-absently and said, "I suppose you have enough money?"

Of course I ought to have guessed beforehand why she so greatly desired my company; indeed I've never known any woman to stake money of her own. Should she lose, she finds no difficulty in forgetting the loan; should she win one may be glad if one gets one's money back.

"A hundred drachmas," I suggested reluctantly.

Claudia Procula turned right around to me with a look of amazement. "Marcus Mezentius Manilianus," she said. "Do you mean to insult me? Or have you turned into a Jew? Say a hundred gold pieces at least—and even that's too little for such glorious horses."

I hadn't so much with me, but all the bankers and money-changers of Tiberias were moving among the more eminent spectators, and they too accepted wagers. I called out the name I had been given by the banker Aristainos of Jerusalem, and a man was pointed out to me who in feature and dress might have been his twin. I confided in him. He was willing to give me credit, but told me that it would be difficult to obtain good odds on Herod's team. Even chances was indeed the best he could get, from a distinguished Idumean who said he was offering this merely out of courtesy to the wife of the Procurator of Judea.

"Remember me when you count your money after the victory!" he called up laughingly to Claudia Procula, as if he had made her a present; and he recorded the wager on his wax tablet.

Once more I surveyed the teams, which only with great difficulty could be kept still in their places. The reason for the long delay was partly to allow time for wagers to be laid and partly to excite the horses and exasperate the drivers. I suspected that some of the chariots would be overturned at the very outset. The Arab chief's white team was evidently unused to the barbarian mass-start, for they kicked their chariot and splashed foam about them as they tossed their heads and champed their bits.

"What will you give me on the white team?" I asked the banker.

He replied smiling, "If you really want to lose your money to me, I'll take your bet myself and give you seven to one. What is your stake?"

"Write forty gold pieces from Marcus on the white team, at seven to one," I decided at the last moment, when Herod had already raised his spear. The banker recorded the wager, and at that moment the spear plunged into the sand, its pennant waving. The charioteers gave a shout and with a rumble the chariots moved off. The more experienced drivers leaned back, reining in their teams with all their strength to allow the foolhardy ones to dash ahead and break their necks at once. But it was almost impossible to restrain the frantic horses. The two foremost teams sprang away at a gallop, and the drivers leaned forward and used their whips so as to gain as long a start as possible and reach the turning-post first. It was the only way to save their lives and avoid being trampled underfoot by the teams hurtling at their heels.

I couldn't help springing up and standing on my bench, for so breathless a start I had never beheld. Herod's black team was thrusting its way skillfully through the packed mass, and the charioteer used his heavy whip mercilessly to force his nearest competitors aside. I saw the lash catch the nearside horse of the white team over the eyes, and fancied I could hear the crack of it from where I stood. The Arab's chariot struck the stone curb, sending sparks flying from the wheel, and it was a marvel that the wheel was not smashed.

At the second turn the heavy bay cavalry team from Caesarea deliberately drove straight at the Idumean, so that it overturned. The Idumean driver was dragged along the course by his reins until the flank horse came down. The bay team got well ahead, but then Herod's chariot broke through and took up the chase. The Idumean staggered to his feet, half his body smeared with blood, wrenched the fallen horse up by grasping its nostrils, and even succeeded in righting the chariot, so that he could drive out onto the course again. But the injured horse was so lame as to be out of the race, and was only an obstacle to the others. I suspected that the charioteer took up the fight again merely to be revenged on the Roman.

In a contest of this kind, in which fairly evenly matched teams are hurtling round the course, it is in fact impossible to lead by more than a lap. The trailing teams bar the way, and the driver who catches them up would be tempting fortune beyond all reason if he tried to overtake them. The white team was now quite checked, for the horse which had had the whiplash in its eyes was still madly tossing its head in pain. The driver was beside himself: he hit out, swore and shook his fist at Herod as he passed the Tetrarch's box. But the black team was rapidly gaining on the bay with its heavy chariot. Claudia Procula stood, shrieked and stamped her gilt sandals.

I couldn't keep count of the laps, nor follow all that happened, but suddenly I saw the Syrian team slung, chariot and all, as if by a catapult from the ruck into the middle of the ring. The horses were thrown head-over-heels, and the driver, his reins still knotted about his waist, flew in among the wildly kicking hooves. I know not whether his dying scream was more terrible than that of one of the horses.

Only a little while later the white team darted forward at one of the turning-posts and crowded another against it, overturning the chariot. But the Arab team passed unharmed. This may have been owing to the blinded horse, for if it had had the sight of its left eye it would hardly have shaved past so closely. At the risk of his life the driver of the overturned chariot managed to get his horses off the course into the middle just as the team behind came up. I had to admire the skill of the drivers. This man saw the grooms running to meet him, took a few paces toward them but fell headlong, and could not get up again.

Wagering began once more, amid intense excitement. The bay team of the Roman mounted cohort seemed to have gained more supporters, and many people backed it against Herod's team, especially Arabs, who signaled the odds with their fingers and waved their mantles. Having abandoned their own entry, they preferred the Roman one to Herod's. Herod's driver had already tried to overtake the other several times, but the Roman swung coolly out in front of him and let his whip whistle through the air. Herod rose in his box, stamped on the floor and shouted to his driver to pass. All the horses were in a lather and the air was full of dust-clouds, although the course had been carefully watered before the race.

Yet the most remarkable thing was that in spite of all setbacks the white team, by its swiftness, had come up into third place, although the light chariot had met with some rough jolts. The fine horses had recovered themselves slightly and were once more moving admirably in step. The one that had been lashed raised its head and uttered a long neigh. The driver leaned forward and talked to it, and it no longer tried to pull away from its teammates.

Another chariot fell out through losing a wheel. The driver contrived to swing around so that the chariot overturned inward, off the course, and so was out of the way of the rest, but the wheel rolled straight on, and the bay team which came next had to swerve for it. Herod's charioteer took advantage of this. Leaning far forward he lashed his horses and succeeded in passing the Roman. Cheering and yelling the crowd sprang to its feet, and Claudia Procula jumped and shrieked with joy, disgraceful though it was of her to show delight at the misfortunes of the Roman team. Yet her behavior evoked applause from those sitting near, and many smiled at her.

The number of competitors had dwindled, but the chariot lying last prevented Herod's charioteer from profiting by his lead. The blood-drenched Idumean, who had had half his face flayed, turned and looked behind him, then beckoned and drew aside to let the other man by. Then he deliberately drove directly in the way of the Roman team behind him, and slackened speed. This happened in the middle of the straight, not at the turn, and the Roman cursed him savagely, for of course this maneuver was against all the rules. But who could prove it? He could always find some excuse for what he was doing. Those Arabs who had staked money on the Roman shouted too, and shook their fists, but at that moment the white team swept past both Roman and Idumean, arrived first at the turn and took the inside position, where it lay close behind Herod's chariot. The spectators were struck dumb and for a moment ceased cheering, for such a thing as this had never been deemed possible.

After the turning-post the Roman took the outer lane and without difficulty drew level with the Idumean. He might easily have overtaken the injured team before the next turn, but he held in his horses and deliberately struck the Idumean on the head with his whip, bringing the man to his knees in the chariot. This brutal act set the crowd in a roar again, and many applauded, but hatred of Rome flared up too, and I saw many who came to blows among the benches.

But this lasted only a moment, so quickly did everything happen. The Idumean struggled to his feet and, urging his horses to a final effort, overtook the Roman team and again swung in front of it. This was no longer racing but murder. The great bay horses dashed full tilt into the Idumean team, bringing it and themselves sprawling to the ground. The sudden stop sent the Roman flying headfirst from his chariot, so that despite leather guards and helmet he cracked his skull on the stone curb in front of the seats and remained lifeless on the course. The Idumean too died before the race was over. He had been badly kicked by one of the horses.

The clearing-up after this collision forced the remaining teams to slacken their pace. Herod's driver roared and brandished his whip, so that the grooms who were carrying off the Roman set him down again and sprang aside for their lives. The driver tried to force the black horses over the Roman's body, but they were no chargers and would not trample on a man. They reared violently and swung the chariot so that it came near to overturning.

Almost at walking-pace the driver of the Arab chariot now steered his white horses past Herod's team. One wheel struck that curb and mounted it, but the chariot remained upright and he reached the turning-post before Herod's driver had rounded the corpse and got his horses in step again. Incredible as it seemed the ill-omened white team was now in the lead, and there were not many laps to go. It was my turn to jump up and cheer, and every Arab there joined in. But the unmetaled course was now as rutted and bumpy as a ploughed field, and as dangerous to drive on.

Now for the first time the driver of the black team lost his temper, and lashing his animals he tried once or twice to pass the white team by force. But the swiftness and even pace of the Arab horses saved them, and as their chariot was light, their driver did not have to hug the turning-post, but could take a wide sweep, relying on speed, without danger of Herod's black team crowding between.

Only three other teams were left in the race. The white tried to pass them fairly, on the outside, but Herod's charioteer yelled to the others to let him through. Two of them were scared into obedience, but the third, who drove a sturdy but slow team of which no one had any hopes, refused to give way. Again Herod's man resorted to the whip, jerked his team purposely into breaking step and drove his hub into the other's wheel, so that effortlessly, by the sheer speed and weight of his vehicle, he overturned his rival's. The driver of this was badly hurt and retired from the race. Both the others continued cautiously, relying on luck to put obstacles in the way of the two leading chariots.

But it was not to be. The flag was waved, and swiftly as swallows the white horses sped forward to victory. The onlookers yelled wildly, and cheered Herod's horses too, which were only a couple of lengths behind at the finish. Both charioteers drove up handsomely abreast, reined in and saluted each other with feigned respect and thanks for a good fight. The Arab chief leaped over the rail of his box on to the course and ran with his mantle streaming behind him to his horses. He talked to them and patted them and with tears kissed the swollen eye of the one that had been lashed. A number of brawls started among the benches, but the stewards quickly put a stop to them. Those who had lost their wagers tried to put a good face on it, and applaud the excitement of the race.

The banker came forward to congratulate me and the Idumean merchant, and in my presence paid him the hundred gold pieces that Claudia Procula had lost. For me he counted out one hundred and eighty gold pieces, so that after subtracting my stake my winnings were one hundred and forty, which for many people represents a small fortune.... Therefore I bore Claudia Procula no grudge.

It must be remembered that I had dreamt about a white horse on the night after the storm. For some reason the dream had been so vivid that I was aroused from it by my own weeping. So I may have remembered the dream, and taken it as an omen, when I first saw that beautiful white team, and perhaps of my own accord I might have wagered on its winning. This is possible but not certain. The horses had stumbled to their knees at the entrance; and however skeptical he may be of omens, no sensible man flouts them. Therefore I felt it my duty to seek out the girl whose brother was dead, though I had nothing to go on beyond the solitary fisherman's word that on that night she was mourning her brother at the Greek theatre in the city.

Claudia Procula urged me to accompany her to Herod's banquet, though I had not been invited. No doubt she considered this favor worth a hundred gold pieces. But I had no wish to force myself unbidden among the many hundreds whom for political reasons Herod Antipas found it necessary to entertain, and Claudia Procula was not offended at my taking leave of her, although she must have thought me foolish not to avail myself of the opportunity.

With the emptying of the circus, the streets of Tiberias were inundated with people of every race, and I fully expected that a night of rioting would follow despite the watchmen and legionaries posted for duty. I found my way to the little Greek theatre without difficulty, but no performance was announced there. Nevertheless the gates stood open, and poor visitors to the city who had found no shelter seemed to be camping on the spectators' benches. Some had even lighted fires and were cooking, so one could guess what that beautiful theatre would look like next day.

I went down between the stage and the seats, and no one prevented me from entering the cellars where stage properties are kept and where traveling players sometimes spend the night if they have no patron to give them lodging. All was deserted and empty and a little ghostly, as always beneath the stage of a theatre when the actors have gone; as if characters and words from all the performances were still lingering invisibly in the air. These dark theatre cellars have always made me think of the kingdom of the dead, as poets have described it. However rapturously I may have hastened down to them after a performance, bearing a gift for some actress who had set my soul in tumult, I've been filled each time with a chill sense of unreality. A player who has shed his costume is not the person he was on the stage.

As I wondered through these subterranean rooms I felt how far and in how short a time I had traveled away from my former life and from everything which used to give me pleasure and enjoyment. The past was just a memory which stabbed at my heart when I realized that I should never be able to experience it in the same way again. I fancied I was seeing a wraith when an old Greek came jogging along the dark passage. His paunch sagged and his eyes were puffy from immoderate toping; he shook his stick at me and demanded with many curses what I was looking for and how I had found my way under the stage.

I asked him in a pacifying tone whether anyone lived down here. He became even more enraged, and yelled, "You don't mean those Egyptian vagabonds who cheated me and brought me ill-luck by leaving a corpse in here? I'd be gladder than you to get my hands on them."

I said, "I'm told that I can find a girl here who has lost her brother. I have an errand to her."

The old man looked at me suspiciously, and asked, "You're not one of them, are you? I'm holding that girl in pawn; I've taken clothes and shoes off her and don't mean to let her go until the debt is paid to the last farthing."

"I've been sent to ransom her," I explained, clinking my purse. "Take me to her, and you won't regret your trouble."

Doubtfully and with misgivings the old man led me farther along the underground passage and opened the door of a little cubbyhole. There I beheld, in a ray of light coming from a chink in the wall, a thin, naked girl crouching in a corner with her hair over her face, as if petrified with grief; for she never moved when we came in. There was not so much as a bowl of water in the place, no food and no covering.

"Is she ill?" I asked.

"She's a wicked girl; she tore my beard when I tried to make her dance by the gate," said the old man. "The city is full of foreigners and someone might have thrown money to her if she had danced. You must understand that I was obliged to pay for her brother's burial, so that no one should know that a corpse had been left in the theatre. And that was by no means all that those cheats of Egyptians owed me."

I touched the girl's shoulder and threw down my purse in front of her. "I've been sent with a hundred and forty gold pieces for you," I said loudly. "Pay what you owe and demand your clothes and belongings, and you're free to go where you please." But the girl did not stir.

"A hundred and forty gold pieces!" cried the old Greek,

making a sign with his right hand to ward off evil. "This is what I feared. The wine is finished and I see visions and hear spirit-voices." He tried to snatch the purse, but I took charge of it again, since the girl did not touch it. I asked him how much she owed.

He began rubbing his hands, stared piously upward with his swollen eyes, mumbled and reckoned to himself and said at last slyly, "I'm not a greedy man, though this wicked girl has brought ill-fortune upon me. At a round figure her debt is just ten gold pieces. I will fetch her belongings at once, with a little food and wine thrown in. She is probably too greatly exhausted with hunger to utter a word, and you'd have no pleasure of her in that state."

He poked at my shoulder and whispered, "A hundred and forty gold pieces is an outrageous price for a girl like that. You must be out of your mind. It will be enough if you pay what she owes; then you can take her away and do with her as you choose. For just one gold piece I can get you the necessary papers, so that you may have her lawfully marked as a slave, with your own sign branded on her backside, for she has no protector."

Without raising her head the girl swept the hair from her eyes and snarled, "Give the filthy old rogue five gold pieces. That covers my debt and all the others' many times over. Then kick him in the groin for me."

I opened my purse and counted out five gold pieces. So delighted was he that he never even tried to haggle, but hastened off directly to fetch the girl's clothes. When he tossed her bundle in to us he cried that he would bring food and wine at once. Again I threw the purse to the girl and turned to go. But she held me back, and asked, "What do you want of me? I can't give you pleasure worth a hundred and forty gold pieces. Tonight I was going to hang myself in my own hair."

"I want nothing," I told her. "I was just sent here with the money."

"Such things don't happen," the girl said incredulously, and for the first time she raised her head and looked at me. To my amazement I recognized her: it was Myrina, the dancer whom I had met aboard the ship to Joppa. But she did not know me at once because of my beard and my Jewish dress.

"Myrina!" I exclaimed, "I never saw it was you. What has happened? Why are you so unhappy as to want to take your own life?"

Myrina shrank back, hid her bare knees with her hair in shame and besought me, "Don't look at me as I am now. At least turn your back while I dress." Opening her bundle she found a comb, combed her hair and bound it up with a ribbon, drew on a short tunic and fastened a pair of gay sandals on her feet. Then she broke into bitter weeping and embraced me with all her thin body, pressing her face to my breast and wetting my mantle with her tears.

I stroked her shoulders, gave her comforting words and asked, "Is your brother really dead, and is that why you are crying?"

Hiccuping with sobs Myrina forced out the words. "For him I have wept already. I believe I must be crying now because there is still someone in the world who wishes me well. Another night and I should have been dead, without so much as a farthing to put in my mouth for the ferryman."

She clung to me hard and wept even more bitterly. I had difficulty in getting a rational word from her, but at last she calmed herself enough to tell me of the misfortunes that had overtaken the troupe of players ever since we parted. They had gone on to Perea and performed in the furlough town of the legion, but there the whole troupe had fallen sick of a fever. On their way back they had existed by appearing on threshing floors, but the Jews stoned them. In Tiberias they had hoped to arrange a display to coincide with the races, but her brother had been drowned while swimming. They had dived for him and rolled him on the ground, and Myrina had tried to blow life into him with her breath, but he never revived. They carried him into the theatre by stealth, and the old Greek had helped to bury him at night, so that the theatre need not be purified because of the known presence of a corpse. The other players had fled, leaving Myrina and her belongings behind as a pledge. But she could dance no longer, having been so frightened by the stoning.

She explained, "As long as my brother was alive we relied on each other and I wasn't quite alone in the world. But when he was dead and buried I felt unsafe, and realized that wherever I go I shall be dogged by misfortune and wickedness, and so I don't want to live any longer. I can neither eat nor drink, my limbs are paralyzed and I want to see nothing more in the world, hear nothing, taste and smell nothing. I have had enough of it all, and I mourn my brother.

"And you I cannot understand," she went on. "Your money must be some new kind of lie and lure, to make me continue my useless life and bring fresh miseries upon me. No, no; take it back and leave me here to die alone, so that I need suffer no further disappointment, now that I know how dangerous and desperate a place the world is."

The old Greek returned with bread and porridge in a dish, poured wine into a bowl with shaky hands and bade her drink. "Come with me to the stage-keeper's room," he said. "It's lighter there, and there's a bed. I will make it comfortable for you."

"For us any place will do, I believe," I answered. "Leave us alone, for we have much to talk of."

He readily gave us leave to remain until morning if we chose; and, he told us, should we desire more wine we might get it from him. He went his way with the wineskin under his arm, and Myrina began to eat, reluctantly at first and then with better appetite, until the dish was empty and not a crumb of bread was left.

When she had finished she asked, "Where is the harm in my dancing, and why should I have been cursed so that I daren't trust my limbs any more, and am afraid? You saw me dance on the ship—you know that I don't do it for seduction, but to give entertainment and stir people's emotions with my tricks and feats. What if I do dance naked? Flapping garments would get in the way and make me lose my balance, and my thin body isn't much to look at, for it's nothing but trained muscle; I haven't even any breasts. I don't understand why the Jews stoned me so mercilessly."

She showed me her bruises and a badly healed graze on her head beneath her hair, and told me, "We asked for food in one village, and would have paid for it by diverting the people as best we could with singing, playing and my dancing. But they would have stoned me to death if there hadn't been so many of us. I'm tormented by the sense of having done something forbidden, and I know I shall never be able to dance again as I did."

I pondered her story and said, "I believe I know the cause of their wrath. I've heard that the Lady Herodias made her daughter dance before dissolute Herod Antipas, to induce him to execute a Jewish prophet who had spoken ill of Herodias. Therefore pious Jews in this part of the world abominate all heathen dancing."

Myrina shook her head: "I used to be proud of my art, and loved the free and varied life of a strolling player. But we met with one misfortune after another, until at last I was full of fear and dreaded every day that dawned. My brother's death was the final blow, and crushed me utterly."

But having poured out all her distress to me she began to marvel. She undid the purse, fingered the gold pieces and asked for what reason I wanted to give them to her, and how I had found her at all. I told her of the solitary fisherman and of my wager at the racing, and ended, "I believe that man could hear your weeping across the lake. But how, and how he knew that your brother was dead, I dare not even try to explain. At any rate the money is yours, and you're free to come and go as you please."

Myrina frowned thoughtfully and said, "Describe that man

to me. Did he look as if he had suffered much and was worn out? Was he grave and gentle, so that you can't forget his face? Had he wounds in his wrists and feet?"

I said, "You're thinking of the same man. You must have met him."

Myrina told me: "After we had fled from the angry Jews we had nothing to eat but ears of corn which we plucked in the fields. At last we came to a well and decided to stay by it that night. We were utterly despondent. Then this man came wearily along the road, and said, 'Let me drink too.' But we were all enraged against the Jews. The men prevented him from coming to the well and my brother mocked him, saying, 'Though you were in your Jewish hell I would not dip a finger in water to refresh you, because you're an accursed Jew.' But at last I pitied him. I fetched water for him, gave him to drink and washed his wounded feet, for he lacked the strength to do it for himself. No one hindered me. Players are kindly people at heart. Very likely my brother was only joking and would have let him go to the well in the end, only just then we were all full of bitter resentment against the Jews. When he had drunk and I had rinsed his feet clean he gave me a gentle look, blessed me and said, 'What you've done for me you have done for him who sent me. For this one act, much will be forgiven you. Kings and princes will envy you because you gave me water to drink when I was thirsty.'"

"Did he really say that to you, Myrina?" I asked in wonder.

"Those very words," Myrina said. "They have stayed in my memory, although I didn't understand them. But I imprinted them on my mind because he was so singular a man. I turned to the others for a while, and during that time he disappeared. We were so hungry that we chewed bark when we lay down to sleep by the well, but a little later an old woman came along the road, looking about her as if in search of something. She had barley bread and mutton in a basket, and she offered it to us, but we told her that we hadn't a farthing to pay her with.

Then she said this: 'Take it and eat. I have been promised that what I give away of my own will be repaid many times over.' We took the food and ate, and were all filled. The men thought that the Jews were afraid after treating us so badly, and that they were now trying to conciliate us. But the woman gathered what remained into her basket and went on her way. I had a feeling that it was that weary man who had met her and bidden her bring us food, because I had been kind to him. Who is he, if indeed he be the same man whom you met on the other side of the lake?"

I hesitated as to how much I should tell her, and then said, "I neither know nor understand. At any rate he gave you a princely reward for a drink of water. But not in my wildest dreams would I have imagined meeting you here, Myrina, or that it was to you I had to give my winnings. I can only see it as a sign and a reminder that it was not of my own will alone that I boarded that ship in Alexandria. But peace be with you now, Myrina, and use the money as you think best. I must go, for I expect a message."

Myrina grasped me firmly by the arm and forced me to sit down on the earth floor again, saying, "No, you shall not go, for I won't allow it. The man you told me of can be no ordinary man. No one behaves and speaks as he does."

But I had no wish to disclose the secret of the kingdom to an utterly strange girl of a dubious profession, and said abruptly, "You've had all you could ask of him and more. Let me be."

Myrina, angered, thrust the purse back into my hands and said vehemently, "Then keep your coin, and may it scorch your conscience as long as you live. You cannot buy me off with money, for money is no remedy for the distress I feel. I would rather hang myself. Tell me at once all you know of him, and then take me to him."

I saw that I had got myself into a quandary, and bitterly did I lament, saying, "His acts are not the acts of men, and I don't understand him with my human reasoning. Are there not Jewish widows and fatherless in the land who revere God and seek the kingdom? Why then has he chosen an Egyptian—a girl who has sinned from childhood?"

Myrina said in a hurt tone, "I'm no common Egyptian; I was born on one of the islands, of good Greek parents, and I don't know what you mean when you say I've sinned from childhood. There is nothing to be ashamed of in my profession, for by it I delight and please many people. I would not indeed claim to be the woman of one man only, but it takes two to commit that sort of sin, and I know not which is the greater sinner: I, or the man who profits by my poverty to bribe me into sin. But I have put an end to my former life as completely as if I'd hanged myself already. I want a new and better life. I can't buy that for money. So you must help me as if you were my brother."

I could have wept. Hardly had I rid myself of Mary of Beret before I had another even more alien and dangerous girl on my hands. But I had to tell her. I thought over what I should say, and began to explain it thus: "I don't know how much you understand of all this, but you've seen the world and must have experienced other inexplicable things. I've reason to think that the man you gave water to by the well and whom I spoke to by the lake is a certain Jesus of Nazareth."

"But him I know!" Myrina broke in, to my surprise. "The legionaries of Decapolis talked of nothing else. He has wrought miracles, healed the sick and even raised the dead, and he promised to establish a kingdom for the Jews. Therefore he was crucified in Jerusalem, and his disciples stole his body from the tomb under Pontius Pilate's nose, to make the people believe he'd risen from the dead. Or do you think he really came out of his tomb, and that it was he I met by the well?"

"He rose from the dead," I said. "Therefore he is the son of God and I believe that he possesses all power in heaven and on earth. Such a thing has never happened before. Then he came here into Galilee, telling his people to follow him. He must have been on that journey when you saw him. He has promised to meet them once more on a mountain."

"But," objected Myrina, with sturdy common sense, "how could he have been thirsty if he was the son of God?"

"How should I know?" I returned, annoyed. "I have myself felt the weals of the scourge across his back, if it was indeed he. I can testify that he is of flesh and blood. He is a man among men, yet at the same time the son of God. Don't ask me how and why it is so, for I believe that this is the greatest miracle about him, and the thing that has never happened before in the world. Therefore his kingdom cannot be merely an earthly one, as the Jews imagine."

Myrina gazed about her wide-eyed, reflected with awe upon my words and said, "If it is as you say, then he has sent you here in place of my brother and not just for the sake of the money. Thus he has bound us together as one binds a pair of doves by the feet. I too long for his kingdom, of whatever kind it may be, for of this one I have had enough. Let us go to that mountain together and throw ourselves down before him and beg him to take us into his kingdom, as he has given you to me for a brother and me to you for a sister."

"Myrina," I said resolutely, "I neither lack nor need a sister. Truly I do not. That is a great mistake. And in any case I don't intend to take you with me to the mountain, for I don't even know yet whether I shall find it myself. Who knows whether his disciples may not slay me, believing that I'm spying on their holy mysteries? You must understand that they believe his kingdom is for circumcised Jews alone. They admit no Romans to it, nor Greeks, nor even Samaritans—no one who does not acknowledge the supremacy of their temple. The whole story is far more complicated and dangerous than you know. But if you promise to be quiet and not bother me, I will visit you again when I have met him, and tell you about him, unless he is to take his own people into his kingdom at once. In that event I shall not return; but I hope that you'll remember me kindly notwithstanding."

With a violent movement Myrina hurled the purse at my head.

"Be it so, then," she said bitterly. "A drowning man clutches at a straw; that's why I would be ready to clutch at Jesus of Nazareth and take you for my brother, though you're not my brother's equal in anything. He and I understood each other with half a word and a glance; we laughed at the same things and made fun of everything—hunger and humiliation too—so as to endure the wretched existence of a player. Go your way, hardhearted man—you who think you can buy a person for money! Hasten to your mountain with a cheerful mind. But I wonder what kind of kingdom it can be that will receive you, when you've left me to sorrow and death. O rich man, what do you know of insecurity?"

I stared at her, and saw in her flashing green eyes that from grief and wild defiance she was indeed ready to hang herself, if only to annoy me. And she spoke with such conviction that doubts began to gnaw at my mind. Perhaps Jesus of Nazareth had meant me to weaken and take Myrina for my sister, outrageous though this might seem. I began to sense that his kingdom was not a purely agreeable realm, and that it made claims that were hard to satisfy.

"Myrina, my sister," I said sourly, "let us go together then, and do not blame me for what may happen."

But Myrina was not satisfied with this. She said, "Don't talk so harshly to me. If you take me with you, do so like a brother, gladly. Otherwise there is no point in my coming."

I could not do otherwise than embrace her thin body in a brotherly way, kiss her cheeks and comfort her with gentle words. She shed another tear or two, but then we set forth together, and the old Greek, sitting and babbling over a jar of wine in his porter's lodge, did not try to stop us.

The sun had just set behind the hills and countless lamps

and cressets of pitch were being lighted in the seething city. I was in so great a hurry to regain the inn that I forgot Myrina's need of new clothes. Because of her player's dress and gay sandals many passers-by shouted at her, and I had some trouble in getting her out of the town and on the way to the thermae unmolested. I had the notion that Jesus' disciples would be moving this very night, for they could choose no better time; many people would be streaming away from Tiberias next day and no wayfarer bound for the mountain would attract attention on the roads. For this reason I hurried.

Not until I arrived breathless and hot under the bright lamps of the Greek inn did I realize that I'd done a foolish thing. The dignified landlord, who was accustomed to behold unmoved the whims of the rich, came forward to us, looked Myrina up and down and said reprovingly, "Roman, you're like a bottomless sack. First you had a Jewish woman for your pleasure, and I said nothing, since you kept her up in your room behind drawn curtains. But to come on a night of festival with a sluttish player-girl who as soon as you're asleep will go out and offer herself to other guests for a couple of drachmas, make trouble and steal the bedclothes—that is too much. We've had player-women here before."

I surveyed Myrina with his eyes and saw how tattered and stained her short dancing-mantle was; how the color of her pretty sandals was rubbed and how grimy were her knees. Her face was still swollen from weeping, so that one might have supposed that she had come straight from some orgy. Under her arm she carried her brother's five-reed pipe, and pipes are no recommendation for anyone seeking house-room at an expensive inn. I understood the man, and Myrina stared at the floor, feeling it best to hold her tongue, though quite certainly she could have found plenty to say. Yet I was annoyed by the landlord's words, since they showed his poor opinion of my judgment, much-traveled citizen though I was. The madness of the situation was brought home to me; I clutched my head in both hands and exclaimed, "You mistake me utterly, my good man! This girl is my sister. We quarreled on our way hither, aboard the ship from Alexandria, and she defied me by joining a troupe of strolling players. I found her at the theatre in Tiberias, and she has had enough of adventure. Wait until she has bathed and dressed her hair and put on decent clothes. For the sake of her reputation keep quiet, and you shall not regret it."

The proprietor only half believed me and muttered angrily to himself that not the most drunken guest who ever smuggled a harlot into an inn had hit on the notion of calling her his sister. But when he saw that I was not drunk and that I had known Myrina before and not just picked her up in the street, he let us in and sent a slave-woman to show Myrina to the bath, a barber to curl her hair and a wardrobe master to lay out clothes in my room for me to buy for her. All I wanted for her was a decent, inconspicuous traveling dress, but when she came from her bath she insisted upon trying on various garments and surveying herself front and back in a mirror held by the slave, until I wearied of it and threw myself face-downward on the bed with my hands over my ears, to escape their intolerable chattering.

When Myrina saw that I was seriously annoyed she threw down the clothes, dismissed the slave, touched my shoulder lightly and said, "A woman's grief and disappointment are soothed by fragrant ointments and newly dressed hair and good clothes. But try to remember that my ragged mantle and worn sandals would be incomparably dearer to me if I might wear them and share a piece of barley bread with my brother. You might at least try to laugh, as I do, when I seek to amuse you and drive the dark thoughts from your head."

I pressed my hands to my head and said, "Ah, sister, I'm glad to see you find relief from your sorrow, but your anguish has passed into me. The night is far spent and my fear grows with every hour. I know not what it is I fear, but in my heart I pray to Jesus of Nazareth that he may not forsake us. Don't talk to me of hair and clothes. It's nothing to me what I put on or eat or drink, now that the hour of accomplishment is near and he will soon show himself to his own."

Myrina pressed against me, threw her arms around me, laid her thin cheek against my shoulder and said softly, "Was it from your heart that you called me sister just now? If so, I ask no more. In just this way I used to sleep in my brother's arms, with my head safe against his shoulder."

In hardly more than a moment she was slumbering in my arms, sobbing a little even in sleep. But I was too uneasy to sleep. Dozing, I seemed to see a wild vision. I was old, my head was gray and I was wandering in the desert along an endless trail, barefoot and wearing a ragged mantle. Beside me, haggard and gaunt, walked Myrina with a burden on her back, and behind, riding a shaggy donkey, came Mary of Beret, so fat and with such lines of discontent about her mouth that it was only by her eyes that I recognized her. Somewhere far ahead walked a radiant figure who now and then turned and glanced behind him; yet hasten as I might, I knew I should never overtake him.

When I awoke from this vision I was soaked through with sweat. If this was really an omen of my future, and if that was the kind of kingdom that Jesus of Nazareth offered to his followers, I was not so sure that I desired to seek him. I remembered that he had foretold other evil things for me, that night by the lake; if indeed that man was he. A temptation seized me, and it seemed to me that a darkness deeper than the darkness of night took upon itself a living shape and tried to entwine itself about me.

"Jesus of Nazareth, son of God, have mercy!" I cried aloud in my torment. The darkness withdrew. Pressing the palms of my hands together I repeated the prayer that Susanna had taught me. When I had uttered the last words, "in truth," I fell asleep, calmly, and slept until dawn.

I was roused by Myrina starting up at my side. Through the chinks of the shutters I saw the pale morning. But Myrina was staring in front of her with shining eyes and a smiling face, and with a cry she said, "O my brother Marcus, what a wonderful dream!"

And she told it to me: "We were walking up a burning stairway, you and I and someone else, but the fire didn't hurt us and we went higher and higher, and it grew lighter and lighter. When you grew tired and reluctant to go on, I took you by the hand and helped you. It was the most beautiful dream I've ever had. It means something good."

"I dreamed too," I told her, and the thought struck me that both dreams might have held the same significance; for one may look at the same thing in quite different ways. Just then there came a knock at the door and a sleepy, scared servant came in to say, "Be not angry, lord, but there is one below asking for you. I would never have dared to wake you but for this obstinate man and his two donkeys. He says you must leave at once."

Throwing my mantle over me I hurried down. The sun had not yet risen. Shivering in the cold I caught sight of Nathan and gave a cry of delight. Even he was so full of impatience that he forgot his taciturnity and told me, "They left Capernaum this night. Word has gone out to all. They went in separate groups, each with his family and kin. They took Susanna too, and I gave her one of the donkeys. I lent another to Simon Peter whose mother-in-law is elderly and sick. I thought it might be prudent for you to keep on good terms with him, although he doesn't yet know whose donkey he has borrowed. But I don't believe they will turn away anyone who has received the message, for this is a day of grace. This very night the kingdom may be founded in Israel."

"Shall I bring my sword?" I asked quickly.

"No," replied Nathan. "He said: 'He who takes the sword

shall perish by the sword.' He can call a legion of angels to his aid at need. Let us hasten now and go to the mountain."

I asked him if it was far to the mountain, and he told me that he knew where it was and how to get there, and that it would mean a long day's journey. In his opinion it would be wise not to arrive before evening, so as not to attract attention. I asked him to be patient for a moment while I dressed and told my companion to make ready.

Not until I came down again with Myrina did I realize that Nathan believed Mary of Beret to be still with me. He gave Myrina an astonished glance, and then looked reproachfully at me. I felt guilty, as if I had betrayed his trust, but defended myself eagerly, saying, "This young girl is a foreigner like myself, but she has lost her brother and I have adopted her as my sister. Have compassion on her for the sake of Jesus of Nazareth. If you won't take her, then I can't go with you either, for I am bound by a promise to take her to the mountain."

I fell in grave Nathan's estimation, and he must have thought me a babbler. But he merely threw out his hands and accepted my decision without protest. His relief after the long time of waiting was doubtless so great that he would have allowed Herod Antipas himself to come with us. I felt cheered, and reflected that even the disciples in their joyous expectation would let Jesus make up his own mind about whom to receive and whom to reject.

Nathan took us by a short cut past the city to the highroad which led into the interior. As I had guessed, many people were on their way out of the place: those who had been at the races and spent the night in Tiberias. When we came higher up among the hills I looked about me at the mighty view across the Sea of Galilee and the city with its arcades. The road behind us was bright with people, and before us dust-clouds hung in the air, showing us our route.

At short intervals along the road, and at every bridge, legionaries were posted. The Roman officials had evidently decided to throw a close net across the land, for the legionaries halted all vehicles, donkeys, camels, horses and ox teams, and exacted toll. Of those who traveled on foot they required no toll, but from time to time called one wayfarer or another who looked to them suspect, questioned him and made sure that he was unarmed.

As we began to descend the hillsides toward the interior of the country it seemed as if all Galilee were one great garden, so closely did the cultivated lands lie alongside the road. Many wayfarers, for fear of the Romans, ran off the road when they spied a guard post. But the peasants in their turn came up onto the road at a run, with oaths and complaints of those who in attempting to circumvent the guards trampled crops and damaged fenced vineyards.

No one examined or questioned us, although because of the donkeys we had to pay toll three times. At noon we halted by a well and let our animals rest while we ate. It was then I remembered something that filled me with anxiety. I asked Nathan whether Mary Magdalene had had word or whether I should turn back to find her. Nathan reassured me, and declared that all who expected the message had received it.

As we rested I watched the folk who were hurrying by without allowing themselves a moment's repose even in the heat of the day, and tried to guess which and how many of them were also on their way to the mountain. I saw some radiant with joyful expectancy and seemingly oblivious of the dust of the road or of any fatigue. But those who were returning from the races walked with drooping heads and seemed weary of everything. Many had broken off green boughs to shade themselves with, for it was a hot day. A handsome youth came by, leading a blind old man.

Just as we were making ready to continue our journey we heard distant shouts of warning and a rumble of wheels and hooves, and the gray team of yesterday's race dashed past. The driver had had to wait amid the press of carts at the guard post, and was now making up for lost time, heedless of travelers on foot. It seemed to me that he was bound to run someone down at that speed, in such a throng.

When we came to the next bend we saw that indeed there had been an accident. A cluster of people stood shaking their fists after the chariot, which was already far ahead. The youth leading the blind man had managed to push his companion out of the way, but had been hurt badly himself. He had been struck on the head—his brow was bleeding—and seemed to have broken his leg as well, for he could not stand upon it when he tried to get up. The blind man was uttering angry complaints, not fully understanding what had happened.

When people saw that help was needed, they scattered hastily and continued on their way. The young man wiped the blood from his face and felt gingerly at his foot. I looked at him curiously, thinking he might thank his good fortune that he was yet alive. With clenched teeth he met my gaze, then turned to the blind man and with a few vehement words besought him to be calm. We would have passed by, but that Myrina called upon Nathan to stop and swung lightly down from the back of her donkey. Falling on her knees beside the lad she felt his leg with both hands, and called to us, "It is broken."

"If you've satisfied your curiosity," I said acidly, "let us go on, for we're in a hurry."

The young man said to us, "Israelites, for mercy's sake take pity on my blind father. We are honest folk, but my father has lost his sight, and he has been promised that someone will heal him if he can reach that healer by this evening. Tomorrow will be too late. I count for nothing in this; but I beseech you to take my father with you as far as the edge of the plain of Nazareth. There someone is sure to come and help him and lead him the right way."

"There are many ways and many false guides," Nathan broke in. "Are you quite sure of the way yourself, young man?"

The boy gave a radiant smile, despite his pain, so that he

looked beautiful sitting there on the ground with his bloodied face. "There's only one Way," he said cheerfully.

"In that case we are all going in the same direction," remarked Myrina, with a questioning look at me. Reluctantly I dismounted from my donkey and said, "Come, blind man! I will help you onto my donkey, and walk."

Myrina suggested, "If we're bound for the same place—if these two are on their way to the mountain—why should we leave the boy behind? Surely we can bind up his wounds and lift him onto my donkey. I am used to walking."

The youth said, "I would not like to be a trouble to you. But if we're children of the same father he will surely bless you if you help me."

I found it hard to accept the idea that a poor Galilean with a broken ankle, and a blind father who muttered so angrily to himself, were my equals and that they had as good a right as I—if not better, since they were Jews—to seek Jesus of Nazareth. But when I saw the justice of it I thanked Myrina because her innate kindliness had vanquished my obtuseness, and together we washed the young man's face, bound up his head, splinted his shin and cut a sturdy staff for him, with which he was able to hop on one leg to the donkey. Meanwhile his blind father had mounted the other animal and was ready to start; he listened impatiently to what we were doing, and suddenly cried out in a voice of authority, "What girl is that whose voice I hear and who knows but a few words of our language? Let her not touch you, boy; don't speak to her—don't even look at her—lest we defile ourselves on our holy journey."

The young man looked uncomfortable and said, "My father knows the law and has obeyed it scrupulously all his life. It is from no lapse of piety that he has been afflicted. Understand him. He refuses to risk defilement before meeting the healer."

For all his ill-will, the blind man clung fast to the donkey with both hands, so that even by force it would have been difficult to lift him off. But my kindly thoughts melted away and

I rebuked him sternly: "Your own race forsook you on the road. The girl is a Greek and I myself am an uncircumcised heathen, though I dress in the Hebrew manner. I hope that my donkey at least will not defile you, since you sit on it so firmly."

Nathan said conciliatingly, "You need not fear them, blind man. I myself am of the children of Israel and of the quiet ones. They seek the same Way as I. Know that I once lived in the desert, in a closed house, where I learned to read the scriptures, gave away my possessions to the children of light and partook of their meals in common. But I was not fit to be a scribe, and so I left the desert to seek a new teacher of righteousness, and followed the prophet in camel's hair who proclaimed that the kingdom was at hand; and he baptized me. Then he was killed and I took a vow of silence, so as not to be tempted to speak of what only a true teacher of righteousness can know. But the hour has come and now is. And so I release myself from my promise. Believe me, blind man: at this time and among this people there is not in a single one of our tribes a man who is clean and without sin. Ablutions and sacrifices cannot purify you, and not even the truest teacher can do so. But the word was made flesh and dwelt among us, though we did not know him. He was crucified and rose from the tomb to deliver us from our sins. If you believe in him, he will give you back your sight. But if you believe yourself to be pure in comparison with us, I don't think he will heal you."

The blind man lamented loudly and with one hand felt for a seam in his mantle, that he might rend it. But his son restrained him, saying, "These strangers showed mercy when the undefiled abandoned us. Don't be hardhearted and grieve them. Our father's sun shines on good and wicked alike; on the children of Israel and on the heathen. Don't think that you shine more brightly than his sun—you who have been struck with blindness already."

But the blind man ordered him to hold his tongue and bade Nathan lead his donkey a little way ahead so that we might not be too near him. Myrina and I dropped back, but the youth reined in his donkey to keep level with us, looked at us frankly and explained, "It's hard for an old man to free himself from the old things, but your guide is right. There is no righteous person on earth. Though I strained every nerve to obey the commandments and the law it would not free me from my sin. I regard myself as no better than any heathen, and I'll never believe that your compassion could defile me."

I looked at him. His face was gray-green with pain, and he gritted his teeth with the effort of keeping himself on the donkey. I said, "Your face is pure, your eyes clear. I don't believe you willingly yield to sin."

He explained, "God created man in his own image. But because of the fall of our first parents, Adam and Eve, God's image has been weakened in me, and in the presence of God I feel naked and ashamed."

"I've read that, and heard it said," I answered, "but I've never understood it. A Jewish scholar in Alexandria told me that this story too should be taken merely as a parable."

The young man tried to smile. "How should I, an unschooled lad, understand anything? But I have seen Jesus of Nazareth by the lake. He gave the blind their sight and made the lame walk. He said that he was the bread of life. I would gladly have followed him, but Father is strict. If he had been kind and gentle I should have run away. But as it was, my heart told me that if I ran away to join Jesus of Nazareth I should be doing so merely to escape my father's sternness. Father believed more in the teachers of the synagogue, who condemned Jesus for keeping company with sinners. Many a time my father thrashed me because I neglected my daily tasks to go and listen to him. Father thought he was an agitator. But then all at once he was smitten with blindness. In the evening he said his prayer and lay down to rest, but when he woke in the morning he could see nothing, and thought at first that day had not yet dawned. He was distracted, and no one could cure him. He was ready then to believe in Jesus, and to seek him, but Jesus had gone on to Judea and Jerusalem, and was crucified there. So then he sought out the quiet ones, who hinted that Jesus was risen and told us of the day and the hour, and of the road we're now traveling. Father firmly believes that Jesus can heal him if only we get there in time. I believe so too, but I could wish that my father would seek the kingdom rather than the sight of his eyes."

Myrina asked me eagerly what the young man had been saying, and I told her. She wondered greatly and said, "This bright-eyed boy is pure of heart. I never even believed such people existed. Why should he of all people meet with an accident?"

"You mustn't ask that," I said, "when he himself accepts it without question. He forgets his own pain in wishing good to his surly father. It is the law among the Jews to honor their father and their mother."

But Nathan, who knew Greek, heard my explanation and turning said, "So the law commands. But, as I've heard, Jesus of Nazareth teaches that a husband should leave his wife and a son his parents and brothers and sisters, and a rich man his house and goods, for the sake of the kingdom. When he called, the fishermen had to leave their nets in the lake and the ploughman his ox in the field; and one man who wanted first to bury his father was not allowed to follow him."

The blind man lamented afresh, crying, "I am fallen among blasphemers, and Satan himself leads my donkey. Can one expect any good thing of a way whose travelers slay the law with their words?"

His son's face darkened, but he consoled him and said, "I never heard Jesus say such things. He called meek people and peacemakers blessed. He forbade us to speak evil words, or meet evil with evil; he commanded us to love our enemies and to pray for those who persecute us. He told us that his father knew all our needs and would supply them if only we would seek the kingdom, without troubling ourselves about the morrow."

Marveling at this I said bitterly, "I have heard a great deal about him and his teaching. The teaching is full of contradictions, and depends entirely on who delivers it. I no longer know what I should believe."

But Myrina looked at us in surprise and asked, "Why are you suddenly arguing about him, just as we're on our way to see him? I believe I am the happiest among you, knowing little of him and being like an empty vessel which he may fill if he please."

Her words struck home. Walking there behind the donkeys I stared at the dust of the road, reviewing all that had happened to me and all the different moods in which I had received it. I could find nothing good in me any more, nor enough love. Yet I assured myself for one last time that it was not from mere curiosity I was seeking the risen man. In my heart I prayed in the name of Jesus of Nazareth, desiring that I might be purged of all my conceit and selfishness, all my learning and my worldly perspicacity—yes, even of my common sense—so that I too might be merely an empty vessel, ready to receive his truth if he would fill me with it.

After that prayer I raised my eyes and saw a hill rising beyond the plain, its rounded crest gilded by the afternoon sun. I knew at once that this was the mountain for which we were bound. Lofty, harmonious, perfect in shape, it commanded all that countryside. We followed the highway a little farther, across the dried-up bed of a stream, and then turned off southward on a track along the hillside to avoid the town which Nathan told us was situated on its northern slopes. We came to the end of cultivation; the path now ran through scrub and we walked in the shade of the mountain. There was silence all about us. We heard no cries of animals and saw no people. Everything was so quiet that I began to wonder whether we were going the right way. Yet the very ground, the trees and the beautifully curving slope told me that the hill was holy. Peace descended on my mind and I was impatient no longer.

Nor was Nathan in any hurry. I believe he chose this difficult path to avoid company on the road and needless questions, for he kept his eyes on the sky and the deepening shadows, and let the donkeys halt and breathe. Being a Roman, I marveled that we should have come upon none of the guard posts of the quiet ones; for where so great and so secret a gathering was concerned, surely the followers of Jesus must have sent forth people on all roads leading to the mountain, to show the way or to turn back those who were unbidden. When three stars appeared in the sky we continued on our way, and in darkness arrived at a place near the summit where we found a great multitude encamped in small groups, and waiting.

Everything was incredibly quiet; people spoke in whispers, so that a gentle breeze seemed to be blowing there. Nathan tethered the donkeys in a clump of trees and helped the blind man to dismount. Myrina and I supported the youth. So we drew near to the crowd and sat down at its fringe, a few paces away from the nearest groups. Away on the other side of the crowd we could see more shadows approaching, outlined against the night sky. Those arriving camped on the ground without talking to anyone, and waited like the rest of us. From the sound of whispering I knew that many hundreds of people must be gathered here, and I would never have believed that so great a crowd could be so quiet.

Thus the first watch of the night went by, but no one wearied in waiting, or rose, or went away. The moon was waning, but the starlight was bright and it rained upon the ground like silver. I began to be increasingly aware of the presence of some power, and putting my arm around Myrina I found that her body had stiffened in expectation. As once in my room in Jerusalem, heavy raindrops seemed to be falling upon me, yet when I touched my face there was no moisture on it.

I noticed that many were standing up to see better, and I

did so too. In the midst of the people a tall figure stood erect under the starlight, and spoke in a powerful voice: "Men, brothers!"

All were silent; there was stillness everywhere. He went on: "The grain is ripening to harvest, the festival is at hand and the forty days he gave us are nearing their end. The hour approaches, and with it the departure. Where he goes we cannot follow. He was the bread given us from heaven. He who eats of that bread shall have eternal life. The bread he gave us is his flesh, given for the life of the world. And we dispute no longer as to how he can give us his flesh to eat, for we eleven have known this thing and can bear witness to it. To us he has entrusted the secret of his kingdom. Truly, unless you eat the flesh of the Son of Man and drink his blood, you have no life in you. But he who eats the flesh of the Son of Man and drinks his blood possesses eternal life and shall awake at the last day. His flesh is the true food and his blood is the true drink. He who eats his flesh and drinks his blood shall abide in him. But if there be any one among you who is offended by this, and finds such words objectionable, let him rise and go, and no one shall condemn him."

But no one got up to go; nor did I, although I feared this mystery. I could not have risen, even had I so wished, for my arms and legs felt powerless and I hardly dared to breathe.

The speaker was silent for a long time, and stood steady as a rock in the starlight in the midst of the people. Then he resumed, speaking as simply as a child and seemingly as full of wonder as anyone else: "We ate the paschal lamb together with him the night he was betrayed. He took a loaf, blessed and broke it and gave it to us, saying, 'This is my body.' And he took a cup, gave thanks and handed it to us, saying, 'Drink all of you of this, for this is my blood, which shall be shed to forgive many their sins.' "

When he had related this, he continued with both arms raised, "Eat now and drink, all you who love him and long for him and believe that he is the Christ and the son of God. Bless your bread in his name, and break it, and share it amongst yourselves; bless the wine in his name and give one another to drink; let him who has give to him who has not, that no one be left lacking. When we have eaten and drunk we will watch and wait for him."

Having spoken he sat down upon the ground, and life and movement came among the crowd as all got up to wash and to help each other pour water over their hands. We had but little water, but Nathan poured some over our hands and over the hands of the blind man and his son; and afterwards I took the waterskin and poured water over Nathan's hands, and he was not offended. We had food enough for all, but the blind man began trembling, and begged in a whisper that he might eat his own bread and drink his own wine. Still no one spoke aloud, but the murmur of the crowd was like a rising wind.

I felt no resentment at the blind man's refusal to share our bread. Nathan blessed his bread in the name of Jesus Christ, broke it in half and handed it to him and his son. Then in the same way he blessed our own white bread, gave some to me and Myrina and ate of it himself, saying, "May this bread be the bread of immortality, as it is spoken. May it be to your life and not your death."

I said humbly, "His will be done, for he is the son of God. If he wills it to my death because I'm a stranger, so be it."

When we had eaten of the bread, Nathan blessed the blind man's drink and gave it to him and to his son. For us he mixed water with the wine and blessed the cup. I drank, then he, and the cup remained with Myrina. We ate and drank as all about us ate and drank, sharing their food with each other.

But the blind man had eaten only a few mouthfuls when he burst out weeping, wagged his head and wailed aloud, "I have eaten of the body of God's son and drunk his blood. I believe that with him all things are possible. May he have mercy on my unbelief."

Myrina handed the cup to me. I drank and passed it to Nathan. He drank, and the cup returned to Myrina. When she had drunk she slanted the cup, looked into it in wonder and whispered, "This cup in my hand gets no emptier."

Equally mystified I said, "I thought we had eaten all the bread, but here is a whole loaf beside me. Nathan, did you put it there?"

He answered, "No, but perhaps we had more with us than I thought."

Once more we drank, and still the cup was not empty. But I was no longer surprised at anything that happened, for everything seemed as in a vivid dream, although I sat on the ground and felt the chill of it, saw the starry sky above my head and heard the murmur of the crowd like the beat of heavy seas on the shore. There was no thought in my head beyond the rapturous certainty that Jesus of Nazareth was on his way, and that I should see him. His bread had not stuck in my throat, and his wine had not choked me.

So passed the second watch of the night, and I believe no one slept: all were waiting. And there was no impatience in that waiting; it was a preparation. Suddenly the blind man raised his head and asked, "Is it already daybreak? I seem to see a brightness." He turned eagerly, peering in toward the crowd.

We craned our necks too, and saw that the risen man had come and was standing among his own people. How and when he came I can't explain, but there could be no mistaking him. He was dressed in white and the starlight was cast back by the whiteness, so that he himself seemed to be giving forth light, and his face too was radiant. Very slowly he walked among the crowd, pausing now and then as if greeting his people, and stretching forth his hands to them in benediction.

Little by little all had raised their heads and were looking in the same direction, but no one ventured to leap up and run to him. Suddenly we heard a scream, unnaturally loud, and a woman flung herself face-downward on the ground before him, and cried with weeping and joy in her voice, "My Lord and my God!" A shudder ran through the crowd. The Nazarene stooped and stroked her head, and she was quiet at once. We heard the people's sighing breath, but more and more were whispering, "That is he. The Master has come to us."

The blind man craned his neck, knelt on the ground with upstretched hands and said, "I don't see him. I see only a light, as if the sun were shining straight into my eyes."

I cannot say how long he lingered among us, for time seemed to stand still; yet I lived wholly and fully while he moved among the throng, pausing by each of his own people, forgetting none. Everything was simple and natural, and so much a matter of course that not one doubt crossed my mind; nor was I surprised at anything that happened. I can only suppose that on that night, for as long as I could see him, I was in his kingdom.

At last he came near us, and as he approached I quaked inwardly, like the surface of ruffled water. He seemed to be talking to the people while he blessed them, but there was no sound, although I saw some who nodded eagerly as if in answer. Then he was standing before us, regarding us. His face was tired and radiant and his kingdom shone from his eyes. I saw the lips of the blind man moving, but heard no sound, and I wondered whether I had been smitten with deafness. But he passed his fingers lightly over the blind man's eyes and laid his hand upon the son's head. Both sank to the ground before him and lay there motionless. Others not far away were lying thus; for them too he had touched.

Then he looked straight at me, and I knew that if he touched me I should die. My lips moved and I must have spoken to him, though I didn't hear my own voice. I think I entreated him: "Lord, take me to your kingdom."

He said, "Not everyone who says to me 'Lord, Lord' is

worthy of my kingdom; only he who hears my word and does my father's will."

I asked, "What is your word, and what is your father's will?"

He said, "That you know already. What you do to the least of these, you do also to me."

I must have asked something more about his kingdom, for he smiled patiently as to an importunate child, and said, "You cannot say of the kingdom of heaven that it lies here or there. The kingdom is in you and in all who know me."

He said further, "I forsake no one who calls upon me. Where two or three are gathered together in my name, I am with them until the end of time. And you are never so lonely as to be without me if you call me."

He turned from me, paused and looked at Nathan. I saw Nathan move his lips, but heard no word. After regarding Nathan he looked gently at Myrina too, but Myrina's lips did not move. Then he turned away and went back to his own.

The blind man and his son still lay there as if dead, but when Nathan saw that this alarmed me he shook his head and whispered, "They're not dead; they sleep. Don't touch them."

After that I saw the eleven gathering about him, and it was as if he were speaking to them with great love, and they making answer. But tears dimmed my sight, so that I perceived him only as a bright haze among the eleven. When I had wept all my weeping he had vanished, and I cannot say how and in what manner he left us. I rather felt than saw that he was gone, for with him power departed from our circle. I felt as if I had awakened from slumber; I sneezed, and was able to move my limbs.

Time returned. By the sky I saw that the third watch of the night had come and that dawn was near. People stood up and looked searchingly about. I heard shouts and animated conversation, as if all were vying with one another in telling what he had said to each of them.

I too exclaimed joyfully, "Nathan, Nathan, I spoke to him and he answered me. You can witness that he did not shut me out of his kingdom."

But Nathan shook his head in wonder, saying, "I can by no means be that witness. I did indeed see your lips move, but your tongue must have been paralyzed, for I heard no sound. But I spoke to him and he answered."

Myrina clutched my arms with both hands and said rapturously, "I dared not speak to him, but he recognized me and smiled and told me I should never be thirsty in my life again, because I gave him drink when he was thirsty."

Nathan lost his temper and exclaimed, "You're out of your minds, both of you! He said nothing to you; he spoke to me alone, and showed me the Way. He taught me that nothing that goes into a man is unclean, only what comes out of him. In his kingdom there are many dwelling places. To each shall be measured according to his own measure—more to one, less to another—but no one who truly asks him for anything shall lack. I am to believe the eleven, for he has chosen them to be the bearers of his message. His kingdom is like a grain of mustard seed: it grows slowly, but one day it will spread into a tree among whose branches birds from every quarter of the world shall build their nests."

Nathan was silent, staring ahead as if listening, and said at last lamely, "He taught me much else too, though I've forgotten it. But surely it will return to my memory in due time."

I was much surprised, but his kingdom still dwelt in me as he had said, and my mind was at peace. "Don't be angry with me, Nathan," I said. "I really believed that he was talking to me and I still believe he said something. Perhaps he spoke to each according to his need. If I knew and could write down all that he has said to his own people this night, surely no book could contain it. So we may not have been meant to hear what he said to each one."

Nathan, mollified, laid his hands on my shoulders and said,

"At least I saw him look at you, and no evil befell you. So I touch you now, and to me you are not unclean."

We conferred together and agreed that it would be best for us to leave the mountain before daybreak, lest anyone should recognize me. But the blind man and his son were still sleeping like the dead, and we dared not rouse them; nor could we abandon them. So we stayed and waited. As day broke, the excitement and elation of the crowd grew ever noisier. Many joined together in songs of thanksgiving. Others ran breathless from group to group to greet their friends and testify that they had seen the risen man with their own eyes. Flushed with excitement they cried to each other, "Peace be with you. Have your sins too been forgiven? Did he promise you eternal life? Truly, we who saw him here on the mountain shall never taste death."

The ground under me was hard, my limbs were stiff and I clasped my hands to feel that there was life in them. When morning came and all could recognize each other, the eleven went out among the people in twos and threes. I saw them rouse and raise those whom the risen man had touched and who had sunk to the ground in a swoon.

Three of them were on their way toward us, and the first of them I recognized as the man who had spoken during the night and addressed hard words to the crowd. I knew him by his round head and broad shoulders, and in the pale light of morning I could see that his bearded face was stubborn and fiery. He had young John with him. John was pale from watching, but his face was still the purest and brightest that I had ever seen in any young man; it made me happy just to look at him. The third man I didn't know, but from his looks I saw that he was one of the eleven. I can explain this in no other way than by saying that his features had something of the features of Jesus of Nazareth, though they were different, and dimmer, as if seen through a veil of gauze.

Beholding him I was reminded of the solitary fisherman

with whom I had spoken one night by the lake. Now that I had looked eye to eye at the risen Jesus, I tried to recall the appearance of that fisherman, and still cannot say for certain whether he was Jesus or not; yet I believe that it was to him I spoke by the lake, although I failed to recognize him then. But why he should have revealed himself to me I cannot understand.

The nearer these three came the guiltier I felt; I tried to avert my face from them. They had not noticed me, but bending over the blind man they shook him, raised him up and said, "Awake, sleeper!"

The blind man rubbed his eyes, stared at them and said, "I see you. You are three men, but I don't know you."

The first of them said, "We are three of the messengers whom Jesus of Nazareth, the son of God, has chosen. I am Simon whom he called Peter. But who are you?"

The blind man rubbed his forehead, looked about him with seeing eyes, rejoiced greatly and said, "Last night I saw a great light. A power worked in my eyes and it hurt so much that I fainted. But now I am awake, and see with both eyes, though I was blind when I came here."

In great joy he bent over his son, shook him awake, raised him to his feet and embraced him, crying, "The risen Jesus of Nazareth healed me last night. Blessed be his name! All my days I will praise God who sent him."

Half asleep, the boy snatched the bandage from his head. The wound in his forehead was healed and cicatrized, and he stood on both legs without pain. Finding that something still hampered him, he stooped and took off the splint, rubbed his calf and said wonderingly, "My leg is mended!"

Simon Peter said, "Last night he healed all those whom he had called to testify to his resurrection, that there might be witnesses enough. We have all beheld him at the same time. Not only has he healed eyes so that they have regained their sight, and restored to deaf ears their hearing, and made the lame walk; he has healed us also of our sins, and opened to us the gate of life everlasting."

But John was staring at me. Touching Peter's arm he said, "We don't know those two; we never called them, yet he has healed them. Others too have come here unsummoned, but last night he turned no one away." Pointing accusingly at me he went on, "But him I do recognize. He thrust himself upon us in Jerusalem, ensnared us with importunate questions, misled the women and tempted Simon of Cyrene and Zaccheus, so that Levi had to go and warn him not to abuse our master's name. This is that same Marcus, a heathen and a Roman. I do not understand how he can be here."

Simon Peter started, clenched his big fists and exclaimed, "Have we even here a traitor among us?"

But John and the other man held him back and said warningly, "Let us make no disturbance. Take them aside, or the people will be frightened and stone him, and then we shall be questioned as to the shedding of his blood; for he is a Roman citizen."

Breathing heavily, Peter gave me a somber look and said, "There are hotheads among the people. What would you say, Roman, if I handed you over to them? They would take you with them to some cave from which you would never return."

"I'm not afraid of you or of anyone," I answered. "Why should I fear, when your master did not turn me away last night? Surely he had power to hinder my coming if he had so wished? Or do you doubt that?"

Anxious and worried, they took all three of us to the copse where they had tethered the donkeys, and conferred among themselves as to whether they should summon the other disciples. From their conversation I gathered that Nicodemus, Simon of Cyrene and Zaccheus, whom I knew, were among the people on the mountain. But John said, "The more men we summon, the more stir it will cause. The Roman is right: the Lord did not turn him away. Why, I don't know; but the servant ought not to think himself wiser than his master."

Now that we were by ourselves the blind man who had been healed and his son spoke up for us, and told what had happened upon the road, saying that I had taken pity on them and brought them to the mountain. But Simon Peter said fiercely, "Was it not sign enough for you that the horse trampled you down and broke the boy's leg? You had not been called and he didn't want you here."

The young man was saddened, and throwing himself on his knees before Peter he implored him: "Forgive me, holy men. I meant no harm. It was for my father's sake that I did it. I never asked him to heal my leg; I never even thought of it. But of his goodness he touched me and made me whole. Perhaps in that way he gave me his forgiveness. Forgive me also—me and my father."

Nor did I find it hard to humble myself before these three worried men. "If you wish it I will kneel to you, holy men of God," I said. "I beg your forgiveness, since you are his chosen ones and the foremost in his kingdom. I am no traitor; I wish you no harm. I will be silent about all that I have seen, if you think it best; or if you will, I am ready to testify to his resurrection before the whole world—before Caesar himself."

Simon Peter fumbled at his tunic as if to rend it, and exclaimed, "Be silent, madman! What would people say if a Roman and a heathen were to bear witness of the kingdom? Better if you had never heard of the Way. Though this night you may have fled from your defilement, yet it will ensnare you again and you will return to the world like a dog to its vomit. For us you are no more than dog's vomit."

In wrath he turned to Nathan and said accusingly, "You I have seen in Capernaum, and I trusted you, but you've betrayed us and brought a heathen to the feast of eternal life."

Nathan rubbed his nose with his forefinger and said, "You,

Simon, fisher of men! Did I not lend you a donkey in Capernaum, so that you might bring hither your sick mother-in-law?"

Peter looked abashed. Glancing guiltily at his two companions he nevertheless returned with some heat, "Well, and what then? I trusted you, and Susanna spoke for you."

"That donkey was this Roman's donkey," Nathan told him in measured tones. "Marcus here is a good-natured man, but if you cross him he may claim the beast again, compassionate though he may be. Then you will be left here on the mountain with your mother-in-law. Of course Susanna might stay to keep you company; she rode here on another of the Roman's donkeys."

Simon Peter was perplexed; scraping his toe on the ground he said, "My mother-in-law has a malicious tongue, and once lashed even *him* with it for enticing me to a life of idleness, as she thought, because I left my nets for his sake. But Jesus cured her when she was sick of a fever and thought she was dying. Since then she has held her tongue. I wouldn't like to leave her in the lurch, for we eleven must set forth at once and travel day and night, if we're to reach Jerusalem before the forty days have elapsed. Then we must remain there and await the fulfillment of the promise. If my mother-in-law has no donkey to take her back to Capernaum, I know not what I shall do."

Warmly I assured him, "I don't return evil for evil; you're welcome to keep the donkey, even though to you I may be no more than dog's vomit. Keep these two other donkeys as well, for the women to ride. We need them no longer, being well able to walk. Take them. Nathan will fetch them in Capernaum. I'll go my way from here without disturbing anyone. And don't curse me or send anyone to hunt me down, for I don't believe that is in accordance with your law."

John now joined in the conversation, and appealed to me: "Roman, try to understand. Some things are not yet clear to us, and the promise is not yet fulfilled. All we know is that the way is narrow and the gate small. Of ourselves we dare not widen them."

The third man said, "He commanded us to make all peoples his disciples. But when and how this is to be done we don't yet know. First, surely, he was to found a kingdom for Israel. All this we shall learn of in Jerusalem."

Seeing these three standing there hand in hand like brothers, and recalling the heritage which Jesus of Nazareth had entrusted to their stewardship, I was filled with envy and dread. I threw myself on the ground before them and appealed to them once more with a prayer, saying, "To you three, and to all eleven of you, he has bequeathed the words of eternal life. I don't rebel against his will, though you're all simple men. Scholars would interpret his teaching, each after his own wisdom, adding thereto something of their own. But you will surely fulfill his will only, as best you can. He did not turn me away; I was allowed to behold him; he did not prevent me from coming. Last night I even believed that he spoke to me; but that I am willing to erase from my mind if you so wish. I don't even ask you for any medicine of immortality. Only allow me to keep his kingdom in my heart, and do not utterly reject me, and I will believe everything as you expound it, adding nothing of my own and claiming no share in any secret knowledge. All that I own I am willing to give away for your support; and as a citizen of Rome I may be able to help you, should you be called to account before the authorities, and persecuted for his sake."

Simon Peter raised his hand in protest, and said, "Not for gold or for silver."

The second of them said, "I remember he promised us that we need never be anxious about what to say if we're haled before the justices; in that hour the words we need will be put into our mouths."

But tears came into the eyes of John; he looked at me with a look of beauty and said, "Roman, I love you for your humility, and I believe you mean us no harm. He descended into the realm of death; he burst its portals and delivered the dead. This I heard from his mother, whom he entrusted to me as my own, at the cross. Should he not then deliver the heathen too? But how this is to come about we do not know. Be patient. Pray, fast and purify yourself. But never speak of him to others, lest for lack of understanding you lead them astray. Leave the speaking to us."

I rose with bowed head and did my utmost to overcome my own vanity, though I was tormented by the suspicion that the heritage of Jesus of Narazeth would be scattered and dispersed by all the winds of heaven if these unlearned men alone were to be its guardians. Yet assuredly—thus I consoled myself—he must have known what was best.

To Nathan I said, "Take the donkeys, go and help the women; protect them and accompany them to Capernaum or to whatever place they are bound for. Rest then after your journeying. Afterwards come back to fetch me from the thermae of Tiberias."

"It will be hard for you to walk through Galilee with only that girl for company," said Nathan warningly. And when I looked about me I found that the erstwhile blind man had seized the opportunity to slip away, taking his son with him. But I was all defiance. Surely Jesus of Nazareth would not forsake me, though men might do so.

"Peace be with you all," I said, and taking Myrina by the hand I set off down the mountain, along the same path by which we had climbed in the darkness. Looking back once more I could see life and movement among the people on the slopes, though many, wearied by their vigil, had wrapped themselves in their cloaks and lain down again upon the ground to sleep for a while before setting forth on their return.

As I walked I recalled all that had happened during the night, and felt no surprise that the blind man should have received his sight, or that his son should have had his leg healed, if indeed it had ever been broken. These marvels seemed to me perfectly natural and the least part of what had happened. So great had been his tenderness that when he revealed himself to his own pople he healed also those whom he had not summoned.

The forty days were nearing their end and he was to return to his father. I tried to accustom myself to the idea that in spite of that he would come to me if I called him, so that never more should I be alone. It was an astounding idea which, if suggested by anyone else, would have sounded senseless. As it was, I had to believe it, so profound was the impression the sight of him had made upon me.

Busy with these thoughts I walked down the hillside through the scrub, leading Myrina by the hand. A fox slunk across the path in front of us. Myrina looked at me and said, "You must have forgotten that you're not alone, although you're holding my hand."

Startled, I looked at her, and reflected that Jesus of Nazareth must have given me to Myrina in place of her brother, lest she perish. He could not entrust her to the Jews, since they would have cared nothing for her; so he had chosen me, a Roman. All this he had done in return for a drink of water.

But, I thought in bewilderment, I have never given Jesus of Nazareth anything. On the contrary, he had been the giver, even to the point of sharing his meal with me on the shore of the sea of Galilee, and letting me warm myself and dry my clothes by his fire, if that solitary fisherman had been he. But I could keep Myrina as my sister, and thus serve the Nazarene.

"Myrina," I said, "from this hour you are my real sister and I will never forsake you. What is mine is yours. Try to bear with my faults and my vanity."

Myrina pressed my hand hard, and said, "Marcus, my brother, have forbearance with me too. But above all explain what it is that has happened to us, and what those three men wanted and why they looked at me with such ill-will."

But since the messengers had forbidden me to speak I dared not explain, even to Myrina, anything about Jesus of Nazareth and his kingdom as I myself understood it. I said only, "Those were three holy men, of the eleven holy men to whom Jesus of Nazareth has revealed the secret of his kingdom. They turned us away because we don't belong to the children of Israel, but are heathen and in their eyes unclean. They forbade me to speak of Jesus of Nazareth out of my own head. But tell me what you think has happened."

Myrina pondered, and then said, "First we ate a sacrificial meal, as is done in Syria when Adonis is buried and raised from the dead. But this was different, for Jesus of Nazareth offered himself as the sacrifice and rose again. Last night I believed him to be the son of God. Our cup was never emptied of its wine, and bread from nowhere appeared beside us. But to me this proved nothing. My only proof is that I loved him with all my heart when he looked at me, and in that hour there was nothing I would not have been ready to do for his sake. This is a great mystery, certainly a greater one than any of the Greeks or even of the Egyptians. I believe that his kingdom is invisible to me, and yet present, so that I am in his kingdom although my feet walk upon the path and the ground here. No, I could never break away from his kingdom even if I would. But I'm not afraid, for it is good to be in it, and when I am there, there is no sin in me."

I looked in wonder at Myrina's narrow face and green eyes, and said enviously, "Surely he has blessed you, and you are happier than I. His truth must indeed be as simple as bread and wine, so that even the poorest may possess it. My worldly wisdom stands within me like a dark wall: learning is a net to ensnare me, and the logic of the Sophists a trap for my feet. Help me, my sister, to remember this when these seductions beset me."

While talking together we had reached the foot of the mountain, but when I looked about me I saw that we had strayed from the path by which we had come the evening before. Yet this did not disturb me, for I could determine the right direction by the sun and I knew where the great highway ran. But we were no longer in a hurry. I was suddenly aware of this. Never again would I be in a hurry for anything, for surely I had had everything already and would receive no more. I possessed a treasure. With careful husbandry it would suffice me and Myrina for the rest of our days.

At this moment of perception, my whole body was filled with an infinite weariness, and I believe never in my life had I felt so tired. "Myrina," I said, "I cannot walk another step. Henceforth all places are equally good to me. Let us stay here and rest, and sleep in the shade of that fig tree. We have our whole life before us and will wander through it together. Let us rest now, while his kingdom is still at hand and we ourselves well content."

We lay down under the fig tree and I took her in my arms. Both of us sank into a deep sleep. When we awoke, the shadows had moved and the eighth hour had already come. We began walking again, following paths and the headlands of fields in the direction of the highroad. We didn't talk, but I had awakened as if reborn, and in Myrina I felt the presence of my sister. The yellowed fields of Galilee and the brown slopes through their blue haze were beautiful to my eyes. The air was light to breathe and I had no evil thoughts of anyone.

But I was astonished beyond measure when the first people I saw on the road proved to be Mary Magdalene and Mary of Beret. Mary Magdalene was riding a donkey, and Mary of Beret walked barefoot in the dust behind it, urging it on with a switch. I clapped my hands in surprise and hurried forward to greet them. But Mary Magdalene gave me a cold look and was not pleased to see me.

"So it's you, then, is it? And you're coming from the mountain?" she asked sourly. "A fine quandary I should have been in if I'd had only you to rely on. And who's that girl with you now, when you have only just escaped the other by a hairbreadth?"

Both she and Mary of Beret measured Myrina with their eyes, and I realized that Mary Magdalene had expected me to accompany her to the mountain. Yet we had made no such agreement, nor had she sent me word. But for Nathan's loyalty I should never have reached the mountain. However, reproaches were useless now.

"Let me accompany you to your home and protect you on the way, as you have no man to escort you," I suggested. "It will soon be evening. We will find an inn, eat together, spend the night there and tomorrow I will go with you to your house."

But Mary Magdalene was deeply offended at my words. She said harshly and haughtily, "Formerly I had many escorts. Formerly I was offered litters and had no lack of protectors. But since I beheld the Lord upon the mountain he is escort enough for me, and you need not insult me by saying that I have no man to go with me."

I guessed that all had not gone as she would have wished at her departure from the mountain. But I was even more surprised when Mary of Beret addressed me with great stiffness, saying, "You seem very frivolous and fickle, and have consoled yourself very soon. I am glad of that, for your sake, for you can have no more hopes of me. I've had my sins forgiven and am purified so that I'm like a virgin again, and can have nothing further to do with you, a Roman and a heathen. So you're not to look at me desirously; and tell that short-nosed girl not to stare at me in that insolent, critical way, with those ugly eyes of hers."

Fortunately Myrina understood but little of what she was saying, but the looks of both women she did understand, and she gazed at the ground. I was grieved for her sake and asked, "What has happened to you, and why do you speak to me so unkindly?"

Mary of Beret told me, "On the mountain this morning I met a young man and his eyes are as clear as spring water and his cheeks are like pomegranates, and as yet no beard has roughened his chin. He looked at me and took a liking to me, and he promised that he would send his friend to Mary Magdalene's house at once, to come to an agreement, so that he and I may break the winecup together. He is all impatience in his love, and I will gladly hasten too, so long as I am pure. His father has a field and a vineyard, olive trees and sheep, and I ask no more than that to live a good life. His father approves of me too and is willing to believe that I'm a virgin, because Jesus of Nazareth restored his sight last night and because he need pay no bride-price for me."

Mary Magdalene interrupted her, saying, "All this is true, and I did not have to let her out of my sight for more than an instant for her to find a suitor. Otherwise I should have been compelled to marry her to you, and that would have been a pity; for Israelite women may not marry heathen men, though the men have an easier time of it. Truly it was a piece of good fortune that the boy's father was cured of his blindness and out of pure joy believes that Mary too has been cleansed of all her sins. Anyone else, though he believed this, would scarcely have been willing to marry her, because of her past."

Surveying Mary Magdalene's face, which was more like white stone than anything, I knew that she would indeed have had the power to marry Mary of Beret to me, even against my will. I sighed with relief and said, "I can only praise my good fortune and yours, Mary of Beret. But I don't understand it, for I dreamed an omen, and in the dream I was walking in the desert with this Greek girl, and Mary of Beret was with us."

Mary Magdalene was suddenly attentive, and said, "Tell me your dream as accurately as you can remember. Are you certain that Mary of Beret was there?"

I described my dream as well as I could, but as I was speaking it faded from my mind and became indistinct. But without hesitation I said at last, "Mary of Beret was quite certainly there. She was riding a donkey, as you are doing now. She had become fat and bloated, and I saw deep lines of discontent at the corners of her mouth, but in spite of that I recognized her by her eyes."

Mary of Beret was angry, and cried, "You have no right to have such dreams about me, and I don't believe you. It is you who will grow fat and bloated with your own sins; you will lose your teeth and become bald."

I spread my hands and said, "May my dream be unfulfilled. Why should we shout harsh words at each other, when we've all been on the mountain and seen him who is risen? Not one of us did he turn away, not even Myrina."

Quickly I told them how I had met Myrina and what had happened to her, and how her winecup remained full. I also told of the chariot that had knocked the youth down upon the road, and of how we had helped him and his blind father to the mountains. Mary Magdalene nodded with understanding, and said, "Surely all this has come about for a purpose. In this way he leads heathen to heathen and the children of Israel to the children of Israel. But the shadows are long and I do not care for these parts, for I have too much money in my purse. I didn't give them the money, for they would not take me with them to Jerusalem, and Peter ordered me to go home. But what they expect to do in Jerusalem I know not. Come with us, and let us put up at an inn together. When you have brought me to my house we must part as good friends."

We set off in company, and there were no longer many people on the road. During our conversation Myrina had stood silent, staring at the ground, and for that I respected her. When we resumed our journey she asked me in a whisper who these women were. I told her that Mary Magdalene had walked with Jesus on his wanderings and had been the first one at the tomb to see that it was empty. At once Myrina was filled with reverence for Mary Magdalene, and walking up beside her as she rode, she begged her humbly, "Tell me of him who is risen, O happiest among women."

Her meekness pleased Mary so that she looked kindly at Myrina and told her many things about Jesus, speaking in Greek. On the mountain she had met a young married couple from Cana, at whose wedding Jesus had wrought his first miracle and turned water into wine to delight the wedding guests. Then she spoke of Jesus' birth, of how an angel had appeared to his mother Mary and she had become with child in a supernatural manner, and how Joseph her betrothed had thought of sending her away, until revelation came to him in a dream. As I listened I began to feel that I now better understood the men whom Jesus had chosen to be his messengers, and I saw what they meant when they said that Mary was too talkative. But Myrina swallowed it all, and listened with bated breath and shining eyes.

At last I could not help remarking, "The gods of Greece and Rome, according to the stories, mixed with the daughters of mortals and begot children by them. It is even said that the progenitor of the Romans was descended from Aphrodite. Nowadays such tales are regarded by sensible people as parables, just as the Jewish scribes in Alexandria interpret their holy scriptures. I don't believe that Jesus of Nazareth needs any stories to make him the son of God."

Mary Magdalene was offended, and laying her hand on Myrina's shoulder she said, "We women are alike, whether Greeks or children of Israel. Men can never understand us. And you, Roman, should not speak of earthbound gods who chain man to the illusions of earthly life. Now that Jesus has become the Christ of the world they have no longer any power over men, unless men themselves choose evil and bring themselves under their sway. But what I tell, I know; and it is the truth. Mary, the mother of Jesus of Nazareth, told me and other women of it herself when we were walking with Jesus. Even Herod, the old and cruel one, believed that a king had been born in Israel, and had all the male children of Bethlehem slain, thinking to be rid of him in that way. Of that there are still countless witnesses."

Her words caused me to reflect. Mary Magdalene herself might well see too many visions and angels, and dream too many dreams, but I did not believe that of Jesus of Nazareth's mother. I had seen her face by the cross as she mourned. I had also formed the idea that she did not talk unnecessarily, but was silent when others spoke. What reason could she have for telling such a tale unless it were true? The miracles wrought by Jesus of Nazareth were sufficient testimony to him. If I believed them—and I could do nothing else after having spoken to Lazarus—why should I doubt this one? Why should not a spirit cause a woman to be with child if God was to be born on earth as a man? Compared with that marvel, all others were secondary.

Myrina asked more questions about Jesus, and Mary Magdalene, with a look of rebuke at me, continued, "Often he would talk of a sower who went out to sow. Some corn fell on a rock and found no soil to grow in. Some fell among thorns, and the thorns grew up and choked it. But some fell in good soil and bore a manifold crop.

"Not everyone who has heard his word and believes in him it fit for his kingdom, therefore," Mary Magdalene went on. "Your heart is not hard, Roman; it is all too soft. When you return to your own people, thorns and thistles will grow up thickly about you, and block your way to the kingdom."

Her words filled me with dread. I looked about me at the red hills of Galilee and the dark green vineyards where the shadows were lengthening, and said, "How could I ever forget? To the day I die I shall remember this Galilee and the mountain and him as I saw him last night. And I shall never be so lonely that he will not be with me when I call upon him."

I thought for a little, and said, "I am a bad servant to him, the king who is bound for the far country now that the forty days are at an end. I don't know whether he has entrusted any minae to me, but if he has I must bury them in the earth by order of his messengers. This torments me. But I have been given a promise which I believe in, although I shall not tell you of it lest you mock me. . . ."

I was thinking that I am one day to die for the glorification of his name, incredible though it may seem. Yet that was what the lonely fisherman had said to me that night by the lake. For my body's sake I rejoiced that I am a citizen and entitled to execution by the sword, for that agonizing crucifixion I could never endure. I no longer regarded this prediction as something bad, but realized that this is the only way in which I can show Jesus of Nazareth that I belong to him.

Before evening we turned off the highroad along a donkey track which Mary Magdalene said led over the mountains to Magdala. She knew an inn where we could spend the night. We reached it soon after sunset, before it was quite dark. The place was crammed and the food had run out, but the people respectfully made room for Mary Magdalene. I saw the many guests sitting round their fires, bright-eyed, holding whispered conversations, and even from the roof a lively murmur could be heard; and from this I guessed that all these people had come from the mountain. All spoke kindly to one another, and those who had provisions shared with those who had none, so that Myrina and I too could dip our bread into a common dish.

Among the Galileans I felt like a stranger, and when the chill of night came I would have liked nothing better than to be allowed to sit by them, and like them talk of Jesus of Nazareth's revelation and of his kingdom, of the forgiveness of sins and eternal life. But they did not look upon me as their brother, and I could not force myself upon them. Nevertheless our host led the strangers' donkeys into the courtyard, swept out a stall and gave us clean straw to lie on, so that Myrina and I did not have to sleep under the open sky.

Since everyone else was still whispering, in the faint light of a single lamp I taught Myrina the prayer that Susanna had taught me. Myrina felt it suited her and made her feel safe. She said too that it was a great relief not to have to take notice of whether the moon was waxing or waning, or to sprinkle salt and repeat incomprehensible incantations, and carve images from vine roots when one was going to pray. With such rites one never knows if one has done something in the wrong way or said a wrong word so as to deprive the prayer of its virtue.

When I awoke next morning the first thing I saw was Mary of Beret, who was sitting beside me in the straw and staring into my face. When she saw that my eyes were open she began wagging her head and wringing her hands; she whispered softly, "I was hot in there and couldn't sleep. I wanted to see what you were doing, and how you hold your hands when you're with that foreign girl. I would rather have slept like that in the straw with my head on your shoulder than with Mary Magdalene in a narrow bed, getting sweaty and louse-bitten. It was thus that you and I slept by the Jordan on our way to Tiberias. Take no heed of my malicious talk. Yesterday evening I was confused—I knew not what I was saying when you appeared so suddenly with that Greek girl, and I didn't know what to think. I still don't really know. All night I have suffered terrible pangs of conscience because I so suddenly took a fancy to that young man and promised to await his friend in Magdala. Perhaps he will repent of it, and no one will ever come."

I assured her quickly, "That young man is without deceit. His friend will quite certainly come, and in due time he will lead you to the bride-bed, according to Galilean custom. The villagers will drink wine and stamp out the beat, the music will sound and all will sing songs of joy in your honor."

Mary of Beret was annoyed; she ceased wringing her hands and raised her voice: "You purposely misunderstand me. I have suffered agonies over this matter all night long, so that I have hardly slept a wink. You must think me very ugly now that I've had two sleepless nights running, and am red-eyed. It is true, on the other hand, that I know my sins are forgiven and that I'm as virginal again as if I had never known a man. You know that too, since you know the Christ. And anyway I never told the young man much about my past life; only what was absolutely necessary since I didn't want to grieve him needlessly. But I am terrified at the thought that his kinsfolk and all the villagers will spread out the sheet next morning and perhaps may find no token of my innocence, so that I shall be shamefully driven away with stones and sticks, and lose my ring. You Romans are less fussy about these things, but I know my own people, and in this the people of Galilee are no different from the villagers of Beret."

I said, "Mary Magdalene is a woman of experience, and a dove breeder. Trust in her. Even the Romans are in the habit of sacrificing a pair of doves to Venus at their wedding, for safety's sake, so that the bride need suffer no shame."

Mary of Beret's voice was even louder as she cried, "Don't twist and turn away from it like this! And don't tell me you didn't take me with you from Jerusalem to be cleansed from my sin and made fit for you. Certainly I should be breaking the law if I became the wife of a Roman, but in the name of Jesus of Nazareth I am ready to do this thing, to save one of the least of his people."

With a bitter look at Myrina she went on, "I bear no grudge against that girl. She is not worth it. I won't even reproach you if you want her as a secondary wife, for that is accounted no great sin for a man, and not even the Pharisees are blameless in this respect. I will show her her place so that she remains as meek as she is now."

Myrina had long since awakened: she was watching us through her lashes and trying to understand what Mary was saying. Now she opened her eyes wide, sat up and said, "When I fell asleep I felt safe and happy, but in the gray pallor of morning I am cold. The moment of truth must be in the gray of morning and not in evening warmth. I couldn't catch it all, but so much I have understood—this Jewish woman has claims upon you. If I stand in her light, or am a burden to you as your sister, I am ready to go my way. I have the gold pieces, with which I may buy myself a secure living in one way or another. So have no concern for me, and do not take me into account when you and that beautiful Jewish girl discuss your affairs."

Mary of Beret understood not a word of Greek. She stared suspiciously at Myrina and screamed, "Don't believe her—not a word. She speaks gently and beautifully, but I know how wily the Greeks are, and you have too little knowledge of women."

She burst out sobbing, clapped her hands to her face and wailed, "How hardhearted you are! Don't you see that for your sake I am ready to leave everything and come with you to save you from heathen dirt?"

Myrina looked at her in alarm with her green eyes, touched my hand and said, "Why do you make her weep? Don't you see how beautiful she is and how her eyes shine, and what a soft red mouth she has? I envied her even yesterday. I haven't even breasts like a real woman; my nose is too short and my eyes are ugly."

Distracted almost from my wits I looked at them both, and reflected that this was what my dream had signified. Marriage I had never thought of. As long as she lived, Mary of Beret would think herself better than I, for she was a daughter of Israel. She would make Myrina her servant, and in the end, after sufficient nagging, compel me to be circumcised for the sake of peace. Such things have happened to many weak men in Rome, although they do all they may to hide it.

Then a frightening idea struck me. Perhaps this was the intention. Perhaps it was only through the imageless God of the Jews that the way to the Nazarene's kingdom led. Perhaps his disciples would no longer turn me away if thanks to Mary of Beret I became a true proselyte. I had left Rome, and was free to shape my life as I would. If only a painful little cut with the Jewish flint knife divided me from the fellowship of Jesus' followers, it was a small price to pay. I have endured worse pains. And Roman officers on garrison duty in the desert often enough have their foreskin removed for purely practical reasons, being tired of the perpetual swelling caused by fine sand. Egyptians and Arabs have the same custom.

Nevertheless I rebelled against this simple idea. It was the highest exponents of this religion, the high priests, scribes and elders of Israel, who had condemned Jesus of Nazareth. In my heart I knew that I should be betraying Jesus if I entered their temple—that glittering slaughterhouse—to beg them to receive me into their fellowship. I would remain simple and humble of heart rather than allow myself to be circumcised on false pretexts in order to be accepted by the disciples, who would have nothing to do with me as I was today.

Mary of Beret had ceased weeping and was staring at me in suspense. Myrina too looked at me as if she had already lost me. Comparing her with the voluble Mary I felt only tenderness for her, and knew that she would always be closer to me than Mary. My common sense returned and I said resolutely, "You need not make any sacrifice for me, Mary of Beret. You would only bring destruction upon yourself if you parted from the people whom your God has chosen, to go with me who am an unclean heathen. Remember that it was I who brought the young man to the mountain on my donkey, after he had broken his leg. You cannot break your promise to him. I must give you up, but I will gladly present you with so large a wedding gift that you will not be utterly dependent on your husband."

Mary was compelled to believe me. She stopped crying, and said merely, "Thanklessness is this world's reward, and now I too believe that Romans are dogs. Think of me, then, in vain some day when sweet ointments drip from you as you recline on soft cushions behind your curtains. Think then upon my hands, which were made for caresses but must grind at a quern all day long, and upon my eyes watering in the smoke as I bake bread."

Her words left me unmoved, for I didn't believe them. On the contrary, I guessed that she would drive her husband to toil beyond his strength and her relations to wait upon her lightest word, and that in her old age she would be a torment to her sons' wives and a plague to her daughters' husbands. But of course I may have been mistaken.

Having tried to distress me as much as possible, she forgave me, and said, "By rights I should throw your words back in your teeth, but for my own sake I am bound to accept your wedding gift, lest I be held of little account in the eyes of my husband's family. It is no gift, but rather a debt you're paying, having broken all your promises."

I wanted to ask her when I had ever promised her anything, but by now I had learned wisdom and was silent. While we'd been talking, the other guests at the inn had set forth to continue their journey. Mary Magdalene now came to us with a radiant face. She scolded us, saying, "Why do you squabble? Look at the world out there, how gloriously it shines in the light of his sun, now that his kingdom is come upon earth. I bear no one any grudge now—not even Peter. Last night I had a dream, and it showed me that grace has come to the world. White doves glided down from the sky and settled upon the people's heads. On your head too, Roman, a dove descended. I reject no one. To each and every one according to his deserts—or even if he be undeserving—there shall be measured such a flowing abundance of love that no one will be left without his share. A father may punish his child if it is disobedient, but he would never utterly forsake it. Therefore today I see no difference between Roman and Hebrew, and all people under the blue sky are my brothers and sisters. I don't except even the Samaritans, although it was a Samaritan sorcerer who made use of the demons that had taken up their dwelling in me, and put them to his service."

She threw her arms around my neck and kissed me on both cheeks, and I felt such a force emanating from her that everything was transfigured before my eyes and I wanted to dance and laugh like a child. Myrina too she embraced and kissed, and Mary of Beret she drew tenderly toward her, calling her her daughter. Thus we all exulted, and resumed our journey without thought of food or drink, so filled were we with his kingdom. That day we walked in his kingdom, although we were still on earth.

In the afternoon we reached Mary Magdalene's place and saw again the sea of Galilee. Her servants welcomed her with delight, for she had left home secretly with Mary of Beret as her only companion, saying nothing to anyone; so they had been anxious on her account and feared lest she had been possessed again by demons. But she commanded them, "Take new clothes for yourselves from the storerooms and prepare a great banquet for this evening. Do your best, for the days of gladness and rejoicing are here. Our Lord Jesus of Nazareth has risen from the dead and shown himself to his own people. More than five hundred of us can bear witness to this. Go therefore to Magdala and invite all who are willing to my banquet. But do not invite Pharisees or leaders of the synagogue, nor elders, nor the rich. Ask to my table the poor and wretched, the publicans and tax gatherers, and also foreigners. Say to them all, 'Mary Magdalene invites only sinners this evening, and not the righteous.' For neither did the Lord invite the righteous, but only sinners, and in his sight nothing was unclean. With him, forgiveness of sin came upon the earth."

Thus rapturously she spoke to her servants, who shook their heads but obeyed. Me she led aside, looked lovingly into my eyes, laid her hands upon my shoulders and said, "The time has come for us to part, but I at least regard you as a child of the kingdom, though all others should thrust you away. Evil days will come upon you yet, and no one is without sin. But let not your heart be hardened, never give yourself out to be pious in the eyes of men, and make no rash promises. Acknowledge your sin when you fall into such as you cannot avoid, and never excuse yourself by saying that you're no worse than others who do the same. But if you suffer from your sin as you commit it, then you are ripe for healing. And there is no sin so terrible that he will not forgive it you, if you ask him with repentance in your heart. It is only a hard heart that he cannot forgive, because by that a man knowingly and deliberately cuts himself off from God. Yet I believe no one can depart so far from him as not to be able to find his way back, so measureless is his grace. But if you follow the way of the kingdom you will avoid much evil. And I will confide to you the miracle that was disclosed to me in my dream: the road that leads to the kingdom is already a part of it."

With tears in her eyes she looked at me and went on, "That is my teaching—Mary Magdalene's teaching—which was surely ripening in me when I listened to him, sitting at his feet. After all that has happened, this man will say one thing about him, and that man another, each according to his intelligence. I am no more right than anyone else—and no more wrong either, I believe."

She said further, "I am only a woman. They bid me be silent, and henceforth I shall be humbly silent in their presence. But to you I want to say that he was born a man, and submitted to the misery of the body, to deliver the world. He knew what was to befall him and spoke of it often, clearly and plainly. He desired to sacrifice himself for many and so enter into a new covenant, taking upon himself the sins of the whole world as the son of Man and the son of God. My heart is blissful for him."

In this way, rapturously, did she instruct me, and I took her teaching to heart, though I didn't understand it all. After that we talked of everyday things and agreed upon the wedding gift I would send Mary of Beret when I reached Tiberias. As soon as she had married Mary off—which, knowing Mary, she wanted to do as soon as might be—she intended to make the journey to Jerusalem yet again, to see that the disciples lacked for nothing; for they did not know themselves how long they would have to stay there. Thomas was the only one who had said, "We will stay there and await the fulfillment of the promise, though it should take twelve years."

At last she came with me to the door, and when we parted

Mary of Beret wept so bitterly that her eyes were swollen, and Myrina wept too, out of sheer friendship for Mary. But I had the cheering certainty that whatever might befall me I could always return here to Mary Magdalene, if I could not win peace in my soul in any other way. It was not my intention to come back, but it is good for a man to know that he has a place to which he may return if ever there is need.

Myrina and I walked in silence to Magdala and took the road to Tiberias. Neither of us was tired, so there was no need to hire a boat, which we could easily have done. As we walked and I looked about me, breathing in the pure smell of the lake, I reflected that I had nothing further to do in alien Galilee. Nor was I in any hurry to leave. So it was good to saunter along beside the glittering waters. And I was not alone; I had Myrina.

We came to Tiberias in the red glow of evening, and my intention was to pass straight through the city to the thermae on the other side; but in Herod Antipas' forum a man deep in thought collided with me before I had time to dodge, and I had to catch at his arm so as not to fall, for he was big and powerful. He started as if from sleep and looked at me, and to my astonishment I saw that it was Simon of Cyrene.

"Peace be with you," I greeted him warily, fearing his wrath if he should recognize me. But he was not angry; he smiled uncomfortably and answered, "Is it you, Roman? With you also be peace."

I let go his arm, but did not walk on; we stood regarding each other. We had not met since the events in his house, but it seemed to me that he had aged greatly during the short time that had elapsed. His gaze was somber and he carried his head stubbornly bent. It was as if nothing in the world were to his liking.

I need not have addressed him at all, but it struck me that the encounter might not have been without purpose. So I asked him humbly, "Have you forgiven me for what happened in your house? I bore the blame for it, though I believe it was not all my fault. But if you bear me any grudge, forgive me now."

He replied, "I'm not angry with you. I myself am answerable for what I do. I sent you word that I meant no harm to you."

"But you meant me no good either," I said. "You would have nothing to do with me. Do you believe now that I'm no magician? What do you think of all that has come to pass since then?"

He looked about him suspiciously, but at this hour the forum was deserted. I raised my hand and said, "Have no mistrust of me. I come from the mountain as you do. Well, what do you think now?"

With a sigh he admitted, "Yes, yes; there were more than five hundred of us there. No wonder I didn't see you. But if you were there, you must know what I think.

"I ran headlong out of Jerusalem when I heard that he had promised to go before us into Galilee," Simon went on, without waiting for my answer. "Many others did the same, but the time of waiting was full of confusion and the reports contradictory, and not everyone believed that he had appeared to the disciples by the lake. Some were disappointed and returned to Jerusalem. But I have learned patience. A slave has to do that. Besides, I had business to attend to in Galilee. I wasted no time. I was already hoping with all my heart that the disciples had lied. I found peace in waiting thus in vain, and hoped to return to Jerusalem and my former life, which suited me. I would give my two sons the best things I had found: the faith of Israel, the culture of Greece, the peace of Rome, and a fortune prudently invested. But then I received word and went to the mountain, and there I saw him."

Simon of Cyrene continued with an effort, his cheek muscles quivering. "I saw that he was really risen. I was forced to acknowledge him as the Christ. And so now I must begin everything again from the beginning. On earth, then, there is more than the eye can see or the hand touch or weights and measures assess. It is terrible to know this. I could curse the day I met him and took his cross upon my back. It is his fault that nothing of what I thought I'd built up so prudently for my sons holds good any longer. You asked what I think of it all. I think of what I must do to be fit for his kingdom, and to see that the boys too may be his subjects. His laws are most unjust —merciless for a man who has toiled himself out of slavery into freedom and fortune. But now that I've been convinced of his resurrection I must submit to his laws. I hoped at least to bargain with him a little, as men do among men in any reasonable dealing. But he is not only a man. When I had seen him on the mountain I knew at once that there could be no bargaining here. I am forced to be his slave, hair and hide of me. I can do no other. Afterwards it will be for him to decide whether to make me a freedman. I have no say in that. I was thinking so hard about these things that I ran straight into you, Roman."

"But," I said, greatly wondering, "don't you distrust me who am a Roman and a heathen?"

Simon of Cyrene looked at me in surprise and explained, "Why a Jew should be any better in his sight than a Roman or a Greek is something I can't understand, now that I'm looking at everything with new eyes. It is for him to distinguish between true and false. I should be out of my mind if I thought I could tell which people are his and which cannot be his. In this too he is unjust. No, I shall never make him out just by thinking. I'm not of those who believe they can find bliss by withdrawing into the wilds, away from everyone. I'm an everyday man. To me, deeds are more than words. I must live my life among people, be they Jews or Romans. Besides, I have evil premonitions concerning my own folk, should there indeed be a new covenant through bread and wine. He himself is said to have wept for Jerusalem. It may be that I shall be prompt in claiming what is mine from a house doomed to bankruptcy, should the temple really prove incapable of saving anyone. Then I shall flee with my sons to some other country. But this I don't yet know for certain."

His words were very curt and blunt, and his thoughts seemed to stray from one thing to another. I asked curiously, "Did you speak with him on the mountain?"

Simon of Cyrene looked at me as if I'd taken leave of my senses, and retorted, "How could I dare speak to him? It was enough to see him."

I told him timidly, "The eleven will have nothing to do with me. Peter has forbidden me even to speak of him, because I'm a Roman."

But Simon of Cyrene cared nothing about this. "When they come to my age and have experienced life as I have, they will know better," he assured me. "They're only men, and there are no men without fault. But slow, simple fellows like them will do less harm than clever and ambitious ones, in so responsible a position. It will be enough for me if they do not entirely scatter their inheritance. No, we shall not get far if the kingdom is to be managed by those eleven only. Yet even that is better than that scribes should squabble over this inheritance. Perhaps they will grow with their task. Such a thing has happened before."

"And of what do you believe this inheritance consists?" I ventured to ask. "Tell me."

Unthinkingly we had begun to pace up and down the forum with long strides, like Sophists in disputation, and Myrina had sat down upon the navel-stone of the city to rest her feet. Simon stopped and stared at me with a somber gaze, and his outstretched hand dropped powerlessly to his side.

"If I only knew!" he lamented in a tone of agony. "I heard much about his message during the time of waiting, but I began to hope ever more fervently that it was no more than the babbling of a crazy prophet. His mother and relatives believed him to be out of his wits, for that matter, and tried in vain to get him home after he'd begun preaching in Galilee. He was too merciless to the righteous and too gentle to sinners. There are people of sound judgment who maintain that he performed his miracles with the help of Beelzebub. That is an evil spirit—one of the ancient gods who live on in the land, as you may have heard. For this reason I didn't memorize carefully all that he is supposed to have said, because one day he said one thing, and the next another. There are those who have listened to him on the selfsame day and make widely differing statements as to what he did say. You may understand what an overwhelming shock it was to me to see that he is still alive, although I myself carried his cross to the place of skulls. I cannot deny him, but I cannot understand him either.

"Forgive us our debts," he went on, pressing the palms of his hands together, "as we forgive our debtors. That I understand, though I resent it. Am I to forgive Herod Antipas what he owes me? For every time the Tetrarch visits Jerusalem his treasurer Kusas comes running to me for money. It is true that I never have great hopes of getting it back, and no large sums are involved; it's more a subtle sort of bribery, to dissuade him from interfering in certain transactions of mine in Perea and Galilee. Yet it rankles deeply in my mind that I should be forced to go to the Tetrarch and, not only with my lips but with my whole heart, cancel what he owes me. I know that he mocked Jesus before the crucifixion. I have canceled the debts of some poor Galileans, although at first I meant to amalgamate their plots of land into one large estate in the name of my son Rufus. But they were family men who through no fault of their own fell into debt by reason of the triple tax and the locusts. I'm not telling you this to boast of it, for Jesus said—so they tell us—that not even the left hand should know what the right hand does, far less strangers. But counsel me! Would it not be more sensible to claim all I can from the Tetrarch and share it out among the poor, than to forgive him what he owes?"

He put this question to me seriously, and I considered his problem. "I believe you worry needlessly about your property and your claims," I said cautiously. "I myself am well-to-do, but for the present I don't allow that to trouble me. Perhaps it is because I became rich through no merit of my own, and in a way which many consider to be without honor. But in any event I would counsel you to wait and do nothing hastily. I've heard that even the eleven are prepared to wait in Jerusalem twelve years if they must, for a certain promise to be fulfilled and for them to receive clear understanding of all things. Why should you hasten ahead of them?"

"Because I'm a hard, wicked man," Simon replied at once, as if he had long pondered this question. "I'm in haste to have my own debts—my own heartlessness—forgiven."

"Now you're thinking in your old way, as a merchant," I told him. "You expect to receive something in return for what you give. I don't believe that Jesus of Nazareth gives anyone anything because of what he deserves. I believe that he was born into the world as a man, to expiate the sins of the world, because no human being can expiate his own sins by himself. It is madness; but as you said yourself, there's much more than this in his teaching which is madness in the eyes of the wise."

Simon of Cyrene laid a hand on his forehead and sighed deeply. "I understand not what you are saying. My head just aches more and more. Do you really think that it is only through a sort of slave-and-merchant arrogance that I want to purchase forgiveness of my sins in the only way I can? Who are you to instruct me? Didn't you tell me you'd been forbidden to speak of him?"

Bitterly I regretted my thoughtlessness, and besought him, "Forgive me, Simon of Cyrene. Who indeed am I to instruct you? You asked me for advice and I ought not to have answered you, for surely I understand no more of it than you, and perhaps less, since you are older and more experienced. Seek then his kingdom in your own way, and I will seek in mine."

Absent-mindedly Simon of Cyrene stretched forth his calloused hand and stroked Myrina's cheek, where she sat on the stone. "If only I had a daughter," he mourned. "I always wanted a daughter. I might be a gentler man had I had a little girl as well as my boys."

He stared in wonder at his hand. Darkness had fallen, and lamps were being lit outside the houses. "Again we have talked much together," he said. "The more we talked, the uneasier I grew; but I had only to touch your daughter's cheek for my head to cease aching and for me to feel contented and at ease."

"She is not my daughter; I'm not yet as old as that," I told him. "This is my sister Myrina, and she does not understand your language."

"She must certainly have been with you on the mountain," said Simon of Cyrene, staring sleepily at his hand. "I felt that as soon as I touched her. I never felt it in you when you ran into me and gripped my arm. From her, peace entered into me, and now I shall concern myself no more about unnecessary things. It was not intended that I should listen to your sententious words, but that I should touch your sister's cheek."

This I thought was unjustly spoken, but I would not trouble his peace of mind by protesting, if he really had found serenity in the touch of Myrina's cheek. But I felt tired, as if talking had wearied me more than the daylong wayfaring. I wanted to go on to the thermae; Simon of Cyrene came with us, holding Myrina's hand. The three of us walked hand-in-hand, with Myrina in the middle. When we came to a lighted inn he insisted on giving us a meal; for it was one of those places where freethinking Jews and heathen may eat from the same dish.

So we broke bread together, and ate fish and salad, and no one was offended because Myrina ate with us. Simon of Cyrene even ordered wine to be mixed for us, though he himself drank water. Myrina's eyes shone, her thin cheeks were flushed and I too felt the mild glow of good food and wine. While we were eating, Simon talked in a different voice, gentler than before. To amuse us he told us a story in his Cyrenean Greek:

"At the other end of the world lies a vast realm, from which silk is brought to Rome. It is so far away that the Silk Road runs through many countries, and it takes two years for the merchandise to reach Tyre. In the Roman realm the earth is red, but in the silk realm it is yellow, and the inhabitants have yellow skins. This is no invention, for I myself have met a yellow-skinned man in Tyre, and his yellowness was not caused by any sickness; he assured me that in his homeland everyone was yellow from top to toe, that his country was mightier than Rome and with so lofty a culture that Greek culture was as barbarism compared. No doubt he was exaggerating the merits of his own land, for he was a fugitive from it. He told me—and this I heard also from other far-traveled men—that a new king had been born in his country who deposed the former ruler and called himself the son of heaven. He changed the existing order in the realm and proclaimed that the soil was common property. Thenceforth no one might possess any land, but all should cultivate it in common, and the king would see to it that each and every one obtained his livelihood. And it is not so long since this happened, for the king reigned for twenty years, and it is only a few years since news reached Tyre that the peasants had revolted and rioted and overthrown him, and a new ruler had restored the old order. The fugitive at once left Tyre for his own country, where he had held an exalted position before the time of the lunatic king.

"Of course much of this is fancy and fable," Simon of Cyrene went on. "That yellow man declared, for instance, that the silk in his country was spun by worms, and that all the people had to do was to gather together the threads and weave them into stuff. But I've thought a great deal about that son of heaven and his mad idea. The same thing might happen in the Roman empire, where more and more land is being gathered into the hands of a few, so that at last everyone else will be either a day laborer or a slave. To the great majority it would be a matter of indifference whether the land were owned by everyone in common or by a few individuals; so, thinking of Jesus of Nazareth, I sometimes fear that when he becomes king he may introduce a similar system, whereby no individual possesses anything and everything is owned in common. Only a man who has been a slave can fully appreciate how dangerous—how impossible—it is to live like that. Even a slave must have something he can call his own, however trifling, to exist at all. In Cyrene a slave might be proud even of his leg iron, if it was larger and heavier than others'. However, I'm relieved to know that Jesus' kingdom is not of this world. If he'd aimed at that sort of administration he'd have had to have himself born emperor of Rome, not king of the Jews."

I said warningly, "Is it wise to talk politics at an inn? As I understand it, Jesus of Nazareth's kingdom came on earth when he was born here, and is still with us, though it's invisible and no ruler from outside can gain control of it. His adherents may be persecuted, but no one can overthrow his kingdom, for it is within us—if you can understand what I mean when I do not understand it myself."

Simon of Cyrene shook his head mournfully and said, "How inexperienced you are, and how little you know of mankind! The kingdom of that son of heaven was overthrown in twenty years, though there the system was comprehensible. How is an invisible kingdom to endure when he himself has gone? Believe me, when we who have seen him are dead, his memory will not survive us by many years. How could one ever induce anybody who has not seen for himself that this was the son of God, to believe in an invisible kingdom? Something of him might endure for as long as a hundred years, if his doctrine were sensible and did not conflict with human nature; but now it runs dead against anything that has ever been."

His common sense depressed me. "So you don't believe that the world will be changed because of him, and through his name?" I asked.

"No, I don't," answered Simon of Cyrene candidly. "No; this world and human nature not even God himself can alter now.

"Why," he exclaimed, "these Galileans did all they could to crown him king after he had fed the five thousand. If even they so completely misunderstood him, how should those understand him who never saw him at all? Note that his is a dubious, dangerous teaching. He summoned sinners. On the very cross he promised one of the robbers who were crucified with him that he should enter his kingdom. In a word: only the rabble who have nothing else to hope for can listen to his teaching. Those in power will surely see to it that such a doctrine never spreads too far."

Myrina, smiling, raised her hand and stroked his bearded cheek. "Why are you so worried about the spreading of his doctrine?" she asked. "That's no business of yours, nor of my brother Marcus, nor of mine. Let us rather rejoice in him, and in having seen him on the mountain. He is a good light, and now that I've seen him I shall never feel quite defenseless again. You talk only of the evil darkness."

Myrina had been sitting so humbly silent that we were both surprised when she spoke, as if a lifeless table had suddenly acquired the faculty of speech. Gladness returned to us both, and as we looked at her radiant face we felt ashamed of our foolish talk. The kingdom was within us once more and my heart overflowed with love for Myrina and for Simon of Cyrene too. We sat for a long time in silence, looking at each other, undisturbed by the noise of the other guests at the inn.

Both Myrina and I slept behind drawn curtains in our room until nearly noon, so exhausted were we from walking and all we had seen and done. Our joy did not melt away as we slept, but was with us still when we awoke, and we rejoiced to see each other wake.

My cheerfulness continued until I remembered Claudia Procula, and my obligation to render account to her of what I had seen on the mountain. Myrina asked me what troubled me, and when I told her of Claudia Procula and her illness, she suggested trustfully that we should go to her together to bear witness of the joyful message.

But first I felt the need to wash myself clean after the hardships of the journey, which seemed to have begun with my departure from Jerusalem. My Jewish mantle smelled of sweat and my body garment was grimy. I wanted to put on fresh clothes, and remove my beard, having now no reason to hide the fact that I was a Roman. So I went to the thermae and had my face shaved, my hair dressed and the hairs of my body plucked. Then, after massage and the rubbing in of ointments, I put on new clothes and gave my old ones to the servant. Now that I looked as I used to do, I felt ashamed of having tried to ingratiate myself with the Jews by wearing beard and mantle tassels. On returning to my room I even took my gold ring from my purse and slipped it onto my thumb.

Myrina came back from her bath and I saw that she too had had her hair done; that she had beautified her face and put on a white gown embroidered with gold thread. We looked at each other for a long time, as if no longer knowing who we were. I ought to have been pleased to see that I need not blush for her before the rich bath-guests, or Claudia Procula. But I did not rejoice at her beauty. Her dress and her painted face made her a stranger. I realized that I preferred to see in her the girl with the thin face and slender limbs who had slept in my arms on a hillside of Galilee, with a stained mantle for covering.

But she had certainly done her best for my sake, so I could not blame her, or tell her that I loved her worn player sandals more than fine shoes and gold thread. But Myrina regarded me in a distant way, and said, "That's how you looked aboard the ship to Joppa. That's how you looked when you gave me the big silver coin from your purse. Of course you're right to remind me of who you are and who I am. It was thoughtless of me to suggest that you should take me to call upon the wife of the Procurator."

I reminded her of the joy we had felt on seeing each other wake from sleep, and said, "You must understand that I was tired of that sweaty woolen mantle and of my beard; I wanted to feel clean again. If all orthodox Jews draw aside from my very shadow now that I look like this, it may be that one day the same thing will happen to them, and the people of the world will spit when they see a Jew. I thought you'd like to see me like this."

But a coolness fell between us, and the thought did indeed strike me that it might be unsuitable to take her with me to Claudia Procula. But in my heart I knew it was a betrayal of her to think thus, and on no account whatever would I betray her. After much persuasion she consented to come, and just then the servant arrived to say that Claudia Procula was willing to receive me.

As we approached the summer palace I noticed that the visitors to the baths no longer swarmed about it inquisitively, trying to peer into the garden, nor were Herod Antipas' red-cloaked guards of honor to be seen. A Syrian legionary from Claudia's own retinue waved his hand lazily to indicate that I might go in. Everything showed that the sojourn of the Judean Procurator's wife in Tiberias was now a part of everyday life. She was merely a distinguished guest among other guests.

Claudia Procula was resting in a cool room behind a floating curtain. She had not troubled to make herself beautiful for me. I saw the wrinkles at the corners of her eyes, her discontented mouth, and her age. Yet she was calm and alert; she no longer twitched and started, nor did her hands shake. She scrutinized Myrina curiously from head to foot and raised her eyes to mine with a look of inquiry.

"This is my sister Myrina," I told her. "She was with me on the mountain. That is why I have brought her before you, Claudia. For now we may talk alone together, the three of us, without a listener."

After a moment's reflection Claudia Procula dismissed her companion, but did not invite us to sit. So we remained standing before her as she began talking with great animation, never taking her eyes from Myrina: "You don't know what you've missed. How much you might have learned of the customs of this country if only you'd come with me to the Tetrarch's banquet after the race. I must admit that Herodias is considerably better than her reputation, and she suffers from the awkwardness of her position. She gave me a triple-rowed Persian necklace and we spoke quite frankly together about everything. Of course her daughter Salome is a shameless hussy and can wind Herod Antipas around her little finger, but that's entirely to her mother's advantage. Herodias herself is not as young as she was. And it seems that the offspring of Herod the Great do not shun incest in any form. It's as if it were a tradition with them, and we Romans are not the people to judge of eastern customs. They can be quite charming when they like.

"However, Herodias is not without influence, and her aim seems to be to obtain royal rank for her husband: and that we talked over as well. For Pontius Pilate it is vital that Herod Antipas should not write disagreeable letters, from sheer malice, to the emperor Tiberius. And Herodias for her part understands perfectly that Tiberius is now just a sick old man. Sejanus supports Pilate, and it is he we have to thank for the procuratorship. As matters now stand, it's to the advantage of both Herod and Pontius to be on good terms with each other and wash each other's hands. That point was settled between Herodias and myself. So my cure here has been profitable, and I am ready to return to Caesarea."

She was in fact disclosing no perilous secrets, for all these things are obvious to any thinking person. The emperor Tiberius is a frail old man and the very name of Sejanus arouses such fear that all men of sense in the Roman empire are content to be silent and wait for him to secure the status of people's tribune, and ultimate power. I thought that Claudia, with her sideways glances, had been trying to discover whether Myrina understood Latin, but now she suddenly pointed to her and said, "By Hecate and her black whelps, that girl is the living image of Tullia!"

Startled, I stared at Myrina, and for a moment she did seem to remind me of you, Tullia. At that instant I knew that I should never send any of these letters to you, and I know also that I never want to meet you again. I felt only repugnance and fear when I beheld you in front of me, in the guise of Myrina. But the spell faded, and as I regarded Myrina feature by feature I realized that there was nothing of you in her. Nevertheless, Claudia Procula continued malignantly, "Just so. If her eyes were dark and shining and her nose more finely chiseled, her hair black and her mouth full, she really would remind one faintly of Tullia."

I wasn't sure whether she just meant to tease Myrina. I believe though that she was in earnest, and was herself wondering what there was about Myrina that could remind her of you, Tullia, for you and she have not one feature in common. I flared up, and said, "Leave Myrina alone. She doesn't know that she's beautiful. And Tullia I don't want to remember. Let us speak Greek. Do you want to know what happened on the mountain or not?"

"Certainly I do," replied Claudia, recollecting herself. "What did happen there? Did you see Jesus of Nazareth?"

"We both saw him," I said. "He has risen from the dead, and is alive."

Myrina too said slowly, "Yes, yes; he's alive."

Then Claudia Procula asked a singular question: "How do you know that it really was Jesus of Nazareth?"

I hadn't thought of that. For a moment I was perplexed.

Then I answered, "Of course it was. Who else could it have been? There were over five hundred people there who recognized him." I laughed. "I saw him myself; I met his gaze. That was enough. He's no ordinary man."

And Myrina said, "No man could look at one like that."

Claudia Procula regarded us sharply and questioned us like an interrogator: "It was night when you saw him. Wasn't the moon waning and the night very dark?"

"It was dark," I admitted. "Yet I saw him plainly enough. There was no mistaking him."

Throwing out her hands Claudia Procula said, "No, of course I don't doubt that he was he, and so forth. But Herod Antipas' physician has continued to treat me, and has visited me from time to time. And Herodias told me in confidence that a strange man is known to have been going about in Galilee, and that many have taken him to be Jesus of Nazareth. Yet the reports are contradictory and no one has been able to describe his appearance accurately. They believe he is someone mad, or possessed, who has purposely wounded his hands and feet. Or else that his disciples, after stealing the body from the tomb, have continued the game by inducing someone to impersonate him."

Seeing my look, Claudia Procula added in excuse, "I am only repeating what I've heard. I don't say that it's my opinion. But there are many possibilities. The physician has discussed the matter professionally with other men of learning. Do you know that in the desert by the Dead Sea there is a Jewish sect living in an enclosed house, and that through fasting, prayer, asceticism, communal meals and baptism its members have become so holy that they're not ordinary people any more? Their white clothes are said to shine in the dark. They have secret associates in Jerusalem and elsewhere. Indeed, Herod the Great considered them so dangerous that he persecuted them. They had to flee to Damascus, and did not return to the desert until after his death. Not much is known about them, for they receive no one as their guest; yet it may be that they—or at least the holiest of them—know more than other people. There are different grades of holiness among them.

"Yesterday, after talking to other scholars, Herod Antipas' physician suggested that this desert sect might have been closely observing Jesus of Nazareth's activities, and protecting him, perhaps even without his knowledge. A particularly suspicious factor is that it was two members of the Supreme Council who laid Jesus in his tomb after the crucifixion. Mary Magdalene saw a shining white figure in the sepulcher in the dawnlight and thought it was an angel. Jesus of Nazareth's disciples are simple men and may have been too frightened to steal his body, but for the holy men of the desert it was not difficult. They may have put life into the corpse by magic, or one of them may be masquerading among the simple folk of Galilee. Why they should want people to believe that Jesus of Nazareth is risen is hard to tell. Perhaps they have their own reasons for undermining the prestige of the temple. But a person used to thinking politically will find political reasons for everything, as the physician said. They may just as likely have religious motives known only to themselves. But they're too clever to prolong the deception. So far as I know it has now been ended by this final appearance—or whatever it may have been—to the Nazarene's closest adherents on that mountain in the dark."

When Claudia observed the bewilderment with which I was following her explanations she threw out her hands once more and said, "I don't believe all that. I'm only repeating what others have told me. His own closest disciples would surely not be mistaken, even in the dark—that is, unless they were in the plot themselves. Tell me just one thing. Did you speak to him about me?"

Embarrassed, I answered her: "I cannot explain the thing to you in any comprehensible way, but I don't believe I could have spoken to him of you even had I wanted to. And I did not want to, for when I saw him, all other thoughts went out of my head."

To my surprise Claudia did not reproach me. On the contrary she said with satisfaction, "Johanna told me the same thing. But she collected a little earth in a cloth from a place where she remembered that Jesus had stood, and brought it to me, that it might cure me if I touched it or laid it on my forehead at night. But I no longer need it."

She gave me an enigmatic look and quite staggered me by saying, "You see, I was on the mountain myself, and he healed me."

Seeing my astonishment she broke into a gay laugh, clapped her hands and cried, "That surprised you, did it not? Sit down here beside me, Marcus, and you sit too, girl, wherever you like. No, I don't mean that I was present there in the body; but that night I had a good dream: the first for a very long time. You know I am a highly strung, capricious sort of woman. In my dreams I'm often pinched or have my face slapped and my hair pulled. It's all real and vivid, and I cannot stir a finger, try as I may, until at last I contrive to utter a cry and am awakened by my own scream, bathed in cold sweat and so full of fear that I dare not fall asleep again.

"We were talking about the mountain," she continued soberly. "I'd been thinking about it a great deal, so it is not surprising that I should have been on it that night in my dream. It was so dark that I rather felt than saw the many motionless figures kneeling on the ground about me, and waiting. And in my dream I was not at all afraid. Then a shining presence stood before me and I dared not raise my head to look at him—not because I was afraid, but because of a strong feeling that it would be better that I not look him in the face. The presence spoke to me in a gentle voice and asked, 'Claudia Procula, do you hear my voice?' I answered, 'I hear your voice.' He said, 'I am Jesus of Nazareth, king of the Jews, whom your husband Pontius Pilate caused to be crucified in Jerusalem.' I answered,

'Yes, you are he.' Then he talked to me of lambs, which I didn't understand, for I know nothing of sheep rearing and therefore did not remember it all. Yet it was like a rebuke when he said at last, 'I am the door of the sheep. I let no thief or robber kill my lambs.' I knew at once that by thief and robber he meant Pontius Pilate, and I declared, 'Surely he will persecute your lambs no longer, and he wouldn't have executed you either had he not been forced to do it for political reasons.'

"But he never heeded my explanation; so I took it that the whole matter was as empty air to him now, and that he bore Pilate no grudge. He went on speaking of sheep, and said, 'I have other lambs too.' Not knowing how to reply, I said, to be friendly, 'I believe you are a good shepherd.' He seemed gladdened by these words, for he answered at once, 'You have said so. I am the good shepherd, and a good shepherd gives his life for his lambs.' In my dream I felt a great desire to weep, and I would have liked to ask him whether I too might become one of those lambs. But I dared not. I just felt him lay his hand on my head, and at that I awoke, and even after I was awake I could feel his hand on my head. It was a good dream—the best dream I've ever had. When I had recalled it accurately so as to forget no part of it, I fell asleep again and slept for a long time; and since then I have not had a single nightmare. As I understand it, he has healed me on condition that Pontius does not persecute his followers."

Claudia Procula tittered like a young girl, then put her hand to her mouth, abashed. "That was an easy promise to make," she went on. "Pontius has no reason to persecute the Nazarene's friends. On the contrary. Should they ever form a party, it will cause further splits among the Jews, and that suits Roman policy. Dreams are only dreams, and if he talked of lambs it must be because I've heard that he often did so when teaching. However, it was a vivid dream, and it visited me on the night when you and this girl saw him on the mountain. Above all, I have been cured of my nightmares.

"Of course," she continued, "Herod Antipas' physician assures me that the improvement has been brought about by the hot sulphur baths and his own treatment. I cannot offend him, naturally, and he shall have the usual presents. All the same, I believe—laugh if you like—that Jesus of Nazareth took pity on me, and cured me in my dream because I've thought of him so much and have had bad dreams on his account."

Then triumphantly she said, "So whoever it was you saw on the mountain, I at least beheld Jesus of Nazareth in my dream. Nevertheless, Johanna is certain that it was Jesus of Nazareth she saw there, and I don't doubt her word."

Thinking about her dream I trembled for joy, and asked eagerly, "Did he really tell you that he has other lambs? If that is true, he gave his life for them too. Myrina, did you hear? In his eyes we are not strangers."

Claudia Procula burst out laughing and cried, "No, no; all that lamb nonsense is too much. I know Jesus of Nazareth and believe firmly enough that he has risen from the dead and is the son of God. Johanna has taught me, so that I can pray to him when necessary, and I mean to obey some of his commandments, insofar as I can do so secretly and without detriment to my position. I must in any case sacrifice to Caesar's genius, even though I may not trouble myself about the other gods of Rome. But the most difficult problem in all this is how much I am to tell Pontius Pilate. He's a hardheaded man who has studied law and is not at all the kind to believe in miracles."

"I should think," I said hesitantly, "that you had better say as little to him as possible about Jesus of Nazareth. This whole matter is a sore subject with him, and wounds his sense of justice. He will only be annoyed if you remind him of it."

"It is hard to know what he really thinks," said Claudia Procula. "As a Roman official he's so used to hiding his feelings that I sometimes wonder whether he has any feelings at all. He is not a bad man. Judea could have had a worse procurator than he. It was wrong to call him a thief and a robber, but that's just the usual Jewish excitability. Perhaps you are right. I shall tell him nothing unless he asks.

"Well, and now to something else," she went on, looking at me attentively. "I'm pleased to see you clean-shaven and decently dressed again. It must have done you good to meet him on the mountain, for I was becoming quite uneasy about you and afraid that the Jews had addled your brains. You looked so ecstatic that the physician whom you met that time asked me afterward what ailed you. Ought you not soon to return to Rome? In Baiae the roses will be blooming now. From there it is not far to Capri. Some friend of yours here in the east might show practical gratitude for detailed and accurate news of Caesar's health from time to time. Conveyed of course in veiled terms agreed upon beforehand, for it is dangerous to write in any other way of how the Emperor does."

Tilting her head sideways she looked at Myrina, and probably did not like what she saw, for with a shrug of her thin shoulders she said cruelly, "A year's exile must be enough to cool off an overardent lover, so you will suit Tullia again by now. I've reason to think that in the meantime she has had her marriage dissolved and has married again, so you may resume in peace and quiet. No one in Rome seeks your life, if that's what she wants to make you believe."

She must have been speaking the truth. No danger can threaten me in Rome now. A pang shot through me. Not on your account, Tullia, but on account of my own outrageous conceit which persuaded me that you would follow me to Alexandria.

"I don't believe I shall ever return to Rome," I said bitterly. "The mere thought of roses disgusts me."

"Then come at least to Caesarea sometime," Claudia Procula returned invitingly. "It is a new, civilized town, incomparably more splendid than the Tiberias of Herod Antipas. From there you may take ship to whatever place you wish. You may also receive advice which may help you to make something of your life. Beautiful Jewesses and little Greek girls are not enough for a Roman in the long run."

Myrina surprisingly put an end to the conversation by rising calmly to her feet and thanking Claudia Procula with courtesy for the honor done to her. Then, just as calmly, she slapped me first on one cheek and then on the other, took me by the hand and led me to the door. There she turned and said, "Honored Claudia Procula, do not concern yourself about where Marcus goes or what he makes of his life. I, Myrina, will see to it that this lamb does not go astray."

Eleventh Letter

MARCUS MEZENTIUS MANILIANUS
GREETS THE FORMER MARCUS:

My last letter was interrupted, and I shall not resume it. This letter I do not address to Tullia, for there would be no sense in so doing. Even as I wrote the earlier letters I knew in my heart that they were not meant for her. Her mere name is now a torment, rendering the thought of my former life repugnant to me. For Myrina's sake, too, I am unwilling to write this letter to Tullia.

Therefore I greet only my old self, so that some day, after many years, I may call to mind all that happened to me during this time exactly as it came about. Time and distance cause events to fade, memory dims, and with the best will in the world one recollects things wrongly. While writing these letters I am troubled by the thought that I may be mistaken; that I may be exaggerating, or adding this and that from my own imagination. If so, it is unintentional. Even reliable witnesses on their oath in a court of law may give conflicting evidence.

It is the more important for me to write, in that I have been forbidden to speak. Of his kingdom I can testify no more than that I saw him die, and later saw him risen again beyond any possibility of doubt. Yet even this I have been forbidden to say, being neither a Jew nor circumcised.

If therefore anyone else with fuller knowledge of the secret of the kingdom should give an entirely different account of all these things, I am ready to admit that he is right and that he knows more than I. My record is fit only for myself, so that in my old age—if I attain it—I may be able to call everything to mind as accurately as I can now. This is why I have written down so much that is superfluous and irrelevant, meaningless to any but myself. And I shall so continue. When many years have passed, these letters will say to me: though I have meticulously memorized uninteresting and unnecessary things, I have recalled at least as much that is important.

In writing I seek to lay bare my mind, for when I examine it I know that I am frivolous and ever curious to hear of new things, and that there is no steadfastness in me. I am vain and selfish, too, and a slave to my body, as Myrina says, and I have nothing to be proud of. For this reason too it is salutary for me to write, lest at any time I should tend to become complacent.

I have been commanded to keep silence. I submit, and freely confess the justice of that command. I lack stability; I am like water poured from vessel to vessel and assuming the shape of each. Could I but remain limpid, at the very least! But all water clouds and degenerates in time. One day, when I'm but a stagnant pool, I shall read all this again, and remember that once I was permitted to sense the presence of his kingdom.

Why was it that I, a foreigner, should witness his resurrection and experience his kingdom? I know not. I am still convinced that it did not happen without some reason. But myself I do know, and am aware that my conviction will crumble away with the years.

Yet no matter how I may degenerate through weakness, in this comfortless generation of skepticism and self-indulgence, the prophecy of that solitary fisherman on the shore has been dear and precious to me. How such a thing could ever come about I cannot tell; it is no more than the glimpse of a hope—for it is hard for man to live without hope. The others are superabundantly rich, and in comparison with them I am poor indeed. Yet I have Myrina. Perhaps she was given me to pin my hopes upon: she has the steadfastness I lack.

Myrina says that I was given to her to watch over, for lack of a better shepherd, and that this demands great patience. I write this in Jerusalem, whither she has suddenly brought me; yet for her sake I desire to return in this writing of mine to the thermae of Tiberias.

I cannot now account for our quarrel, since we were filled with such great joy. It may have been because of Claudia Procula. At any rate Myrina lost her temper, boxed my ears and dragged me from Claudia's house.

I remember that when we were in our own room again she told me that the more grand ladies she saw, the greater her self-confidence because of being what she is without trying to be anything else. She hunted vainly everywhere for her old clothes in order to leave me without delay. I made no attempt to restrain her, because my feelings were injured, and because she used such stinging words to me that only Tullia at her worst could have vied with her.

She punctured my smugness. She even declared that I had betrayed Jesus of Nazareth in Claudia Procula's presence by stooping to listen to her empty gossip. She refused to believe that Claudia had ever had a dream. She baffled me—she who until then had always been so reserved and quiet; I fancied that I must have been mistaken in her and that now she was appearing in her true colors.

So malignantly and acutely did she point out all my faults that I thought some demon must have taken possession of her. How else could she have spoken so perspicaciously, and described so much that she could not possibly have known? In a word, she plucked me so thoroughly that I hadn't a feather left;

and in all she said there was just enough truth to make me listen to her, although I had already resolved never to address a single word to her again.

At last she calmed herself enough to sit down with her head between her hands, and staring before her she said, "So this is what you're like! I'd already thought of leaving you, and it would serve you right. . . . But for the sake of Jesus of Nazareth I can't forsake you, since it was he who hung you around my neck. Truly you're like a sheep among wolves in this world: you can keep no one at bay. Anyone could twist you around his finger in a moment. And I can't bear to see you lick your lips at the memory of that Tullia woman and all your old dissipations. Take that gold ring off your thumb!"

Rising, she sniffed at me and scolded, "You smell like an Alexandrian catamite. I liked your hair better when it was full of burs than now, all in curls. Truly I would leave you if I hadn't walked with you along the paths of Galilee, and seen that you can swallow dust and wipe sweat from your forehead and not complain of sore feet."

Thus she railed at me until she ran short of words. I would not condescend to answer; I didn't even want to look at her, since much of what she said of me was true. I will not repeat it all, for in any case my weaknesses are manifest in what I have written, though until now I had been unaware of this.

But at last she said, "Be alone with yourself now and ponder whether what I've said is true, or whether I exaggerate. I will share your room no longer."

She went, slamming the door after her so that the whole house resounded. Presently a bewildered servant came to fetch her belongings; but I felt no uneasiness on Myrina's account, knowing that since she had been received by Claudia Procula the landlord of the inn would take care to find her another room.

When I had thought over all that Myrina had said I was crestfallen indeed; then I set myself to write down everything that had happened. Of her I wrote as disinterestedly as I could, and tried not to mingle my own bitterness with the record. I wrote for days on end in my room, behind drawn curtains, and told the servants to bring my meals to me there. Myrina came once to tell me that she was going into Tiberias to order a Greek tombstone for her brother's grave. Another time she came to say that Nathan was there with the donkeys, and was asking for me. But I hardened my heart and would not answer her, merely signing to her that I didn't wish to be disturbed while I was writing.

After that Myrina never came again to ask my leave to go anywhere, and only later did I learn that she had paid a visit to Mary of Magdala. She went to Capernaum, too, with Nathan.

I did not count the days while I was writing. Time meant so little to me that I wrote at night too, when I couldn't sleep. At last the bitterness in me melted away, and as I fell asleep or woke I thought again of Myrina and of what she had said. I reflected that it had been high time for someone to tell me all this about myself. Now and then I could be quiet and humble of heart, but I soon became puffed up again, fancying myself better than others.

At last one morning I heard Myrina enter my room. I felt that she was looking at me in the belief that I was asleep, and next I felt her gently stroke my hair. Joy returned to me with her mere touch, and I was ashamed of having hardened my heart for so long. But I wanted to see how she would behave toward me; therefore I turned over and pretended to awaken gradually. When I opened my eyes she recoiled a little and addressed me curtly: "Without doubt you've done well to dedicate yourself to silence, Marcus, for thus you talk no foolishness and harm no one, however much ink you may squander on your scrolls. But now you must get up. The forty days are at an end and we must go to Jerusalem. Nathan is waiting below with the donkeys, so gather your things together, pay the reckoning, and come! You can sulk as easily on the road as here behind your curtains."

"Myrina," I said, "forgive me for being what I am. Forgive me too for all the malicious things I have thought about you in silence. But what have I to do in Jerusalem? I'm not sure that I should allow you to order my comings and goings according to your own ideas."

"That too we can discuss upon the road," said Myrina. "The Jewish feast of the wave offering is near, and many people are journeying to Jerusalem. Make haste!"

Her suggestion came as no surprise to me. While writing I had begun to feel a desire to learn what was to happen to the disciples of Jesus of Nazareth in Jerusalem. I was not averse to a sudden departure, for I was weary of my writing and my silence. Looking at Myrina I could control my joy no longer, but threw my arms about her, embraced her, kissed her cheeks and exclaimed, "Speak to me as surlily as you like; I still believe that you wish me well. Joy returned to me just now as you stroked my hair in the belief that I was sleeping."

At first Myrina tried to convince me that I had been dreaming. Then relenting she kissed me and said, "I spoke evilly to you, but I had to speak my mind. I like you just as you are, if only you'll realize that you *are* so, and nothing else. I wouldn't wish you otherwise, and never would I have been so merciless if I hadn't liked you so much. Of course you shall order your own comings and goings, so long as you decide to come now to Jerusalem, at once!"

"I'm yearning for Jerusalem," I said hastily. "For a long time the idea has been smoldering in me that the end has not yet come. Where else should I go? I have no place that I may call home, and I have become so much a stranger on the earth that all lands are alike to me."

Myrina touched my brow and my breast and said, "I too am a stranger on the earth. His kingdom is my only home, little though I know of it. He has entrusted you to me. Therefore I desire to be the steadfastness in your weakness, your friend, your sister—whatever you will—and your home, in both good and evil days."

I too touched her brow and her breast, and kissed her once more. Then hastily we gathered up my belonging and I put on my traveling clothes. Not until I settled the reckoning did I realize how highly my landlord valued me as a guest. He would have taken my money and my purse as well, and still not been content, had not Myrina come to my aid and pointed out his errors to him. I rejoiced at the sight of Nathan and the familiar donkeys waiting in the courtyard, and we set off on our way without needless talk.

Of the journey I need say no more than that we took the way through Samaria to avoid the heat in the valley of the Jordan; to avoid also the Galileans who were on their way to the feast of the wave offering. On beholding once more the temple and the city and the mount of the crucifixion, I was seized by so violent a trembling that I came near to falling off my donkey. I dismounted and walked, still trembling in every limb, so that I fancied I had the ague. Blackness came before my eyes and my teeth chattered; I couldn't speak, only stammer, and I felt as if a mighty cloud had unrolled above me, ready to break out in lightning and thunder. But the sky was clear.

The fit soon passed and when Myrina felt my forehead it was cool. But I dared not mount my donkey, preferring to walk. We entered the city through the stinking Fish Gate, and when the legionaries saw my sword and heard that I was a citizen they let us pass through unhindered. Too many people were pouring in for them to examine everyone.

Karanthes the Syrian trader greeted me joyfully, and I too was glad to see his bearded face and crafty eyes again. But at the sight of Myrina he blinked several times, stared and said, "How thin you've grown from the hardships of your journey, Mary of Beret. Your eyes have changed color, too, and your hair, and your nose is shorter. Galilee is indeed a land of magic, and I begin to believe the tales that are told of it."

I think he said this just to tease me, but Myrina disliked such jesting.

We now had to part from Nathan and let him go his own way. Scratching his head he began to render account of the purse I had given him. While I'd been lying sick at the baths he had put the donkeys to work for me in Capernaum, and the money so earned he now produced, desiring for himself no more than his daily wage. To please him I accepted everything according to his calculation; but then I said, "You have served me well, good servant. I won't insult you by pressing money on you, but keep these four donkeys at least, to remember me by."

Nathan looked longingly at the animals, wriggled in embarrassment and said, "I may not keep any property beyond what I need for my livelihood. I'm glad to be able to give the poor their share of what I have earned with you. In this way I lay up treasure in the kingdom. But four donkeys are a fortune for a man in my position; I should only worry about them, fearing lest one or other of them might be stolen or fall sick, and so my thoughts would be distracted from important things to things less important, and I should lose myself to the extent to which I became attached to the donkeys."

His words shook me. I said, "Take the beasts, Nathan. They have served us meekly on a good journey, and I dislike the thought of selling them to a stranger. Many have come here on foot from Galilee, among them sick people and women. Present the donkeys to the messengers of Jesus of Nazareth, as a gift from yourself. Those holy men will know how best the animals may be used to help the weak, and will certainly not quarrel over them."

Nathan approved of my suggestion, and smiling he answered, "Yes, let us allow these gray donkeys to serve those who are closest to him. That is good."

Yet he hesitated still, and asked, "Shall I come and tell you if I hear anything of importance?"

I shook my head and replied, "No, Nathan; no longer will I try to discover things from which I've been shut out. If I am meant to hear about them I shall. Don't concern yourself about me; just see to it that you yourself amass treasure in the kingdom."

We parted. The sunset turned the sky to purple and my heart was heavy, although Myrina was with me. I wouldn't even raise my eyes to the magnificent temple of the Jews, and as evening darkened I was aware of the same ghostly sensation that I had known before the journey into Galilee. The great city was once more full of people, not only from Galilee and Judea, but from every land where Jews live in dispersal.

In spite of this I felt desolate. A vast power seemed to vibrate high in the heavens above the city, and I felt as if at any moment it might sweep me away in a whirlwind and extinguish me like a spark in a storm. Obsessed by this feeling I grasped Myrina's hand. Presently she put her arm around my neck and we sat close together in the darkening room. I was alone no longer, and did not desire to be so.

Then came Karanthes the Syrian, bringing a lamp. Seeing us sitting there close together he lowered his voice and moved on tiptoe, without bursting into his usual chatter as he had no doubt intended to do. He merely asked us if we would eat, but we shook our heads, and I felt that in this mood I could not have swallowed a single morsel. Nor did he press us, but was content.

He squatted before us on his haunches and looked at us with eyes that glittered in the lamplight, and there was not the least mockery in his glance, but rather fear and awe. He asked humbly, "How is it with you, Marcus my master? What has happened? What is the matter with you both? I feel stabs in my limbs when I look at you. There's a feeling of thunder in the air, though the sky is full of stars. When I came in here your faces seemed to shine in the darkness."

But I could not answer him, nor did Myrina. After a while he rose and went out with bowed head.

We slept side by side that night. I awoke several times, and each time I felt Myrina close to me, and had no fear. In my sleep I felt her touch more than once and knew that she too felt safe near me, and was not afraid.

The next day was the Sabbath. We beheld great crowds on their way up to the temple, but we never stirred from the room. There was no reason why we should not have gone out and taken a stroll around the city, for we were not bound by the Jewish law concerning travel on the Sabbath. But neither of us felt so inclined. Now and then we talked, just for the sake of hearing each other's voice. Myrina told me of her childhood, and we addressed one another by name; for my own name became dear to me in Myrina's utterance, and Myrina enjoyed hearing hers from my lips.

Thus, during this quiet day in Jerusalem, our two lives grew gently together into a life in common. For me this is grace indeed, because alone I would find it hard to go on living; although then I had not fully appreciated how great a gift was bestowed upon me by the unknown fisherman when he bade me seek out Myrina at the theatre in Tiberias. We spoke not one harsh word to each other that day; we ate supper together that evening on which began the Jewish feast of Pentecost.

As soon as I woke the next morning I was aware of a great restlessness. I felt compelled to pace up and down the room, my limbs shook and I was cold, although the day promised to be hot. Nor was I calmed when Myrina touched my forehead and stroked my cheek; I reproached her, and said, "Why did we come to Jerusalem? What business have we here? This is not our city but theirs, and theirs is today's festival."

But Myrina answered, "Is your patience so short? You were called as a foreigner to witness the resurrection. Can you not wait for the fulfillment of the promise that was made them, so that you may testify to that too? They are prepared to wait twelve years, but you weary in a day."

"I know not what they have been promised, and I have no share in it," I said impatiently. "I am thankful for what I have had; it is enough for me to live on. Why should I desire more, having already experienced things which kings and princes might envy me?"

But Myrina persisted. "If it was in this city that he was crucified, and suffered, died and rose again, then this city contents me though I should wait here twelve years."

But my mounting restlessness would not allow me to be still. Irresolutely I wondered whether to go up to Antonia and see Adenabar the centurion, or seek out Simon of Cyrene or the learned Nicodemus. At least I suggested, "At least let us get out of this closed room. I ought to call upon Aristainos the banker and go through my accounts with him. He must be in, for a feast like this is his best time for business."

Myrina had no objection. We went out, but when we reached the end of the alley, where there was an open square, my state of disturbance and distress became so violent that my breast threatened to burst and the ribs loosen from my body. I had to stop and gasp for breath, holding Myrina tightly by the hand.

I looked up at the sky, but it was still veiled by a light haze which gave a reddish tinge to the sunlight. There was no sign of any storm, and the day was no hotter than is usual at this time of year. I could not account for my distress.

By main force I controlled myself, and to please Myrina I showed her the court of the heathen at the temple, and the colonnade, where trading and money changing were in full swing despite the earliness of the hour. We walked hand in hand, and on leaving I took her to the eastern side, to show her the great Corinthian bronze gate which the Jews regard as one of the wonders of the world. But by the wall we were met by the stench of garbage from the Vale of Kidron which, when I had walked there after the passover, had been cleansed by the winter rains. So we turned, and made our way toward the house of Aristainos.

Hardly had we reached the forum when we heard something resembling a violent gust of wind. The noise was so loud that many turned to look toward the upper city. No whirlwind or cloud was to be seen. Some indeed pointed and said that they had seen lightning strike down there; yet there was no sound of thunder. This mighty rushing wind seemed so supernatural that I suddenly remembered the house in which I had visited the upper room, and began making my way toward it at a run, dragging Myrina with me. Many others seemed to be running in the same direction, for the strange noise had been heard all over the city.

So many people were on the move that there was a dense throng by the gate in the old wall. Folk were jostling each other feverishly to pass through, and inquiring in many languages as to what was going on. Some shouted that a house in the upper city had collapsed, others that the noise had been caused by an earthquake.

But the big house had not fallen. Mutely its walls stood and enclosed their secret. Hundreds of people had gathered outside it, and more were streaming up. The gate was open. I saw the disciples of Jesus of Nazareth staggering out of the house on unsteady legs, with glittering eyes and flushed faces, as if they were drunk or in some ecstasy. They mingled with the crowd and spoke excitedly to whomever they met, so that people drew aside from their path.

They could be heard speaking in many languages, addressing each in his own tongue. This aroused such amazement that those nearest shouted to the rest to be quiet. For a time the whole throng was silent, and only the ecstatic shouting of the disciples rang out in many different languages.

One of them, whose name I didn't know, came up to Myrina and me. I saw the terrifying rapture in his distorted face, and felt the power that issued from him. To my eyes it seemed as if a thin tongue of fire were waving in the air above his head. He looked me straight in the face and addressed me in Latin, yet without looking at me, for his eyes were staring straight into the kingdom and not into this world at all. But he was speaking Latin, and so rapidly that I couldn't distinguish separate words, or what it was he was trying to say. Then he turned to Myrina and changed to Greek, still shouting, and with the words pouring in so tumultuous a flood from his lips that they were impossible to catch. I cannot imagine how this great sunburnt, untaught countryman could speak both Latin and Greek so quickly and fluently.

He hastened on, and his power swept us out of his way as if we'd been leaves in the wind. A path cleared for him, and he paused again and spoke to some other people in a language I'd never heard. The other disciples were moving in the same way through the crowd, which billowed and whirled about them. Elamites and Medes, Arabs and Cretans and pious Jews from distant lands raised their hands in amazement and asked each other how it was that uneducated Galileans could talk to each one of them in his own language. They realized that these excited men were proclaiming the mighty works of God, but they could not grasp any single phrase amid the torrent of their speech.

The throng increased to many thousands, and the latest comers argued animatedly together and asked each other what all this might mean. There were mockers who laughed and said that these Galileans were drunk with sweet wine too early in the day; yet even the mockers left a way free for them.

While the disciples were talking in their many tongues, so that it sounded like Babel, I was overcome by a feeling of weakness; the ground shook under my feet and I had to catch hold of Myrina so as not to fall. Seeing my pallor and the cold sweat on my forehead she led me away from the open place into the courtyard of the house, and no one hindered us, although a flock of women and bewildered servants were standing there and peering out through the gate. Such had been my agitation that I swooned, and when I came to my senses again I had at first no idea where I was or how long I had lain unconscious.

But my limbs were cool and my soul was at peace, as if I had rested, and shed all my cares. With my head on Myrina's knee I turned my eyes and saw a group of women seated on the ground near us. Among them I recognized Lazarus' sister Mary, also Mary Magdalene and Mary the mother of Jesus. Their faces shone with such rapture that at first I didn't realize that they were earthly beings, and took them for angels in women's shape.

From the gate came the murmur of a mighty crowd; I saw that Simon Peter had gathered the other disciples about him, and heard him addressing the people in a powerful voice. And this was no ecstatic harangue in a foreign tongue; he was talking persuasively in his own Galilean speech, and quoting the prophets. He told of Jesus of Nazareth and his resurrection; of the promise made to Jesus by his Father, concerning the pouring out of the holy spirit, which the people themselves had beheld and of which they could bear witness. But in saying all this he spoke merely as an Israelite to Israelites. In my disappointment I ceased to listen, and looked with entreaty at the holy women.

Meeting my gaze, Mary Magdalene took pity on me; she came over to me and greeted me by name, as if to show everyone that she at least had not forsaken me. I asked her in a faint voice what had happened. She sat down beside me, took my hand in hers and began to tell me.

"They were all together in the upper room, where they had been meeting for some days: the eleven and Matthias, whom they chose by lot to be the twelfth in their circle. Suddenly a great rushing sound filled the whole room where they were sitting. They saw something like tongues of fire dividing and descending on each man's head. They were filled with the holy spirit and began to speak in tongues, as you heard."

I asked, "Was this what Jesus of Nazareth had promised them, and what they were waiting for?"

Mary Magdalene smiled at me and said, "At least you can hear that Peter, without veiling his words, now proclaims to all the people that Jesus of Nazareth is the Christ, and you see that the eleven others stand about him unafraid. Whence could they have gained this courage and strength if not through the spirit?"

"But he still speaks only to the people of Israel," I complained, like a child from whom a toy has been taken away.

And indeed at that moment I heard Peter declare, "So now let all the house of Israel know assuredly that God has made Jesus, whom you crucified, both Lord and Christ."

At this I forgot my own discontent and was afraid for him. Raising myself on my elbows I cried, "Now the mob will fall upon them and stone them!"

But nothing of the kind happened. On the contrary the crowd fell silent and stood motionless, as if Peter's accusation had struck them to the heart. Then a few hesitant voices were heard asking the disciples, "Men, brothers, what shall we do?"

Simon Peter shouted in a voice which might have carried over all Jerusalem, "Repent, and be baptized every one of you in the name of Jesus Christ, that your sins may be forgiven. For this promise is made to you and to your children, and to all both near and far whom the Lord our God may call."

Thus it was that he proclaimed the secret of the kingdom, and I bowed my head, realizing that not even now did he relent toward me but was calling the Jews only, addressing the promise to those both here and in dispersal who were circumcised, who obeyed the law and served the God of Israel. So my last hope faded, insofar as I had still hoped in secret to become one of them. But of the knowledge of Jesus of Nazareth and his resurrection Peter could not deprive me.

Seeing my sorrow, Mary Magdalene consoled me, saying, "He is a slow, stubborn man, but his faith is like a rock and he will surely grow with his task. Just now he referred to the prophet Joel and proclaimed that the last days are at hand, but that I don't believe. No, for when he parted from them on the Mount of Olives he warned them, and said that it was not for them to know the times or the seasons which the Father has put in his own power. For forty days Jesus has been appearing to them and speaking to them of the kingdom; but so little did they understand that before the cloud came and took him they were still nagging him and saying, 'Lord, is it now that you will restore the kingdom to Israel?' So you must not lose hope, Marcus."

This was new to me. I listened avidly and asked, "Do they no longer conceal from women what happened and what cloud it was that carried him away?"

"They hide nothing from us," Mary Magdalene assured me. "The secret of flesh and blood in bread and wine they revealed on the mountain. The faithful already number one hundred and twenty. On the fortieth day Jesus went with them to the Mount of Olives near Bethany, forbade them to leave Jerusalem and commanded them to await the fulfillment of the promise he had made them. John baptized with water, he said, but you shall be baptized with the holy spirit not many days hence. This baptism came about today; of that there can be no question, for now power dwells in them. Of the cloud I know only that on the Mount of Olives he rose up before them and a mist removed him from their sight, and from this they knew that he would not appear to them again. I don't want to bandy words with them, but I think I may be allowed to smile a little, hearing them try so awkwardly and clumsily to put into words all that I felt in my heart to be true while he was yet alive."

As she talked I looked about me at the trees of the courtyard with their silver-shining leaves, at the steps leading to the upper room and its massive wooden door, to impress the sight of these things on my memory for all time. In my exhaustion I was quiet and humble again, and felt it was enough for me to have beheld the place where the kingdom became reality.

I stood up, weak at the knees, and said, "I must go now, lest I cause argument and disturb the holy men. The power struck me to the ground, and they would no doubt regard that as a sign that I shall be turned away from the gates of the kingdom."

Very gladly would I have blessed and thanked Mary Magdalene for her kindness, but I felt too insignificant to give anyone my blessing. Perhaps she read my intention in my face, for she touched my forehead once more and said, "Never forget that you have helped one of the lost children of Israel to come to him. Mary of Beret has happily celebrated her wedding and moved to her new home. I don't believe that any of these men would have done as much for her. Of the women, Susanna too blesses your kindness. Know, then, that wherever you may go there will be some of us praying for you in secret, foreigner though you are."

But I protested, "No, no; all my actions have been selfish and impure. I believe that not one of them could be accounted to me for merit. In me there is nothing good beyond my knowledge that he is Christ and the son of God. But that is no great merit, since I've been permitted to see and witness this."

Myrina said, "Marcus has no other merit than his weakness. Perhaps one day it will grow to strength, when the kingdom spreads to the world's end. Until that time comes I will be the one to comfort him, for never again in this life shall I know thirst. Within me is a fountain which will suffice also for him."

I looked at her with new eyes. In my weariness I seemed to see her transfigured, so that just then she seemed not a human being but my guardian angel incarnate, sent to keep me from straying from the Way. This was an odd idea, as I well knew what her past had been, and had first met her on the ship bound for Joppa.

But it was with human hands that she grasped me under the

arm and led me out of the courtyard into the restless, murmuring crowd. More and more of them were asking in dismay what they should do, and some had torn their garments in grief for their sins. There were so many of them that the twelve, headed by Peter, led them down through the alleys to the city and beyond, to baptize in the name of Jesus Christ those who desired to repent and to be forgiven their sins. Myrina was anxious about me, but consented to guide me in the wake of the crowd, to see what was to happen.

Thus is was that I beheld the twelve standing by a pool outside the walls, baptizing every man of Israel who desired it, and laying their hands on his head that his sins might be forgiven. Women too they baptized. And as the number of those with whom they shared their spirit increased, so also grew the joy among the throng, and the more willingly did others press forward for baptism. The men sang Israelitish songs of rejoicing, and embraced each other. This continued until evening, and I heard afterwards that their number grew that day to three thousand.

And they hindered no man of Israel, but received both rich and poor, cripples, beggars and even slaves, without distinction. And their power never waned but sufficed for all to share in it. For this reason I was greatly saddened, and returned to the city and to our lodging before dusk. I reflected ruefully how readily had been forgiven the sins even of men who had stood before Pilate shouting: Crucify him! Crucify him! For there were many of those among these frightened and remorseful Jews.

Perhaps on this day of rapture I could have stolen in among the Jews and been baptized with the rest, but I did not want to deceive the messengers; and such a baptism would have had no value for me, even if in error they had laid their hands on my head too. But perhaps the spirit in them would have detected that I was a Roman, and turned me away. I do not know, for I did not want to attempt such a deception.

Next day I still felt dazed, so that Myrina seemed radiant as an angel to my eyes as she moved about the Syrian's guest room and tended me. But when I felt better I began to examine myself, and found that something had happened to me while I'd been lying unconscious in the courtyard below the upper room. My mind was more naked than before and I thought less about unnecessary things.

One day my landlord Karanthes came in, looked at me searchingly and said. "You've not yet told me anything about the Galilean. Why have you become so close-lipped? You must know that miracles are happening here in the city again, on account of that crucified Nazarene of whom you were gathering knowledge. His disciples have returned and are proclaiming that their teacher has given them the power to work magic. They're turning people's heads to such an extent that parents leave their children and children their parents to join them. Many even renounce all they possess, so truly it is a matter of really alarming witchcraft. The disciples stand every day in the temple arcade, blaspheming, without fear of the Council; they own everything in common and assemble in people's houses to perform their questionable mysteries. Even highly respected Jews of whom one would never have suspected such a thing have caught the Nazarene infection and acknowledge the man as king of Israel."

I could not answer him, for who was I to be his teacher? He was free to go and listen to the twelve himself. Receiving no reply from me, he was crestfallen; he shook his head and asked, "What has happened to you, and what do you mean to do next, lying here and staring in front of you day after day?"

I pondered this question, smiled sadly and said, "I may take your advice: build me a house and plant trees. That is as good counsel as any other for one facing a period of patient waiting." With a sigh I added, "Let me only take care that my heart does not become too firmly attached to anything in this world; that nothing becomes so much a part of me and so dear that I'm not prepared to renounce it if necessary."

Karanthes sighed too and answered soberly, "We must all renounce everything when the day comes, but far be that day from both of us." He thought for a little, and said timidly, "They say those Galileans have a medicine of immortality."

But neither to this did I dare make any answer; he could learn of it from Jesus of Nazareth's own men. Karanthes rose, puffed a little and said, "You've changed, Marcus the Roman; you're not the man who went to Galilee. I don't know whether you're better or worse than before, but you cause me to sigh. This I do know: Myrina whom you brought from Galilee is a quiet-minded girl, and it's good to be near her. Since she came to the house, business has prospered and my wife no longer beats me about the ears with a slipper several times a day. If she were a little plumper she would be quite beautiful."

I couldn't help laughing, yet I reproved him. "Karanthes, don't concern yourself about whether Myrina is fat or thin. In my eyes she is lovely as she is. Even when she is gray-haired and toothless I believe I shall find her beautiful—if we live so long."

Karanthes, having coaxed laughter from me, went away content. Thinking it over I perceived that Myrina was indeed growing more beautiful every day. Now that she had abandoned her vagabond player's life and was getting enough to eat, she had grown imperceptibly but becomingly plumper, and her cheeks were less narrow than before. The thought stirred a tenderness in me, and was strangely reviving. It showed me that she was no angel but a woman, and one of my own kind.

Myrina had gone to the temple, where every day two or three of the twelve stood in the arcade and taught the baptized and the merely curious, proclaimed the resurrection and testified that Jesus of Nazareth was the Christ. Feeling suddenly in good spirits, I dressed myself and combed my hair, and called on Aristainos my banker to prepare for my departure from Jerusalem. He received me kindly and began talking with great animation, saying, "The baths of Tiberias have evidently done you good, for you're less of a fanatic than you were. You dress like a Roman once more. That is a good thing, for I'm going to give you a warning, should the matter not already have reached your ears. The Galileans have returned to the city and are causing a great deal of consternation. They proclaim openly that Jesus of Nazareth rose from the dead, although everyone acquainted with the circumstances knows what really happened. But they call him Messiah, and twist the words of scripture for their own ends; they go so far as to assert that he has forgiven them their sins. I am a Sadducee and venerate the scriptures, though I do not accept the oral tradition, nor the intolerable, tangled interpretations of the Pharisees. This resurrection talk is lunacy, although the Pharisees incline a little to that way of thinking. People are apt to accuse us Jews of intolerance in questions of religion, but our tolerance is best shown by the fact that we allow different sects to compete freely with one another. Most likely Jesus of Nazareth would never have been crucified if he hadn't blasphemed against God, for that is the one thing we will not endure. But now it seems as if a fresh rift is to form among us in his name. Time will show whether we can allow it to widen or whether we shall be compelled to hunt these people down. They baptize, but that is nothing new and has never been regarded as an evil. It is said that they heal the sick, but so did their teacher, and it was not on that account that he was persecuted, although the Pharisees did consider it unseemly of him to do so on the Sabbath.

"No, the pernicious part of their doctrine is their insistence that all property shall be held in common. Hitherto levelheaded people are now selling their fields and laying all the proceeds at the feet of the disciples, who distribute to each man what he requires. Such a teaching is neither more nor less than a subtle evasion of tithes and taxation. There are neither rich nor poor among them. Our leaders are nonplused, for we had supposed that everything would settle down once we had crucified the Nazarene. We have no desire to persecute anyone but we cannot conceive how they have become so bold, unless it is that they've heard that Pontius Pilate will not allow any persecution of the Galileans. This he announced in veiled terms to the Supreme Council. Another instance of the intolerable Roman policy. You'll forgive my frankness, being familiar with our customs, and being also my friend. Now indeed the Procurator may wash his hands and mock us; for as you see yourself, the last aberration is worse than the first. They have the gullible people on their side, and therefore it would be imprudent to molest them. If they did, everyone would be the readier to believe these fishermen's tales."

He barely gave himself time to draw breath, so eager was he to talk. I couldn't refrain from observing. "You seem more excited about Jesus of Nazareth than I am. Calm yourself, Aristainos, and remember the scriptures. If this enterprise of the Galileans is of human origin, it will run out into the sand and need not trouble you. But if it is of God, then neither you nor the Supreme Council nor any power in the world can vanquish these men."

Breathing hard, he pondered my words; then with a burst of laughter he raised his hands conciliatingly and cried, "Shall a Roman teach me to read the scriptures? No, the doings of ignorant fishermen cannot be of God. They cannot, for then life would no longer be worth living, and the temple would collapse. Of course it will all run out into the sand. Others before these have come forth claiming to be somebodies, and all have disappeared. Unschooled men cannot prophesy for long without entangling themselves in their own words and falling into their own pits."

Having calmed himself in this way he asked me what I wanted, then at once ordered his bookkeeper to look up my account and calculate a rate of exchange advantageous to himself. I told him how well his business acquaintance in Tiberias had served me, and he nodded with satisfaction, waving a thin letter-scroll which he then handed to me with the words, "I nearly forgot this. It was delivered to your banker in Alexandria, and he forwarded it here. I didn't want to send it on to Tiberias, not knowing how long you meant to stay there, and fearing it might go astray."

Cold with apprehension I broke the seal and unrolled the short letter, for at first glance I had recognized Tullia's nervous, hastily scrawled writing. The letter ran as follows:

> Tullia greets false Marcus Mezentius.
>
> Can one then rely on no man's promise? Does fidelity no longer exist? Did you not swear to await me in Alexandria until I had ordered my affairs in Rome and become entirely yours once more? Rome was no longer Rome after you had gone, but by taking prudent steps I was able to secure my own position. And on arriving at Alexandria, ill and weak after a rough voyage, what do I hear? That you have lightly broken your word and set off for Jewish Jerusalem. Come back immediately on receiving this. I lodge at Daphne's Inn near the harbor. It will gladden me to see you again, but I shall not wait forever. I have friends here. However, if you want to continue your researches into Jewish philosophy, which it seems is now your study, send word and I will come on to Jerusalem. I believe I can soon drive Jewish wisdom out of your head. Come, then, as quickly as you can. I am impatient. I burn with waiting.

Each word made me shudder with dismay. When I had regained command of my tongue I read the letter through again, and asked in an unsteady voice, "How long has this letter been awaiting me?"

Aristainos counted on this fingers and said, "Possibly two weeks. You must forgive me, but I never thought you would stay so long in Tiberias."

I rolled up the letter, and thrusting it inside the breast of my tunic I said with a wave of my hand, "Let the reckoning wait. At present I'm incapable of calculation."

Filled with icy fear I left Aristainos' house and fled back to my room at Karanthes'. Tullia's letter had come like a thunderbolt from a clear sky, just as I'd begun to believe that I'd won peace and become reconciled to my destiny.

Fortunately, Myrina had not returned. For a moment I was scorched as with a flame by the temptation to leave my purse in Karanthes' keeping for her, flee from Jerusalem and make for Alexandria by the shortest route, to hold Tullia in my arms again. I took out her letter and caressed it, recognizing her very self in every fevered, scribbled character; and at the mere thought of her my body was on fire.

Yet at the same time I could judge her coolly. It was characteristic of her to take the offensive—to reproach me in the very first line. For a whole year I had waited patiently for her in Alexandria without receiving the smallest sign of life from her. And what did she mean by the phrase: I was able to secure my own position? Surely divorce and remarriage. One could put no faith in anything she wrote. Ill or weak she may have been after her voyage; nevertheless she was able to show her claws and point out that she had friends in Alexandria. In whose arms should I find her if I went? Tullia has plenty to choose from. I'm no more than a whim among her thoughts. I could be sure that it was not for my sake alone that she had come to Alexandria; there would be many reasons.

In Tullia my former life was personified: its pleasures and its emptiness. I was free to choose. If I chose Tullia I should be renouncing forever my search for the kingdom, for I knew as well as she that she was capable of banishing all such ideas from my head at once if I returned to that heavenly death. So reflecting, I loathed myself and my weakness; never before, I believe, had I been so plunged in self-disgust. Not because I still desired her, but because I still hesitated whether to return and let her continue to torture me. This was the greatest humiliation, for if I'd had any firmness I would not have hesitated for a moment. After all I had seen and known, the choice ought to have been obvious: stay away from Tullia, away from all the past. So weak was I, so easily tempted still, that the hot wind of memory made me waver like a reed.

With my brow bathed in a cold sweat I braced myself against temptation, hating myself. I was so bitterly ashamed that I did not want Jesus of Nazareth to see my shame; nevertheless I hid my face and prayed, "Lead me not into temptation but save me from what is evil. For the sake of your kingdom." I could do no more than that.

Just then I heard footsteps on the stairs. The door opened and Myrina hurried in with outstretched arms, as if bringing me great news. "Peter and John!" she cried. "Peter and John!" Then she saw my look. Her arms sank, her fact lost its radiance and grew ugly to me.

"Don't talk to me of them," I said bitterly. "I don't want to hear."

Hesitantly Myrina took a step forward, but dared not touch me. Nor did I wish her to; I recoiled, and stood with my back against the wall.

"They've just cured a man who'd been lame from birth. It was by the Corinthian gate of the temple," Myrina tried to say; but her voice died and she stared at me anxiously.

"Well?" I returned. "I don't doubt they have the power. But how does it concern me? I've seen miracles enough. They leave me cold."

"Peter took him by the hand and raised him up from his bench," Myrina stammered. "And his feet supported him. Everyone in the temple ran to Solomon's colonnade; he's there now, leaping and praising God. Disbelieving people are feeling his feet and Peter is proclaiming the forgiveness of sins."

"A fine circus for the Jews!" I sneered.

Myrina could contain herself no longer, but seizing me by both arms she shook me and asked with tears in her eyes, "What's the matter with you? What has happened, Marcus?"

I hardened my heart and said, "Weep, Myrina. These will not be the last tears you'll shed for me. I know that."

Myrina released me abruptly, wiped her eyes and tossed her head. Flushed with anger she stamped and said, "Speak plainly. What has happened?"

Coldly and sourly I surveyed her, scanned each feature which only that morning had been dear to me, and tried to discover what I thought I had seen in her. Through her face I saw Tullia's brilliant eyes, Tullia's proud, voluptuous mouth. I showed her the letter, saying, "Tullia has written. She is waiting for me in Alexandria."

Myrina gazed at me for a long time. Her face shrank and narrowed. Then she sank to her knees and bowed her head; I thought she was praying, though I saw no movement of her lips. All my thoughts seemed to have been frozen. I merely looked at her golden-yellow head, and the notion came to me that a swift swordstroke would sweep off that head and set me free. The thought was so amusing that I laughed.

Presently Myrina rose and without looking at me began to gather together my belongings and lay out my clothes. At first I was surprised, then dismayed, and at last I couldn't help asking, "What are you doing? Why are you putting my things together?"

She counted absent-mindedly on her fingers: "One tunic and one traveling mantle at the wash." Then she replied, "You're going away, aren't you? You're going to your Tullia. I'm getting your things ready: it's what I'm here for."

"Who says I'm going away?" I exclaimed hotly; and seizing her by the wrists I forced her to drop everything. "I said no such thing. I simply told you about the letter so that we could decide what to do."

But Myrina shook her head. "No, no," she declared. "In your heart you've decided already. If I tried to stop you, you'd only bear me a grudge. It's true you're weak, and perhaps, by speaking of the kingdom, I might persuade you to stay; but never for the rest of your life would you forgive me. You would always be gnawed by the suspicion that it was for my sake you renounced your precious Tullia. You had better go. You mustn't fail her if she's waiting for you once more."

I couldn't believe my ears. Myrina seemed to be drifting away from me—depriving me of the only friend I had to turn to. "But—" I stammered, "but—" More I could not say.

At length Myrina took pity on me, and explained, "This is something I cannot help you with. You must decide for yourself, and be answerable for your decision." She smiled sadly and continued, "I'll make it easy for you. Go to your Tullia; let her scorch you and stab you with red-hot needles, and destroy you. You've told me enough of her to show me what she's like. But of course one day I'll come after you, and when the time is ripe and she has gone I'll take care of what's left of you. You need not fear to lose me. Jesus of Nazareth has given you to me. Go, if the temptation is too strong for you. Surely he will forgive you, as I in my heart forgive you because I know you."

While she was speaking thus collectedly I was filled with ever-increasing reluctance, and reviewed in thought all the humiliations and torments which Tullia would inflict upon me, to spice her own pleasure. At last I cried, "Peace, Myrina, you mad creature! Are you trying to send me as a victim to a cruel, lascivious woman? I wouldn't have believed it of you. Should you not rather stiffen my resolve? I don't recognize you. How can you treat me so?"

Indignantly I went on, "I hadn't decided to go to her at all, though you say I had. I hoped that you would help me. I *won't* go to Alexandria. I'm just wondering how to explain everything to her. I ought to send her a word, or she might think I'd disappeared on my way hither."

"Would that matter?" Myrina asked softly. "Or does your masculine pride demand that you humiliate her, in writing, by telling her you want no more to do with her?"

"Tullia has humiliated me a thousand times," I said sourly.

"Would you return evil for evil?" asked Myrina. "Rather let her believe that you've vanished without trace; thus you will not insult the woman in her. She must have other friends, and will soon console herself."

Her surmise was so accurate as to stab me. But the pain was no worse than when one passes one's tongue over the place from which an aching tooth has been drawn. An ineffable sense of deliverance filled me, as if I had regained health after a long illness. "Myrina," I said, "you've shown me that I can't endure even the thought of leaving you. Myrina, you're not just a sister to me. Myrina, I fear I love you as a man loves a woman."

Myrina's face began to shine for me like the face of an angel. To my eyes she was beautiful as she said,"Myrina and Marcus, we two. In your heart you know that I am whatever you would have me be. But we must decide what we're to do with our life."

Taking my hand she drew me gently down beside her on a bench and began to talk as if she had been thinking about the matter for a long time: "I have a deep longing for his disciples to baptize me and lay their hands on my head in the name of Jesus of Nazareth. Perhaps in that way I should gain strength from their strength, to endure this life and to be a partaker in the kingdom and in the spirit that descended upon them like tongues of fire. But I'm not a Jew, and neither are you. Yet without demur they baptize devout proselytes from other countries—men who allow themselves to be circumcised and who obey the law in its entirety. But I've heard also of gate-proselytes: God-fearing men who will not be circumcised, but who despise idolatry and do not mock God or shed human blood. Incest, theft and blood-food are forbidden them, and they must live a life of devotion. Perhaps they would consent to baptize us as such gate-proselytes if we earnestly begged them to do so."

I shook my head and said, "I know about that and have often thought of it. Since meeting Jesus of Nazareth, the son of God, I have no other gods. It ought not to be so especially difficult to keep those commandments, and why should I not be content to eat the meat of animals slaughtered in the Jewish manner? Meat is meat. But I can't see how it would make me acceptable.

I cannot bind myself to living a devout life, no matter how greatly I desire good. This is one of the few things I know about myself for certain. You're mistaken too if you think they would consent to baptize a mere gate-proselyte, however loudly I might thunder at that gate. They are less merciful than their master."

Myrina nodded, holding my hand hard, and owned submissively, "No doubt this is a childish wish of mine. I don't believe that I should be more his than I already am, even if they baptized me and laid their hands on my head. Let us give up that hope, and follow his way as he himself showed us. Let us pray that his will may be done and his kingdom come. He is truth and mercy. I believe it is enough for us that we have seen him."

"His kingdom," I said. "We can only wait. But there are two of us. It must be easier for two to follow the Way than for one alone. That is his mercy toward us."

Nevertheless we did not leave Jerusalem at once, for first I wrote all this down for remembrance, even though it may have been no more extraordinary than what went before. But I do want to remember exactly how the spirit came like a rush of wind and descended like tongues of fire over the twelve messengers of Jesus of Nazareth, so that never more shall I doubt them or judge their actions out of my own head.

During this time the Jewish authorities imprisoned Peter and John, but because of the people they had to release them again the very next day. And the messengers did not let themselves be frightened by threats. Courageously they continued to proclaim. I believe about two thousand people have joined them since they healed the lame man at the Corinthian gate of the temple. And these also, in their own homes, have begun to break bread and bless wine, and consecrate it as a drink of immortality in the name of Jesus Christ. None of them suffer want, for the rich among them sell their farms and fields, and each receives what he needs. I believe they do so because they still see everything as in a mirror and believe that the kingdom will come any day. I have not heard, however, that Simon of Cyrene has sold his land.

When I had written all this down I received word from Antonia that Procurator Pontius Pilate desires me to leave Jerusalem at once, and Judea, his administrative area. Unless I go of my own accord I shall be arrested by legionaries and brought before him in Caesarea. Why he has come to this decision I know not, but for some reason or other he evidently thinks it undesirable from a Roman point of view that I should remain in Judea. But I do not want to meet the man again, so Myrina and I have decided to go to Damascus. We chose Damascus because of a dream that Myrina had, and I have no objection to going there. At least it's in the opposite direction to Alexandria.

Before we left I took Myrina to the hill outside the city gate where on my first arrival at Jerusalem I had seen Jesus of Nazareth crucified between two thieves. I showed her the garden, too, and the tomb where his body had been laid and from which he rose when the earth shook. But his kingdom was no longer there.